A
DARK
PATH

ALSO BY STUART THAMAN

NEF HOUSE PUBLISHING

Cover by J Caleb Clark (www.jcalebdesign.com)
Interior layout by Bodie D Dykstra (www.bdbookdesign.com)

A DARK PATH

FORSAKEN TALENTS
— GRIMDARK LITRPG —

STUART THAMAN

"Saxi placed this stone in memory of Ásbjörn, Tóki's son, his partner. He did not flee at Uppsala, but slaughtered as long as he had a weapon."

~Inscription of the Sjörup Runestone, c. 1000 AD

CHAPTER 1

We stood there, two of us amidst a swirling crowd, staring at the circular portal. I'd seen it plenty of times before—hell, the world practically revolved around the seven portals—but it never ceased to strike a certain chord in my mind whenever I got ready to walk through. I didn't really know what that chord was, though. Awe, maybe, but it felt more . . . *inspiring* than that. The portals had done so *much* that I just couldn't help but be overwhelmed.

As my literature teachers had said, I was a romantic at heart. I never used to believe them, but when the portals were finally finished and opened to the public, I knew it was true. The sheer magnitude and grandeur of the manmade structures were enough to make me swell with emotion no matter how many times I saw them—though *them* wasn't exactly the right term. I had only ever seen the one, towering before me now like an ambitious politician surveying an innumerable crowd.

Like many people who played Wonder, I had only seen one portal. Honestly, there wasn't a need to visit the other portals, not for a relatively new player like me. It had taken me over a year to save enough money to purchase my own lifetime pass, and then I'd spent another six months in and out of the game putting together the funds to get a pass for Ingrid, my daughter. Now, after waiting so long to use her pass, she was sixteen years old. That meant she could walk through the portal and finally experience the "The One True Wonder" as the game developers called it. Just another hundred feet and we'd be inside the game.

"It's so big," Ingrid said, her hand wrapped in mine.

I nodded. "And our portal is only the third largest. The one in Spain where the developers live is supposed to be five times the size of our little portal." Of course, everyone on the planet had seen the pictures all over the internet. The game had only been online for a few years, but it was already indelibly lodged in the history books. Documentaries had already been made about the game in more than forty languages. It was, without a doubt, the single most important event of the 2060s, if not the entire twenty-first century.

Standing there in the shadow of the portal, I knew the acclaim was well-earned. So many people played the game every single day that there hadn't been a war—not even a border skirmish—in more than eighteen months. Crime had almost evaporated as well. For once in human history, society was essentially at peace.

But the world inside the portal, the world of Wonder, was a different story. The game featured hundreds of different zones; each of them with their own theme, but not truncated or separated out from the others, and the multitudes of factions living in the different zones were constantly at war. A lot of people thought the game was some sort of conspiracy run by all the governments of the world to placate the masses, and I had to admit that I agreed with even some of the more radical theories tossed about on the forums. Humanity used the game to vent its frustrations, and death in the game just meant you were sent home to the real world and then had to find your way back to the nearest portal.

All the different zones were more or less situated around one of the seven kingdom capitals, which were just on the other side of each portal. Here in the outskirts of Atlanta, our portal led to the heart of a sprawling metropolis of stone called 'Echelon.'

I gave Ingrid's hand a squeeze, checked one last time to ensure that both of our transponders were functioning, connected to our home dock in case we died inside Wonder, and then took a step for the portal.

Hundreds of storefronts lined the marble walkway leading to the portal. Almost all the items being sold were only useable in-game, and they came in the form of little black discs that could be taken to certain NPCs in Wonder for activation. With so many millions of people going through each portal every day, the veritable cities that had grown up around them on the Earth side were beyond impressive. We passed one particular shop, a cosmetic modification business, and Ingrid pulled me closer to get a look through the window.

A couple workers were inside, and it appeared as though they only had a single customer. "How long will it take to afford that?" Ingrid asked, pointing on the glass to a mannequin wearing a red cloak fastened with a golden brooch the size of my fist.

I glanced at the price. "Four million," I mouthed, shaking my head. "That's enough to buy our entire apartment complex. Not just our unit, but the whole damn complex. Maybe another one next to ours as well."

Ingrid smiled before bounding back toward the throng of people, pulling me along by my hand as she went. She had never been a superficial kind of girl, and I knew she didn't care one bit about an insanely priced cosmetic upgrade. She was adventurous by nature, always ready to forge ahead no matter the risks—and she reminded me a lot of her mother. I had a plan for us in mind already. We'd head out of Echelon to one of the starter areas to get her some experience, and once she leveled up a few times, I'd buy her a dress for her birthday. Not the most practical gift for doing battle inside a fantasy realm, but Ingrid was planning to become a caster, and she'd need to at least look the part.

When we reached the front of the hurrying mob pushing to get through the portal, Ingrid's joyful exterior finally began to crack a little. "What will it be like?" she asked. Her voice was small and reminded me of the days before Wonder even existed, the days when she was just a child.

"You've seen so many vids. You've seen me go through a thousand times. You'll do just fine," I told her.

We waited for a few minutes as the people in front of us were all bottlenecked into the portal, and then it was our turn.

"Here we go," I said, taking a step forward and pulling her along behind me.

In an instant—faster than any human could ever possibly perceive—we were standing in Echelon. The weather back on Earth had been warm and balmy, slightly overcast, but Echelon was a city among a vast plain, and there were rarely any clouds in sight. Though hundreds of people entered through the Echelon portal every single minute, day and night, the game engines spread out their entry locations to prevent huge mobs from instantly forming and rampaging through the cities.

Luckily, Ingrid was still by my side. About half a dozen other people came through right next to us, but they all took off without giving us a second look. On the inside, Wonder was seven times the size of the Earth. Each of the seven major territories, complete with their own capitals, leadership, and all the other trappings of civilization, was supposed to be the size of its own planet, though the game was still new enough that huge swaths of it hadn't been explored yet. Honestly, the immensity of the game was too staggering to really comprehend. Thinking in ideas larger than one region at a time was overwhelming.

"Come on, let's get to the fields," I said. My sword and all my other in-game gear had instantly appeared on my body, and Ingrid looked wildly out of place in her jeans and one of my old shirts. The world around us, after all, was made of stone and wood, not steel and carbon fiber reaching up to the clouds.

Ingrid stood transfixed, her mouth open slightly as she clearly struggled to absorb even the most mundane of sights that Echelon had to offer.

"Hey," I said, giving her shoulder a jostle. "We can come back and explore the city tonight. For now, you need to get some levels. Can't go wandering around the city looking like that, can you? Let's go."

Finally, Ingrid seemed to snap back into reality. I led us toward the nearest gate, and she dutifully followed at my heels. "Use the walk to summon your character sheet," I told her. "It takes some getting used to before you'll feel comfortable scanning it quickly in the middle of a fight."

I summoned my own stats to my vision and read through them for what felt like the millionth time:

Ben Hales, Level 9
Physical: 18
Cunning: 19
Influence: 15
Renown: 1
Investigation: 6
Trade: 9
Craftsmanship: 6
Fortune: 7
Infamy: 0
Status: healthy
Holdings: none

Allegiance: King Ahmose II of Echelon

For all the hours I had sunk into Wonder, I hadn't progressed very far. I'd spent so much of my in-game time and energy trying to earn Ingrid's lifetime pass that I had neglected my own stats. I didn't even have an official class yet, though that wasn't really such a huge deal. Classes could be gained at any level beyond five—but you had to find a trainer in the game world, and some were much more hidden than others—and the cost to unlearn a class was so high that I didn't feel like committing yet. It would take me a month or more to earn enough cash in the real world to be able to afford a class change.

Ingrid ran through her own meager stats with a smile still plastered to her face. At the first level, all of her stats would be less than five, but she would progress quickly. The way the developers had designed it, I was actually close to hitting a new level myself. The first three skills on the sheet, physical, cunning, and influence, were considered "primary" attributes. They were harder to increase, but they directly influenced level, and level was the barrier to everything awesome about Wonder. Each level gave a new talent, and talents separated the newer, still-learning players like me from the raid leaders and guild champions.

"Your level is always half of your highest primary stat," I explained to Ingrid as we passed beneath a huge gatehouse that took us into the countryside surrounding Echelon. "If you want to be a caster, you need to focus on Cunning and try to get it up to level ten, maybe a little higher, before you bother with the other primaries."

The secondary skills, everything from renown and investigation to fortune and infamy, didn't have any bearing one way or another on level. The people who loved crafting were usually around my level, laughably low for someone with so many hours, though their trade or craftsmanship skills could be in the hundreds. Even so, the absolute best crafters in the entire game focused on both primary and secondary skills. All the craftsmanship in the world meant nothing if you never reached a high enough level to use a legendary forge or hold an enchanted loom—and level was the only way to gain access to the more powerful magical locations and dungeons. Those areas held untold possibilities for the players with enough experience to reach them.

Now outside Echelon, we took a smaller path that wound to the east through a few patches of farmland, which eventually brought us to one of the many designated starter zones. Prices to buy gear from NPCs in the zone were a little cheaper than everywhere else, and the enemy mobs we would encounter were specifically toned down to be easy prey. Beyond that, only players level ten or below were allowed access to quests in the starter zones, and that meant the chances of being ambushed by players from other kingdoms were extremely low.

When I thought of the possibility of getting jumped and sent back to my apartment in the real world—to be reconstituted by the most advanced technology mankind had ever developed—my expression soured. There was a single player in Wonder who actually wanted me dead—Vic Fuentes. I had seen him a couple times in the past few weeks, so I knew he was lurking around Echelon, despite his allegiance to the current king who ruled Olympia City, the capital connected to the portal in Oslo, Norway. Echelon wasn't at war with any of the other six factions, and that meant that neither the NPC guards nor the higher-level characters cared if they saw Vic coming around waving Olympia City's colors.

I just wanted to train with my daughter. I didn't want to worry about a potential fight with such a petulant, persistent troll like Vic, so I pushed my thoughts of him as far from my mind as I could. Besides, we had arrived at the starter area, and it was time to help Ingrid earn her first handful of experience points.

Surrounded by grassy plains and beautiful rolling hills, the village of Whitechapel wasn't the nearest starter zone to Echelon, but it was my favorite. As an added bonus, it was relatively deserted. The only other player I saw was a level six thief working on a few of the longer quest chains.

"Alright, where do you want to start?" I asked Ingrid.

She looked to the largest building, the namesake chapel painted in white, and started heading in that direction. "Let's do the best quest they have," she stated confidently. Of course, she had watched my stream for thousands of hours, so she knew the general outline of what we'd be up against. The quests in Wonder changed from time to time, altering their parameters as directed by the most advanced AI ever coded. Starter quests were usually so far removed from the huge world events that they stayed predictable.

"Want to stop the necromancer or investigate the murders?" I asked. "When I first began, I went after the necromancer, but I wasn't able to stop all the experiments before the timer expired."

"I don't want a timed quest, let's investigate the murders," Ingrid answered. She bounded up the chapel's steps with all the enthusiasm I had felt when I had done the same just a year or so earlier.

Inside, the sun gleamed through tall, narrow stained-glass windows, creating an intricate pattern of reds and blues on the marble floor. "Go to the back for the murders," I told Ingrid, letting her handle herself as I stayed back a ways.

Ingrid presented herself before Amida, the high priest of the chapel, and immediately caught the old man's attention.

"Ah, adventurer! I have need of your assistance. Have you come to Whitechapel in response to the bulletin posted in Echelon?" he began, slowly stroking his wispy beard.

General quests designed for low-level players were always posted on town bulletin boards or tavern walls, but it wasn't necessary to find them and accept them before heading out in search of rewards. Right on time, Ingrid said, "Yes! I've come to help solve the murders."

Amida nodded, and though I couldn't see it, I knew a quest notification had just appeared in Ingrid's vision, slowly flashing in the bottom right corner until she focused on it. I waited for Amida to finish his quest tale, then Ingrid and I left the chapel in search of the first clue.

"You'll need to talk to—"

"I know, Dad!" she interrupted.

I put my hands up and smiled, eager to watch her complete her first quest. I planned on staying a respectful distance back, ready to jump in and save her from her first respawn if I needed to, but she wouldn't earn any experience or progress her skills if I helped too much.

Our first destination was the home of the chandler's wife. She lived in a thatched hut a couple buildings down from the chapel, and her husband had been one of the murder victims. Ingrid knocked on the wooden door, and a few moments later was admitted to the house.

I waited dutifully outside, occasionally stealing a glance at the higher-level guy running his own quest chain throughout other parts of the town. He was on a mission I didn't recognize, and it looked terribly boring. With a sack of grain under each arm, he struggled to lead a pair of unruly oxen from one wooden pen to another. On the forums and all the streams from the high-level players, the quests were all about slaying dragons, raiding ancient lairs, and hunting down legendary artifacts. In Whitechapel, things never really got that exciting, though the necromancer quest line supposedly had an alternate option where you could choose to help the bad guy and attempt to sack the town.

Ingrid emerged from the chandler's house a moment later with a garnet necklace in her hand. "My investigation skill went up to two!" she cheerfully announced.

"Ready for the next step?" I asked with a smile and a nod.

I had to watch with mixed emotions as Ingrid bounded away for the graveyard where she would return the talisman to the chandler's grave and then discover her next clue. Her mother—my wife—had never stepped a single foot into Wonder, and now she never would. She had been a literature professor, an old soul at heart, and had decried the portals back when the developers had announced the first stage of construction. *If you could see your daughter now*, I silently mused. For as much technological advancement the portals had brought to humanity, they hadn't brought a cure for cancer. With her gone, Ingrid was all I had left.

I pushed away the grim thoughts and hurried to keep up with Ingrid. Entering the Whitechapel graveyard threatened to revive memories of my wife's funeral, but Ingrid spoke before they had a chance to come flooding back into my mind.

"What do you think?" she asked. "Once I return the amulet and talk to the ghost, should I try to find the killer right away or go back to Amida for more help from the town?"

"Oh, just place the amulet on the grave. You need to make the decision for yourself. Just remember, getting more help is easier, but you'll get better rewards and more experience going solo. And I'm always here for backup." I gave the sword at my side a gentle pat to reinforce my fatherly position as my daughter's eternal guardian.

Ingrid placed the garnet necklace on the top of the headstone, and a swirl of ghastly smoke puffed up from the freshly turned soil in response. Before long, the ghost of the slain chandler stood in full form on top of his grave.

"Thank you for returning the heirloom, Ingrid," the intangible NPC stated with rigid formality.

"It was my pleasure, sir," came Ingrid's response.

The ghost turned away slightly, dropping his pale head into his ghastly hands. "But I am not at peace . . ." he murmured.

"Who was it that killed you?" Ingrid was clearly eager to get on with the last part of the quest chain, skipping any of the small-talk dialogue options the NPC was capable of producing. Although, truth be told, no one *really* knew the extent of the AI system that ran Wonder. In the early days of the game, a few programmers from some of the world's best universities had been skeptical, and they'd made a huge public event of testing the system's artificial intelligence during a live stream online. On the third trial of what ended up being more than ten thousand runs, the AI passed the famous Turing Test, and then it never failed again. While most of the NPCs had scripts they followed, especially upon first interaction, their capability for going off-script was apparently limitless. If Ingrid wanted to, she'd be able to ask the chandler's ghost about absolutely anything that struck her fancy, and she'd get a completely human-like response.

The ghost pointed to one of the buildings in Whitechapel with a stone facade and a chimney reaching up into the afternoon sky. "There. The man who lives there, his name is Alric. I owed him money, and when I couldn't pay, he killed me." With that, the ghost vanished back into the dirt covering his casket.

"What's your plan?" I asked.

Ingrid was already moving in the direction of the house. "I'll avenge his spirit," she said with determination.

Taking the risky route meant she would get her first weapon—but only if she survived.

I decided to wait outside Alric's house as Ingrid went about completing her first quest chain. "Be safe," I told her. "And if you don't make it, wait for me in the apartment. I'll come right out, and then you can try again if we have time."

She nodded, then snuck around the side of the house to the back door, the one that everyone who had ever played Wonder knew was always unlocked.

I positioned myself at a side window to watch. The glass wasn't great, so I couldn't make out any details of the scene, but I knew well enough what was happening from the forums and all the Wonder guides that existed everywhere online. Slowly, Ingrid crept through the rear of the small, one-room house. She was quiet despite her terribly low cunning score, and she was light enough that the floorboards didn't even creak beneath her feet.

Alric, her target, was asleep on a small cot nestled against one wall between a table and a three-legged stool. A half-eaten loaf of dark bread sat on the table, and the hilt of a knife stuck out from the end of it.

Ingrid grabbed the handle of the knife and slowly slid it from its unconventional sheath. Still sneaking on the balls of her feet, she crept closer to the sleeping Alric, the knife poised high above her head for a clean strike.

Just like every time any character reached the vengeance point in the quest chain, Alric awoke with a sharp yell. He thrashed upward, his bare chest exposed as his meager sheets fell to the ground, and grabbed Ingrid's wrist. She twisted back at the same moment—she'd rehearsed the quest probably fifty times before stepping through the portal—and dropped her knife, took a fist to her ribs that only staggered her a little, and then caught the hilt of her tumbling weapon with her free hand.

Alric's eyes went wide in surprise. His AI software had no doubt seen the maneuver before, but he was never quick enough to stop it. He tried to move his hands down to block the incoming attack, but his own kitchen knife sank into his gut. Blood splattered all over the floor.

Keeping the knife in her hand, Ingrid ran back out the rear door and to my side. "Well done!" I said, clapping her on the back.

"I did it! I should get a point in physical when I turn it in, right?" She jumped up and down like all excited girls do when they can't contain themselves. The whole idea of her celebration was a little weird, if I was being honest with myself. She had just killed someone—a line of code in a video game that would respawn eventually—and she was covered in blood. But Ingrid was too young to know the world before Wonder had changed it forever. Before the game, people were killed with knives just like the one in her hand. Real people. The game had taken over so much of society that the real murder rates in all the developed countries had fallen nearly to zero. There just wasn't time for that kind of thing back on Earth anymore.

Living in a world with so little crime meant that moral education was a little different than when I had been a child. Ingrid didn't see the quest as anything other than that—a quest. Maybe she was right. Alric was, after all, a bit of scripted code and not a human. He'd be back in his bed in a day, maybe sooner if the zone's population suddenly escalated. Still, seeing her standing in front of me practically giddy at having completed her first quest was unnerving. My little girl wasn't meant to hold a knife. She wasn't meant to feel the slick glide of blood covering her fingers.

"Dad?" she asked, her voice breaking my reverie.

"Yeah? Oh, don't forget to go check under the bed!" I told her. "You won't get full credit unless you get the matching necklace and give it back to the widow."

She bounded back through the door at once to grab the stolen jewelry, and I simply shook my head at my own thoughts. Wonder was everything now. The last I had heard, somewhere around a quarter of the world's population either worked in-game or for the developers, and all the things everyone used to love about society had nearly faded into the history books. Wonder had it all—everything from sports leagues to schools, guilds, jobs, and art galleries, all created entirely in-game. Teaching my daughter how to play Wonder wasn't just a fun daddy-daughter activity like a video game might have been ten or twenty years ago. No, I was teaching her the world. The only one that really mattered.

When Ingrid emerged from the house with the necklace in her hand, we walked down to the widow's front door with our fingers entwined. For a second, the illusion of being inside a video game was lost on my mind, but then I felt the blood transferring from her skin to mine, and all I could do was shake my head once more.

CHAPTER 2

I jingled a few coins in my pocket as we walked back from Whitechapel to Echelon. Ingrid's physical attribute had increased by one upon completing the quest, and the widow had told her to keep the knife she had stolen from Alric. She had her first weapon, was well on her way to level two, and with the little bit of silver I had saved I'd be able to buy her a nice dress that wouldn't make her stand out so much. My own clothes, a simple linen tunic with a pair of cloth pants and a leather belt to hold my cheap scabbard, had barely cost a single coin.

I planned on taking Ingrid to one of the better shops in Echelon—not anywhere close to the best, of course—when a system-wide notification began flickering along the bottom edge of my vision. Ingrid stopped as well, and I could see her eyes moving to activate it at the same time I did.

System Notification: New Event! A rogue band of thieves led by the infamous criminal Vic Fuentes is attempting to lay siege to the northern gate of Echelon! King Ahmose II of Echelon requests the aid of his loyal subjects in repelling the attack! Earn renown and influence in the service of Echelon!

I waited while Ingrid finished reading the message before trying to figure out what to do, though I already knew what I *wanted* to do. "Since you just got here, you haven't officially pledged for Ahmose II, so fighting at his call would probably be enough to seal your allegiance if you want to do it," I explained.

She thought it over for a minute. "What's the point of declaring for Echelon? I've never seen you do much with it," she answered.

I tried to think back to a time when I had taken advantage of my allegiance to the king of Echelon, but she was right. I hadn't used it much. "You'll get a discount when you shop anywhere in the city, and it opens up a few dungeons for when we get higher level. Pledging any of the other cities would take forever. Walking to one of them would be impossible, and we don't have enough money for a mount."

"What about joining one of the guilds or other groups?" She fiddled with the hilt of her stolen kitchen knife as we walked.

"Some of them are alright," I said honestly, "but some of them are horrible. Like Vic's group attacking the city right now. They move from town to town sacking the NPCs and raiding their stores. And they kill player characters, too. You don't want to join one of the smaller groups and risk pulling the ire of someone like Vic."

"Like you did?" she asked, a hint of a laugh edging her voice.

I sighed. Vic had been hating my guts since long before Wonder came online. "It wasn't joining Echelon that made Vic such a pretentious prick. We worked together at the Ministry, remember? I fired him. He's hated me ever since. Killed me a couple times in here, too."

"So, you want to help bring him down?" she asked. The laughter in her voice was replaced by a bit of optimism.

"Yeah," I said. "Let's get him."

"Then I'll help your king. If Vic doesn't like you, I'm not

his friend either." Ingrid charged forward down the road a bit, slashing at invisible enemies with her new weapon.

"Ha, then let's go!" I caught up to her, and we nearly ran down the road back to Echelon to make sure we reached the world event in time to join and rack up some solid experience points.

When we arrived, a battle was in full swing. Vic had probably a hundred or more brigands under his command, each of them with insanely high infamy scores. Somewhat ironically, Vic himself wasn't a thief or any other class based on skulking around and stealing away through the shadows. He was a warlord, a leader class designed to inspire others and empower them in combat, and that made him a formidable opponent on the battlefield.

Sadly . . . I'd never be able to stand against him anyway, formidable or otherwise. I was still level nine, and he was in the thirties the last time the two of us had crossed paths. While skill and creativity always played an important role in any battle or duel, there was pretty much nothing that I had ever been able to do to make up for such a stark level difference. And that bastard had some strange obsession with killing me every chance he got.

"Looks like Vic finally bit off a little more than he can chew," I said, surveying the unfolding battle from the safety of a hastily erected battlement right outside Echelon's northern wall. "He's losing. Or maybe he has something planned."

"Maybe he's finally lost his marbles," Ingrid chimed in. Behind us, two NPCs were organizing the city guard and discussing plans for reinforcing the gatehouse. It was odd to watch NPCs interacting so freely with each other when their programming could have certainly allowed them instantaneous communication, but I didn't have time to consider the strangeness before another player came up to give me orders.

"Fall in, soldier!" the man shouted. I could see his name,

level, and class, but nothing else about his stats or abilities was available. His name was Edward, and he was a raidmaster class, something I hadn't come into contact with much before. I had seen a couple of them on the forums and the streams, and they were typically the standard choice for leading the high-end dungeons all over Wonder. From what I knew, playing a raidmaster was really difficult in the early levels, so not many people opted to go that route. On top of that, finding a class trainer to bestow the title reportedly involved running through some grim dungeons over and over. Stuff like that wasn't really my cup of tea.

I fell into step next to a handful of other characters awaiting orders, and Ingrid stayed right next to my side ready to fight.

"You sorry lot are all we have. The king's own are holding the gatehouse well enough for now, and more reinforcements are on their way, but we can't count on NPCs for shit." The raidmaster walked back and forth in front of us like a drill sergeant displeased with the presentation of his troops. One of the other players, a ranger, even offered a somewhat awkward salute.

"You . . ." The raidmaster stopped in front of Ingrid and me. "What are you doing here?"

I offered a curt nod. "Vic's killed me plenty of times. Just trying to do my part and maybe get a little revenge, sir."

The raidmaster seemed pleased with my answer, so he kept pacing. As he spoke, a few more stragglers came out of the city or in from the countryside to join the ranks of players ready to help repel the attack. By the time we were dismissed and ready to be deployed into the field, we had about thirty players. It looked like more than a hundred guards had taken the field against Vic and his band, and the city was still winning.

"What do you have hiding up your sleeve?" I muttered toward Vic as Ingrid and I moved out with six other players to our designated position on the right flank of the guards. Our crew was comprised of the lowest level volunteers, and as such we were given what was ostensibly the easiest of the tasks. Edward and the other high-level players were charging up the middle with their mounts and lances. The sound of their horses was thunderous among the panoply of other noises emanating from the battle.

Our warband arrived at a small ridge laden with unassembled supplies and two portable ballistae the guards had dropped off at the beginning of the battle. "Get to work!" yelled our de facto leader, a twelfth level engineer.

We split into pairs, each of our four duos knowing exactly what to do by relying on our craftsmanship stats to construct the small rampart and get the ballistae into position. Under the engineer's direction, we had the battlement constructed in no time, and Ingrid was still able to help despite her low stats. My craftsmanship ranked up to level seven, still pretty weak compared to just about everyone in our group, but not too bad by my standards. I'd earned my first six levels in the stat by doing an in-depth quest chain involving a lot of manual labor for a wall crew under the direction of one of Ahmose's close advisors.

When two other members of our low-level crew, a pair of druids with decent cunning stats, had the ballistae loaded with bolts, the rest of us grabbed spears and manned the front line to either side of the heavy weapons. Our gunners were a shaman and a ranger, the only two with enough fortune to maybe score some critical hits against the thieves, and the ranger at least had a good amount of experience with a bow that we all figured would translate somewhat to manning the siege equipment.

Ingrid and I watched side by side, our hands gripped tightly around our spears, as the ballistae began to fire. Vic's crew still had about fifty yards or more to cross before reaching the gate. The first three bolts sailed far over the heads of the oncoming thieves, but the fourth hit its mark. One of the thieves mounted atop a pale white horse was skewered through his chest. When he fell from the saddle, our small battlement sent a cheer into the air.

Bolt five found its mark as well, and another mounted thief was instantly sent rocketing to the ground and a quick respawn. The player would appear back in his own home—or wherever he had left his transponder—and I just had to hope it would take some time for him to get back to the portal and through the throng of people always surrounding it. Or better yet, if the thief had entered Wonder from a different portal, I knew I wouldn't see him for weeks, or maybe never. Although, all it would take to quickly reinforce the thieves was a single talented mage with the ability to teleport players across Wonder. Mages powerful enough to teleport others were rare, and that meant their services were usually priced in the tens of thousands.

A nagging notion at the back of my mind told me Vic had something devious planned. A mage instantly teleporting his fallen soldiers back into the battle wouldn't necessarily surprise me. *Something* had to be coming.

More and more bolts sailed over the town guards and landed among the throng of thieves, and most of them hit their targets with devastating effect. The bolts were so long and heavy that even a glancing blow, especially against a mounted target, was absolutely brutal.

Then Vic, conspicuous in a plumed hat at the rear of his little army, turned his attention to our battlement.

"Get ready!" our engineer leader called. The atmosphere behind the barricade instantly shifted from one of celebration to one of fear. We were all low levels. Vic alone would probably be able to slaughter us all if he got close enough, so we'd have to make the ballista bolts count.

"Aim for the guy with the feathers on his helmet!" I yelled to the two gunners. They swiveled their ballistae in Vic's direction and waited a moment for the thief leader to get into range. In front of him, Vic had a ring of heavily armored bodyguards who looked like they might be his best soldiers saved for last. If my estimation was correct, we were screwed.

I didn't want Ingrid's first death to be at the hands of that damned troll, either.

The six of us guarding the ballistae planted our spears in the ground and prepared to make a stand against the on-coming marauders. Thankfully, a few of Vic's goons broke off to join the fray with the town guards while they were still en route to our position—a sign of the man's insatiable ar-rogance, no doubt. Two massive ballista bolts took down an-other pair, but Vic still stood, and I could see the fire in his eyes when his gaze fell upon me.

"Shit," I spat. "He knows I'm here. Get behind me, Ingrid." I positioned myself in front of my daughter as best I could, futile though I knew my defense would likely be. Still, I clung to the hope that the other six of us in the battlement would be sufficient.

There wasn't enough time to reload either of the ballis-tae before Vic and his goons were upon us. A bolt of magic launched out from the druid in our group and caught one of Vic's guards squarely in the chest. The man didn't go down, but he staggered, and that was better than nothing.

Vic's guards fell upon us all at once. I kept my planted spear to my left side and tried to use it like a stationary shield. Not having a class meant I didn't have a single magical ability to activate, so all I could do was try to swing my sword, block-ing and parrying as best I knew how. After only two exchanges with the level thirteen marauder right in front of me, I knew I was sorely outmatched.

The marauder came on in a frenzy, his outline shimmer-ing with blue magic that told me he had activated a talent. Since I had spent every minute of my time in Wonder trying to scrounge up enough money for Ingrid's lifetime pass, my knowledge of different auras and effects was extremely limited. I was essentially fighting blind. The man's long, narrow mace swung for the side of my unarmored head, and I was barely able to get the crossguard of my sword up in time to block. At once I could feel that the marauder's physical stat was higher than mine, and he began crushing downward through my block without much resistance.

I had to take a gamble. I wasn't the risking type normally, greatly preferring to stick to safer options when I could, but I didn't see any other way out. Ingrid was screaming behind me, clearly terrified as the very real possibility of her first death inched closer and closer. Gritting my teeth, I pulled back on my sword arm and slid to the right, opening myself up to a crushing strike that sent waves of pain blazing through my shoulder—but I had an opportunity. With all the strength I had left, I slashed horizontally, and my blade connected.

I wasn't strong enough for my sword to go through the marauder's studded leather armor.

He cackled at the top of his lungs, and then his weapon ignited with a cylinder of fire and crashed down onto the back of my head. I sprawled onto the ground. I could hear Ingrid above me, and I knew she would be next. As my vision dimmed, I hoped Ingrid would at least meet a swift death, but Vic had never been known for his mercy. The only logout features in Wonder were either death or leaving through a portal in a capital city, so there wasn't any way for either of us to simply click a few menu options and avoid the pain.

Before I could think any further, the marauder above me stepped on the back of my neck, and I died.

I awoke on top of my transponder, which I had left on my bed in my apartment. Thankfully, none of the pain or injuries sustained inside Wonder affected my physical body in the real world. From the only window in my bedroom, I could see the top of the arched portal about two miles away, and my heart sank for Ingrid. I could run back to the portal, race through the streets of Echelon, and try to rescue her before it was too late, but what if she died and respawned while I was out looking for her? We had phones in the real world, but the technology didn't work if one or both of us was inside the game.

All I could do was wait. Pacing around in the kitchen of our cramped apartment, I flipped on the only monitor we had and decided to watch the streams coming from Echelon. 'Normal' news had essentially ceased to exist since the creation of Wonder—there just wasn't any point in talking about a single thing outside of the game. I flipped to my favorite Echelon streamer, a player who went by the name AggroKing, and flopped down in a stiff wooden chair to try and catch a glimpse of my daughter.

Luckily, AggroKing was in Echelon when the stream connected to his character, and he was near enough to the north gate that I could at least get a general idea of how the battle was playing out. The city guards had easily held the gate, especially with the arrival of some of the higher-level players from Echelon, and Vic's raiders had been corralled to one small corner of the battlefield. AggroKing moved to a different section of the wall to get a look at something else in the fight before I could find the meager battlement where my defeated crew had been stationed.

A little while later, AggroKing moved to one of the guard towers flanking the northern gate and cast a spell to enhance his vision. He was a level thirty-eight sorcerer, and the spell was one he had trained well. Every detail of the battlefield came to life in his eyes and on the stream. "Look at the battlement! The ballista!" I yelled at the monitor when his vision focused on the wrong side of the field.

Finally, he found one of the last knots of combat and focused his gaze upon it, bringing the engineer and Ingrid into full view. They were the last two still standing from the original group of eight. My corpse was there as well since it wouldn't despawn until I walked back into the game. The two defenders were outnumbered. Vic and a pair of his men had them surrounded, basically toying with them while keeping their distance. For a moment, I thought AggroKing might summon some huge burst of magic to his fingers and end the fight all the way from the wall, but alas he did not. Instead, he only watched, and he didn't say anything so no one on the stream had any idea what he was thinking.

All I could do was watch with the rest of the people on the stream.

Vic had grabbed one of our spears from the battlement and was poking it over the heads of his two soldiers. I shuddered when he tore a line across Ingrid's collarbone. She dropped her knife and fell to the ground, and AggroKing zoomed in a little more to catch the action. Between the battlement and Echelon's walls, a group of mounted cavalry had emerged from the town and was galloping toward Ingrid's position, but it didn't look like she had enough time.

More than fourteen thousand people were watching AggroKing's stream of the battle. Vic hit Ingrid once more with his spear, goring her right leg, and she screamed in pain. The engineer managed to take down one attacker, and then it was all over for the battlement crew.

A soft popping noise accompanied Ingrid's return to the apartment. I heard her groan a second later. I waited just a little longer to make sure I could watch Vic get trampled into the ground by the Echelon cavalry before switching off the stream.

"Hey, sorry I died so quickly," I told her, moving down the hall to her room.

She emerged from her bedroom with a smile on her face despite the ravaging pain she must have felt only moments before. "I gained points in physical and cunning!" she said cheerfully. "I hit level two!"

"What did you think of your first quest?"

She walked past me to the small kitchen and began looking through a couple cabinets for some snacks. "That was awesome. I just want to advance as much as possible. Can we go back? How long do we have to wait?"

I grabbed two bowls from a cupboard near the fridge and set them down on the table. Ingrid brought over a box of honey biscuits and shook out a few into each of the bowls.

"We should let things calm down for now. We can go back through the portal tomorrow," I said. I took a bite from one of the biscuits and savored the flavor. Food outside of the game, especially anything sugary, was always expensive. With everyone eating the majority of their meals inside the game where coins were much easier to come by, even things as mundane as bread and honey had become wildly pricey on the outside. I still didn't really understand how the food we ate on the other side of the portals sustained our real, physical bodies, but then again, being inside the game didn't really *change* us . . . it was simply entering another world.

Ingrid continued to beam over her quest completion. "So when do the death penalties kick in?" she asked. "Which level?"

"I'm almost there. Starting at level ten, dying in-game has a fifty-fifty chance to reduce any of your secondary stats by one. You can lose stolen goods as well, but that doesn't come up as much. Not really a huge deal unless you die all the time," I explained. "Some of the items you have, if they get stolen quickly enough after you die, will also be lost. It just depends on how fast you can get back to the portal to despawn your corpse and how malicious your killer was. NPCs almost never steal your loot, but some of the meaner players won't think twice about it."

She nodded. "We should do something tomorrow that could get both of us experience. I want to see you hit level ten. And you need to start finding a class! No need to keep going after gold for me."

I knew she was right. If I was going to protect her in-game, I needed a class. The problem was, one of the reasons I had waited so long to find a trainer was simply that I didn't know what to select. Becoming a knight or a paladin would help me stand toe-to-toe against Vic whenever he showed up, but casting spells was also extremely awesome. Once a class was selected, it cost a ton of money to change. The developers weren't too keen on letting people change frequently, so there were also one-time stat penalties any time a change was completed. Whatever I decided to finally take, I would need to stick with it for some time.

The next morning, Ingrid woke me up before dawn. She was wildly eager to continue, and I couldn't deny that I was just as ready to head back into Echelon. The crowd at the portal was as thick as the day before, and it took us a good two hours to get from the apartment back to Echelon. When we stepped through, we appeared in the center of the city near some of the markets. The capital was huge, and there were dozens of shopping districts of all different qualities and styles. The one we were near was on the lower end and not far from the dress shop where I had planned to take Ingrid.

I led her there, and her eyes went wide when she realized that it was a gift for her we were after. I had thirty silver coins in my pouch—not much by any means, but clothes not meant for combat weren't usually expensive. "Anything under thirty. You pick. Need to have you looking like a proper citizen of Echelon."

She spent a decent amount of time browsing the different selections before finally settling on a red dress trimmed with gold that only left me with two coins. The garment was also mildly enchanted, improving her fortune by one. It came with a braided cloth belt that she tied around her waist and used to hold her knife. The game AI had seen fit to let me respawn with the spear I had been given at the battlement, and tucking it into my own belt didn't really work well, so I had to just carry it along. If it got to be too much of a burden, I had already decided to pitch it. The spear was worthless, and it didn't match my playstyle at all.

"What's on the agenda for today?" Ingrid asked. Her curly brown hair contrasted beautifully with the bright red of the dress. I had to admit she looked impressive in the new threads. Red had been her mother's favorite color, and Ingrid had adopted it as her own a couple years ago.

For today, I had a few quests in mind. "There are a handful quests between our levels that might interest you. Some of the tasks might be too hard for a level two, but I can help with those. If we do something around level five, we'll both get experience."

"Anything that will help my physical? I don't want to die so easily next time we meet Vic," she said.

"There's a fifth-level quest, a small dungeon beneath one of the municipal counting houses, that we might be able to complete. It'll be tough, but it should be fun. What do you say?" I had never completed the dungeon on my own before, but I had seen streams of other low-level players running through it, so I knew the general layout well enough to be confident that we wouldn't be charging in totally blind.

"What types of enemies will we fight?" she wanted to know.

I had to think for a minute to remember what I had watched online. "There should be some choices along the way that could alter things, but it'll be mostly goblins and kobolds," I explained.

"Alright, let's do it," Ingrid said with a smile.

With that, we were off. I led her in the direction of one of the larger counting houses in Echelon, a building that served as both a bank and place where people could make investments. The more complex financial capabilities of Wonder hadn't been scripted into the original game code, but once the portals had so thoroughly taken over the entire economy of the real world, the developers had added them with a patch. Echelon's stock market was something I had never been wealthy enough to bother exploring, so I still only knew the absolute basics of what went on inside the counting houses.

We reached Richter and Fryer, the counting house home to our targeted dungeon, after about twenty or thirty minutes of walking. The front door was guarded by two huge NPCs, both level twenty-five warriors with swords strapped to their hips, halberds in their hands, and steel armor hanging from their shoulders.

I went up to the guard on the left and caught his attention. "Anything going on inside that might need the help of two adventurers?" I asked, prompting the response I knew I would get.

The guard looked me over once, glanced to Ingrid, and then began: "Master Shrifkin is having a little trouble, eh, with some new residents. If you're looking for work, you'll find him on the second floor wearing a leather vest with a flower pinned to the lapel."

I nodded in appreciation before pushing open the door and heading inside with Ingrid right behind me. The counting house was busy and noisy. Several rows of NPC bankers sat at wooden desks talking with clients, their armed guards hovering over their shoulders. In front of the bankers, we could see all manner of players conducting their business. The highest-level player in the room appeared to be one of the more well-known streamers, an online icon easily recognizable in his shimmering red armor and horned helmet. The man was a ranger by the name of Kevin, and he'd been a legend on all the Echelon streams for years. He didn't bother looking up from the parchments he was discussing as Ingrid and I walked right past his desk to the stairs that would take us to the second level.

Above the rows of desks was another security checkpoint. Two huge bouncers, both half-orc NPCs, confiscated our weapons with a disapproving sneer before letting us beyond the velvet rope to the counting house leadership. In all honesty, there wasn't any need to remove our weapons, and the NPCs had known it. Even Kevin and his high-level guildmates wouldn't have been able to sack the counting house and get very far. The whole city of Echelon would be down their throats before they'd make it more than a dozen feet out the door. On the other hand, though, that didn't mean full-scale raids had *never* taken place. In fact, some of the most viewed videos in the world came from those exact events and the thousands of streams they produced.

Perhaps Vic's attack was a prelude to something larger, or maybe it was just nothing. The man we were supposed to see for the dungeon quest walked over to us before I could think any more about the possibility of Echelon being sacked.

"May I help you?" asked the banker, a tall NPC elf with pointed ears named Sparg.

I straightened my back and tried to look impressive enough to make sure we would get the correct quest. If the NPC perceived Ingrid and me as being too powerful for the minor dungeon run, he would give us something else, and that could be anything. Of course, looking too *powerful* wasn't really a concern. I needed to make sure we weren't too damn *weak* to get the quest in the first place. "I heard about your problem. We're here to help," I stated with confidence.

The elf looked us over once as he straightened his velvet

jacket. "Alright, I suppose I could use your help. It'll be tough though, make no mistake about that, adventurers."

I nodded eagerly. "What do you need?"

"Oh, some of the typical vermin of Echelon have taken up a residence of sorts in our lower levels. I need an exterminator if you're up for it," he explained.

"How many have you seen?" The dungeon runs I had watched on the low-level streams had been against goblins and their stronger hobgoblin cousins, a race known for breeding quickly and using sheer numbers to overwhelm anything they wanted to destroy.

"Dozens, maybe more of the damned ratlings, I don't know," Sparg said.

In all the streams I had watched, I'd never seen anyone killing ratlings below the counting house. It could be a different version of the dungeon quest, or perhaps the AI had changed the script and redesigned the entire area as a result of some sort of player interaction that had occurred. That was the best part of Wonder: no matter how many times you watched a stream or memorized an NPC pattern, there was always an element of mystery. It kept the game from getting stale.

"What do you think they're after?" I asked, hoping my investigation skill was high enough to get me a few clues before we headed down into the darkness of the dungeon.

The elf appeared curious. "I don't know," he said, shaking his head and running a long-fingered hand through his dark hair. "We keep and protect all sorts of artifacts here in the counting house, of course, so they might be looking for almost anything."

"Any ideas?" I didn't know if pushing the issue would help or not, but I figured it couldn't really hurt.

Surprisingly, the elf leaned in close, waving to Ingrid so she could move near enough to hear, and began to explain the quest in a little more detail. "Alright . . . Truth be told, I know what they want. The goblins that were here before, remember them? Well, they left something behind. Something the ratlings want. I don't know what it is, but those skittering bastards haven't stopped coming after it since the goblins were finally chased out. See if you can figure out what they want. Bring it up here once you find it. Got it?"

Your Investigation skill has increased to 7!

Again, I put on my best air of confidence and nodded. "We're the right ones for the job. Speaking of which, has anyone else gone down to look recently?" I wasn't really sure if other people being on the same quest would necessarily interfere or not. I knew that decisions made by other people doing the same runs could affect those that came after, but I didn't really understand the full extent of how the AI interpreted anything. If I had only spent more time learning the game and not trying to fly through quests to buy Ingrid a pass, I would have been more prepared. In the end, I had to smile. I was worried about nothing. I'd have plenty of time to explore Wonder with Ingrid by my side. She was only sixteen. We had our whole lives in front of us.

Sparg the elf told us about a pair of other low-level adventurers that had gone into the tunnels and chambers below the counting house about an hour ago. I knew the quest usually took longer than a single hour, so they probably hadn't finished it yet. I doubted we would ever run into them. The dungeon was designed to be confusing with a lot of secondary passages where people could easily get lost for hours at a time.

With nothing left to discuss, I let Sparg lead the two of us back down to the first floor, past Kevin, and into the cellar. Beneath the main floor was where the counting house kept all of its most valuable items. A handful of guards stood around a stack of square boxes playing dice, and the valuables were kept locked behind an iron gate on rows and rows of shelves. Sparg, hands tucked awkwardly into his vest pockets, led us down deeper to a part of the basement that looked like it had been recently blasted apart.

"Here it is," he began. "My men have investigated the tunnel for some distance, but the ratlings are industrious. The path shifts frequently, and their traps are devious. Be careful down there."

As a final parting gesture, the elf pulled a small silver coin from one of his pockets. "Please accept a small token," he said, placing it in my outstretched hand. "It might be useful to you. Finish the job and bring it back, and I'll make sure you're paid handsomely."

I thanked him and stepped into the dim light illuminating the tunnel. "Here." I gave the coin to my daughter. "Take it. It raises your fortune by one, and you need it more than I do. Hopefully it helps keep you safe."

She deposited the coin in the small pouch on her belt and smiled.

CHAPTER 3

After about forty-five minutes in the dungeon, all we had found were ratling corpses. Whoever had come before us had cleared out a ton of the ratlings, and their hairy little bodies were scattered everywhere. From what I could tell, the players killing them were using long, thin swords like fencers. The fencer class was rare, and I'd read on some of the forums that it was considered one of the best classes in all of Wonder, though I had never actually met one in real life. I wasn't even sure where I would need to go to get the class, though it wasn't really one I considered for my own choice.

Ingrid and I came to a large chamber lit by torches in cage-like iron sconces on the wall. In the center was a big cistern with a grate of iron bars covering it, and several ratling bodies were scattered around the outside of the room in a circular pattern.

"If we don't find anything to fight, I'm not going to get any experience to level up!" Ingrid said.

She was right, of course, but there wasn't much I could do about it. I'd probably need to think of something else for us to do today if I wanted to hit level ten and get her to level three at the same time. Still, it didn't mean our dungeon run was useless—not at all.

"Just need to focus on investigation and cunning, I guess," I told her. "There will be time to train your physical stat later. Keep in mind that you're still on just your second day in Wonder. Plenty of time."

She grinned up at me. "I know. Thanks for taking me on a higher-level run. A lot of people on the streams don't get to run a real dungeon until they've spent at least a week inside."

"A week if they know what they're doing, at least two if they're bumbling around without a plan," I added.

Ingrid knelt down over one of the ratling corpses and began poking around its fur with her knife. "So what are we looking for?" she asked.

"I'm not really sure . . ." I pushed over one of the dead ratlings with my boot. The creature was about the size of a large German shepherd, maybe a little bigger, and its long whiskers extended a good foot beyond its face on either side. For weapons, the ratlings rarely used forged iron or steel. Instead, they wielded just their natural teeth and claws. In a swarming pack, the little beasts would certainly be formidable against someone without armor, but lacking numbers they were relatively easy to strike down for just about anyone in Wonder, no matter their level or class.

Finally, I found something that looked interesting. "Here," I said, calling Ingrid to my side. "Check out the scroll." The dead ratling I was inspecting had a tightly rolled bit of parchment gripped in one of its rear claws. The document, whatever it was, was clearly damaged—as though the creature had been running through the tunnels with it still clutched in a back foot. If we'd be able to read it all, we'd be lucky.

Ingrid plucked the scrap of paper from the ratling's pink foot and began smoothing it out on her knee. Thankfully, she lifted her new dress out of the way to save the red fabric from the dirt and grime of the underground chamber. I had already planned on washing it as soon as we got back to the apartment.

The parchment turned out to be a crude map drawn in rough, splotchy charcoal. "Here's the cistern," she said, pointing to the dark circle near the center of the paper. She traced her finger along one of the jagged paths that radiated from the cistern and ended with a misshapen triangle inside a circle. "What do you think that means?"

I shook my head. "I have no idea. Which tunnel is it?"

We both looked around and counted the number of passages leading from the cistern room. "See if you can figure out which path we need to take. I'm going to drag a few ratlings down the path we came from so we don't get lost," I said.

My morbid work took a few minutes, and by then Ingrid had a guess as to which path was which based on the general outline of the map and the ways in which the tunnels twisted as they left the cistern. The last streamer I had watched complete the dungeon run had been killing goblins and poisoning their food supply, so I had absolutely no prior knowledge that would help us out at all.

"Your guess is as good as mine," I said.

Ingrid oriented her map for the direction we were about to try and then stepped forward without a care in the world.

"Hey," I said, moving ahead of her, "let me take point. Just tell me where to go. You keep your eyes on the map, I'll keep my eyes on the ratlings." I drew my sword from my belt. I jammed my spear through my belt on my back, keeping it awkwardly in place, though it wouldn't really do much good in the tight quarters, at least not with my skills.

Almost at once, it was obvious that the tunnel we were using hadn't been traversed by any other humans in some time. All the footprints beneath us were ratling, though that didn't necessarily rule out *all* possibilities of players. While everyone walked through their first portal as a human, there were a few magical ways of acquiring a new race. Most players regarded the race-change magic as too expensive to be worth it, but every high-end guild made sure to employ a fair selection of non-human players. Some of the more exotic races offered some rather unique benefits. Though the possibility was real, there would simply never be any point for a human to spend considerable time and resources becoming a ratling. Their racial bonuses were pathetic, and all the major cities considered them vermin; attaining an allegiance anywhere was incredibly difficult for a player with long whiskers. Elves, dwarves, treants, and other more traditional fantasy races were the typical non-human player choices.

A sound from up ahead made me pause. I held out my hand to the side, and Ingrid stopped next to me, lowering her map and reaching for her dagger.

"Something's coming," I quickly whispered.

We crouched down along the side of the tunnel, but there wasn't anywhere to hide or anything to even offer some cover. Up ahead from a bend in the passageway, two chittering ratlings came into our view. Distracted, they took a few seconds longer to notice us than we did to see them, and that was all the time we needed.

I pulled Ingrid along by her left arm and charged. The ratlings barely had time to think before we crashed into them. Our larger human bodies outweighed their collective mass by at least a hundred pounds, and they scurried backward as they struggled for purchase in the dim tunnel, filling the air with their high-pitched screams.

Ingrid stabbed the ratling on the right several times with a series of quick jabs to the creature's gut. My sword, twice as long as my daughter's dagger, easily ripped through the top of the left ratling's skull, and then it was wrenched from my hand as the beast collapsed on the dirty ground. Another pair of stabs, and the ratling Ingrid was fighting went silent.

Almost as quickly as it had begun, the easy fight was over. "Still didn't raise my physical stat," Ingrid muttered under her breath. I knew she had seen enough streams to know that it would take more than a single ratling to see some stat movement. There wasn't much of a point in looting the ratling corpses for anything useful since the beasts didn't carry weapons and our investigation stats were so low. At higher levels, having enough investigation might allow us to find something valuable even within the corpses—perhaps a bit of a poisonous organ or a particularly worthwhile bone—but we were both still far from that kind of level.

"We'll find more up ahead, I think," I replied.

We didn't have to wait long to find more action. The end of the tunnel opened into another room a little larger than the cistern area, and at least a dozen ratlings were moving back and forth working at various tasks. The center of the chamber was dominated by what I could only describe as a throne, and the ratling leader—I had no idea if the creature was a king, chieftain, or something else—was inspecting the construction of a wheeled device somewhat similar in appearance to a horizontal siege engine like a battering ram.

"Whatever they're trying to steal from the counting house," I whispered, using my hand to muffle my words, "it looks like they're going to bring down the whole building."

"What should we do?" Ingrid asked. She crouched at my side at the edge of the tunnel like a cat clinging to the shadows of an alleyway.

I had a few ideas, but I didn't want to take the lead too much and deny the girl her much-needed experience, so I simply shrugged. She would need to rely on her own cunning stat and natural intellect to figure out what we were supposed to do next.

After a few tense moments of watching, she finally looked like she had a plan. "Those two," she said, pointing out a pair of ratlings, "they're patrolling the area. When they come close, we can grab them and haul them into the tunnel. Quick and quiet."

I nodded and readjusted the grip on my sword.

When the ratlings neared our little hideout, we both leapt forward to grab the creatures by their pelts and hurl them into the passage behind us. It worked perfectly, and the ratlings barely made a sound as we ended their lives. "What's next?" I asked.

"We need to know what it is they're building," she whispered back. "Charging headlong into the room probably won't end well. Let's wait for an opening and then move up closer. We can hide behind the barrels to our left, and that will give us a better vantage point."

I had to admit I was impressed. I was about to respond and tell her, but her face lit up with a huge smile before I had the chance.

"My cunning just increased again! I'll level again before long!" she said with an excited whisper. Her voice was loud enough behind her covering hand to make me worry that some of the ratlings might have heard, but we got lucky.

After a silent nod, I waited for a few minutes until Ingrid took off in front of me for the barrels at the side of the dimly lit chamber. She made it to safety on quick and silent feet, but I wasn't so graceful. About two feet from the barrels, I lost my traction on a slick patch of fetid, green moss that I hadn't seen before. I hit the ground with a thud, trying desperately not to grunt or make a sound. Sadly, my sword didn't share my concern for stealth, and it made a horrible racket as it slid across the stones. To make matters worse, the spear on my back caught awkwardly on the stone ground, cracking the shaft.

Three of the nearest ratlings squealed to alert their

brethren before charging at us. I was just barely able to reach the hilt of my sword and get to my feet—with Ingrid's help—before the fight began. With the barrels to our left and a wall of solid stone at our backs, we were actually in a decent position to fend off the diminutive swarm.

Using a wide, sweeping stroke, I cut down the first ratling charging for my legs. Ingrid's weapon was much smaller than my own, so she had to wait for the ratlings to come to her, and she wasn't equipped to really fend them off. The beady-eyed vermin snapped and slashed at her, but she dropped two of them to the ground without taking much damage.

It looked like every ratling in the room except the boss on his throne was coming to kill us. Within seconds, my arms were tired and splattered with blood. One of the creatures had managed to bite the meat of my calf, and though it wasn't a grievous wound by any means, it hurt enough to make me start losing my focus. I had to wonder if the ratlings carried some sort of infection in their saliva as well. I would be able to check my character sheet for a new ailment once everything died down.

One of the ratlings was scrabbling over the barrels to my side. I turned to bash him in the skull with my blade, but another ratling was already pressing in from the front. Ingrid had two of her own bearing down on her. Trusting my daughter not to fall, I made a split second decision and whirled on the climbing ratling with a vicious overhand chop. The ratling dodged to its left, and my sword bit into the wooden ring of the barrel's top. I pulled back, but the metal wouldn't budge.

The ratling coming over the barrel paused for a split second before leaping for my face with its claws outstretched. I felt its small, razor-sharp nails digging into the skin on either side of my neck, and I stumbled backward with the creature on top of my chest.

Without my sword, all I could do was punch. Luckily, it

seemed like my physical stat was significantly higher than the NPC's since I was over-leveled for the dungeon in the first place. My fist crushed through the ratling's teeth and sent it reeling. It slid down toward my legs, giving me enough room to scramble to an awkward sitting position.

Arms outstretched, I held the biting critter at bay as I struggled to my feet and then hurled it over the barrels. The one I had ignored chomped down onto the meat over my right hip. I gave its head a punch, but it didn't move. It only ground its teeth further into my body. My sword was still there, lodged tauntingly in the rim of the wooden barrel. I wrapped my fingers around the handle and pulled, but it still wouldn't move.

With a ratling hanging from my hip and both hands wrapped around the hilt of my sword, I gave it everything I had.

Suddenly, I was overbalanced and fell into the wall behind me. "Cheap-ass sword!" I yelled through the pain. The hilt had broken off from the blade, leaving me with a worthless hunk of metal in my hands. Although . . . *worthless* wasn't exactly true. I essentially had a set of brass—technically steel—knuckles, and combined with my already overpowering physical stat, I knew I'd deal some damage.

After the first hit, I saw that I was right. The ratling's stunned expression told me that one more hit would be all that I needed. I wound up and let loose right on the top of the beast's skull, and I could feel the flesh and bone give way under the combined weight of my fist and the hilt of my sword. The ratling's jaws released, its eyes rolled back in its head, and blood began running down its forehead.

Finally, I had enough time to see how Ingrid was faring on her side of the barrels. She had two of the beasts dead at her feet, and she was locked in a grapple with a third. With all the damage she had taken, her arms simply weren't strong enough to keep the ratling from gaining ground.

I didn't want to step in and steal any of her experience, but she wouldn't gain much if she died, either. Moving toward her with my steel knuckles, I smashed the ratling in the center of its spine. A moment later its blood splashed all over the ground as Ingrid slashed its throat with her knife.

The last ratling left in the chamber was the boss, and the hairy creature looked pissed.

"You dare to challenge the Grimmock Clan?" the ratling chief yelled with a thick, almost indecipherable accent. While hundreds of languages existed all around the seven continents of Wonder, the AI converted them into English for most of the lower-level quests and other areas where the communication barrier would cause too much needless difficulty. In some of the high-level raids meant for dozens of players at the same time, knowing the various languages of Wonder was critical, and there were players who had dedicated their in-game lives to mastering them all.

Ingrid stepped forward and brushed some of the blood from her dress. "We challenge you, vile beast!" she shouted.

The ratling rose up from its throne slowly. It stood on its hind legs like a human, and it was at least twice the size of the other beasts we had killed.

"Why are you here?" I yelled at it. With fifteen influence, I figured I had at least a decent chance to intimidate the chief into giving us more clues.

The ratling hesitated for a second before answering. "You'll never get the Bits! The Gibbering Bits!"

I had absolutely no idea what the ratling was talking about, but 'Gibbering Bits' seemed like a useful piece of information, so I counted my intimidation attempt as a success.

Before any more verbal ripostes could be exchanged, the ratling chieftain produced a small cylinder of elemental lightning in the shape of a mace and charged.

"Ingrid!" I yelled. The beast was almost upon her. "Dodge!"

If she stood her ground and tried to be the hero, she probably wouldn't stand a chance. Her level disadvantage would mean a quick end.

I breathed a sigh of relief as the ratling's lightning mace only singed the end of her red dress. She came up in a crouch to the side, and I ran in as quickly as I could.

Broken hilt still in my right hand, I slammed it into the ratling boss's back—or I would have, if the strange creature wasn't so *damned* fast. It spun on its heels and blocked, and a violent jolt of electricity fired through the entire right side of my body.

Ingrid began slashing wildly in front of her, and she managed to land a few hits on the ratling's back, though they didn't do much against the chieftain's thick, hairy hide. Luckily, I had drawn the creature's ire, and it didn't turn back to give Ingrid a quick death. Instead, it kept swinging down, bashing me over and over with lightning. Without a shield or even decent armor, my body was taking a serious beating. My left arm was scorched, and the cloth of my shirt was starting to catch on fire. A few more hits would break my wrist, or maybe it wouldn't last that long before snapping back into my face.

I fell to my knees under the relentless magical assault. My broken sword hilt felt pretty weak in my hand.

Suddenly, the ratling boss screeched into the air. I could see Ingrid's hair flying out wildly to the sides behind the chieftain's body, but I couldn't tell what exactly she was doing. Still, I welcomed the reprieve.

As the boss turned back to fend off Ingrid's new assault, I rolled away to try and collect my senses and take stock of how badly injured my arm was. Healing in Wonder wasn't too bad, it simply required moving out of a city portal and then back in again, but the Echelon portal wasn't anywhere close to the underground sewer system.

I crawled over to the barrels in the corner and tried to

catch my breath. Pulling myself up using one of the barrels as a makeshift cane, the lid shifted under my grasp. Inside was a shimmering pool of inky black liquid with a pungent smell.

"Oil . . ."

I dug into the deepest reserves of my leftover strength and wrenched the barrel onto its side, spilling the thick oil all over the floor of the chamber. "Push him back, Ingrid! Back!" I yelled. I didn't have enough time to see what the girl was doing as I ran for the nearest torch and yanked it from its sconce. When I turned back, I saw Ingrid rushing my direction, the ratling right on her heels. She had a gruesome line of black ash on her cheek, and blood was running down her neck to her shoulders.

I reached out my throbbing left arm, and a fresh wave of pain cascaded through my body when Ingrid latched on. With so little strength remaining on that side of my body, I couldn't really pull her along, but I liked to think I was helping.

Ingrid wasn't entirely out of the oil slick, but I couldn't wait any longer. I tossed the torch right at the ratling's feet.

Fire at once began spreading all over the room. It licked up the bottom of Ingrid's dress and the backs of her feet, but it fully engulfed the ratling boss. The girl collapsed into my arms, and we both crawled away from the fire as best we could. Frantically, she ripped off the bottom few inches of the dress and tossed it aside. Her ankles were a little burned, but she wasn't too badly wounded.

"Is it dead?" Ingrid asked between breathless pants.

I shook my head. The ratling shrieked once in the burning oil. With a somber countenance, I turned Ingrid's face from the horror of the melting creature. "Come on, let's go!" It wouldn't take long for the huge siege contraption to begin to burn as well. Smoke was quickly filling the room, and the whole underground complex would be consumed by it before long.

We ran back to the cistern room as quickly as we could. I didn't know how long it would take the smoke to start filling the entire dungeon, and I wasn't too keen on finding out.

A split second before Ingrid and I came crashing in, voices from the cistern room told me someone was there. We didn't have time to stop.

The pair of adventurers the elf from the counting house had mentioned had their backs to us, kneeling and inspecting the dead ratlings all around the cistern. I had to assume they had missed the map earlier and backtracked to try and find the clue that would lead them to the ratling boss. Of course, that missing clue was in our possession, and the ratling boss was likely already dead.

"Kill them!" I yelled to Ingrid as the two adventurers—a level three woman and a level four man—slowly turned to face us with their eyes full of shock.

Ingrid met her target first, lunging ferociously with her small knife leading the way. She pounced on the level four player and drove her blade into his side as the poor man was still trying to turn and get his bearings. Before he had the chance to fumble for his own weapon and try to defend himself, Ingrid slashed him again across the chest.

Luckily for us, both of the players were also classless, so I didn't have to worry about any magic spells or talents coming my way. The problem was, I still only had my broken hilt for a weapon, and the level three woman I slugged was wearing a hardened leather breastplate.

My knuckles throbbed with pain as they crunched against the woman's armor. She let loose a scream and shoved me backward, and some of the oil still coating the bottom of my right boot made me lose my footing. She didn't waste any time.

I let out a yell of my own as the woman's small, rounded mace smacked against my ribs. It didn't feel like anything had broken, but between the pain in my wrist, my hand, basically my entire body, and now my side, I was in bad shape. I rolled to my side to try and get away, and the woman missed her next strike.

"Ingrid!" I yelled, trying to get back on my feet at the same time. "Help!"

I held my arms up in front of me in a crossed position hoping to block the next swing of the woman's mace. If I could catch it on the crossguard of my broken hilt, I might be able to deflect it to the side long enough to get my feet planted and fight back.

Ingrid yelled, and I saw her jump on the woman's back. I scrambled to my feet and rushed forward, not wasting any time punching the woman on the chin with my weighted fist. Blood splattered across the stone floor.

Before I could punch again, Ingrid slit the woman's throat, and the cistern room fell eerily silent. Smoke was just starting to creep in along the low ceiling.

"Damn," I panted. "Thanks for saving me." I picked up the woman's mace and tossed aside my broken hilt. The weapon was small, but it felt sturdy and more than capable of at least knocking someone out if it met the back of a skull. As Ingrid looted the fourth level player's dagger, a weapon that would likely be a decent upgrade compared to her kitchen knife, a grim thought crossed my mind.

"Hey, Ingrid . . . I know we've talked about it a few times before, but I just want—"

"I know, Dad," she interrupted. "Nothing here is real. Just a game. You know I'd never hurt anyone in real life, right? I'm not a monster."

My eyes wandered back to the woman at my feet in a pool of blood. "I know . . . It's just . . . that was pretty brutal. I don't want you to change. You're still my little girl, right?"

Ingrid, her red dress in need of repair and a thorough cleaning that I fully intended to purchase for her when we returned to the streets of Echelon, wrapped me in a big hug that dispelled all my fears for her sanity. "Just a game," I whispered into her hair.

◄◆►

We emerged into the basement of the counting house perhaps an hour or so ahead of the smoke trailing behind us. A few guards were lazily throwing dice in one corner, and another man we hadn't seen before was pacing in front of the locked valuables. He wore a nice leather doublet over a tailored shirt, and he looked pleased to see us emerge from the dungeon.

"Ah, adventurers, everything has been handled well, I take it?" he began.

All the NPCs in the room stopped moving. They froze perfectly in place, and I could feel my own boots rooted to the stone floor as though I was a statue. The time stoppage was jolting, but I knew what was happening. "Message from the admins," I said to Ingrid. System-wide messages locked all NPCs and granted them immunity for the duration, and it froze all players' feet in place while leaving the rest of our bodies free to continue doing whatever we pleased.

In dark orange script, everyone across all seven continents of Wonder saw the same message:

System Administration, Incoming Message, All Players . . .
Alert!
Unknown Error (513a) has occurred in the world script. Some world elements have been corrupted.
Alert!
System primary and secondary servers will undergo full reset in 10 minutes. Players may experience a short period of unconsciousness. New logins have been temporarily disabled.
Alert!

10 minutes remaining until system reset . . .

"Whoa, that's weird," I said. The text stayed on my vision for a few seconds before gradually fading out from top to bottom.

Ingrid looked worried. "What does a reset feel like?"

"Nothing to worry about," I answered. "I've been through one before. Your vision goes black and you can't do anything, but it only lasts for about five seconds, maybe ten. We'll be fine. And when the server comes back online, we'll be in the exact same position as before the reset, so we won't get separated or anything. Again, nothing to worry about. Just weird to see an unknown error. Wonder what it means."

The freeze dissipated, and the NPCs in the room immediately picked up right where they had left off just a moment before.

"Yes," I answered, shaking my head and returning my thoughts back to the dungeon run we had completed.

The man smiled and held out his hand. "And the lucky coin? Have you returned with it?" he asked.

I figured the coin was likely involved in some sort of side quest we hadn't had enough time to explore. There was a probably an offshoot of the cistern room that led to another chamber where the coin could be traded for clues or some other kind of reward, and the choice would then be between getting help with the dungeon itself or getting a better reward upon our return. Since we had completed the dungeon quickly and subsequently burned the place, we hadn't had time for any secondary adventures.

Ingrid grabbed the coin from her belt and placed it in the man's open palm.

"Ah, excellent. And did you discover what exactly the ratling vermin were after in our vault?" the NPC asked.

Alert!

8 minutes remaining until system reset . . .

"Uh, the ratling boss—which we killed, by the way—said something about Gibbering Bits, whatever that means," I explained.

The man's expression became inquisitive, and he rubbed a hand across the stubble of his chin. "Interesting. We'll have to send more adventurers into the tunnels to unlock the rest of the mystery, I suppose. Come back when you are both stronger, and I'm sure we will have more tasks that need completing. As for your reward, take this back to Sparg on the second floor, and he'll see to it that you are compensated adequately."

He handed me a small rectangle of paper with a little bit of writing. "Come on, Ingrid. Let's get some loot!"

As we walked back up through the rest of the counting house, we got the next notification telling us that the reset was six minutes away. The main floor of the building was a little less populated than before. Kevin, the streamer with the awesome armor, had left as well.

We found Sparg reclining on a couch with a long briar pipe between his teeth. Two elven women, both NPCs like Sparg, sat on the couch with him.

"We've completed the quest," I announced as we approached. I handed the elf our slip of paper, and he looked on it with a smile.

"Very well," the elf replied. He motioned to another NPC in a different part of the balcony area, and the man walked over with a red silken pillow the color of Ingrid's dress held out on his arms.

A few items rested on the pillow: a small pouch of coins, a sturdy short sword with a simple design etched on the blade, and a pair of leather bracers. "You may select two items," the man carrying them said flatly.

"Take the sword," Ingrid said almost at once. "I'm keeping the dagger we looted, and you need a new one."

She was right, so I grabbed the sword from the pillow and its information appeared in green text under the weapon in my vision:

Reinforced Short Sword of Extermination: Built specifically for killing ratlings, goblins, spiders, and other denizens of the dark, the sword deals extra damage to vermin and humanoid NPCs smaller in stature than the wielder.

"Nice!" The sword would be a welcome replacement for the unenchanted one I had lost, though it was still pretty far from being something valuable. I slid it into my belt and then reached for the gold. "Let's take the cash. We can get your dress fixed up and find something to buy for you at the market."

Ingrid nodded, and I officially completed the quest by grabbing the purse from the pillow.

Your Cunning skill has increased to 20!

Congratulations! You have increased to level 10!

I did a little fist pump as we walked back down the stairs toward the counting house's front exit. "Hit level ten," I told my daughter. Judging by her smile, she had leveled up as well.

"I reached level three when we completed the quest. Increased my physical. Maybe I'll stick with the two-dagger approach and become a rogue or a thief or something," she said. "I don't know, I liked watching mages on the streams, but getting up close and personal was fun."

"Yeah, not a bad idea. If I keep focusing on cunning, I might as well try to become a caster. I've never really liked the wizard play style, but maybe a shaman or a druid would complement whatever you end up choosing." As we opened the front door and stepped into the sunlight, another system message appeared:

Alert!

4 minutes remaining until system reset . . .

I didn't think much of it. I was just excited to head back to the market and see what else I could buy for Ingrid to help her progress. If she really wanted to become a melee class, maybe we'd be able to find a trainer that could at least give her some options and some explanations. Overall, it felt like a fairly productive day.

Then I saw one of Vic's goons leaning against the brick exterior of the counting house, and my breath caught in my throat.

I tried to pull Ingrid along behind me as quickly as I could, heading in the opposite direction from Vic's henchman.

It didn't work. He saw us at once—he had clearly been waiting for us to emerge—and began to follow.

Ingrid and I rounded a corner a little way down the street, and I quickened our pace. A few seconds later, I felt a strong hand on my shoulder.

"Think you'd just get away? Not after yesterday," the thug growled in my ear. I thought about spinning around and testing out my new sword, but I didn't want to spill blood on the streets of Echelon in broad daylight. Besides, the guy was bound to be a much higher level than I was, and murdering people inside the city walls could have some serious consequences with the local government. King Ahmose II wasn't a tyrant by any means, but he ran a city of laws, and one of them provided severe punishments for murder.

I turned slowly, keeping my hands down at my sides to try and diffuse the situation. "Come on, man. We're low level. I don't know why the hell that idiot Vic wants to constantly grief me, but I just want to do my own thing, you know?"

Alert!

2 minutes remaining until system reset . . .

The man showed me a toothy grin covered in grime. Above his head, the AI showed me his name and level:

Madrid Bonebreaker, Level 24 Pirate

His name was a pseudonym, of course, something I had

never bothered to look into much since I didn't really have anything to hide, but I was starting to think that changing it wouldn't be such a bad idea after all. If it made it a little more difficult for Vic and his goons to hassle me, it'd be worth it.

"Vic sends his regards." Madrid took off running down the street.

At first, I didn't even realize what was happening. Then Ingrid collapsed to the cobblestones. The hilt of a knife was sticking out of her stomach.

I ripped it out, and my heart sank further. The bastard had left the knife as a message. The handle was clear glass, filled with a sloshing green liquid, and I knew it was poison. Even though Ingrid's wound wasn't fatal, the poison coursing through her body certainly would be.

I let out a sigh and added the poisoned weapon to my rapidly growing collection. "Fuck those guys."

Ingrid was clearly in pain. Her face was contorted, and she clutched her stomach so hard her fingers were locking. "It hurts . . ." she muttered through clenched teeth.

"I know," was all I could say. "We need to train, to get strong. We'll kill that bastard once we're powerful enough. If we kill him enough, he won't be a threat."

Ingrid looked up at me, her hands as red with blood as her dress, and died.

The thug who had killed her was long gone, and there was nothing left for me to do. With the server reset coming so soon, I decided to sit down against the nearest wall on the side of the street and wait it out. After the reset, I could go back through the portal and return to the apartment. Some food sounded nice, and we had done enough for one day. A little relaxation felt in order.

System Administration, Incoming Message, All Players . . .
Alert!

Unknown Error (513a) has occurred in the world script. Some world elements have been corrupted.

System primary and secondary servers will undergo full reset in 10 seconds. Players may experience a short period of unconsciousness. New logins have been temporarily disabled.

CHAPTER 4

E verything was black. I couldn't see, and I couldn't hear.
I mentally ticked off the seconds as they went by since
I had absolutely nothing else to do.

I counted to twelve before the light of the world returned
and the servers came back online. Staying logged in through
a server reset was kind of weird, and part of me felt like it was
somehow risky, but Wonder had existed for years, and no one
had ever reported any bugs regarding the reset system. Still,
I shook out my arms and stretched my legs just to make sure
everything was working. No complaints.

System Administration, Incoming Message, All Players . . .
Alert!

"Damn, another freeze? What the hell . . ."

Unknown Error (????) has occurred in the world script. Body re-
constitution module detached from primary servers. Player regener-
ation corrupted.

"What the hell does that mean?" I said aloud. In front of
me, Ingrid's body was gone, but that was to be expected after
a reset. She wouldn't have to wait and walk back through the
portal to force her body to disappear.

Still . . . something didn't feel right. In fact, everything felt *profoundly wrong*.

I walked back toward the counting house in the hope that one of the higher-level players would be there so I could ask some questions.

A normal afternoon in Echelon felt almost as busy as New York City. Now, as I walked down the side of the street, everything was quiet. The majority of people had gone indoors, and the others left on the street were apprehensive and visibly distrusting, talking in hushed whispers in small knots of two or three.

Without Ingrid, I felt alone. I didn't think she would have any more answers than anyone else, but I hated simply walking without a single person to at least give me some company. I was in the center of a massive city, and I felt lost.

Finally, I reached the counting house and slowly walked inside. Even the NPCs were quieter, as if all the players conducting business had stopped engaging them, rendering them silent at their desks. In the back of the room, a fifteenth level player was standing awkwardly by himself, so I headed in his direction. Despite the guards all around us, his hand still drifted toward the hilt of his sword as I approached.

"Hey, any ideas what's going on?" I asked, trying to sound casual despite my mounting trepidation.

The player, Karros by name, only shook his head. His eyes were wide with fear.

"What do you think was all that business about the player regeneration module getting corrupted?" I pressed. I ran a hand through my hair and looked to the NPCs in the room for any kind of clue, but none of them had seemed to notice the system announcement. Bankers were still counting coins, and other employees were busy moving sheets of parchment and going about their normal business.

"I . . ." Karros began speaking, but his voice trailed off.

"What? What are you thinking?" My own voice wavered just a little as I spoke.

"Maybe . . . it means . . ."

System Administration, Incoming Message, All Players . . .

Alert!

I felt a little relieved that a new message was on its way. Maybe we would get some answers. Karros turned away and put his head in his hands like he was going to cry.

System Administration, Incoming Message, All Players . . .

Alert!

This is a personal message from Nepheli Galianos, Director of Primary Server Management and Calibration at Wonder Technologies, Inc. Two errors have occurred in the primary mainframe as a result of intentional tampering. Right now, the technical and developmental teams are working at full capacity to resolve the issues. Wonder Technologies' legal counsel are also currently establishing an open channel of communications for players wishing to explore claims.

Interpol is being deployed around the primary servers and Wonder Technologies' headquarters in Corinth, Greece to prevent any further corruption of the servers. Rest assured, Wonder Technologies is doing everything in their power to correct the developing situation.

Several errors are now present in the game world that players need to understand. To explain the situation further, Sven Jorgensen, the head of Wonder Technologies' legal department, will address you shortly. Please remain attentive.

"Oh shit . . ." I muttered.

Karros had slumped against the back wall of the counting house and was crying into his hands. I got the feeling that if his character was able to move freely he would be running out into the street any second.

System Administration, Incoming Message, All Players . . .

Alert!

Hello. My name is Sven Jorgensen, and I am the chief legal counsel for Wonder Technologies, Inc. An open channel of communication will soon be established allowing direct communications between players and representatives from my department. I advise all players to refresh themselves of the terms of service agreement that can be accessed in any of the seven home cities. That document will be made available on character sheets as well.

There was a long pause in the incoming text scroll, and I got the distinct feeling that the developers at Wonder were scrambling for answers, preparing to deliver the worst of all the news. After a few minutes of standing awkwardly frozen in the counting house, the text appeared once more in my vision:

The legal team has made the decision, for the safety of all players, to be very honest regarding the effects of the damage sustained by the mainframe. First, the secondary server equipment was not harmed. As you are all certainly aware, NPCs and the world itself are housed on the secondary servers. The world will continue to exist as you have enjoyed it all these years. However, the damage sustained by the primary servers is significant and localized in the regeneration module. All player information is stored on the primary server. The regeneration module has been corrupted, and that means player deaths are now permanent. Furthermore, any deaths that occurred after the first server announcement some twenty minutes ago are permanent.

As all of you certainly know, the beauty and draw of Wonder is the ability to use one's own body to play the game—the most advanced alternate reality technology ever invented. For the last twenty minutes, since the first error was detected in the code, all player deaths in the game have also meant real, physical deaths in the world outside the game.

Everyone at Wonder Technologies is extremely saddened by these developments, and we're working hand in hand with law enforcement to find the individuals responsible and bring them to justice. Again, legal channels will be opening in the next few days.

The current death toll stands at more than twenty-five thousand. Right now, everyone reading this message has survived the most significant loss of human life since the wars of the 2020s and 2030s.

For the foreseeable future, the game world will continue to exist as normal in accordance with the terms of your service agreements. All portal entry technology has been disabled as a precautionary measure. Logout services have been temporarily disabled as a result of the attack. Wonder Technologies, Inc. is actively pursuing every possible avenue that might lead to an answer.

City leaders in every portal city have been instructed to help maintain peace, and lawlessness within those cities will result in indefinite confinement until the situation can be resolved.

More updates will be delivered via system administration messages as they become available. Everyone at Wonder Technologies is deeply moved and saddened by the losses felt throughout every corner of the game. May God have mercy on us all.

The world unlocked, and my feet could move once more. Instead of taking a step, my legs collapsed under me and sent me sprawling to the ground.

Ingrid was dead. She would be dead forever.

She wouldn't respawn, and she wouldn't come walking back through the portal to go adventuring. I'd never see her face again, hear her laugh, or . . . anything. She was gone. Just like my wife.

I had nothing.

I had no one.

Without Ingrid, I *was* nothing.

CHAPTER 5

Sometime in the dead of night, the NPCs working at the counting house forced me to leave. The building didn't close at any particular hour, but eventually the collective patience of the NPCs broke, and they would no longer tolerate my desperate sobs and cries.

Knowing that Ingrid was gone was surreal. When my wife had died some years before, I had felt the exact same utter despair—but it hadn't lasted more than a few days. Ingrid had been there to hold my hand, young though she was, and that had been my comfort. I had awakened every day with Ingrid on my mind, her image giving me hope hour after hour, day after day, and year after year.

And Ingrid was gone. Taken from me.

Taken from me by Vic.

I walked out of the counting house and into the darkness of the Echelon night. The city, at least from where I was standing, was quiet. I imagined everyone had gone to their houses, guildhalls, or wherever they had to stay to wait until more information came out from the developers.

I had no such refuge. I had always logged out and gone

home to sleep in our own apartment, but that option was off the table. Maybe forever.

I still had a little bit of money in my pocket—the coins I had planned on using to get Ingrid's dress fixed and to buy her some new gear—and that would be enough to get me a room for a night. Most of the cheaper inns were located on the northern side of Echelon near the gate where Vic and his goons had staged their ill-fated attack, so that was where I went.

The first inn advertising a vacancy was a little beneath the quality that would have normally caught my eye, but I simply didn't care. If I ended up being murdered in my sleep, so be it. A man with nothing left has nothing left to lose.

I pushed open the door to the inn, and a handful of nearby patrons sprang to their feet with their weapons ready, clearly on edge and waiting for something to happen. It didn't take them long to figure out that I was far from a threat. The mace and poisoned dagger tucked into my belt weren't nearly as formidable or magically enchanted as the weapons brandished my direction.

The barkeep was equally nervous. The man, a player with a name and a class floating above his head, eyed me suspiciously and never took his right hand from the hilt of a sword hanging on his hip. "Don't worry about me," I said, all the life gone from my voice. "How much for a room? Just one night."

The man looked me up and down once more. "Ten gold," he said.

I took my entire purse and set it on the counter. "I don't have ten. You can keep however much is in there. Around six, I think."

He counted out the contents of my purse and then plucked a key from under the bar. "You don't look so good. Gonna be alright?" he asked.

I shook my head. "No. I don't suppose I'll ever be 'alright' again. Now, about the room."

"Right, right, just don't make me regret it," he said as he handed me a small brass key. "Number four. Down the hall. Be gone by noon tomorrow."

I grabbed the key and trudged onward to room number four. It was small and dingy, a little wet in the corners, and had no window. For the quality of the room, I had grossly overpaid.

The deadest hours of night brought no sleep to my eyes. When I had cried my last and no more tears would come forth, I simply sat on the rough straw mattress and stared at the dagger I had stolen from Madrid.

The man's name echoed through my head like a relentless drip of water splashing against stone for eternity. It would be there, seared into my memory, for as long as I lived. Of that I was certain.

His name, and the vile name of the coward who had sent him: Vic. Victor. I didn't remember his last name. We had worked together for a few years at the Ministry of Public Health, and I had been his direct superior. The bastard had been constantly late, hadn't given a shit about the quality of his work, and he'd gotten what he deserved. I fired him the day before one of his kids was born. He hated me for it, of course, and now I hated him more than he could possibly fathom.

Madrid and Vic.

I'd kill them both, and in that order. I'd make Vic watch as I tore apart his band of thieves and thugs, saving him for last.

I spun the small poisoned dagger with the glass hilt, and it wobbled on the old floorboards. The item was probably worth a hundred gold or better, and it had been left as a message. A message that Vic was stepping up his game. That Vic was determined to either kick me out of Echelon or make me quit Wonder altogether. Now that everything had gone to hell, quitting wasn't an option.

Holding the dagger in my hand, I accessed its stats:

Masterwork Dagger of Searing Pain: Contains three doses of potent venom. A single envenomation is enough to kill most humans, deteriorating their physical stat by one every ten seconds until death or the poison expires.

Maybe a hundred gold had been a conservative estimate. The 'masterwork' designation meant that a smith at least level forty had crafted the weapon. Perhaps the dagger would be worth thousands. Regardless, even if it were worth millions of gold, I wouldn't sell it. There were still two doses of poison contained in the clear glass hilt, and I already knew who they were meant to kill.

When morning came, I was ready to leave. I walked into the main room of the inn, and a different proprietor was behind the counter. I tossed him the key without paying him much attention. Outside on the street, the city was a lot different than the night before. People were about, and that was a little unexpected. I had guessed the city would stay mostly in seclusion for quite some time as the fear became more and more fully understood, but that wasn't the case at all. Everywhere, on every flat surface in sight, various guilds and other organizations had placed their calls to action. Everyone was recruiting for what they apparently viewed as an impending war.

I had to say they were probably right. Permanent death meant those with ambition could rise to the top and take all the power for themselves. The multitudes of smaller towns would be the first targets, naturally, and then the warlords like Vic would turn their sights on portal cities. Eventually, the seven capitals of Wonder would turn on each other, and massive armies would take to the seas to raid and pillage. The world would devolve into chaos.

I ignored the posters and banners as I moved through the city. The coming wars and casualties meant nothing to me.

I had my own war, and it was one I had every intention of winning.

No matter which city, which king, or which faction ultimately came to dominate Wonder, it would not matter. Vic and Madrid would die.

Outside the city's northern gate, I took the first step toward winning my personal war. I needed a class. Vic's group was full of marauders, raiders, pirates, warriors, thieves, and other melee classes. The bastard himself was a warlord, a class that was practically useless in a duel but unparalleled when it came to commanding troops in battle. His cunning and influence stats had to be high, probably both in the fifties or sixties. His cunning meant I would never be able to kill my way through his organization one at a time. He'd see me coming, root me out like a mole, and I'd be killed before I ever got close. A frontal assault might work, but only if I had an army following me. A battle of commanders would be like a game of chess, and that felt a little too fair.

I needed something unexpected, something *impossible* to anticipate, and I had at least a vague notion of where to get it.

Whitechapel was my first destination. Before I could begin to worry about a class and gear and everything else—an army, perhaps—I needed to acquire the fundamentals. I also felt like I had to store my poisoned dagger somewhere safe while I quested. I wouldn't need it until I was ready to take my pound of flesh, and the glass hilt meant it was fragile, despite being a masterwork item.

It took me a full day to reach the starter village, and I was sore and hungry by the time I arrived. The whole journey had been productive, though. I had used my slow steps as an opportunity to harden my resolve and think through my plan in meticulous detail. I half expected the AI to award me with a cunning point just for how forward thinking I was, but it didn't happen.

The beginnings of night were falling on Whitechapel when I arrived at the church dominating the village's center. Amida, the high priest, was still standing in the back of the chapel like the dutiful NPC that he was, but he wasn't my target. Instead, I moved toward the far left of the building where a small metal gate guarded the entrance to the crypt. It wasn't locked, so I took the steps in stride and found myself amidst the dimly lit tombs of Whitechapel's most faithful.

"Yes?" came an old voice from somewhere among the shadows.

"Hello?" I called back.

A small, withered man carrying a candle on a tin plate emerged from the side of one sarcophagus. "Yes? What are you doing here?" He stood a few feet back from me as though he feared I would suddenly lunge for his throat with my sword.

"Anything strange going on?" I asked. I had done the first half of a quest here before, and I had to assume that it hadn't changed very much in the months I had been gone.

The man's countenance took on a mysterious quality as he narrowed his eyes and gave me a sly grin. "Ah, so you've heard the rumors in town, have you?"

I nodded. "Something about a theft. That's all I remember."

The man silently motioned for me to follow, and I padded along like an obedient dog. He led me down a twisting staircase to the floor beneath the crypt, and his single candle barely did anything to keep the encroaching darkness at bay.

"We keep the heretics down here," the old man began to explain. "Those who defy the teachings of Ashur are burned, and their ashes are stored here in our vault so that no one may use the remains for nefarious purposes. It seems there is someone in Whitechapel who wishes to do exactly that."

"So they stole an urn or some ashes?" I asked. I couldn't see anything in the darkness, and I had take small steps to keep from stubbing my toes on every stone monument in the room.

"Two urns and a skull to be exact," the man answered.

We reached our destination, a smooth stone altar at the back of the room, and the man placed his candle inside a lantern. The extra light wasn't much, but it helped. We were surrounded by urns, bone piles, blank tombstones, and several sarcophagi with heavy bronze lids. "All of these are heretics?" I wondered. The town of Whitechapel was small—I'd find it hard to believe that they would catch too many heretics.

"No," the man replied, shaking his head. "Certainly not. The heretics are confined to a single shelf. The others are kept down here for various reasons, some mundane and others more controversial, but they are of no consequence at the moment."

"Alright, so what's missing, and who would want to take it?" Looking at the stark white bones sitting on the shelf in front of me made me think of Ingrid, and I had to look away.

The old man pushed a bone into my hand, forcing me to gaze upon death once more. "The last bone of a particularly vile heretic, a man who called himself Xollmomath. He was a scourge in Whitechapel, and he had designs much larger than our small village. We fear that a new cult has arisen. Perhaps they seek to use Xollmomath's relics to try and bring him back from the dead. All I know for certain is that the thieves took ashes and bones, but they forgot one. Perhaps something in the crypt spooked them, and they dropped it in their haste to escape. There are ghosts down here, you know."

"Any clue where the cult might be hiding?" I asked. Seeing all the death and bones surrounding me was starting to get on my nerves, though I knew what I had to do. Finding the cult would be the first step on my path of vengeance. The first of many steps, and they would only get more difficult after Whitechapel.

The man thought a moment before answering. "South of town, I think. Do you know where our water well is? Find the well and then look west. You'll see some thatched houses. The constable reports unusually activity going on there at night. You might find the cult around there. One final bit of information: if you find the true remains of Xollmomath, the final bone should begin to softly glow. He was a powerful heretic in life, and his corpse retained a fraction of that power in death."

Eager to be gone from the crypt, I thanked the man, took the bone, and retraced my steps out into the crisp night air. Since I had almost completed the quest once before—albeit a slightly different version than the current iteration—I knew the tasks were timed. If I didn't discover the cult quickly, there wouldn't be enough time left to alert the constable and rouse a crew to kill the cultists, and one person couldn't take them down on their own.

The well was easy to find from memory, and from there I turned left just as instructed. Three cottages lined the street, and some noise was coming from behind them. With the bone of Xollmomath tucked into my belt next to my weapons, I crept up along the side of one of the houses as quietly as I could. My cunning was a good deal higher than the quest required, so my footfalls didn't make a sound. I smiled when I realized that I couldn't even hear my own breath. I had never done a stealthy quest before, and being over-levelled for the task made me feel stronger than I had a right to feel.

In the small clearing behind the three houses, a group of five shrouded figures stood around a slowly dying collection of embers. Their meeting was about to conclude, and following them seemed like the best course of action.

After a few minutes, the robed figures began walking toward one of the houses and a cellar door. Whoever it was looked around once, didn't notice me, and then opened the hatch for the others to descend. Watching them move, an idea crossed my mind. The last time I had done the quest, things had gone similarly, and I had followed the cultists into the basement. Now . . .

I waited for the very last cultist. When his back was turned and no one else was above ground to see me, I sprinted across the clearing, vaulted over the dying fire toward the cellar door, and rammed my sword through the man's neck. It was a clean kill, and he barely made a noise as I eased him to the ground.

I didn't have much time to work. Going as fast as I could, I stripped off the cultist's robe and draped it over my own back, keenly aware of the sticky patch of blood rubbing against my flesh and hair.

Closing the door behind me, I followed the cultists into the darkness of the cellar. A few candles illuminated the bottom landing. I pulled the cowl down low over my forehead to conceal my face, and it seemed like no one was really paying me any particular attention in the first place, so my disguise held. I followed the column of cultists down a short hallway to a dirt floor root cellar that looked like it was a communal structure large enough for all three of the houses above to use together. Various pungent herbs and other agricultural goods were strung up on wooden scaffolds, and a huge summoning circle was laid out in the middle. Standing on the other side of the circle was a warlock, the head of the cult, holding a pulsating wand fit with a green gemstone.

Normally, the quest would branch into two options once I figured out what was happening. I could run back to the chapel to get the necessary forces and take the cellar by storm, or I could try to sabotage the plans in some other, much more complex way.

But things weren't the same as before. Besides the slight changes in the quest and NPCs, *I* was different. Ingrid was gone, and I needed my revenge.

I followed the others' lead and stood at my designated spot around the magical circle. Still, none of them noticed me. The leader began a chant, and her wand pulsed erratically, throwing green light all around the cellar.

One of the other cultists began to empty a bag of bones and ash into the middle of the circle, and another produced a short, curved dagger from his robe.

"Blood for Xollmomath, to make him whole once more," the cultist stated defiantly. He slashed the blade across his palm and held his hand out to the circle, dripping blood onto the ancient remains.

He passed the dagger to his left, and the action was repeated by the next cultist.

After two more, it was my turn. I grabbed the dagger, held it to my palm, said the words, and then dripped some of my blood onto Xollmomath's bones.

One more cultist went after me, and then the dagger was in the leader's hands. Something about her facial expression told me the ritual was not going as planned. Or perhaps I had been discovered, and my ruse was about to come to a painful—and permanent—end. A shudder ran through my spine.

"The ritual is not strong enough," the leader said, her voice a mixture of anger and panic. She thrust out the dagger again to the cultist on her right. "Another round of blood! Xollmomath requires more!"

"No!" I interrupted, pulling the missing bone from my belt. I tossed it onto the pile in the center of the circle. "You had forgotten a single bone, my lady. I retrieved it. Now the ritual may commence."

At once, the air in the room changed. It grew heavy with magic, and the candles fizzled out one by one. Then, slowly, the ground beneath our feet began to tremble. The bones were coming alive. They snapped back into place, forming a twisted and contorted skeleton in the center of the summoning circle, illuminated only by their own strange magical light.

After what felt like an eternity, the room settled, and the candles reignited.

"Xollmomath!" the leader called. She fell to her knees, and her long black hair brushed across the top of the white skull.

A moment later, the skeleton stirred. It sat up, and the rest of the cultists fell down in supplication, prompting me to hastily follow suit.

"Flesh," a new, rumbling voice said. "Bring me flesh . . ."

The cultist nearest to their leader grabbed the ceremonial dagger from the ground. "Take mine, master!" he yelled right before slitting his own throat and falling into the circle.

"Hehehe, good," the skeleton rumbled. "Your flesh shall be mine."

What came next was truly sickening to witness. The skeleton knelt over the dead cultist's body and began consuming him, biting down and tearing skin from bone with its teeth. When it swallowed, the flesh magically knit itself onto the skeletal frame. Before long, the process appeared to be complete, and what I had to assume was Xollmomath stood as a fully reconstituted human. His flesh was pale, covered in scars, and he bore a circular tattoo around his waist that reminded me of an intricate leather belt. Altogether, he didn't look as imposing as I had expected, but I could practically feel the sheer magical power emanating from his form.

Suddenly, I wasn't feeling very confident. I didn't even know if joining the cult and completing the ritual was a scripted possibility in the game, but in the end, it wouldn't matter—the AI was the best software ever conceived, and it would handle the unexpected algorithms seamlessly.

Xollmomath stood to his full height and turned, surveying the supplicants kneeling around him.

Then I felt a heavy tap on my right shoulder.

I stood, and Xollmomath placed a finger under my chin to direct my gaze into his eyes. They were blood red, completely lacking an iris or pupil, and they were terrifying. "You," he spoke.

"Yes, Master?" I whispered past the growing lump in my throat. I figured continuing the ruse was the best plan, and besides, it was the only one I had come up with.

"You are not one of my servants, are you?" the necromancer asked.

I tried to gulp down my fear. "No, Sir . . . I am different. An adventurer."

"I sensed as much." Xollmomath swung his countenance back to the leader and commanded her to rise as well. "What are you doing with an adventurer in your midst?" he demanded.

Her eyes darted to mine and then back to Xollmomath. "I apologize, Sire. If you wish me to kill him, to sacrifice him in your honor, I will do so immediately."

I tried to take a step back, but my foot landed on the bottom shelf of a wooden rack. I was stuck. Nowhere to run.

Thankfully, Xollmomath seemed to have other ideas for me. "No. We shall keep him alive for now. I am . . . curious."

Perhaps I had given the AI an algorithm it had never seen before, and it needed time to process what was happening. Regardless, I was quite pleased to have my life.

"Do . . . do you require food, sir?" the leader asked when it became clear that Xollmomath didn't intend to press the issue of my survival any further.

He shook his head. "I am satiated for now, my pet. What I require cannot be grown on a farm nor stored in a larder. I require souls if I am to grow stronger." Again, one of the eager cultists leapt up at the opportunity to sacrifice himself for the cause, but Xollmomath wasn't interested.

"We—"

"You, send these insufferable wretches away. Set them about a task. I require only you and the adventurer," Xollmomath stated, clearly losing his patience with the eager brown-nosers.

When the four remaining cultists were gone, the bad feeling in my stomach grew from terrible to somehow worse. I had the distinct feeling that Xollmomath intended to torture and kill me whether I stayed in the cellar and tried to obey his commands or if I tried to make a run for it.

"What is it you wish of me?" the leader asked meekly. She sounded like a harem girl begging a prince for another round in between the sheets. I had to shake my head—maybe that was *exactly* what she *was* asking.

To my surprise, Xollmomath didn't even bother to answer her question. He paced, still completely naked, back and forth in the cramped space of the cellar. Finally, he said, "I am pleased that you have brought me a devotee, my pet. Long have I been trapped in that forsaken temple, and I desire to see what has become of the world. Yet I shall remain bound to the circle for some time until I am strong enough to truly enter your plane of existence."

He looked right at me as he said the word 'devotee.' Another shudder ran down my spine. "How may I serve?" I asked. Perhaps if Xollmomath wasn't terribly interested in the cult leader's offerings, he would have some diabolical use for me.

Xollmomath stepped right into my face, his acrid breath washing over my mouth and nose in putrid waves. "You wish to serve the darkness? That is why you have come, hmmm?"

Well, I had come to Whitechapel for a class. I felt like I was about to find one. "Yes, Master, that is correct. If you will teach me, I will learn. What exactly . . . can you train?"

Since I had never interacted with a class trainer before, I had no idea how to go about accessing that kind of meta information without throwing the NPC for a loop. Typically, asking an AI-controlled entity things about the server status or subscription fees or anything else they weren't programmed to understand would cause them to become confused and sometimes belligerent. I thanked my lucky stars when my question seemed to work.

"I am Xollmomath," he said, mercifully turning away to resume his pacing. "Several hundred years ago, I practiced the dark arts of desecration and necromancy. I drank the pure blood of priests and twisted it in my veins, shaped it to do my bidding, and all who opposed my creations could only bow. Is that what you seek, adventurer?"

Necromancy wasn't *exactly* what I had been hoping for. It was a rare class to be certain, but not because it was difficult to obtain. It was rare because necromancers were so easily cut to ribbons by the first skilled warrior or fighter they encountered. The class was based on cunning, and it neglected the physical stat so much that it left the player frail and unable to take even a single well-placed strike from a sword or spear.

"Oh, Master of the Arcane, I have no doubt that you are skilled in thousands of disciplines. I have come seeking the most obfuscated, the darkest of your vile arts, if you would impart such wisdom upon your humble servant." I bowed my head and spread my hands to my sides.

Your Cunning skill has increased to 21!

The notification brought a huge smile to my face. I had played the situation correctly, and the AI was impressed.

"You seek the esoteric knowledge of the cabal?" He stopped his pacing, and with my head down I had no idea what he was doing or where he was looking. "A brave disciple indeed. Not all who choose the path of the Stench of Corpses survive. And once you accept Lady Kalma's blessing, there is no return. Vows of such weight are not broken once made."

By the gods, I was treading in unknown waters. I had never heard of any of the things Xollmomath was describing, and I had never even seen them mentioned on the streams or the forums. Maybe I had stumbled upon something new, or maybe the AI really was rewriting the game as I made a choice it had not anticipated. Either way, I didn't know what to do.

"Following Lady Kalma . . . what will I become?" I tentatively asked.

Xollmomath burst out in laughter, his head tilted back to the ceiling. "A heretic! Anathema! Apostate!"

I didn't know how to ask the NPC about individual stat specializations, so I tried my best. "And heretics, do they charge into battle to fight on the front lines? Or do they learn magic like necromancers? Or lead an army?"

Again, more laughing from Xollmomath. Finally, his blood red eyes found mine once more, and his gaze bored into me. "The Stench of Corpses bestows a special gift, young adventurer. When I wore the mantle, the Lady called me *Surma* in her language. If a translation exists, perhaps it would best be called 'deathbringer,' for that is what I was. I stood face to face with the strongest warriors for thousands of miles. I captured the magic thrown into the air by the wizards and sorcerers just to fling it back at their mighty towers. I commanded hundreds of men and abominations alike, scourging cities and laying waste to entire populations!"

A smile crept across my face, and all the fear I had felt a moment before dissipated with it. In my mind, I saw Ingrid's smile as well. She was standing next to her mother, the two of them the most beautiful women I had ever seen in my life, and I knew I would get my vengeance.

CHAPTER 6

F inally, after so much time spent grinding away in Wonder, I had a class:

Ben Hales, Level 10 Deathbringer

Physical: 18

Cunning: 21

Influence: 15

Renown: 1

Investigation: 7

Trade: 9

Craftsmanship: 7

Fortune: 7

Infamy: 1

Status: unstable

Holdings: none

Allegiance: Lady Kalma, the Stench of Corpses

Xollmomath, magically bound as he was to the summoning circle until he could regain his full strength, turned out to be a powerful necromancer in his own right already. The AI listed his level as seventy, easily high enough to be a dungeon boss requiring dozens of skilled and geared players to take down. The cult leader, a woman whose name was Xia—no doubt styled after her master—was a level twenty-three warlock, and she was actively training her group of four underlings in her own dark practice.

As for me, I had received a handful of benefits by accepting my class and newfound allegiance. Classes began to confer boons at level six, so I had a few waiting for me:

Kalma's Forbearance (physical): Grants the deathbringer resistance against necrotic magic and natural corruptions. Such attacks are less effective against and cannot kill the deathbringer. Passive.

A Feast of Spores (cunning): Vile toxins borne on a hazy cloud of corruption are spewed from the deathbringer's mouth. Those affected receive a penalty to physical. The length and severity of the infliction are based on the amount of spores inhaled by the target. Active, consumes moderate energy.

The Black One's Sustenance (physical): Lady Kalma's followers want for nothing. Her presence sustains them, and they no longer require physical food to maintain their bodies. Passive.

Forsaken Barrier (physical): The deathbringer reacts to an incoming strike, shifting positions and leaving behind a faded image that lasts until touched. Active, consumes moderate energy.

Pull from the Darkness (influence): Shifting creations and vile amalgamations are the denizens of Lady Kalma's domain. Reaching within the body, the deathbringer can summon forth a creature of shadow capable of fighting and carrying out tasks. Active, consumes massive energy.

Overall, I had to say I was more than happy with my class choice and subsequent talents. Following an ancient vile deity like Kalma would be perfect for exacting my revenge. The talents favored physical, a stat I would have to rely upon in single combat with Vic or any of his underlings, yet I still had one talent each relying on cunning and influence. As I increased my stats, the abilities would become more and more powerful. In addition, every class in Wonder occasionally received a direct upgrade to a skill in the form of a more powerful version replacing the previous iteration.

The energy consumption mechanic was one of which I only had a cursory knowledge. Martial classes—most of them, at least—consumed either endurance points directly listed on their stat sheets or specific action points that they could also overtly manage. Mages and other arcane casters utilized a mana pool, and the nature-based classes like druids and shaman had an entirely different resource involving their innate connection to the world. I had only seen a couple players on the streams with an expendable resource named energy, though I wasn't sure my version was the same.

Online, the craftsman classes like blacksmiths, bowyers, and engineers used a measurable amount of energy to activate their talents and ply their trades. I called forth my character sheet once more and looked for energy to be listed among my secondary skills, but it wasn't there. Mine was different.

Not knowing exactly how much energy I had made me a little nervous, but it didn't make me too nervous to practice. I stood in front of the now-cold fire pit behind the trio of houses and listened to the sounds of the village coming awake in the morning. I hadn't slept, but the adrenaline of taking a step closer to my goal was better than any coffee I would have gotten at the inn.

I took a deep breath and prepared myself to try casting a spell. A Feast of Spores felt like the logical choice for my first attempt. Activating the spell wasn't difficult at all as it simply felt natural, like the talent was lurking just below the surface of my mind and waiting for me to call it forth.

I activated A Feast of Spores, and my neck immediately arched backward. My jaw swung down, and then a cloud of spores launched out of the back of my throat. They hung in the air right in front of my face, almost like a swarm of moths surrounding a lantern. After maybe ten seconds, the cloud dissipated and scattered into the wind.

All at once, I understood what the energy consumption listed on the skills really meant. The veins in my left arm bulged, and I could feel the blood rushing out of my head and making me instantly dizzy.

The sound of someone clapping from my side caught my attention, and I had to rub my eyes to refocus them and not lose my balance. Xia was standing there, her long hair curled around her shoulders and a smirk on her face. "You seem unsteady," she said, though her voice was far from accusatory. Instead, she sounded slightly concerned, a quality I hadn't expected from a death-worshipping cultist leader.

"Yeah, I'm new to it all. Not really sure what I'm doing." My head was still a bit foggy, though I could feel it dissipating in a similar fashion to the spores I had released. "Any tips or pointers?"

The woman thought for a moment before answering. "Casting spells of Lady Kalma's schools does not require mana or hours of lengthy study like a wizard or a mage," she explained, oddly casual as she skirted the meta-bounds of her AI scripting. "Your spells will draw from your lifeforce, from your soul. *That* is how you will reap destruction and bring death to all those who stand in your path."

"Speaking of that path, we have work to do," came another voice, one I easily recognized as belonging to Xollmomath. The man had finally decided to put some clothes on, a loose-fitting robe over his naked body, making him appear more like a pauper begging in the streets than a powerful necromancer. He had killed another of our cultists, and that had apparently given him enough strength be able to move about twenty or so feet from the summoning circle. With such limitations, he couldn't quite make it out of the cellar, but he could at least stand on the second stair from the top.

"Alright, what are you two planning?" I asked. I still wasn't sure if I would join up with their group as a follower, try to take over the operation and become the new leader, or if I would leave altogether. I had a lot of options, and I didn't technically *need* to stay with the cult now that I had acquired a class. On the other hand, channeling my lifeforce into spells sounded extremely dangerous, and I needed more information. Since Xia and Xollmomath seemed intent on discussing the long-term operation, I had to table my myriad of questions until another time.

From the top of the cellar stairs, the necromancer was eager to share his ideas. "The time has come to reclaim my former glory. I will sit upon the throne of Echelon once more, but I need an army first. Raising an army will require power, and power requires corpses. Whitechapel shall provide the first ranks."

That was a little unexpected. I knew Xollmomath held lofty ambitions, but capturing an entire capital city was about as extreme as it could get. "It will take thousands—hundreds of thousands of soldiers to storm Echelon," I said. "Whitechapel is nothing compared to the capital. How are we going to raise an army?"

I couldn't imagine that the cult of Lady Kalma counted more than a dozen or so followers across all of Wonder. If it had been anything noteworthy, I would have read about it on the forums and watched it on the streams.

"First, a proper citadel. We must raze the village to the ground, and then we can begin our true work," the necromancer cackled. He pointed toward Xia who had been standing motionless by the fire pit. "Three meager houses are not nearly enough. We must begin the work of purging Whitechapel. Build me a citadel worthy of my name!"

With that, the crazed necromancer turned back and descended once more into the lightless cellar.

"So, we control these three houses?" I asked. I hadn't paid the structures much attention, but it would make sense for them to belong to our other acolytes.

Xia nodded. "I shall stay above the summoning circle until Xollmomath is strong enough to move freely through the world once more. You may take the far house, and the others will reside in the central house for now. If our ranks are going to swell, we will need additional room. Supplies, housing, defenses—everything. We need our own city."

Taking over Whitechapel was intoxication, but it also felt reckless. We were too close to Echelon. Granted, we were far enough away that we couldn't see the walls without walking several hours, but we were still too close. The only good thing about the village was that it wasn't popular. In fact, it was downright obscure. Players running low-level quests with new characters rarely ventured all the way to Whitechapel, and the high-level players had no reason to be here at all. That anonymity would prove useful, I had no doubt.

"Have you any experience, Deathbringer, in the field of citadel construction?" Xia asked, pulling me out of my own thoughts. For once, I realized I hadn't been drowning in memories of my daughter—it was probably my first inkling of respite since her death.

I thought of the small battlement I had helped build alongside the engineer and a few others before Vic's attack on the city. It didn't really count as construction experience, but it would have to do. "Not much," I answered honestly. "If we could find or recruit an engineer, we'd have a much easier time. Until then, I suppose I'd be happy enough looking after the fortifications."

"Good," Xia said, placing a hand on my shoulder. "We have enough food in the cellar to last us a few weeks. I'll try to get out a message to our other members and bring them here, and perhaps find a few new recruits along the way. You should see to the defenses. It won't be long before the old priest at the temple comes looking for the missing bones. When that happens, we need to fight."

I glanced at my character sheet and my rather unimpressive skill of seven in craftsmanship. I had built a few things for a handful of quests in Echelon, but I'd never designed a fortress before. Still, despite what the stat said, I wasn't an idiot. My job at the Ministry of Health had involved managing an office of thirty employees, and I had always felt comfortable in the role. Building a citadel for an evil necromancer wasn't too far off—the bureaucratic healthcare system was probably more evil than Xollmomath would ever become, if I was being honest.

My first order of business was to inspect my own living quarters. I had a small house all to myself, though it wasn't anything worth bragging about. What essentially amounted to four walls with a small cot provided little in the way of creature comforts or defense.

I had one window right over the cot that was barely large enough to let in decent sunlight, so I didn't have to worry about any stealth attacks coming in the middle of the night from that direction. The door, though, was a different situation. It didn't fit well inside the frame, and it was lacking any sort of locking mechanism. Fashioning a locking bar would have to be a top priority.

Apart from the door and window, I had a single stool, a few rough sacks of dried meat and vegetables which I planned on giving to the other cultists due to my rather unique talent, and a butcher's cleaver resting on top of a cutting board. Thankfully, we had a well only thirty feet away, so water wouldn't be an issue. Securing that well would have to be a priority, right behind the locking bar.

Once the village officials discovered the den of cultists lurking in their midst, they'd come for us. A protracted siege of sorts wasn't out of the realm of possibility, and cutting off our access to water would be an easy play.

In need of supplies to begin the citadel construction in earnest, I knocked on the front door of the central house. It opened a few seconds later, and I could see my four NPC minions all crammed together inside. "Come outside, I have tasks for you," I told them brashly, testing the limits of my influence skill.

I stepped aside, and the four cultists filed out into the sunlight. "First things first," I began, pacing in front of my small assemblage like a drill sergeant, "lose the robes. I know you're all big on wearing black every moment of the day, but right now our strongest ally isn't a necromancer trapped in a root cellar. What is our best ally?" I pointed at one of the men, and he only stammered under my gaze.

Time to assert my authority, I thought. *I'm doing it for you, Ingrid. Everything for you.*

I cuffed the man on the side of his head with my small wooden mace. The blow was heavy, and the rounded surface of the weapon definitely hurt. The other cultists straightened their backs and stood a little taller.

"Alright, since you morons don't know, I have to tell you. *Secrecy* is our most prized ally. Right now, we operate in the daylight. Whitechapel has no idea what we're up to, and I intend to keep it that way. No robes, no sacrificial daggers, no . . . sacrifices, and don't speak a word about Kalma, Xollmomath, or anything else to anyone! Understood?" I waited a second for a notification telling me my influence stat had risen, but it never came.

In response, the cultists nodded. The one I had hit was still rubbing his temple, but his entire demeanor had changed just like the others.

"Good. Your first tasks should be rather simple. We need supplies. We have food to last a few weeks and easy access to a well, but that isn't good enough. The first order of business is tools. You two, acquire tools. Anything related to carpentry or woodworking that you can find, figure out a way to get it. Bring them back to the firepit by dusk." The first pair ran off, and I singled out the next cultist in line. "You, we need to be ready for a potential siege sometime in the future. That means we have to catalog everything we have and begin adding to it. Find every bucket in all three houses. Fill them with water and add them to the stockpile. Then prepare a list of our resources. Have it done by nightfall."

The final cultist stepped eagerly forward. "My task, sir? Begin eradicating the nearest civilians to expand our domain?"

The man was the one I had cuffed a minute before, and he earned a second on the left side of his head to match the growing bruise on the right. "The next time you consider thinking for yourself, just come to me so I can do your thinking for you. Secrecy and inconspicuousness, remember? I don't think murder fits the bill." Looking down the street, I wondered if the other three I had sent into Whitechapel would go on killing sprees of their own. If they did, our whole operation would be sunk in a single day.

I forcefully turned the final cultist toward the three houses. "You see those three doors? We need locking bars made for all three. In order to make locking bars, we need wood. And we're going to need more than just lumber. We need firewood. That's your job. Gather wood until dusk, then fashion a locking bar for every door. Go."

The man, still rubbing both sides of his head, immediately left for the woods outside Whitechapel, leaving me alone and very, very tired. The adrenaline had died down, and my lack of sleep was finally catching up with me.

Once we had some tools and supplies, I'd be able to help out with the fortifications. Until then, I really didn't have much to do. I thought of returning to the temple in the center of town and trying to misdirect the priest in hopes of buying us some time, but I didn't really have the confidence or the energy to pull it off. I walked back into my house and, much to my surprise, Xia was sitting on my stool with her back turned toward the door. I could have sworn I'd seen her moving away from our little trio of houses to head into the village . . . but maybe she had a warlock ability that had allowed her to enter my house unnoticed.

"Oh, hello," I awkwardly began.

She turned around, and I could see a small knife that she was using to mindlessly pick underneath her fingernails. "So, I was thinking, you haven't told us your name, Adventurer," she said without looking up from her knife.

I had forgotten that NPCs couldn't see player names the same way I could see them. Or if they could, the AI scripting wouldn't let them acknowledge it. "Ben, Ben Hales," I told her. "Uh, thanks for not killing me last night." A long, awkward silence passed between us. "Is there something you needed from me?"

She smiled, glancing up from her nails, and I noticed her piercing green eyes for the first time. "Oh, Ben, I *always* need something, but can we trust you? Can you truly be trusted, Ben?"

The mystifying woman stood and walked past me, brushing against my entire body as she made her way to the door in the tight space. Her hair smelled fresh and clean as it passed beneath my nose. When she was gone, I collapsed onto the straw mattress of my slightly elevated cot. There was still some valuable time left in the day, but I didn't care. I was far too tired to give much thought to the strange encounter that had just taken place. I fell asleep almost as quickly as I closed my eyes.

The next day started early. The four worker drones—a term I had thought of the previous night before falling asleep and felt was adequate to describe the cultists' role—were sitting around the various piles of our supplies surrounding the fire-pit. None of them were doing anything productive, so my primary task was simply to get them moving.

I assigned all four of them to the same task: we needed to begin establishing a defensive perimeter, and we needed to do it surreptitiously. Creating a livestock pen that happened to use our outer two houses as part of the walls seemed like as good a plan as any, and it would be a lot of work.

Xia had the report of our supply situation waiting for me after I dismissed the grunts. While our food stores would probably last for about fifteen or eighteen more days without any additional hunting necessary, our weapon situation was sorely lacking. Luckily, two of the cultists had managed to steal a wooden box full of tools, and while it didn't have everything we would need, it would still be a huge help.

According to Xia, and I had to agree with her assessment, our woeful lack of weaponry was the absolute highest priority. We didn't need crossbows and spears so much as Xia and her warlocks needed ritual components. When the time came to fight against the town's guards and priests, we would fight with magic, a prospect I very much enjoyed, as my skill with a sword was rather weak. I set Xia to the task of acquiring all the magical items she could while still maintaining discretion.

For myself, I grabbed one of the locking bars a drone had made and dropped it off at my house before heading into the root cellar to pay my necromancer friend a visit. I needed to know more about Lady Kalma and the background of the cult in general. Beyond the history, I also needed to know more about my own class. If casting deathbringer spells required my own lifeforce, I needed to know exactly what that entailed.

Xollmomath was, expectedly, still in the root cellar underneath Xia's house. I found him seated in the very center of the summoning circle, his arms resting gently on the tops of his thighs as though he was meditating, but his solid red eyes were open and watching me. The whole scene was unnerving.

"You approach?" Xollmomath said. His unblinking eyes followed my every movement.

"Yes, of course," I answered. "I have questions. If I'm going to help you conquer Echelon, I'm going to need some answers."

The necromancer nodded slowly. "Lady Kalma's knowledge is not entirely known, nor is it completely within my power to disseminate. You may never find all the answers to the questions you seek."

"Just the basics then, alright? How much do you know about deathbringers?" I figured starting at the absolute beginning of my questions was the best route, though I had so many burning in my mind that I feared I would never find enough time to discover all of their answers.

The man readjusted his position on the ground. "The last time I walked through your plane, perhaps a hundred years ago or more, I walked beside a deathbringer. She was Lady Kalma's daughter, and she was a scourge upon the land."

One of the best features of the wildly complex software developed for Wonder was the rich history the company had embedded into the minds of each and every NPC. Even though the game had only been online for a little less than a decade, talking to the NPCs made it feel like Wonder had always been, that it was just as real as Earth, and that it would continue into eternity.

"Xia said that my talents are based on my own lifeforce. I've never experienced anything quite like it, and I need direction," I said. I sat down cross-legged in front of the necromancer like a pupil attending the first day of school, except my teacher worshipped death, and the degree I sought was in vengeance.

Xollmomath cocked his head to the side and stared at me

from the corner of his vision. "You've bound your soul to the Stench of Corpses, and that soul has now become the well-spring of your powers. The more you bring forth the Lady's magic, the stronger you must be to withstand the drain. If you are too weak, Lady Kalma may add your corpse to her collection."

I had to admit that the necromancer's answer was almost exactly what I was expecting. My own body was my mana pool, and I had no way of accurately gauging when it would simply expire. I needed to practice and familiarize myself with my new class, preferably sooner rather than later, to get as good a handle on my limits as I possibly could. Knowing how much I could push myself would be critical if I was going to survive.

"Another question, if you don't mind. How long will it be until you regain your powers? I have the feeling that we will need to fight pretty soon, and a necromancer would certainly help our cause." I was hoping he would quickly find the strength to take over the entire operation as our leader. I didn't really want to wear the mantle myself, at least not when it came to the overall mission and strategy, and at least not yet.

"Keep bringing me sacrifices, and I will give you an army," Xollmomath said with a sinister smile. "Though it will take some time. With each live offering, I can either convert them into a necromantic soldier to help defend the citadel, or I can consume them to increase my own power. Since I cannot see everything happening on the surface, I'll have to trust your judgement as to what we need the most."

His explanation made sense. I needed to balance our sacrifices between powering up the boss and making new soldiers. When I thought about sending sacrifices into the cellar, another question crossed my mind. "Do you know what will happen to the people I send to you?" I wasn't really sure how to ask an NPC about the respawning mechanics in the game, and with the recent server corruption making so many changes, whatever answer I received could end up being wrong anyway.

The man's dark red eyes watched me for a long moment before responding. "Once we control Whitechapel, I do not know where the remaining citizens will go. Perhaps they shall flee to other cities or take up refuge in Echelon."

We wouldn't have to worry about the NPCs respawning in their own houses once we took over the whole village. That gave us at least some advantage, though I was still relying on the assumption that Xollmomath had the scripting to be able to understand the pseudo-meta question I had asked. Perhaps he could, and once we began work on our citadel in earnest, we wouldn't be bothered by the high priest showing up every day to try and bring us down. That gave me a little bit of hope, though we still had the looming task of what basically amounted to genocide standing in our way.

For the rest of the day, I had to oversee the first stages of our construction. The cultists were happily setting up a knee-high fence around the entire property and so far, none of the other residents of Whitechapel appeared too concerned. Losing the robes had made our underlings inconspicuous enough to not warrant anything more than a passing glance from the various villagers as they went about their day.

Around midday, Xia returned from wherever she had gone, and she brought with her an armful of strange components, animal parts, and some small pieces of metallic ore. I stopped her by her arm before she headed toward her house. "What kind of items did you get?" I asked. "If I'm going to help manage our settlement, I'll need to have a clear picture of everything going in and out. Also, how capable are our warlocks? Can they fight?"

At first, Xia looked taken aback by my straightforward style of leadership—I didn't think she was used to someone simply asking her for results and not fearing her power and authority—but she answered me nonetheless. "The warlocks are all simple initiates. They can fight, though it won't be pretty. I can teach them if you like. Training will take time and supplies, however. I was able to barter or steal enough components for a few simple defensive rituals as well."

"Defensive rituals? Like what?" The prospect of casting a spell around the encampment to shield us from the rest of the village until we were strong enough was enticing.

"I'm a lot stronger than the initiates. If you'd like a ritual, I'll be the one to do it," the woman replied defensively. She gave me a little sneer as she spoke, and I wasn't exactly sure what she was afraid of.

"Anything to hide the three houses or maybe set a trap?" I asked, trying my best to sound friendly and non-confrontational.

Still, the woman leered. "Traps I can do," she said. "Hiding the whole citadel or casting an illusion to change its appearance would be the work of a wizard or some other arcane sorcerer."

"Excellent. Can you make traps that will recognize anyone with a devotion to Kalma?" If we could get a few defensive traps set up around the perimeter to allow our members to come and go as they pleased, we would be making huge strides toward the ultimate goal.

The woman nodded. "I have enough for a single trap, and it will recognize those of us who are loyal. Or I could use the components to begin training the recruits. Which would you prefer, Deathbringer?"

"Let the recruits continue their work on the wall. We need that just as much as we need the traps. Concentrate our defenses on the area closest to the well and the temple. Tomorrow, when the wall is at least serviceable, you can train them." If I had a whiteboard and a computer with some spreadsheet software, I would have felt like I hadn't left work. But there,

ever-present in the back of my mind, was the lurking sensa-
tion of fear. I wasn't playing a game anymore, and my daughter was already dead. Getting things wrong didn't mean I'd be
fired from the Ministry or demoted to a lower position with
less pay—it meant the end of my entire family line.

When night fell, I decided to use my relatively high cunning skill to do a little reconnaissance. I needed to know if the
town's leadership had caught on to our growing cult. For all I
knew, a raid would be incoming to eradicate our whole group
before midnight. As long as we lived alongside civilian NPCs,
knowledge was likely going to be our most prized possession.

Sneaking around the outside of the chapel wasn't too
tricky. Not many people were out at night, and the side closest
to my house was the graveyard—sparsely populated indeed. I
crept up to one of the tall stained-glass windows and pressed
my face up against it to try and see what was happening on
the other side. The shapes standing amongst the pews were
blurry, but they were certainly humanoid. Interestingly, the
NPCs were not in the usual configuration that I had seen them
in a handful of times before. They were discussing something,
and I had to find out exactly what it was.

I moved through the shadows to the front entrance of the
church, the only way in that I knew of, and tested the door
knob. It was unlocked. I pushed it open ever so slightly, cring-
ing every time the huge wooden door made even the slightest sound. When I barely had enough room to press my body
through, I darted into a dark corner in the back to crouch behind the rows of pews and chairs.

". . . I just don't see how any of that is possible. We're in
Whitechapel, not some forsaken wilderness!"

"You aren't listening, Magister! You need to calm down and
open your ears."

"How long will it take? How long before we can send someone to Echelon to bring help?"

If the men gathered behind the altar were talking about the necromantic citadel arising in their village, I had just heard excellent news. They were so tied up in their own bureaucracy and bickering that they hadn't even sent a runner to the capital yet. If I could find out when they planned on sending the message, I'd be able to stop them on the road.

A few moments later, I heard exactly what I needed.

". . . I say he's leaving at once, and that's going to be the final word on the issue. I'll not hear any more. If you want to make another formal grievance against me, go ahead. The council will meet again in two days. Go and tell them how horrible I am."

Fearing that whoever was shouting at the others to send their messenger was about to make a big show of storming out, I slipped back out of the door and began to run down the street in the direction of Echelon. I stole a glance back over my shoulder when I figured I was a reasonable distance away, and I saw someone leaving the church with speed, though they weren't heading in my direction.

If my assumption was right, whoever had stormed out would be fetching their messenger and getting them on the road. All I needed to do was find an inconspicuous place to hide.

I probably had somewhere between five and ten minutes before I'd need to fight, which afforded me plenty of time to try my more interesting skill, *Pull from the Darkness*. I found a dark, fairly hidden depression that gave me a view of the road, and I braced myself for the physical drain I knew I would feel when I activated the talent.

After a few deep breaths, I focused on the ability with my mind and cast the spell. Whereas the spore cloud I had vomited earlier had sapped the strength and energy from my left arm, casting *Pull from the Darkness* wrenched the energy from my entire body. I felt like the blood was being ripped forward from my veins all at once, and it left me staggering backward deeper into the ditch. In front of me, in the exact spot where I had been standing just a moment before, was a shadowy ball of writhing tentacles roughly half my size. It moved and undulated with new protrusions rising forth and others receding, the whole mass of shadows tentatively awaiting my command as I breathlessly tried to regain the full functions of my brain and senses.

Slowly, my eyes regained their focus. I knew that with time and enough practice I would get used to the drain. For now, I needed to see what my little shadow pet could handle. "Forward, uh . . . shadow-thing," I ordered, pointing a finger toward the road. Without hesitation, my creation began slithering toward its target. "Stop! Come back!" Again, it immediately obeyed.

I decided to try a more complex approach to see how much the creature could handle making inferences on its own. "Prepare yourself for combat," I said. The creature formed into more of a low-lying animal profile like a badger or a fox, with three shadowy horns coming forth from its featureless, shadowy head. Honestly, I was impressed. I drew my sword from my belt and tossed it about ten feet away further from the road. "Get my sword." The amalgamation reacted instantly, and a few seconds later my sword was being presented to me at waist height, hilt first.

Before I could test another command, I saw a dark figure breaking the horizon and heading in my direction. "Get ready to fight," I told my pet monster. It remained in its vulpine state and crouched low in the ditch at my side. I was still a little wobbly from the summoning, and I wanted to see how well the creature could fight on its own before I jumped in myself.

The runner heading toward Echelon was young and fit, with a tightly rolled scroll held in his hand. When the man was only a few feet from my ditch, I pointed and commanded my shadow monster to kill.

All at once, the peaceful countryside on the outskirts of Whitechapel erupted in chaos. The runner screamed and lost control of his message, and my monster gored him with its short, slightly curved horns. It was fairly clear after only a few seconds that the runner was only that—he couldn't fight. My shadow monster had him on the ground under its head, and its triangular horns were shredding through flesh left and right.

Another unwelcome burst of energy exploded outward from my chest, arms, and legs. The monster required a second tick of life in order to remain on the material plane. Lady Kalma's second demand on my lifeforce was much more taxing than the first. My vision blackened and mingled with the night, and my legs gave out. As I hit the soft ground, I could barely hear the sounds of my pet mangling the poor runner just ten feet away. All of my senses were dulled nearly to the point of nonexistence.

A full thirty seconds passed before I could find the strength to get off the grass. When I finally had my feet secured underneath me once more, the rest of my senses began returning in truncated pulses until they were back to normal.

The runner from Whitechapel was dead. My shadowy fox minion was still standing on the man's gored chest like a hunter posing with a fresh trophy.

Your Influence skill has increased to 16!

I felt like I needed to thank or congratulate my pet, but I didn't really know what to say. After all, the shadow fox was essentially a part of myself, not a separate entity. Any emotion I felt I had to assume was also felt by my shadow. Regardless, I just couldn't let the thing stand there without at least saying something. "Thanks, buddy," I awkwardly said. Immediately, I realized I needed to come up with a name for the creature.

Figuring out a fun name would have to wait. I felt like I could withstand one more crippling lifeforce drain if I had to, but no more. A fourth would kill me. "You, fox, carry the body. We have to get back to the citadel. Xollmomath will want the corpse, no doubt. And if I fall before we get there, ditch the corpse and carry me instead. A third is ok, but don't let a fourth . . . uh, well, if you need energy from me for a fourth time, don't. Go back home before that happens, alright?"

The fox creature didn't nod or speak its assent. In the back of my mind, I could *feel* the being's acquiescence to my command, and I knew it understood everything I had said. Its body shifted once more into something akin to a dwarf, though it propelled itself on five stubby feet and used a sixth shadow-born appendage to haul the corpse behind it.

We made it almost to the well before Lady Kalma required a third dose of my soul to keep my shadow creation alive. Judging by the time between doses, I figured the shadow creation required more energy when it was active and could operate on much less fuel doing simple tasks like carrying a corpse.

Two of the acolytes came running out to meet me, and I mentally detached myself from the magic connecting the shadow creature to the material plane. As soon as the creature was gone, it felt like a huge bolt of electricity coursed through my body, reinvigorating every muscle it touched. "Finally . . . get the corpse to Xollmomath. Tell him to make us a soldier. The church knows we're here. I expect a fight tomorrow."

The cultists nodded and began carrying the body off to the root cellar to be converted into a soldier for the cause.

Watching two necromantic minions carrying a corpse to an ancient being I had helped resurrect really started putting things in perspective for me. I thought of Ingrid, saw her dying face flashing through my mind, and . . .

Everything started to make sense.

I had been thinking of it all—my class, Xollmomath, the citadel—as just another quest. Another dungeon mission.

I sat down against the side of the well and stared at the early stages of the defensive fortifications.

"No, Ingrid . . ."

If I was truly going to exact my revenge, I had to change. The emptiness I had felt in the moments and hours after Ingrid's death was suddenly full once more. What took up residence in my body, my heart, in all the cracks and crevices where my love for my family had once so verdantly grown—all of it was now hate. Every ounce of my soul thrummed with it.

"Ingrid . . . I'm coming for you. They made you suffer as you died. Vic, his lackey, whoever was responsible for the server attack. They're all guilty."

I stood from the well and brushed some of the dirt from my clothes. Behind me, a few of the villagers who were still awake had come out of their own houses to see what was happening. No longer did I care about them, or anyone else who got in my way. There would be time enough to add them to my undead army later.

Xia strode out through the small wooden gate the drones had constructed. "Ben, what—" She paused and covered her mouth with a hand. "You look different." She could see the change that had come over me, the new determination and purpose in my countenance. I seethed with so much hatred that it was basically tangible.

Behind her, the cultists reemerged with our first soldier between them. The undead, a truly twisted abomination of broken bones, shredded skin, and torn muscle, left a cloud of pestilence in the night air as it shambled. "It can fight, yes?" I demanded of the cultists.

"Yes, but what's happening?" Xia nearly yelled. She took a few quick steps forward and placed herself between me and the zombie.

My voice booming, I commanded my army: "Get your robes and your weapons and your magic. Hiding in our meager houses and waiting to repel an attack is the coward's way. We fight tonight."

I turned back toward the village with fire burning in my dead heart. One of the civilians from across the street began hesitantly approaching, his arms held nervously at his sides.

In one clean motion I leapt upon him, drawing my sword in the process, and removed his head from his shoulders. His body hit the ground like a lifeless sack of wheat being thrown from a wagon. "Kill any who resist. Bring the rest of Whitechapel back to the well. Bind their feet. Xollmomath requires power, and I require an army."

Your Influence skill has increased to 17!

I didn't look back to make sure my underlings were going to carry out their grim task. They were evil, truly evil, and that was the only thing they cared to follow. I felt a dark stain of malevolence spreading over me, and I knew in that moment exactly what I had to become.

"Ingrid. I'm coming. I'll be with you soon," I told the night air. Three villagers were murdered right in front of me, cut down by Xia and a pair of cultists as they refused to surrender to Lady Kalma. Their corpses would soon swell my ranks, and I smiled at the thought.

"Yes, Ingrid. Everyone guilty shall pay. Wonder will burn, and the Stench of Corpses will flood their cities. If I ever leave this world, if the portals come back online someday, I'll find every last wretch responsible for the glitch, Ingrid. And I'll add their bones to the walls of my citadel. When every guilty corpse adorns the foundation of my ossuary, that will still be too little. Their sacrifice shall be judged, and it shall be found wanting. Their families, their acquaintances, anyone who ever gave them a drop of aid—they'll all rot beneath my boots. Yes, Ingrid, my love . . . their corpses will rot beneath my boots."

Deeper in the village, screams were rising up to mingle with the stars in the sky.

CHAPTER 7

Whitechapel was mine.

Tall plumes of thick smoke blotted out the sun, casting the destroyed village in a gloomy pattern befitting the occasion. Before me knelt two dozen captives, the small lot who had chosen to cast away their honor and surrender. Three of them were players, all low-level, who had been trying to start their characters on basic quests when the server corruption had thrown the world into chaos. Unlike the NPCs who softly cried for mercy, the three players were gagged, and their eyes were filled with more terror than I had ever seen before.

I drank in their fear. Seeing them so beaten, so broken . . . my mind replaced their faces with Vic's hideous snarl, and I had to look away. He would kneel before me in due time, and every death I wrought would simply be practice for the only ones that truly mattered.

At my side, Xia held her dagger ready and awaited my command. My renown had risen from one to four, and with it came a new measure of respect and obedience from everyone in the cult except Xollmomath. The ancient necromancer still knew he was my superior, and I wasn't eager to change the status quo just yet.

"Ten villagers to the master," I commanded, pointing to a section of the huddling captives. The four cultists began herding them toward the cellar door. "Tell Xollmomath to grow his power. We need him strong." The ancient necromancer didn't exactly obey my orders, but I knew he wouldn't reject a chance to get stronger.

Eleven villagers remained alongside the three players. Behind them, my singular zombie groaned and shuffled around as it waited for a command.

"These eleven will join the ranks. Slit their throats and tell our master to turn them," I commanded. Some of them tried to scramble away, but their feet were tied with cord. Xia killed them one at a time with her dagger. When the cultists returned, the new corpses would be dragged away and converted into zombies, bringing my total to twelve.

"Now, a trio of adventurers." Their eyes grew collectively wider as I turned my gaze toward them. "I have need of lieutenants. People I can trust. People to help bring the Stench of Corpses to every corner of Wonder."

Two of them began sobbing behind their gags. They were both men, probably a few years younger than I was, and both were only level four.

"Your cries betray your weakness," I told them. One of the men fell backward. He tried to push away with his heels, but his bindings were tight, and he didn't make it more than six inches before giving up. "Pathetic."

I drew my sword. The enchanted weapon was designed for killing rats and other sewer-dwelling vermin, but it still accomplished the task well enough.

"Two more zombies for the army brings us to fourteen," I stated. The drones were still working on delivering the first batch to Xollmomath for conversion. At the rate I was growing our forces, we would need a specific place to house the undead so they remained out of our way. Luckily, the village of Whitechapel had been recently vacated, so there was plenty of room to be found.

I pulled down the gag from the remaining player's mouth. She was level six, caked in dirt, and didn't appear nearly as fearful as the two gibbering idiots had been. The name above her head said 'Helvegen.'

Leaning down, I whispered in her ear, "As I said before, I am in need of lieutenants I can trust. Can I trust you, Helvegen? Could you be strong for me, Helvegen?"

I could see her trembling, but she did not cry or make a feeble attempt to flee. Instead, she only looked forward, her eyes locked on the stone well in the center of the street. I liked her resolve. In the middle of so much death, she didn't break. Perhaps I could use her as a lieutenant. She would no doubt try to kill me the first chance she got, but the risk was unavoidable. If I was to be surrounded by actual players and not purely NPCs, I had to allow for some level of risk. I faced the standard tyrant's dilemma: anyone subservient enough to pose no risk of rebellion or assassination would be too weak to be truly useful, and my empire would suffer because of it.

Still, I didn't have the luxury of unnecessary danger. I had to transmit my absolute authority to the woman if I was going to allow her to live. "Xia," I called, and the warlock approached.

"Yes?"

"We have the materials necessary for minor healing, correct?" I asked. She nodded. "Good. Hold out Helvegen's left hand. Spread her fingers."

The captive woman's eyes found mine, and again I saw some resolve lingering on her expression. "Only two choices. Either put that fearsome determination to work for me as a lieutenant, or I'll put your body to work in my mindless army of zombie slaves."

She continued to stare, and she didn't resist Xia's manipulation of her hand, though I could see her beginning to tremble. The fear brought about by uncertainty was starting to take its toll on her mind. Finally, she cast her eyes back down at the well. "I'll serve," she said meekly.

"Excellent. Now, Xia, hold her pinky finger out from the rest." I leveled my sword right above Helvegen's knuckle. She still didn't cry or scream out or even try to resist. "You know, I like the strong, quiet type. I need that kind of composure. You'll be a welcome addition to the citadel's forces."

With a clean strike, I removed the woman's pinky finger from her hand. She grunted and gasped, but she did not call out.

"Xia, fix her hand. I don't want to lose a lieutenant to a simple infection." Before Helvegen had a chance to move, I crouched down to her eye level. "I need you to know that I won't hesitate to kill you. And you saw the message from the developers. Death is real now. The scar on your hand will be there to remind you every single day that you're just barely a step ahead of oblivion."

I stood, and Xia hauled off the whimpering, bleeding Helvegen in the direction of the root cellar. "When she's recovered, take her to Xollmomath. He can train many classes. Let her pick what she wants to be."

The warlock nodded, and the two women left the desolate street.

Your Infamy skill has increased to 12!

Congratulations! The holding of Whitechapel is now yours! Do you wish to rename it? Yes / No

I selected *Yes*. A blank lined appeared next to the holdings area on my character sheet. Coming up with something perfect would be difficult. I casually walked around the well and the nearby houses—all of which were now vacant—to move my legs a little as I tried to think of a name. Blackchapel came quickly to my mind, but it didn't really have the right ring to it. It was too expected. Xollmomath was intent on developing a citadel, so incorporating the word felt logical.

The Dark Citadel? Too cliché. I needed something to evoke fear, but it couldn't be too ridiculous. If all went well, I'd be living here for quite some time. Nightwell Citadel? That one had potential. Actually, something that evoked the old memory of Whitechapel would be the most appropriate. Undercroft Citadel had a nice ring to it.

Congratulations! The holding of Undercroft Citadel is now yours!

Your Renown skill has increased to 5!

Your Influence skill has increased to 18!

Something about the 'Holdings' section of my character sheet was a little different than it had been before. Next to the word was a little green carrot, and when I focused on it, a new menu expanded to the right of the sheet:

Undercroft Citadel

Commander: Xollmomath (Influence: 25)

Bosses: Xia (Warlock), Ben Hales (Deathbringer), Helvegen (Painter)

Resources: Moderate stockpiles of food and lumber, poor stockpiles of weapons, no stockpiles of wealth, exotic goods, or artifacts.

Military Strength: 4 warlocks, 14 zombies

Defensive Structures: Partially constructed wall

"Whoa," I muttered under my breath. On all the streams, I had never watched any dungeon bosses. The closest I had gotten was watching Ahmose II playing a few times, but his days were boring. I had always preferred to watch the bold solo adventurers and some of the larger raid guilds. Epic fights, dragons, and guilds clashing against each other were always the best draw online, not tedious management menus.

I had a ton of information to help me build Undercroft into a powerhouse dungeon. All I needed to do was put my years of management experience from the Ministry of Health to use.

First, another visit to Xollmomath was in order. I had to

assume that whoever had the highest influence skill was the Citadel's natural commander, and for the next few weeks, I was fine playing second fiddle.

The necromancer wasn't in his root cellar as I had expected; rather, I found him inside the house above the summoning circle. As it turned out, the sacrifices we had rounded up from the village were enough to grant the ancient magician a little more mobility. That was certainly a good thing. The more powerful he became, the better chance we had to protect the citadel when the first inevitable raid came to our doorstep.

Xollmomath's house was small, and only he and Xia were present inside. "The warlocks are managing the zombies right now, yeah?" I asked. The thought of my tiny army running rampant through the remaining Whitechapel buildings was a little worrisome, though I supposed it wouldn't actually be that big of a deal if it happened. We would need to clear out the buildings eventually anyway.

"Yes, the cultists are training the zombies," Xia answered. "They're creations of necromancy so they cannot learn any warlock spells, but they may benefit from certain warlock enchantments that can be placed upon them. They will continue training until you tell me otherwise."

It was good that when left to their own devices, the NPCs would at least figure out a way to be productive even if it wasn't the ideal use of our time. For now, training the militia was just fine. On to the next order of business.

"Alright, I saw that Helvegen received a class. I'm not sure I'm familiar with a painter. What's that?" I directed my question more to Xollmomath since he had been the one to bestow the strange class upon her.

"Painters are similar to other arcane classes, sorceresses and necromancers and the like, but their specialty lies in visual manipulation. Once she is strong enough, she will be able to create convincing illusions large enough to hide the entire citadel," the ancient man explained, his inscrutable red eyes fixing me with their awful stare.

"Perfect. She'll make a fine addition." *If she doesn't kill me in my sleep* . . . The very real possibility that I would meet my end at the nine-fingered hand my own underling was something I could never allow. "Xia, you said before that you can create traps. Do you know any traps or other protections you could place on me directly?"

The woman thought for a moment. As she was about to respond, Xollmomath cut her off.

"I can protect you from death," he stated.

"What do you mean?"

Again, the man's blood red eyes bored into me. "You serve Lady Kalma faithfully. I am powerful enough to place a shroud upon your body. If you would die, the shroud would bring you back. So long as you continue to follow the Stench of Corpses, the shroud will last."

Though he was light on the details, it sounded perfect. I would be the only one in the entire world with a second life. "Sounds good. Let's do it," I said.

Xollmomath snapped his fingers, and the status line on my character sheet changed.

Status: unstable, shrouded by Lady Kalma

If that was all there was to it, I was certainly impressed. "Nothing else?" I asked, wondering if there was some pig heart I would need to eat or a pool of goblin blood I would have to drink in order to get the magic to stick.

Xollmomath shook his head. "You are protected. A single death, and do not let your faith waiver."

"Could you protect any of the others as well?" I asked.

The necromancer offered a short, clipped laugh. "I am not yet strong enough to cast the spell on multiple souls at the same time. Bring me more sacrifices, and my power will continue to escalate."

Excellent. As Undercroft Citadel continued to grow in strength and expand outward, we would be able to bring more and more captives to Xollmomath, growing the dungeon boss's abilities with every sacrifice. If we could remain undetected for long enough, we would survive. 'Long enough,' though, was a nebulous term. How much time would we need? Would a raiding party full of high-level players from Echelon show up to retake the village tomorrow? The day after that? In a month? The uncertainty burned in my mind.

I spent the rest of the day laying the groundwork for Undercroft's eventual defenses. For the near future, I had to keep the small perimeter around the three houses that served as our command center. We didn't have nearly the numbers required to secure the entire village—or what was left of it after the outermost buildings were razed to the ground—so we had to concentrate our efforts where they would pay off the most. By nightfall, the small livestock pen had been enlarged to a proper wall, though it was still only about five feet high.

Xia was able to use some magical components to give the wooden fortification a defensive enchantment, though she admitted that the trap wouldn't be much at all against a concerted attack. Better than nothing, I reasoned.

I split up our zombies into four patrol groups that could walk a pattern around the nearest buildings and alert the entire camp if trespassers were discovered. Each patrol squad had a single warlock escort. During the hours of downtime that came with walking the border, the warlocks trained the zombies, teaching them basic formations and rudimentary tactics. Xia thought the training would pay off, and eventually the zombies would be more than mindless brutes. Training them would also give secondary benefits to the warlocks themselves, hopefully increasing their influence and cunning skills little by little.

As for Helvegen, I gave her orders to train directly with Xollmomath. If she tried to escape or cause some other treachery, the ancient necromancer had a mind to kill her, and that kind of control was what I needed.

Deep down, I wasn't quite sure yet how I felt about killing two players and enslaving a third. Some part of me regretted the decision. That part was small, however, in comparison to the burning hatred flooding through every fiber of my body. If I had left the two cowards alive, they would have become a liability. If either of them had escaped back to Echelon, Undercroft Citadel would be doomed. That eventuality was not one I was willing to entertain.

Helvegen was a different matter. She had a warrior's spirit within her, but she still hadn't come to terms with what had happened—to her personally or the game as a whole. I could see the uncertainty lurking behind her eyes when I went into Xollmomath's house to check on her progress.

I spent my time with Xia scouting the nearest buildings for supplies. Mostly we found food to add to our stores, but we did come across the occasional weapon. Some of the villagers had what looked to be family heirloom swords or axes stowed away in their houses, and we gladly took them back to the compound. If we were ever lucky enough to add a blacksmith or an arcane enchanter to our ranks, we would be able to make good use of the salvaged weapons.

When I went to sleep at night, it was with a smile on my face. Undercroft Citadel was coming along at a steady pace. Each sack of dried meat, every scrap of metal—they were all useful. Eventually, I would command a formidable dungeon and an army strong enough to conquer Echelon.

On the third day of Undercroft Citadel's existence, one of the warlocks in charge of a patrol group reported something most unusual.

"Sir, we've found something. Come quickly!" the robed warlock shouted as he bounded into the central compound. I had been inspecting a pair of old axes that Xia had discovered, trying to determine if they were strong enough to actually be used in combat or only suitable for the scrap pile.

I tossed the axes aside immediately. "What is it?"

"Some of the bones and spirits in the church are stirring," the warlock explained between breaths. "The old priest's ghost haunts the grounds."

For all the trepidation in the warlock's voice, I couldn't be happier. The game's AI had begun to change things as it recognized Undercroft Citadel as a new, permanent development. The world was changing, and that meant new quests would be scripted into the game that hadn't existed before. New quests would bring loot, opportunities to level skills, and so much more.

I chased after the warlock as he ran back to the temple in the center of the village. He had set the zombies in his group in a defensive semi-circle around the front entrance to the building, and from there I could see what was happening inside. The front doors had been burned and knocked from their hinges, allowing a view of the interior.

Ghosts prowled within the dappled, shadowy walls and stained-glass windows. There was probably a dozen of them, maybe more. The building's steepled roof gave off a constant mist as though a fog machine had been placed inside and allowed to constantly run on a low setting. Every few minutes, a dark shadow would obscure the front entrance for a brief moment, and sounds of rustling bones reached my ears.

"We have our own dungeon to conquer," I said under my breath. "Keep your patrol here. If any of the ghosts attempt to leave the temple, fight them. Kill them if you can. If your zombies and spells don't affect them, run back to Xollmomath. I'll be back soon."

I returned to the well and the houses to summon the rest of my forces at once. Luckily, Xia was already there with an armful of salted meat to add to the root cellar, and I sent her out to gather the other three warlocks.

Half an hour later, my war council was assembled around the fire pit behind Xollmomath's house. The necromancer was strong enough to join us, though he had to remain close to the building itself to stay within the magical limits of the summoning circle. Helvegen, never far from the necromancer's side, glared at me. She had changed her outfit slightly since joining the ranks. Instead of the rather basic adventuring garb she had worn before, she now had a tight black tunic and matching skirt held in place by a leather belt sporting two pouches full of magical components required for her strange spellcasting.

The three warlocks all stood around the fire pit unmoving, their AI-controlled eyes shifting between Xia and myself as they awaited new orders.

I decided to get right to the point. "The temple in the center of town has become haunted," I began. "The old priest, Amida, is still prowling around the place as a ghost. He's summoned some other spirits from the crypt as well, and something else also prowls within. I think it's a skeleton, but I'm not positive."

Xia's expression perked slightly as I explained the situation. I got the impression she was just as eager for combat as I was. "What's the plan?" she asked.

"We're going on a dungeon raid."

We assembled in front of the temple about an hour later. I decided to leave a warlock and four zombies back at the home base just in case anyone happened to stumble upon the village while we were occupied. I didn't expect any trouble for at least another few days, but it wouldn't hurt to be extra cautious.

I could still see a dark shadow passing in front of the broken entrance every few minutes. The building was small, and there wasn't any easy way to take the enemies inside in small groups so that our superior numbers could end the fight quickly.

The three warlocks and Xia all looked to me as their leader without Xollmomath nearby to usurp my authority. I was happy to step into the role. "Alright. We don't know how much we're up against," I began. "I don't want to lose any zombies if we don't have to, and I want everyone to focus on getting some experience and levelling up. The zombies are just fodder to keep the ghosts busy while we kill them. Understood?"

The warlocks all nodded.

Helvegen stood off to one side with her arms crossed over her chest. She kept one eye pointed in my direction, though she didn't actually stand to face me. I knew I had to talk to her, to sit down and try to explain what the hell was happening, but we didn't have time for that kind of thing just yet. Maybe once the dungeon raid was over we would be able to come to some sort of understanding. Although I needed players with real intellect and skill under my command, I knew that what I needed even more was loyalty.

I decided the quickest way to win the woman over—or at least begin to get to know her—was going to be fighting right next to her. "Helvegen, you and I will draw out the ghosts into the open. If we can pull out small groups one after the other, we'll have a better chance." I intentionally left out any semblance of a question, curious to see how she would react to such a direct command.

The woman fixed me with both of her eyes, and I saw the same determination lurking there that had convinced me to spare her life. "You have something to live for," I stated. "What is it? Why are you still here?"

I caught her off guard. She clearly hadn't been expecting me to ask after her most basic motivations, but she covered her surprise quickly with a mask of distant indifference. "What do you care?" she snapped.

"Correct me if I'm wrong, but you didn't know those other two players we caught, did you?"

She shook her head.

"So, what are you doing in Wonder? What's your goal here?" I pressed.

She stared me down for a moment before responding. "I have a brother in Echelon. He's probably looking for me. We just started a week ago, maybe more."

The woman didn't exactly answer my question, and that was fine. I expected her to be reluctant, perhaps outright lying, for quite some time. Eventually, I would have to either break through to her or kill her.

"You know what I'm building here. I'll need lieutenants I can trust. Players, not scripted NPCs. I don't care how good the AI is, I want real humans serving in the highest positions. If you fight well and prove yourself to be trustworthy, you'll have a place in the empire I'm building." In my own mind, I felt like I had put forth a fairly reasonable argument.

Inscrutable, the woman said nothing.

"Think about it," I added. "Right now, you and I are going into the temple to draw out the first group of ghosts. I need you to fight. If you refuse, either I'll kill you or the ghosts will. Decision time."

I didn't wait for Helvegen to say anything before heading for the busted temple doors. When I was on the steps, I turned back to make sure all the warlocks and zombies were in their correct positions, and I saw the painter only a couple steps behind me. She held no weapon, but I trusted that her magic-based class would prove useful in other ways. I was eager to see what exactly a painter was capable of, even if she was only level six and barely knew anything herself.

I waved for Helvegen to take up position on the left side of the entryway, and I took the right. After a deep breath to steady myself and clear my mind, I ducked my head around the doorframe. Inside, I saw roughly ten ghosts flitting in and out of the various patches of colored light created by the tall stained-glass windows on either side. Near the back of the room, something that was both a skeleton and not quite a skeleton prowled from side to side. It was an amalgamation of arms and legs, though none of the bones had been combined in any human order. The whole thing was more like an elongated oval, perhaps a centipede or some beetle shape, and it skittered on the knobby ends of its bones with a horrible noise.

"We need to—"

Helvegen leapt into the chapel and thrust her arms forward, sending out a strange tendril of energy that immediately encircled the nearest ghost in its clutches. "Back outside!" she half-yelled through gritted teeth.

A group of four or five ghosts had certainly noticed whatever it was the woman had done, and they weren't happy about it. They chased after us, their ethereal hands elongating into wispy claws as they lunged and raked. In the sunlight outside the chapel, the creatures were hard to see. They melded with the shimmer of the afternoon sun and moved in short, blurry bursts of translucent energy.

Just as I had planned, the zombies came rushing in from either side of the doorway as Helvegen and I escaped the church. My undead army couldn't actually hurt the ghosts with their rotting, foul arms, but they served an important purpose nonetheless. The ghosts stalled for a few moments as they appeared to contemplate whether they would pass through the small ring of undead, giving Xia and her warlocks enough time to begin their casting.

Without our group taking a single casualty, the ghosts were banished by warlock magic until not a single one of the first group remained.

"How many more can you kill?" I asked Xia over the celebratory shouts and cheers of the cultists. I knew she didn't have much in the way of components, and the banishing spells would quickly deplete our reserves.

Before Xia could answer, the rest of the ghosts from the temple emerged, and they were moving much faster than the first group. They only hesitated for a brief moment before rushing straight through the wall of zombies separating our warlocks—and myself, of course—from the church.

More ghosts were readily banished by Xia, and another bolt of grey magic launched from Helvegen's fingertips. It wrapped itself around two of the ghosts like a huge, shifting scarf, and the creatures stopped right where they were, suddenly unable to move.

"What did you do?" I called. For someone only level six, having a magical, ranged stun ability that could affect multiple targets was wildly overpowered.

The two wrangled ghosts began moving backward, and then they were banished from the material plane. Both of them instantly evaporated into the afternoon air, and the magical bonds that had covered their bodies were gone.

"Just changed how they saw us," Helvegen answered between breaths. She clearly wasn't used to the rush of combat, and even something as relatively easy as standing behind a line of zombies while casting spells was draining her energy.

I didn't really understand what she meant, but I didn't have any time to figure it out, either. As the second wave of ghosts were banished, Amida's spirit came charging out of the doorway, followed by the bone monster I had seen prowling around the altar just moments before.

Amida didn't give the zombies a second look before sweeping right over them. The monster behind him, however, basically crashed into our defenses like a bowling ball clattering down a lane. Three zombies were quickly tossed into the air by the creature's flailing head. When they hit the ground, their brittle flesh broke apart and scattered across the ground. Luckily, the remaining seven zombies swarmed onto the bone monster's back and sides, slowing it down and preventing it from quickly trampling all the undead we had brought.

"Xia, take the priest!" I called. "Helvegen, with me! To the bones!"

I only had one particularly relevant talent I could activate to potentially damage the bone horror. Summoning my shadow monster wouldn't do much, and it required too much energy to sustain. My only other outright attack was *A Feast of Spores*, but the bone monster had no lungs, again leaving me at a loss.

I charged in, pushing past two of the undead, and swung with both hands for the creature's ever-shifting legs. A few bone chips flew away—and the thing continued to thrash around and bash into the zombies.

Swinging from low to high, I smashed my blade into the creature's underside, but it didn't have much more effect than my first attack. The zombies clinging all over the monster were biting and punching, and they were having even less effect than I was with my sword. "Start pulling it apart!" I yelled to the mindless soldiers.

All at once, the zombies began wrapping their rotting fingers around the protruding bones beneath them. Some of the zombies were too decrepit to make much progress, but a few handfuls of bones found their way to the ground nonetheless.

I slashed once more with my sword at a weak connection

where three bones met, and finally my blade passed through, severing a large chunk of the beast from its own body. Then the thrashing head—covered in jagged, broken bones—smashed into my chest and knocked me backward.

Searing pain shot through my side and back. It felt like one of my kidneys had been skewered by a broken femur.

Where I landed on the ground offered me a view of Xia and her warlocks fighting the priest's ghost, and they had made much better progress than I had. The three warlocks were all joined in the same chant, channeling their abilities together to power a swirling pool of dark magic beneath the ghost. Xia, standing behind the warlocks with her hands raised above her head, was trading magical bolts of energy with Amida.

She rolled side to side and dodged, continually dancing between the ghost's volley of attacks while firing back with magical blasts of her own. With the warlocks focusing on pouring enough energy into their banishing to exile Amida altogether, the spirit was slowed, essentially chained to a swirling portal of magic, and the impediment gave Xia enough time and range to work.

Of the seven zombies still clinging to the bone monster and trying to rip off parts of its body, two of them looked too battered to stay in the fight, though they mindlessly pursued their goal nonetheless. I scrambled back to my feet to join them. Charging in once more with my sword, I swung wildly for the monster's head, if the front of it could really be called that, and cleaved another handful of bones from the mass.

Another zombie went down, shorn in half by a pair of curving bones that reminded me of a mammoth's horns. If we didn't end the fight soon, I'd lose too many zombies. Without them to hold the line, it wouldn't take much for the bone horror to run roughshod over Xia, the warlocks, and myself.

I counted my blessings when Amida's towering spirit finally succumbed to the magical bombardment it had endured.

The spirit popped and sizzled for a few seconds before being sucked down into the magical portal beneath its feet where it vanished forever.

"Bind it!" I yelled to the warlocks while pointing to the bone monster. "Chain it or slow it down! Anything!"

Another zombie took a huge hit that ripped off one of its arms and sent it flying through the air.

"We can't banish . . . that! Only spirits!" Xia called back.

"Just slow it down!" I barely skittered out of the way of a flailing bone arm that would have probably taken me out of the fight.

The warlocks began casting their spells at the beast, and ethereal chains of magic appeared all over the bones. No portal sprang into life beneath it, but I was happy to see at least something being done to stymie the slaughter.

From the corner of my eye, I caught a glimpse of Helvegen standing a way off and not doing much of anything. "What are you doing?" I yelled at her, though I had to admit I was somewhat surprised she hadn't used the tumult of the battle to make an escape back to Echelon.

"I only have one spell. It doesn't do much," she casually replied. I could barely hear her voice over the sounds of bones scraping against dirt, rotten flesh, and each other.

More and more chains began to blink into existence over the bone horror. The creature slowed and slowed until it was barely moving, and I called off my zombies. Six of them were more or less unharmed, and another handful I would have to assess later to see if they were still capable of fighting.

"Everyone, form a semi-circle around the . . . thing," I commanded.

Xia took up a position near me. "We need to kill it," she said. She wore a violent scowl that would have been frightening to see had we not been on the same side of the battle.

"No, we don't have to kill it." I had another plan, and I was brimming with excitement at the prospect. Turning to the warlocks with command over their magical chains, I gave my order. "Drag it back to Xollmomath!"

The three warlocks smiled as they instantly recognized my plan.

"Haha, creative," Xia added with a smirk, her scowl gone. "Well played."

Your Cunning skill has increased to 22!

Your Physical skill has increased to 19!

Your Fortune skill has increased to 8!

Your Renown skill has increased to 6!

Congratulations! You have increased to level 11!

You have new talent options to select!

Reading the lengthy list of notifications from the game system, I couldn't help but pump my fist in the air and give a little cheer. The battle had been a fantastic one, and all of our casualties had been worth it. I dismissed the blinking notification telling me to pick a new skill—that could wait until we had the bone horror secured—and walked alongside Xia on the way back to the citadel.

The journey took some time, and the warlocks were exhausted from recasting their magical chains, but it worked. Xollmomath was leaning against the side of his house when we returned, and his blood red eyes grew wide when he realized exactly what it was we were delivering into his capable hands.

"A charnel golem," he muttered, staring up at the beast as it struggled in vain to free itself.

"Can you dominate it? Kill it and reanimate it on our side?" I asked. Having a charnel golem patrolling the outskirts of the village would certainly deter any raiding parties, at least for a while. I imagined the monstrous creature rampaging through whatever hellhole Vic lived in, trampling his goons under its shifting bones, and I smiled. The thought of so much death, so much vengeance, was intoxicating.

"Yes," Xollmomath said in a whisper. "Yes, I will add the golem to our ranks. You have done well, Deathbringer. I am . . . impressed."

The ancient necromancer waved his hand, and the chains surrounding the golem snapped away to fizzle in the air. The beast didn't move. Instead, its moving body settled and calmed as though it was looking to Xollmomath for a command. Perhaps the undead abomination recognized another of its own kind, and it wanted to serve. Or perhaps it simply recognized Xollmomath's unbridled power and didn't want to be annihilated.

Either way, the necromancer's growing grin told me had the charnel golem perfectly under his control. "Shall I tell it to patrol the borders while we grow?" Xollmomath asked.

"Exactly what I had in mind." I watched in awe as the shambling beast made its way further south to the edge of the buildings. It stood taller than all of the single-story structures, and that height was certainly welcome, as I could then watch its movements from almost anywhere in Undercroft Citadel.

I took stock of everything we had left before heading back to the chapel to investigate. Once we looted everything we could, I wanted to burn it down. I didn't want to take any chances leaving it standing, and a temple to a good and righteous god in the middle of a grim bastion of absolute evil felt wrong.

The AI updated all the information on my character sheet instantly:

Undercroft Citadel

Commander: Xollmomath (Influence: 25)

Bosses: Xia (Warlock), Ben Hales (Deathbringer), Helvegen (Painter)

Resources: Moderate stockpiles of food and lumber, poor stockpiles of weapons, no stockpiles of wealth, exotic goods, or artifacts.

Military Strength: 4 warlocks, 9 zombies, 1 charnel golem

Defensive Structures: Partially constructed wall, minor defensive wards

After confirming our total remaining zombies and that the charnel golem had been officially accepted by the game mechanics as a member of the citadel's forces, I shifted my focus over to my own blinking notification telling me I had a decision to make concerning my talents.

Every class in Wonder was a little different when it came to the method by which they gained power. Many of the martial classes had the option to increase their secondary skills every time they gained a level, and the ability to raise investigation or craftsmanship without actually using the skill was invaluable to some builds. Casters typically weren't afforded that function, though they had boons in other forms. Wizards, sorcerers, shaman, and the like typically received more options to improve their spells with every level, sometimes replacing early forms of spells with more powerful versions of different names.

As far as I knew, my deathbringer class was essentially a combination of a necromancer, a soldier or fighter, and a warlord. I used all three primary stats, and the talents I had received so far weren't focused on one single stat over the other two. As I expected, I had three options to choose from for level eleven, one linked to each primary:

Nothing to Fear (physical): Lady Kalma protects her most faithful servants. Attacks which the deathbringer cannot see deal less damage and have a chance to fail altogether. Passive.

Shadow Jaunt (cunning): If the deathbringer commands a puppet after activating Pull from the Darkness, the deathbringer may switch positions with the puppet at will. Active, consumes moderate energy.

Corpse Stench's Presence (influence): Destruction follows the path of the deathbringer from world to world, and with that stench comes a flood of otherworldly minions. The deathbringer's aura of command grows stronger allowing more minions to be controlled and fewer thoughts of dissension to spread through any of the deathbringer's holdings. Additionally, Corpse Stench's Presence allows certain controlled bosses to be promoted to more powerful positions than would otherwise be available. Passive.

I had to read all three skills twice before I could narrow down my selection to only two. While Nothing to Fear was certainly a useful passive to have, I couldn't justify selecting it over a teleport or way of tightening the reins around everyone else in the citadel.

Perhaps only two or three days ago I would have chosen Shadow Jaunt without even considering the other talents. Now, in the midst of organizing my own dungeon and advancing through the ranks, I knew that I had to select Corpse Stench's Presence. Not only would the passive talent allow me to grow the citadel's forces more quickly, but it would make Helvegen and any other players I managed to press into service just a little more loyal.

I focused my attention on the bottom skill of the list and unlocked it.

Since I had better command over everyone except Xoll-momath, I decided to put it to use immediately.

"Xia, Helvegen, you two are coming with me to search the crypt beneath the chapel. Hopefully we'll find some more magical components to add to our stores." The two women nodded—though Helvegen didn't look very happy. She was still nursing a bandaged hand where I had removed one of her fingers.

I then ordered two of the cultists to take some of our zombies and continue patrolling the border while also training. With a huge charnel golem also walking the beat, I could afford to reduce the rest of the patrols accordingly. The other warlocks I set to finishing the wall around our interior compound. In the long run, the wall would be useless as soon as our holdings expanded beyond our first three houses, but it still gave me a measure of comfort to have it completed.

CHAPTER 8

Back at the chapel, there wasn't anything worth looting on the ground floor. I hadn't expected anything of value to be in the simple altar or between the pews, but it was still kind of depressing to come away empty-handed from an entire floor. With more investigation skill, I might have been able to discover a hidden relic or a secret passage that would yield riches. Unfortunately, those potential rewards would all be lost since we planned on burning the whole thing to the ground.

Moving to the crypt got my hopes up for some loot. We were desperately in need of equipment more than anything else. Our zombies were quite literally falling apart, deteriorating further every single day, and all the rest of us had to wear were cloth robes. If we could grave rob some armor, that would be perfect.

On top of acquiring armor, I also needed to know the capabilities of my lieutenants. "Before we go down into the crypt, I have a few questions." Both the women stopped to regard me. "Helvegen, you said your magic altered how the ghosts saw us. What does that mean?"

"The only spell I know is a basic paint. I have to throw it, and then it changes what the target sees, but I can't change *much*. Not yet," she explained. "Against the ghosts, I made them see nine of us charging into the chapel instead of only two. It only lasted for a few seconds, just enough to catch the ire of the group and get them to chase us outside. I don't know, honestly it was a bit of luck that it worked at all."

I wasn't sure what to think. She had made the ghosts think our invasion was much larger than it had been in reality . . . had she actually been attempting to pull the entire room at once and purposefully sabotage the raid? Maybe.

"Alright, that's useful. Good to know. Xia, what kind of things can you do? Unfortunately, I don't know as much as I should about warlocks." Learning my chief warlock's powers was going to be paramount. She was more powerful than I was without a doubt, and at some point, I would have to surpass her to gain more control within the citadel. That might entail killing her, but more likely than not simply overtaking her in the unspoken power rankings of the organization would be good enough.

"Most of what I've focused on revolves around destruction and keeping myself alive. The cultists are the summoners. Their power brought forth Xollmomath from the eternal abyss. I simply gathered them and kept them alive long enough to complete the ritual," she explained.

I had watched a few streams of some warlocks in the past, and I knew the general idea behind the destructive build she was using. Similar to mages and wizards, warlocks had lots of different play styles, though casting destructive spells typically wasn't a common choice. The much flashier talents revolved around summoning demons, and the best guilds always employed warlocks who specialized in banishment, slows, and stuns like the four acolytes. That kind of warlock wasn't considered terribly fun to play since they basically couldn't go out adventuring on their own, but they were vital to the high-level raids. Having four of them was certainly going to come in handy.

"Since you can kill things the easiest, you'll take point in the crypt, Xia," I told her. She didn't complain at all.

Warlock leading the way, I put myself in the middle and had Helvegen behind—trusting that Xollmomath's protections on my life would hold true if the painter decided to stab me in the back. Some part of me felt like allowing Helvegen the last spot in our order was a bit of a trust exercise kind of like the stupid activities the Ministry of Health would make me practice with the office every now and then. Having her behind me was a trust fall over a pit of spikes.

Only a few stray candles flickered around the various tombs and urns scattered throughout the first level of the crypt. As the candlelight wavered, I got the distinct impression that something was lurking in the darkness, waiting to spring up from behind a tomb and lay waste to us all. "Get ready," I whispered, though I didn't actually need to say anything. All three of us were already on high alert.

Up ahead, something moved. In the low light, it could have been a mouse or a cat, but I couldn't tell. All I knew was that something had moved, and its shadow had run across the far wall.

Xia conjured a small sphere of magic to the palm of her hand. The red-orange orb spun slowly in a clockwise motion, ready to be released in an instant. I held up a fist and placed a hand on Xia's left shoulder to stop our progress. Silently, we waited.

A little bit of noise—something almost like a scratching but not quite—came at us from the direction of the flickering movement. *Probably just a rat,* I told myself.

Xia took another step forward. She kept her magic at her fingertips, and I had to wonder how much her mana reserves were being drained by the constant effort. Maybe she had a talent that would let her keep the spell in a readied state indefinitely. There was no way to view an NPC's talents or individual stat levels, so I'd never know for sure.

The shadows on the wall moved again . . . and I heard a whimper . . . or something. I couldn't tell. It almost sounded human.

Xia loosed her ball of magic against the back wall where it shattered in a brilliant display of colors and fiery destruction. What I had thought was whimpering turned into a scream, and I knew we had found a person. The warlock had another orb ready and waiting in an instant.

From behind a silver urn balanced atop a large, curved tombstone marking the final resting place of one of Whitechapel's priests, two hands emerged. They were blackened, either covered in dirt or recently burned, and they shook with fear.

"Come out!" I yelled to whoever was cowering behind the grave.

Slowly, the hands were joined by wrists, and then a head appeared on the other side of the grave marker. He was young, maybe Ingrid's age judging by his face, and the darkness on his hands was from Xia's spell. He'd been burned, though the wounds didn't look serious. Above his head, his name appeared in red letters: Jakk, Level 7 Thief.

Xia didn't have to wait for a command before dismissing her held magic and grabbing the boy by a wrist. She hauled him in close to her body, and then a dagger was in her hand and pressed to his throat.

"P-Please . . ." Jakk stammered. His eyes began to water, and I could see a line of tears reflecting the candlelight and making his cheeks shimmer.

"Kill him? Another zombie for the army?" my warlock lieutenant asked.

I made a show of rubbing my chin and pondering the idea for some time despite not actually having any real intention of killing the boy just yet. In fact, he was so young and reminded me so much of Ingrid that I wasn't sure I could give the order. Making him a denizen of the citadel would certainly be useful, but there was always a chance he wouldn't be as complacent with his servitude as Helvegen, and if that proved to be the case, he would serve me better as a corpse.

As I contemplated my options, thoughts of Ingrid's tortured face full of pain filled my mind. Over and over the scene replayed itself in my thoughts, and I knew I would never get her back. And finally, the weight of my previous two executions settled on my consciousness. I had been so engrossed with organizing the citadel and plotting my revenge that I hadn't actually stopped to think about what I had done.

Those two players—I couldn't remember their names—would never come back. Like Ingrid, they didn't get to respawn and walk back through the portal.

I let out a sigh. If I didn't rule with an iron fist, would I ever gather an army strong enough to exact my revenge?

No.

"Alright, Jakk, I'm giving you two choices. I'm building an empire, and I need players to help me run things. Option number one: you become one of my lieutenants. You follow my orders, you help build the citadel, and you get to live. On the other hand, I recently summoned an ancient necromancer who spends his days turning corpses into the living dead to fight for me. I also need more of those. Your choice." I stood in front of the captive boy, my sword tip angled for his sternum while Xia's knife pressed up against his throat.

The boy began nodding before I had even finished speaking. "I'll do it, whatever you say. Just let me live."

I nodded to Xia, and she released the boy from her grasp.

"Good. A thief will probably be useful, though I'd rather

you be an engineer or some other craftsman. Oh well. Now, tell me what you were doing down here in the crypt," I demanded.

The boy gulped hard and tried to hold my gaze. Ultimately, his resolve didn't take long to falter. "I-I . . . I was here on a thief quest . . . Sir. I was supposed to steal a valuable talisman, a necklace, I think, but I couldn't find it. Then so much started happening, and I didn't have any way to escape. The priest turned everyone into ghosts, so I stayed down here."

His story sounded plausible enough for me to believe it, and the young guy was so visibly terrified that I knew I didn't have to worry about a possible mutiny. "Welcome aboard, Jakk," I said, extending my hand.

His class flashed into place on my character sheet in the holdings sections, and he was officially a member of Undercroft Citadel. Interestingly, he wasn't listed as a boss like Helvegen, Xia, and myself, but rather he was simply counted as a generic thief after the charnel golem. I had to assume his demoted status was due to either having the maximum number of bosses already or to his relatively low fighting capabilities. No matter the reason, I could figure it out later.

"There's one more level below the main crypt," I said. "Maybe we'll find that amulet you're looking for down there. Probably some monsters too. Let's move."

Jakk nodded sheepishly and fell into line between me and Xia. I knew that he didn't really understand anything about what he was getting into, his fear evident in every step. I wanted the second level, the ossuary, to hold more enemies for us to fight so I could see if the thief would be able to hold his own in a battle, and from the sounds coming up the stairs, I figured we would get to witness just that.

"More skeletons," Xia said quietly. The sounds of bones clinking against stone—a distinctive noise I remembered well from the charnel golem—echoed in the ossuary below.

"Turn the corner and hit 'em hard," I said.

Xia summoned a ball of flame to each hand. Taking only a brief moment to steady herself, she darted around the corner and loosed her magic.

I had to push Jakk from behind to get him to follow our warlock. All four of us burst into the lowest floor beneath the temple with a chaotic volley of fire and screams. Two skeletons had been blown apart by Xia's magic, and Jakk had fallen on top of a third, taking the bone warrior down to the ground in a heap.

Four more skeletons came at us from every direction. One of Helvegen's magical bolts whirled past my shoulder to wrap itself around the nearest skeleton.

I was lucky that the reanimated bones were so slow, because the painter's magic didn't affect them, a fact I attributed to the lack of brains and eyes rattling around in skulls. I caught a sweeping bone hand with the hilt of my sword, severing a few fingers in the process. Turning my shoulder, I used my body weight to shove the skeleton away and reset my sword for another slash.

From the side of my vision, I saw a bony hand heading for my eyes and activated *Forsaken Barrier*. My body was instantly ripped several feet through space, stealing my breath and making the veins on the sides of my neck bulge. The magical image left behind by the talent evaporated almost as quickly as it had appeared, but the skeleton attacking it was overbalanced and tumbled forward. As it hit the ground, Helvegen's boot came crashing down on the back of its skull, and I saw her level floating next to her name tick up to seven.

From my new position effectively behind the battle, all I had to do was simply walk up behind the skeletons and lop their heads from their vertebrae. I *almost* decided to just let the rest of the party finish them off, not only to watch how they fought but also to let them have some of the experience—but

my greed won out in the end, and I killed the last three enemies in rapid succession.

Jakk required an embarrassing amount of time to extricate
himself from the tangle of bones covering the floor. I thought
it curious that Helvegen, our only other real human, didn't
offer him a hand.

"Any idea where your amulet would be?" I asked once everyone was situated on their feet once more.

"Uh, I don't know. Maybe in one of the urns, I guess," Jakk
replied.

I stuck my sword out to the nearest pedestal and used it to
knock one of the urns to floor, where it shattered. "Just ashes
in that one."

With the four of us smashing urns, it only took about thirty
seconds to find the amulet Jakk was after. As a little added bonus, we also found a small handful of gemstones and a silver
ring. The gems would be useful if we ever had someone at the
citadel skilled in craftsmanship—a vacancy I was quickly real-
izing would cripple us if we couldn't fill it soon—but the ring
was already enchanted.

*Sylvia's Wedding Band: Blessed by the moon, this ring allows
whoever wears it to see any nearby spirits or corpses regardless of
visual barriers.*

I figured wearing the ring inside an ossuary would be
nearly blinding, so I pocketed the item with the intention of
giving it to Xollmomath upon my return to the citadel. If he
could use the band to find more corpses buried around the
village, our zombie army would be able to replace the losses
it sustained earlier.

"What's the amulet do?" I asked when I realized Jakk had
been staring at it for a little longer than expected.

He held the item out on his hand so I could access the
game's description in my own vision:

Sylvia's Talisman: Blessed by the moon, this locket grants the wearer a +2 bonus to Cunning. Only females may benefit from Sylvia's Talisman.

"Sorry, champ." I snatched the amulet from Jakk's hand and tossed it to Helvegen. "Our lovely painter needs it more, and unless I'm wildly mistaken, you can't use it anyway."

Jakk stood there with his hand still outstretched looking a little perplexed. "I need to take it back to Echelon to complete the quest," he muttered.

"Not going to happen. No one goes back to Echelon until we're ready to raze the city. Understood?" I fixed him with what I hoped was an intimidating glare.

"Oh. Alright," he answered.

Without any other enemies readily available, we had plenty of time to conduct a thorough search of both the ossuary and the crypt above it, though we didn't come up with much. Xia found a few small tidbits she said she could use for more warlock rituals, but we didn't come across any weapons worth bringing back. The closest thing we found to even scrap metal was a sword so old it had rusted off its hilt.

Back at base camp, things were coming along nicely. The cultists managed to finish the wall, and the charnel golem walking the perimeter hadn't run into any trouble yet, so I had to assume we remained undetected by the outside world. With our growing numbers, we had to push further out to claim a few more houses as well. I made the cultists stay in the newest acquisitions so I could keep a closer eye on Xia and the two players.

When night fell, everyone except the zombies gathered around our fire pit to eat. Since I had no need for food and didn't even feel the slightest notion of hunger, I used the time to reassess our establishment's position.

Undercroft Citadel

Commander: Xollmomath (Influence: 25)

Bosses: Xia (Warlock), Ben Hales (Deathbringer), Helvegen (Painter)

Resources: Moderate stockpiles of food and lumber, poor stockpiles of weapons, minor stockpiles of wealth (gems), no stockpiles of exotic goods or artifacts.

Military Strength: 4 warlocks, 9 zombies, 1 charnel golem, 1 thief

Defensive Structures: Wooden wall, minor defensive wards, minor physical traps (punji pits)

Overall, I was impressed with the progress we were making. Undercroft Citadel would still fall with barely a fight against the first high level guild that caught wind of our existence and decided to raid, but I felt like we were getting off the ground a little quicker than I had expected.

Trying to get a better feel for the group dynamics at play, I paid specific attention to Jakk and Helvegen. They sat next to each other, far from the NPCs and far from me, barely within the range of the fire's heat. Whatever they were talking about, I could tell the woman was directing the conversation, and Jakk looked unsure of himself.

All it would take to bring down my entire plan, to ruin *everything*, was one of them escaping back to Echelon. If anyone had an answer, it would be the ancient necromancer fueling the entire operation.

"You're making steady progress?" I asked the man quietly.

He nodded and continued eating.

I handed him the ring we had found in the chapel, and his facial expression softened a bit. I didn't know if he was impressed or not, but he accepted the gift nonetheless. "The ring lets you see where all the bodies are buried," I said, though he could read the item's description as surely as I could. "See what you can find that's close enough for you to use."

"Most certainly. And would you like more soldiers to patrol the borders?" he asked.

"Not this time." More zombies could wait. "I need you to become stronger. And I also need you to figure out a way to put a leash around Helvegen and Jakk."

"A leash?" the old necromancer took another bite of the dried meat he was eating.

"If either of them escapes, we're all dead. You're the only one who might be able to stop them," I explained. I had also told the four cultists and Xia to kill either of them without hesitation should they detect any kind of escape or mutiny, but their watchful eyes wouldn't be foolproof by any means.

"Ahhh, I might know a spell that could be useful," the man said after a moment of thinking. In his usual cryptic manner, he didn't bother to continue his explanation any further.

If Xollmomath wanted to keep a few secrets for himself, I was fine obliging him. "Good. Spend tomorrow growing stronger, consuming any corpses or spirits you find in the area, and when you can, do whatever you can to keep our new recruits from running."

"Excising their brains would certainly keep them from running," he said with a devious smile.

There was something deeply unsettling about a powerful, ancient entity making a casual joke, and it sent a shiver down my spine. But then again, I was a heartless murderer. I didn't know what Xollmomath had done in his AI-generated history, but it didn't really matter—he had never killed a real human. No genocidal rampage within the original parameters of the game's respawn mechanic could ever compare to a single human death in real life.

Watching the centuries-old necromancer finish his meal, I had to wonder who the real monster was.

Then I remembered Ingrid's corpse again, and I knew my answer. Vic was the monster. His minions were all part of his monstrous brood. If I had to be evil to rid him and his ilk from Wonder, so be it. I could do evil. Hell, I already *was* evil. If it came down to it, I knew beyond a doubt that I wouldn't hesitate to slit Helvegen's or Jakk's throat. I'd leave a trail of corpses from horizon to horizon if it meant Vic's body was among them.

". . . the plan for tomorrow?" someone was asking me.

I pushed my violent thoughts of conquest out of my mind and looked up from the fire to see Helvegen standing not far off with her hands on her hips. I had to admit that in the firelight, she looked good. She had a lithe build, and the way her hair fell to her shoulders and framed her face reminded me of my wife . . .

Get it together, I mentally growled. *Enough. Think about them later.*

"Ah, yeah, the plan for tomorrow? Let's get everyone together," I said, obviously stumbling over my words and stalling for time.

Addressing the entire assembled forces of Undercroft Citadel—sans mindless zombies and charnel golem, of course—was a little like running the early morning Wednesday meetings at the Ministry of Health. "We have more work ahead of us tomorrow," I began, moving my gaze from the cultists to the others. "Our first order of business is straightforward: we need to know exactly what we can salvage from the remnants of Whitechapel. Xia, take two cultists and scout the entire village. Take whatever is useful and map the rest. See if you can find a forge or something else we could use."

She nodded, and I could see a little bit of admiration in her expression.

"Helvegen, Jakk, you two are with me and Xollmomath. We have enough resources to keep working on the defenses." I turned to address the cultist group for the final task. "The two of you who don't go with Xia are to head to the graveyard next to the chapel. Exhume as many bodies as you can and bring them back here. Oh, and take a few torches with you to burn down the chapel when you're finished. No reason to keep it around. Everyone understand?"

Murmurs of assent came all around. With the zombies and charnel golem walking the perimeter, we would be able to get some much-needed work accomplished, and I looked forward to the labor, tedious as I knew it would be. Building something with my own hands wasn't a task I hadn't gotten to do much in life on either side of the portals. Working on the defenses would be a great opportunity to learn something new and get my hands dirty.

"Hey, can I talk to you?" Helvegen asked from my side, again pulling me out of my own thoughts.

"Sure. Right now? We can use my house, though it's rather cramped," I answered.

She agreed, and I led her into my tiny house, keeping a hand near my dagger just in case she intended to assassinate me already.

"I understand that you can't let me go," she began, her eyes glued to the rickety floorboards beneath her feet. "I get it, I do. Whatever you're doing here, I don't want to interfere with it. Those guys you killed . . . I—" She paused to suck in a breath. "I didn't know them. Nevermind, it doesn't matter."

There wasn't enough furniture in my small house for us both to sit to make the encounter less awkward, so I didn't know what to do other than try to get her vagueness more on track. "What is it you're asking? Just be honest. I'll give you an honest answer."

She lifted her head and looked me in the eyes. "My brother is still in Echelon. He might be able to help you. He's low-level, but he's also an engineer."

"Oh." That changed everything. If we could acquire an engineer to legitimately build the defenses of the citadel—augmented by magical talents as well—our chances of survival would skyrocket.

"If you'd let me go back to Echelon for just a day . . ."

I couldn't just turn her loose. "No, if anyone goes to find your brother, it will be a group of us. Do you have any idea where he might be staying inside the city?" I wanted to rush out in the morning and find the man if he really was an engineer, but there were too many variables that I didn't know how to control. Not being loyal to Ahmose II wouldn't be a huge deal as far as the guards were concerned, though it would raise some eyebrows. Our names would appear in a different color than other players', and the NPCs would simply know that we weren't from Echelon. While being noticed wasn't a particularly bad thing, if my infamy or renown was high enough, we would certainly draw the wrong kind of attention. My infamy currently sat at twelve, and I had no way of knowing how much that was relative to being a person of interest.

"I have a few ideas of where he might be. Just ideas, though. I don't know for sure." Helvegen turned to leave, her eyes once more finding the floorboards.

"Not tomorrow and probably not the day after, either, but we'll go find your brother eventually, alright?" I said, trying to lift her spirits a little. Whether she believed me or not, at least I was telling the truth.

She nodded meekly before leaving.

Tired from the day's work, I flopped down on my thin mattress. There was a lot on my mind, and all the things that needed doing in the coming weeks made it difficult to sleep. If we could just survive the next handful of days, I was optimistic for our future. Luckily, the fear of permanent death would at least make people reluctant to attack us, though I didn't know how long it would last. In the real world, the fear of death had never stopped nations from going to war. It was only a matter of time before the leaders of Echelon or some big guild caught wind of the citadel and decided they'd like to have it for themselves.

When dawn broke, everyone in the camp began getting ready at about the same time. More food from the cellar was passed around, and I took a more specific look at how much we had in the way of construction resources. I wanted to build a look-out tower near the well in the center of the street, and that would use up most of what we had left, if not all of it.

After some consideration, I decided that we could maximize our useful lumber by utilizing one of the houses across the street from the well as a support. If we built a tower about three stories tall extending from the roof of the nearest house, we could save all the materials we would otherwise have to use on the base.

The members of Undercroft Citadel broke into their requisite groups for the day's tasks, and I got to work with Helvegen and Jakk figuring out the best way to begin construction on a second floor for one of the houses. Luckily, the core of the structure appeared somewhat solid, so we didn't use too much wood creating reinforcements around the foundation.

The house itself was the one I had given to Helvegen, so I let her make some of the decisions as well. She'd be living in it for some time if all went well, and letting her take some control regarding the physical appearance of the structure felt like a good way to continue building her trust.

Around noon, we had the supports in place to climb up to the house's roof and begin laying the boards that would eventually become the second story. We had enough tools for the three of us, and that meant progress was quick and steady.

Every now and then I would catch a glimpse of the charnel

golem patrolling the grounds. Seeing its lumbering, mis-shapen form brought a smile to my face. The cultists were making good progress as well. A few hours after noon, one of them came over to inform me that they had exhumed all of the graves closest to the chapel which meant the building was ready to burn. Twenty minutes later, smoke started fill-ing the sky.

Your Craftsmanship skill has increased to 8!

That's when I realized my mistake.

We were burning a pretty large building, not just a small house like we had done before with some of the outlying structures, but a wooden church with a substantial amount of fuel. The smoke it would produce would be seen for miles, maybe even in Echelon. If the AI wanted to, it could use the smoke as a catalyst for a new series of investigation quests that would summon players from the city to see what was happen-ing. I could only imagine what the second stage of a quest like that would involve.

From the half-completed tower, I watched the flames growing higher and higher in the center of the town. The smoke was thick against the clear blue sky.

"There's no way to stop it," I said, more to myself than any-one else. "We need to get the others. People will see that pillar of smoke. If anyone comes to investigate, we have to kill them."

I went down the somewhat rickety ladder we had made to the second floor of the tower and darted over to Xollmomath. Two of the cultists were there resting for a few minutes as the necromancer consumed the corpses with magic to grow stronger.

"You two, go find Xia the others. Bring them back. And tell the charnel golem to stand guard at the road. The smoke signal might be attracting curious adventurers. We have to be ready to defend the citadel. Go!" I couldn't believe how foolish I had been. I was so concerned with the safety of the settlement and growing my power that I hadn't stopped to consider what would happen. We should have left the ghosts in their damned chapel to respawn, killing them every single day if we needed to.

Xollmomath seemed unfazed by everything going on around him. The remnants of a few corpses lingered around his feet, though they were little more than minor bone fragments and left-over ash. "If anyone arrives to investigate the fire, bring me their corpses. I'm growing stronger every minute," the ancient being stated.

"There's no way you can go far enough away from the summoning circle to help us, right?" I imagined standing side by side with Xollmomath, his magic tearing apart wave after wave of invaders, and I would be there directing our own forces to a lopsided victory.

The bald man shook his head, and I knew my vision wouldn't become reality, at least not today. "Soon I shall be able to prowl about the entirety of the village if you continue to bring me corpses."

"Alright, if anyone shows up, you're the only one who gets to consume their dead bodies," I replied. *We have to survive first, though.*

I was pleasantly surprised at the small amount of time it took for the entire citadel to mobilize and meet at the burning church. A few shovels were scattered about the graveyard, and I commanded the cultists to continue exhuming bodies as long as we could. The rest of us fanned out through the nearest buildings to watch, our charnel golem stationed in the dead center of the road and waiting.

Hours ticked by as the fire raged. The church's roof collapsed, and the falling timbers and shingles sent out a wave of hot dust that covered us in dark soot. By my estimation, the rubble would continue to burn into the morning until there was nothing left.

One of the cultists I had stationed a few houses away called out the distress signal. We didn't have any fancy code or other system of communication, so the NPC simply yelled and then came running. Everyone tensed, weapons and spells at the ready. To my left, Jakk appeared more frightened than anyone. If he was going to be a productive member of the citadel, I would need to harden his nerves, but that task—like so many others that needed doing—would have to wait.

"There's a group coming up the road!" the warlock yelled.

"From Echelon?" I called back.

The man shook his head. "No, headed toward the city. They've changed direction, heading right for us now!"

"How many?"

"About a dozen, I don't know. What should we do?"

I turned to Helvegen. If I understood her magic, she would be the perfect one for the job. "Helvegen, let's go. With me."

She fell into step behind me, and we followed the warlock out to his observation position. Sure enough, about a dozen people were marching along the road, and they turned from the main thoroughfare to move in our direction. They carried two banners with them as well. I didn't recognize either, not that I thought I would be able to. The whole group was made entirely of NPCs, and for that I was grateful.

"Helvegen, make them see something that will pull them in. If we can get them disorganized and running, we'll slaughter them in an ambush." I knew we had piqued the NPCs' interest with the fire, but if we created an emergency that they felt they needed to hurry to save, they'd abandon their formation.

"Alright, I'll try," the woman said. She stepped forward, and a bolt of magic arced out from her hands toward the incoming NPCs. It landed in the chest of the person leading the group. The others around their leader hesitated for a moment, clearly unnerved or scared by what they had seen. After a few seconds, the leader raised a sword and began sprinting directly for us.

"What did you make them see?" I asked.

Helvegen was laughing. "I've seen their banners before on a stream. They're paladins—do-gooders and real 'hero' types—so I just showed them the charnel golem."

We had about thirty seconds before the group would be close enough to start fighting. "You gave away our best secret? Showed them the ambush right out of the gate?" Anger boiled through my veins.

"Not exactly," the painter clarified before I had a chance to gut her where she stood. "I showed them the priests from the chapel being eaten by a pair of charnel golems. I think I made the golems large enough to block us out, so they should run right past and right into the trap."

All the anger I had felt just a second before turned into a mixture of joy and appreciation. "Not too bad." I gave her a slap on the shoulder. "Once they run past, we'll fall in right behind them. Crush their whole group between us and the golem."

The NPC group ran by, and I finally got a better chance to see exactly what we were up against. They looked to be squires and other attendants for a pair of knights—the paladins, I had to assume—though the knights themselves didn't have any horses, which I found odd. No matter who they were, it was fairly apparent that only a few of them would be any trouble with their weapons. Half of them were young boys, probably squires, and they looked terrified. They were really just charging along because they had essentially been given no other choice.

As the last of the group went past, Helvegen and I took off behind them. They rounded a corner, and all hell broke loose as the charnel golem rose from its flattened, elongated posture and began barreling forward. The zombies crashed in from all sides at the same time, and at least half of the un-trained NPC group was slaughtered in the first few seconds of the battle. Everything was coming together quite nicely.

One of the squires, a boy of perhaps eight or ten years, dropped his sword. He scrambled around the dirt trying to find the hilt once more, and I ran him through with my sword. The squire right next to him saw what happened. His eyes popped, and his mouth hung agape. He began turning back toward the direction from which they had all come, and I met his waist with a sweeping swing of my sword. He doubled over, taking my blade with his bloody guts, and began to scream.

I moved on to the next squire. There were only two knaves left alive along with a pair of armored warriors standing their ground at the very center of the chaos, so far holding their own against the charnel golem and the onslaught of zom-bies. As the undead raked their claws against steel armor, bits of flesh and bone were flayed from their bodies like brittle cheese sliding down a sharp grate.

"Call back the zombies!" I tried to yell over the tumult. I needed the warlocks to rein in the zombies before they all killed themselves on the armor. The charnel golem would be more than enough to handle two paladins, and saving our rank-and-file soldiers was a priority. Unfortunately, the war-locks didn't hear me. I mentally flew through the options and menus on my character sheet for some sort of command in-terface I could use to direct the battle, but there was nothing of the sort.

Together with Helvegen keeping the squire from running, and the warlocks launching minor destructive spells into the mix, I executed the final squire with a single quick strike and began advancing on the two paladins. They stood stalwart, shoulder to shoulder, their shields held firmly in front of them and their swords constantly slashing at the charnel go-lem bearing down from above.

Blast after blast of magic came crashing down against their armor. Every burst of energy that connected with them elicited a violently bright response of blinding light. They certainly were paladins, a favored class among the player characters of Wonder for their dramatic talents, flashy gear, and over-the-top quest lines involving purging the undead, consecrating temples, and exorcising demons. Even if the class had never been too attractive to me, I had always understood why so many people liked playing them. The NPCs were basically putting on a light show as they fought.

One of them shouted, and the banner attached to the back of his armor began to shimmer. Whatever was about to happen, I didn't like it.

I ran and leapt, putting all of my strength into my legs, and swung hard for the wooden pole supporting the blue and white standard. When my sword connected, it felt like I had just jammed a fork in an electric outlet. Magical energy—holy energy—rocketed through my sword, into my arms, and straight to my head. All at once I was flying through the air, but at the same time my mind was so rattled and disoriented that I had only a vague notion of which direction was up.

Finally, my body crashed into the ground, and I was lucky that my shoulders and back led the way. I was only a few degrees in rotation from landing on my neck. Even using the largest parts of my body to cushion the fall, the wind still blasted from my lungs. Everything hurt.

I staggered to my knees, my mind still whirling in a confusing blur of chaos overlapping pain. We had to end the fight soon. My entire zombie force would be dead—or more dead, I supposed—before long. They kept mindlessly advancing on the paladins, an inexorable mob of flailing arms and gnashing teeth, but they made absolutely no progress. The warlocks were faring better, and Xia's magic was certainly potent compared to theirs. The problem was that the paladins were perfectly attuned to fighting undead. It was their singular purpose, and every talent in their arsenal was designed for it.

More brilliant magic flowed out of the paladins' swords, and a huge chunk of the charnel golem flew out across the street.

I got my feet once more under my torso and began the search for my sword. Among the dead bodies and the shattered bones of the charnel golem, the weapon wasn't readily evident.

We only had a few zombies left. Half of them weren't in any fighting shape. I *had* to find my sword and get back into the fray. But their armor . . . I had never fought against enemies so heavily clad in steel, and I didn't think my physical stat was high enough to do much against plate mail. Still, I knew I would offer more of a challenge than the flayed corpses throwing themselves into the meat grinder.

As I spotted my sword half-buried beneath a mound of bones and torn flesh, something else caught my attention. Helvegen was preparing to cast once more. She coalesced an orb of glowing yellow magic between her fingers, and it sang through the air when she let loose. The magic left behind a sparkling tail, twisting and coiling as it went, before settling like a constricting snake around the nearest paladin's neck.

At once the man stumbled. He fell several paces backward and had to use his sword like a cane to steady his balance. Then—all the while still weathering the barrage of zombie flesh crashing down against his plate—he began to scream. He wasn't in pain, that much I could tell. No, he was enraged. Something within his mind had snapped, and he wasn't fully capable of processing whatever it was Helvegen had made him witness.

Then, unexpectedly, the man took up his sword in both hands and began stalking toward his comrade's back. He swung down with tremendous force, and the paladin's spaulder cracked under the weight. A second strike quickly followed the first. The metal gave, and blood erupted from the paladin's armor like a fountain. A third heavy chop cut through the air, and it found the sensitive area between the man's rent spaulder and his gorget, instantly killing him.

On the side of the street, Helvegen collapsed. She was clearly out of mana, and the exhaustive expenditure had depleted her entire constitution.

It didn't matter.

With only one paladin standing, the warlocks and Xia focused their attacks with renewed vigor, and the strangely altered paladin died within seconds.

Your Renown skill has increased to 7!

Your Infamy skill has increased to 13!

The fight was over, and it was time to take stock of our losses. Only three of the zombies appeared to have come through the short skirmish relatively unscathed, though none of them were actually as whole as they were before. Our zombie corpses were counted at six. Their bodies were scattered around the paladins in a gruesome circle, completely destroyed and incapable of rising again. The squires and paladins themselves, however, I had every intention of taking back to Xollmomath.

I wrenched my sword free from the general gore pile and slid it back into my belt. "Actually . . ." I started unbuckling one of the paladins' sword belts to steal his sheath. It was roughly the size I would need for my own weapon, and it looked well built. "Take all the bodies back to Xollmomath," I commanded Xia and her underlings. "Leave the paladins for last so we can properly loot them."

Helvegen already had a few pieces of steel plate mail in her hands.

"What did you make him see?" I asked as we worked together to free a heavy breastplate from the corpse trapped within it.

"I made it to level eight, and that unlocked a new talent. It took everything I had to cast the spell. I didn't actually make him see anything, though. I made him *hear*," she said with a smile. Her grin was born of confidence, and I was starting to think that she was becoming too powerful too quickly. If she could edit my own mind and make me see and hear things . . . I couldn't trust her.

"What did you make him hear?" I had to pull a bit to get the second sword belt from the other paladin's corpse. As I bent low to get a better angle, I saw the man's twisted face. He had died in a state of horror. His mouth was open and bent to the side, and his lifeless eyes spoke volumes more than his screams ever could.

Not far to my side and happily looting a few of the other corpses, Helvegen answered, "I knew the paladins worshipped some lesser hope and charity deity, and I had heard the god's voice a few times on different streams. I copied the voice to whisper to him. I told him that his friend was possessed, a demon walking in stolen skin, and that it was all a trap orchestrated by the paladin. Since the words were in the voice of a god, he believed every last syllable."

"Obviously," I remarked, standing to inspect my newfound wares. I had to admit I was impressed with Helvegen's ingenuity. I couldn't have planned a more flawless execution myself. Her painter skills were downright phenomenal. I had to wonder if the painter class—and the deathbringer class as well— were old prototypes from one of the alpha or beta rounds of the game that the developers had decided not to release. It would make sense considering the false history implanted in Xollmomath's NPC mind.

"I think we can finish the tower before dark," Helvegen added. Her voice still had an unnervingly jovial quality to it that I found both worrisome and intoxicating at the same time. Was she becoming evil? Was she becoming like me?

I wondered what the woman had lost. People without dark pasts didn't go along with evil warlords so quickly. Or perhaps she was using her deceptive magic on me already, and nothing I saw or heard or felt was real.

"Hey, Helvegen, let me ask you a question," I began, not really knowing exactly how to probe into her life without inadvertently sending her further away. "You and your brother— what kind of characters had you planned on making? What did you want to do in Wonder?"

She thought about my question for a moment, and the warlocks returned to collect the last of the corpses for Xollmomath's processing. One of them appeared a little different than the others. It took me a moment to realize exactly what had changed, and then I spotted a bit of green design on his robes that wasn't there before. "What's that?" I asked, pointing to the runic embroidery.

The warlock smiled. "I struck the killing blow on the final paladin," he replied. "I became a conjuror."

NPCs didn't have the exact same level and experience point progression as played characters, but I knew what he meant. He had reached a high enough level to select a specialty, and he had chosen the conjuration field. If I recalled correctly, the options for warlocks were conjuration, destruction, alchemy, and enchantment. The final two were non-combat specializations, and if the citadel ever began harvesting resources at a good enough rate to warrant it, we would need an alchemist brewing potions for the cause.

I nodded my appreciation and let the warlocks continue their grim work.

Helvegen's touch on my right elbow startled me out of my own thoughts, and for a second my mind raced through the darkest possibilities, readily anticipating a knife in my back. "My brother and I . . . we aren't 'good' if that's what you're asking. We started playing the game for the same reason as so many others: to escape reality. Our family was—or still is—poor. We had to steal food most of the time, and then we sort of stole our lifetime passes as well."

If she was telling the truth, it made a lot of sense. No normal person pressed into service by an ancient necromancer and his underlings would have come to terms so quickly with everything going on. Maybe before the server glitch, things would have been different and more easily explained away, but not now. Helvegen knew that she would have to kill a real person someday, and she knew that death would be permanent.

And come to think of it . . . "Have you seen our thief? I don't know where he went in the midst of the battle. Lost track of him, I guess."

She looked around the remnants of the skirmish, but he wasn't there.

"He ran." The words tasted like salt in my mouth. Deep down, I knew it was the only possibility. "He's probably on the road to Echelon right now. Damn it!"

Helvegen's face took on a serious expression. "If he tells people . . . maybe they won't believe him."

"No, they'll at least investigate." I shook my head. "At a bare minimum, he'll be able to convince some NPCs to start a new quest chain to see if he's telling the truth. Shit! We're so close, and now everything's gone to hell. I'll gut that bastard. Cut his head from his shoulders and jam it on a pike in the center of the city."

"I could go to Echelon and try to head him off," Helvegen offered.

I considered her proposal for a few seconds, but it felt too well planned. Was she betraying me as well? *Damn it all, I can't trust anyone.*

I sighed. I wanted to flat out deny her, but I couldn't let her on to my suspicions if they turned out to be correct. "If he gets a guild involved, we're dead, but the chances of that have to be slim. We need to prepare for another NPC attack and the possibility of players snooping around the outskirts to investigate the operation. Finishing the tower is the top priority. We'll need a lookout by nightfall."

Helvegen looked a little crestfallen before quickly turning away.

I knew we had to make a trip to Echelon before long. If we didn't try to go and find her brother, the woman would leave. I couldn't allow that to happen. "Tomorrow. We can go to the city tomorrow after the guard tower is finished. The two of us and Xia will make the trip. If we can find Jakk, we'll kill him. If we can find your brother, we'll bring him back to the citadel. Agreed?"

Still facing away from me, Helvegen nodded.

The short walk back to the houses at the center of my growing empire was an awkward one. Helvegen didn't say anything, and no words to break the tension came to my mind.

When we arrived back at camp, Helvegen immediately headed for the guard tower, and I was eager to take stock of the new changes in our resources. With the scavenged gear from the paladins, we had more materials to work with, and I needed to know how many of the corpses were successfully converted into more zombies for our shambling army.

Undercroft Citadel

Commander: Xollmomath (Influence: 25)

Bosses: Xia (Warlock), Ben Hales (Deathbringer), Helvegen (Painter)

Resources: Moderate stockpiles of food and lumber, poor stockpiles of weapons, minor stockpiles of wealth (gems), no stockpiles of exotic goods or artifacts, minor stockpiles of crafting resources

Military Strength: 4 warlocks, 11 zombies, 1 charnel golem, 1 thief (missing)

Defensive Structures: Wooden wall, minor defensive wards, minor physical traps (punji pits), partially constructed guard tower

We had some advancements, and adding two zombies to the total was certainly welcome. As it turned out, the paladins had each been wearing a necklace with a minor magical enchantment as some sort of gift bestowed upon them by their god. Since no one working at Undercroft Citadel was even remotely close to being aligned with any 'good' deity, none of us could use either of the necklaces. Instead, Xia took them to add to our supply of magical components for use in warlock rituals.

Curious to know if the game acknowledged any kind of difference in the warlock cultists now that one of them had upgraded to a conjuror, I focused my vision on the military strength panel to expand its details.

Military Strength: 4 warlocks (one conjuror, rank 1), 11 zombies (minions), 1 charnel golem (rank 3), 1 thief (rank 1, missing)

The added information about ranks was interesting. I didn't know exactly what it meant, but I could assume that the higher rank indicated more combat experience and therefore more potent ability. The 'minion' identifier next to the zombies made sense as well. They weren't capable of receiving any upgrades or modifiers to their status since they occupied the absolute lowest tier of underling.

I dismissed the menus from my vision as Xollmomath appeared, a smile accenting his bald head and creepy countenance. "You have done well today," he said evenly. "Bringing me two paladins . . . that is most appreciated."

"Oh yeah? What can you do with them?" I asked.

Perhaps the two-zombie increase to our military strength wasn't all the benefit we had left to reap. Judging by the necromancer's devious smile, I was right.

"Such virulent followers of religion have different souls than other men. They're connected to magical energy in a unique way not dissimilar to my own connection, though inverted. I can bring them back as something more powerful than the mindless zombies already under my command." I could tell by the way he was speaking that he was excited— and I got the feeling that it took quite a bit to evoke surprise within the centuries-old necromancer.

"What are the downsides?" There *had* to be some huge drawbacks, I knew it.

His eyes narrowing, Xollmomath answered, "Nothing to worry about controlling them. They shall be my slaves, and disobedience will mean their deaths."

"And what else might you be able to do with them?"

"I suppose I could consume their spirits as well, and the power I would gain from such a feast of energy would be substantial," he explained.

Both options sounded fairly advantageous to the citadel as a whole, and we *did* have two bodies to use . . . "Alright, consume one to expand your power. Raise the second one as an undead. We'll try both."

"A fine plan," Xollmomath replied after a moment of thought. I could tell he was considering whether or not to obey my order. Thankfully, he saw the wisdom of the plan and valued it over his own pride. He turned for the center of the complex where the warlocks had been using a small patch of grass as the makeshift holding cell for soon-to-be-zombie corpses. The paladins, stripped of their armor and covered in wounds, were the only bodies left. Xollmomath beckoned to the nearest one, the paladin whose flesh was most shredded by the fight, and a pale green smoke began wafting out of his eyes.

The smoke drifted speedily through the air to Xollmomath's outstretched hand, and from his palm he directed it to his mouth. It didn't take long for whatever energy was in the paladin to be depleted. As the necromancer drank, the dead flesh on the ground broke apart into small particles light enough to blow away on the breeze. Before long, there was nothing left.

Xollmomath smiled and laughed with devious delight. "I should be able to move about the entire village now," he stated with a grin. "Yes, the paladin's spirit was strong. Now it is mine."

Converting the second paladin's corpse into a useable undead soldier was much less dramatic. Xollmomath popped his neck and twisted his back, then issued a one-word command to the corpse that instantly animated it. The paladin rose, and I saw the military strength tab on my character sheet blink.

Military Strength: 4 warlocks, 11 zombies, 1 charnel golem, 1 thief (missing), 1 truthbreaker paladin

"Very nice." The 'truthbreaker' adjective wasn't one I had seen before, and if the name was any indication of the risen creature's combat potential, I was excited. "What can it do?" I asked the necromancer.

Xollmomath smiled. He lifted a hand to point toward one of the structures about twenty yards away which we hadn't yet razed. "Destroy," he commanded.

The risen paladin charged off—actually ran with a distinct purpose and power in its steps, unlike the constantly shambling zombies dragging their feet—in the direction it had been ordered. A few steps before the house, the zombie flexed its arms out wide, and then a burst of deep purple and black magic erupted from its center to encase the house in a shifting shell of darkness. The shell shimmered with power, shaking loose the stones and mortar. Bricks and wood went flying in all directions, and the roof began to cave in on top of the zombie almost at once.

"Wow. That's impressive. Do we need to armor it?" I asked. I still hadn't portioned out the salvaged armor to any of the citadel's residents, and I kind of hoped I would at least get to keep some of the plate. One of the paladin swords was mine, that was for certain. A matching breastplate and helm would make fine additions to my personal armory.

Xollmomath shook his head as he watched the dark paladin obliterate an entire building. "In life, his faith was strong. In death, that strength has been inverted. It will sustain him for quite some time." He reached out a hand and called the creature back, presumably to preserve its magical energy for when we actually needed to use it.

"Good to know. If we run across more paladins, we're making an army of truthbreakers. They're perfect." I let my eyes drift up from the rampaging undead to where Helvegen was diligently working on the second story of the guard tower. She was working quickly, but without a second set of hands she was inefficient.

"Teach the truthbreaker what you can, and then set it on a defensive path around the village," I told the necromancer. "We need some high walls before we can afford to set our minions to anything other than defense. I'm going to help finish the lookout, and then tomorrow we have a job. A dangerous one."

The man didn't bow or nod or do anything else that might indicate that he felt even a shred of obedience toward me, and that was fine. He had the highest influence score in the settlement—which had risen to twenty-six after he had created the truthbreaker—so he was the boss worth the most to the outside world. That made him the leader.

I climbed up the small ladder we had built on the outside of Helvegen's house to join her in the construction work. We didn't have a whole lot left to do, and since our plan was for a simple two-story structure, I knew we would be finished by nightfall. I looked back toward the chapel, and I could barely see the remnants of the fire burning there. I just had to hope that destroying the structure itself would prevent the NPCs from respawning or returning. From everything I knew about the adaptive nature of the game's powerful AI, it would work.

As predicted, Helvegen and I finished the guard tower right around dusk. We had built it in such a way that adding a third story on top of the first two wouldn't be terribly difficult in the future should the need arise. For our efforts, both of us received another point in craftsmanship, which brought my total to nine. Eventually I would have enough points in the skill to be able to design some really creative and innovative structures or items, but I was still a good bit from that kind of level. If we brought back Helvegen's brother to serve as our citadel architect, I wouldn't even need to worry about my own craftsmanship skill.

When morning arrived, the whole camp awaited my orders. I let them eat and then called Xia and Helvegen to my side. "You both know we have a problem. A big one."

The women nodded. Helvegen was the first to speak. "Jakk took off during the fight against the paladins, and we have to assume the worst. That means we're operating under the assumption that he's already made it back to Echelon and is in the process of recruiting an army to come kill us all right now. Obviously, we have to stop him."

I looked to the painter and held her eyes for a long moment. "And I want to get your brother, Helvegen. You're right. We need to find him."

She looked genuinely relieved. I hoped my passive aura enhancing my element of control over the citadel's subjects was doing its work to influence her mind, but I had no way to measure the results.

"Echelon is a massive city," Xia said, her lack of confidence rather obvious in her voice. "Where do you suppose we look for him?"

A few different ideas crossed my mind. "We can start in the thieves' district with the other lowlifes and scoundrels. He didn't strike me as a really bright kind of guy, so I doubt he'll do anything out of the ordinary. If he's from Echelon originally, he'll go back to the places he knows. That means other thieves. And if he's already raising an army to march against us, he'll be even easier to find."

"And my brother?" Helvegen asked.

"Priority number two," I replied. "We can find him *after* we solve our thief problem."

It took a brief moment, but an expression of understanding finally settled on Helvegen's face.

"I've given Xollmomath plenty of direction in case we need to spend more than one day in the city. He'll be training with the warlocks, managing the patrols, and also working on pushing the walls closer to the edge of town one section at a time." Overall, the necromancer had great ideas for Undercroft Citadel, and I was somewhat eager to loosen his leash a little in my absence, not that he really needed my commands in the first place. He wanted Undercroft Citadel to succeed just as much as I did. He'd keep things running smoothly in my absence.

"We don't have enough supplies to take any kind of gear with us to Echelon, especially not for a few days," Helvegen said.

She was right. We had enough food for another week, perhaps ten days, but we didn't have much else. I had laid claim to the breastplate from the paladins that wasn't destined for scrap, though I didn't want to take it on a mission that had the potential to end up requiring stealth. Besides, not getting into a fight in Echelon was another top priority, and I wouldn't need any armor if no one ever took a swing at me. I figured there was at least a decent chance that going in unarmed without making any kind of scene at all would help us remain inconspicuous.

"We're just going for a single day. That's the goal, at least. Hopefully we won't need much. Just to be on the safe side,

I've packed food for you and Xia that should last three days." I could tell by Helvegen's expression that she was confused by my failure to mention myself in our food plans. She hadn't noticed my lack of food intake yet. "Being a deathbringer gives me a talent that makes it so I don't have to eat," I explained.

"Alright. And what do you plan on doing with my brother if we find him? Bring him back here?" she asked.

If I was being honest with myself, I didn't really have a great answer. "I plan on making him an offer to return with us to the citadel. If he will agree to be our engineer and help with the design and the defenses, I'll make him one of my lords, a dungeon boss. That's quite a high title for anyone less than level fifty."

"And if he does not want to come with us?"

I'll probably kill him, I silently stated, furthering my own resolve. As soon as he knew we existed, he would become a liability. "I don't know," I lied. "We'll figure that out when we come to it."

Helvegen wasn't convinced, and she clearly didn't share much, if any, of my confidence.

After an uneventful trek to one of the lesser-used entrances into Echelon, my own fear bean to mount. No one in our trio had Ahmose II listed as our allegiance, and that meant our character names would appear in a different color since we were in his territory. My infamy score didn't help much either. While thirteen was still low by most standards, it was unusually high for someone who had just hit level eleven. I would draw the suspicion of NPCs, and more insightful AI algorithms would be downright distrustful. I just hoped my stats weren't skewed enough to bring any interest from the official town guards.

Luckily, the entrance we chose wasn't particularly well-staffed. Echelon was huge, and the game only allowed for so many AI-controlled guards to be in the world at a time, so most of Echelon's resources had been devoted to patrolling the streets and watching the major entrances. Ever since the system announcements proclaiming true player death, the city had been on high alert. The evidence of the general panic was everywhere. Doors to player-owned businesses which had stood open and inviting for years were now shut with bouncers standing guard in front of them. Windows had been shuttered, and some of the rooftops sported archers on the lookout for anything unusual.

"We're waltzing into a warzone," I muttered. I could tell by body language alone that both of my companions had made similar assessments. Of course, Xia didn't understand why. She simply knew that 'something' was different, and I had to tell her more than once to stop asking so many questions.

As planned, we set our sights first on the thief starting areas. I made Helvegen take the lead, and I had given Xia explicit orders to kill the woman if she ever tried to run. At least by delegating the murder, I hoped to avoid any sort of bounty landing on my head should it come to that. While we were in the city, I wanted to keep blood off my hands as long as possible.

Thieves beginning in Echelon almost always utilized a well-known class trainer who lived in an abandoned temple on the city's south side. The temple had never housed any worshippers in the real years the game had been active, but the developers had scripted a detailed backstory for its rise and fall over the decades that existed within the minds of NPCs.

The temple stood in the middle of a sprawling, somewhat incoherently designed quarter of the city devoted to all kinds of religious orders and affiliations. I knew most of them, though I had never been too interested in any of their practices since I hadn't planned on playing a monk or a cleric or a priest, and the building the thieves' guild had taken over wasn't familiar to me. The symbol on the front was a crescent moon with the opening facing the right and a single eyeball nestled into the curve. I figured the religion probably had something to do with the night at some point, so it kind of made sense that it was the chosen home of a bunch of thieves.

So far, we hadn't seen many people, and we had remained under the radar. No one had given us any trouble despite some noticeable looks of curiosity given toward the color of our player names as we moved through the city. The front door to the thieves' guild was guarded by a single NPC, and I wasn't so confident that we would be able to enter without incident.

"What's the plan?" Helvegen asked quietly. She wore a hooded robe with the cowl pulled over her hair to further make her appearance more inconspicuous.

"Tell me about your brother," I said. "What's his name? What's he look like? How will we recognize him?"

Helvegen sighed. "He's taller than me, blonde hair, broad shoulders. He should have been a warrior or a warlord, some martial class swinging a two-handed axe on the front lines, but he's always been more of a bookworm."

"Anything else we need to know?" I asked.

She thought for a moment without replying. Nearby, I noticed someone watching our little trio from a partially-shuttered window. I figured the man was a thief, a lookout placed along the street to keep an eye on things out front, and I didn't mind his presence. At the moment, we had nothing to hide.

"He's generally a nervous kind of guy. If he's hiding some-where, he might not be too eager to come out," the woman answered.

"Alright, we'll keep our eyes open for him. For now, Jakk is our first priority." I knew there wouldn't be any way to sneak into a den of thieves. Their security, whether we could see it or not, was going to be thorough. The only plan that came to mind was to go right up to the doorman and try to figure out a way inside. It was the best thing we had, so I started walking right toward the guild.

The guard out front was disguised as a beggar, though I had seen enough streams online to know better than to trust him. He was an NPC, but a high-level one for sure. Underneath his tattered robes was bound to be an array of traps, tricks, and poisoned knives. Speaking of which, I had a poisoned knife that just might serve as our ticket inside.

A warlock and a painter following close behind, I approached the guard with an air of confidence. "I have business with the master. Is he in?" I demanded, all the arrogance I could muster dripping through my words.

The beggar fixed me with a scowl. "Your coin?"

I didn't know if the man was referring to a bribe I needed to pay him or a special coin that would mark me as someone able to go inside freely. Relying on my fortune stat to bring me a bit of good luck, I didn't let my confidence waver for a second. "I lost my coin in the field, if you must know." I pulled the masterwork dagger from my belt and held it out on the palm of my hand. "I have a delivery, and I don't think the master will appreciate any further delay. Now let me pass."

The beggar peered down at the dagger, and I could tell he was impressed. The masterwork weapon certainly warranted a good level of respect.

The ploy worked. "Get in," the man said. "Master will have your hide for losing a coin, but I reckon that dagger is worth a whole lot more."

I pushed past him and scoffed, muttering about the incompetent help as I opened the door and barged into the guild. The two women followed close behind. Inside, the front room still resembled a destroyed and disused temple from a long-forgotten era. An old chandelier hung in a midst of cobwebs above our heads, and several ruined bookcases had crumbled into heaps of musty parchments.

"This way," Helvegen said, pointing toward a passage on the right. "I read a few walkthroughs online just in case I had ended up joining the guild."

A tightly wound staircase led down a floor to where the actual guild activities took place. About twenty people sat around the tables all through the main hall, and an assortment of contracts and trophies lined the walls on either side. Built into the nearest corner was a bar supplying drinks to the noisy patrons. Sitting on a stool with his elbows leaning on the top of the bar was Jakk, his back toward the staircase.

"Wow. There he is," I said quietly.

"He hasn't seen us yet." Xia's eyes narrowed, her eagerness to kill the deserter clear on her face.

I still needed answers before running a blade through his guts. "Come on, let's pay him a visit. I walked up behind him and set a hand down on his shoulder. He turned back, terror quickly flashing through his eyes, and Xia took up a position between him and the other thief he was talking to.

"Let's take a walk outside," I whispered. I held the tip of my poisoned dagger—though I had absolutely no intent of using it on the likes of Jakk—against his ribcage.

On the other side of the bar, the NPC bartender had noticed the altercation. Thankfully, the character didn't appear too interested in the unfolding events. I had to imagine that the NPCs working inside the thieves' guild had seen quite a bit of violence, and a little confrontation with a knife wasn't all that out of the ordinary.

Jakk stammered, his eyes wide. "I-I . . . I don't . . . I don't want any trouble," he finally said.

"Excellent." I used the point of my blade to direct him out

of his seat, and the little prick of pain in his ribs was more than enough to do the trick.

Helvegen walked in front of our prisoner, and Xia stayed right at my side as we escorted him back out the front door. The beggar guard gave us a curious look, but I didn't care. I threw the thief down onto the stone alley between the guild and the temple next to it. He landed hard on his hands and knees.

Without my prompting, Helvegen kicked him across the side of his face, sending him sprawling. I figured she was gunning for a little more trust and approval—it worked. Her loyalty was starting to show.

I added one of my own boots to the boy's ribs for good measure. When he stopped wheezing, I knelt down right in front of his face, blocking all of his vision so that I was the only thing he could see. "I'm only going to ask you once," I said. I sheathed my poisoned dagger and drew my sword. I let the heavy point of it fall on the boy's chest. "Who have you told about the citadel?"

Jakk's eyes went even wider. "No one! I thought you guys were just messing around doing your own thing in some starter village, right? What the hell is going on!"

"He could be lying," Xia said, her arms crossed over her chest.

The painter offered a different assessment. "I don't think so," she said. "He would have had protection or at least been hiding if he feared us."

Jakk started to speak again, but I cut him off with a few more ounces of pressure applied to my sword. "You're probably right. I don't think he has the guts to try and stand against us in either case. Look at him, he's practically pissing himself right now."

"Please . . . I'll die . . . for real . . ." he pleaded with a heavy wheeze.

"I know." I pushed to my feet and planted all of my weight on the hilt of my sword. After a soft squishing sound, I felt the tip of the weapon hit a paving stone. Jakk was still barely alive, but with his lungs and diaphragm eviscerated, he wouldn't do much talking. Still, I couldn't take any risks at all. I ripped my sword free and slashed the boy's throat, then flicked his blood all over the alley walls. What remained on my weapon I cleaned on his shirt.

"No loose ends," I stated flatly, locking eyes with Helvegen.

Her resolve didn't waiver. "No loose ends," she repeated.

Xia taking the lead, we exited the alley without giving another second of attention to the thieves or their guild. "Where will we find your brother?" I asked Helvegen.

Despite the carnage of the alleyway, the woman wore a smile. "We didn't know too many places around Echelon before I left for Whitechapel and some quests. He was working on a project for a small-time quest giver, but I don't really remember exactly where."

"What was he building?" I asked.

She thought for a moment before answering. "I think he was helping build a new aqueduct near the portal."

"Let's check it out. Maybe we can find him from there." I lead us toward the center of Echelon where the huge portal used to bring players from the real world into the game. I could see the top of it poking up above the buildings before we even got close, and the sight of it brought a pang of sadness to my chest. The shimmering blue field that had once danced between the portal's stone arms was gone. In its place was nothing. I could see all the way through to the other side.

Around the sides of the portal, a heap of items had been left behind like a makeshift memorial to the dead. Everything from swords and armor to letters, flowers, and little trinkets had been amassed in a sprawling, disorganized pile. *I should leave something for Ingrid* . . . I thought. I had to brush a tear from my cheek.

The two women were quiet.

"I'll bring something for you, Ingrid," I told the memorial. "I'll bring Vic's head and fasten it to the top of the portal. For you . . ." I turned back to the others. "Come on, let's find the aqueduct. Let's find your brother."

It didn't take long to find the project site. A fresh trench had been dug near the side of the street, and fired clay tubing had been laid in the trench, but none of it had been covered. It seemed the work crew hadn't finished their project just yet, so our chances of finding Helvegen's brother were good.

We followed the fresh plumbing around a corner and down another street. At the end of the avenue stood a handful of city guards—all of them NPCs, with about half a dozen player characters. Their names in blue above their heads indicated they all held allegiance to Echelon's government. With their backs turned away from us, I couldn't tell what was going on. It looked like the group was investigating something on the ground or perhaps in someone's hand. Whatever it was, we were too far away to tell.

I led us closer, and then an incoming system notification froze everyone in place.

System Administration, Incoming Message, All Players . . .
Alert!

Hello. My name is Sven Jorgensen, and I am the chief legal counsel for Wonder Technologies, Inc. Over the past few days, everyone at Wonder Technologies, Inc. has been working non-stop to resolve the issues that have corrupted the regeneration module within the primary server mainframe. In an effort to be as transparent as possible with players, I am informing everyone today of an update.

The damage to the code has been isolated and contained. While the regeneration module is still non-functioning, the development and technical teams believe that no further damage can be realized within any Wonder systems at this time.

Legal and diplomatic representatives from around the world have been meeting at Wonder headquarters to discuss a myriad of issues presented by the shutdown. For now, the seven portals will remain closed to entry. The technology allowing players to logout is expected to take another month to repair, and that is not a guarantee.

Furthermore, world leaders have agreed by treaty that any actions taken within the game world are not subject to any nation's legal purview or jurisdiction. Leaders of all seven capital cities have been instructed to foster environments of peace so that every player may get through these trying times without incident. The idea of generating more AI-controlled entities to institute martial law across the game world was heavily debated. Ultimately, Wonder Technologies, Inc. has decided against that course of action.

In the pursuit of further transparency, it is with a heavy heart that I am instructed to inform the players that Nepheli Galianos, Director of Primary Server Management and Calibration at Wonder Technologies, Inc., has taken his own life. Many of you knew him from several popular online streams. His loss weighs on each and every one of us.

Many of you have experienced grievous losses as well. Please know that Wonder Technologies, Inc. shares in your sorrow. The company is doing everything in their power to restore all game systems to operational capacity. Players will be notified as soon as possible with any changes or new developments.

Certain NPC characters have been reclaimed by active personnel at Wonder Technologies, Inc. These NPCs will serve as legal representatives on behalf of the company and can hopefully answer any questions you may have regarding present changes to the game world and your Terms of Service agreement. You may find them in any capital city. They will be designated by appropriate signage.

Thank you for your patronage, patience, and perseverance.

May God have mercy on us all.

"Nothing has changed . . ." I muttered. They hadn't found a way to bring Ingrid back from the dead, not that I had any hope that the development team ever would. She was dead, and all I could really hope to do was send her a few more corpses to keep her company.

I shook my head in a vain effort to get images of my slain daughter out of my mind. I had more immediate tasks, and whatever investigation was going on at the end of the aqueduct needed my attention. The sinking feeling in the pit of my stomach told me that whatever had drawn the crowd wouldn't be good. Simple digging for a minor public project didn't warrant guardsmen from the city barracks to show up in force.

When we got a little closer, my suspicion was confirmed. I heard the words 'necromancer' and 'relic' being thrown around, and that could only mean one thing. Xollmomath's return had changed certain aspects in the AI scripting—that much was obvious from the new classes we had discovered at the citadel—and the game was introducing new quest lines related to the ancient mage all on its own.

The NPC guards gave my little trio a few inquisitive looks I had to assume came from our allegiance to Kalma and not the city, but they let us approach the scene for a closer look nonetheless.

One of the player characters, a higher-level warlord with some impressive armor, was holding a fragmented wooden stake in his hand for everyone to see.

"What is it?" I asked.

The human snorted. "An ancient evil has returned. We found a relic, and one of the guards knows a legend from the before the game existed. Who the hell are you?"

The man's abrasive attitude instantly pissed me off. With thoughts of Ingrid still whirling in my mind, all I wanted to do was add his corpse to the memorial in front of the portal. But he was far stronger than I was, and his gear alone was far better than all the talents I had amassed so far. "Just curious to know what's going on, that's all," I said.

The wooden stake in his hand was about the length of my forearm, and it had been broken into three pieces.

Luckily, the NPC guards seemed a little more forthcoming with their information than the warlord. "We think the relic is something belonging to an ancient evil, a powerful necromancer known only in legends and myths. If more relics are discovered, they could prove to be a very troubling portent indeed. Perhaps someone is trying to complete the forbidden ritual."

I had to turn my head to hide my smile. When I did, I saw Helvegen at my side was looking elsewhere further down the street.

"Ásgeirr!" she called, waving her hand. A man in a craftsman's apron came running and wrapped her in a hug that lifted the woman off her feet.

"I thought you'd died, sister," he said into her hair, tears running down his face. "I thought you were dead . . ."

Two quests down. Time to secure Xollmomath's relic.

I needed a way to either distract the warlord or kill him outright and take the stake. Bloodshed in the middle of the street would almost certainly generate a bounty on my entire group, setting the city of Echelon against Undercroft Citadel. Even though cunning was my highest stat, I still wasn't confident that I would be able to concoct any kind of riddle or ploy to peaceably attain the artifact.

I turned my attention back to the warlord as Helvegen and her brother reunited. "What do you plan to do with the stake?" I asked.

The man tightened his grip and pulled it away from my reach. "The guards are putting together a quest. Not that it is any concern of yours."

"These guards?" I pressed, indicating the handful of soldiers. "They know enough of the old legends?"

"They've sent a messenger to one of their historians for more information. Should be back any minute now." Again, the warlord's callous, arrogant tone grated against my mind. Perhaps it was the fresh sting of Ingrid's death clouding my thoughts . . . but I hated the man. I hated the way he stood so full of confidence in his black and red armor, a sword sheathed on his right hip and his gauntleted hand resting on the pommel. He was attired like a typical knight, and the warlord class meant he was used to commanding others, always getting his way.

I glanced to Xia and winked. A smile twitched at the edges of her mouth.

Summoning every ounce of emotion coiled within my body, I ripped a shadow from my chest and launched it toward the warlord's head, using sheer force of will to command it to attack. In the space of a heartbeat, the writhing spawn latched onto the man's face. Screams erupted from the street.

I drew my sword and held it in both hands, swinging it down as hard as I possibly could on the back of my own shadowy minion. The weapon passed directly through the creature and into the warlord's skull. It didn't stop until it clanged off the man's steel gorget beneath his chin.

Your Physical skill has increased to 20!

Your Influence skill has increased to 19!

Your Renown skill has increased to 13!

Your Infamy skill has increased to 29!

Status: unstable, shrouded by Lady Kalma, feared, hated by Echelon, hunted by the Pyreborn Legion (guild)

The street exploded into a frenzy of combat. I ignored the notifications scrolling through my vision at rapid speed and swung for the nearest NPC. My sword caught him on a leather pauldron, but it didn't cut through. He rotated away, and I managed to bash him in the teeth with my hilt.

As the guard reeled, I tossed my sword to the ground and

reached for the warlord's weapon still resting in its sheath. It took me a few seconds to wrestle the weapon free. Thankfully, my shadow creature had leapt to the next nearest guard, employing the same face-mauling tactic I had ordered against the warlord.

Sword in my hand, I read the notification displaying its stats as it scrolled by:

Infernum, Masterwork Pyreborn Blade: The sacred weapon of the Pyreborn clan, this sword can be brought to life with fire, and it increases the wielder's effective Influence skill by 10 (level remains unchanged). Anyone who wields the Pyreborn Blade may also summon the mantle of Kagu, First to Walk Among the Flames of Righteousness.

"Oh . . . Hell yes." Two of the NPC guards were dead on the ground, Helvegen and her brother Ásgeirr were staying clear of the action, and Xia was locked in combat with the three remaining enemies, her forearms covered in defensive wounds.

"Xia!" I called. "Stand down! Let me have them."

My new sword was longer than both the short sword I had received in the counting house and the one I had taken from the dead paladin back at the citadel. It wasn't large enough to be unwieldy with only a single hand, but I knew without a doubt that the devastation it would reap with all my weight behind every swing would be massive.

My right hand above my left on the long hilt, I willed the blade to life. Flames leapt out from the hilt to cover the entire length of the steel blade.

Xia twirled and skipped away from the guards. My shadow monster sent its groping tentacles over the face of the guard farthest from me, and I took a swing with my flaming sword. The weapon landed squarely on the side of the leather brigandine of one of the guards. The man screamed as he was nearly rent in half.

Bloodied and inhumanely destroyed, his corpse clattered to the stones. The brazen slaughter was more than enough to pull the attention of the two remaining guards back to me, saving Xia from more punishment.

I mentally recalled my shadow pet to my side and held my sword out wide. The heat from the magical blade was welcoming, warm and gentle on my arm even though I knew it should have been singeing my flesh. "Time to die," I stated.

The two guards lunged at the same time. Their coordinated attack would have easily been enough to eviscerate me where I stood just a day ago. With the Infernum in my hands, I felt immortal. The guard on my right slashed first, and I met his standard-issue Echelon gladius with the full strength of my blade. His weapon broke in his hand, and Infernum continued up into his chest. The man's ribs shattered, and his spine was severed by the tip of my sword before he had a chance to scream.

The guard to my left managed to take advantage of the opening I presented, and my cloth shirt didn't offer any kind of resistance. Pain seared through my left side.

Without any real concern for the slash I had sustained, I whirled left with Infernum horizontal in front of me. A single strike was all it took to end the NPC's life, and the street was quiet once more. A fresh pang of energy left my body to sustain the shadow monster I pulled forth, reminding me that I couldn't keep the creature in existence indefinitely, so I dismissed it back to wherever it lived with a thought.

Your Physical skill has increased to 21!

Toward the portal a street away, some people—either players or NPCs, I couldn't tell—were running away in fear.

"We have to go. Now," I commanded. Xia and Helvegen both nodded, terror in their eyes.

"You know this guy, Hel? You're . . . with him?" Ásgeirr muttered.

I extinguished my sword and grabbed the man by the front of his apron. "Yes, she follows me. And either you follow me with her or you get to join the corpses covering the ground. Make your decision quickly." Still holding the man, I told Xia to start stripping the armor from the fallen warlord.

Ásgeirr didn't take long to decide. "Y-yes, with y-you, I'll go," he stammered.

I took my hand from his chest. "Good. We don't have much time, but I'm not leaving that armor behind. Grab as much as we can, and then we're out of here."

From the looks of it, we would be able to get most of the warlord's armor pretty quickly. The only piece that looked to take too long to remove was the sword belt, but everything else came off quickly with so many hands working toward the same goal. I would need to clean the blood from the gorget and breastplate, but that could wait.

Xia grabbed the three fragments of the broken stake from the ground, and we had everything worth taking. Given more time I probably would have looted the guards as well, but time was the one thing we didn't really have. The four of us ran hard back toward the portal and the entrance we had come through in the temple district. Everyone who saw us stopped to stare. None of them dared to get in our way.

The two guards manning the gate out of Echelon almost blocked our path, but even the scripted, AI-controlled NPCs knew better than to try and arrest us. They lunged out of the way right before we ran past, and I could hear one of them cursing us as we went.

Once we were outside the city, I checked my character sheet again. Next to my influence of nineteen, the number twenty-nine showed in a smaller grey font. The sword would let me command as though my influence was ten points higher. For someone attempting to build a citadel of darkness and evil, it was perfect.

I desperately wanted to try Infernum's second ability, calling forth the mantle of a god I had never even heard of, but that could wait as well. Besides, the line about 'flames of righteousness' gave me a little concern. I wasn't exactly righteous by any means, and I wasn't convinced that the sword or the god living inside it wouldn't try to kill me if I pushed my luck.

As far as any of us could tell, no guards or anyone else followed us out of the city, though I still elected to take a somewhat circuitous route to reach Undercroft Citadel, just in case.

CHAPTER 9

I was happy to see that everything was in order upon our return. Though we hadn't been gone long, Xollmomath had managed to extend about half of the wall another twenty feet outward. The warlocks had also secured a small forge from the remnants of the village, and our stockpiles of food and supplies had grown a little.

It was almost night, so I figured more task delegation and citadel building could wait until the morning. For now, I wanted to give Xollmomath the stake we had recovered. If it turned out to be anything remotely as powerful as my new sword . . . well, I knew my fortune stat wasn't nearly *that* high. Still, it had to at least be important. Beyond returning the stake to the necromancer, I had an entire set of steel armor to investigate. All in all, the trip to Echelon had been far more rewarding than I had ever imagined. We were well on our way to an empire—well on *my* way to revenge.

I found Xollmomath walking through some of the abandoned buildings of Whitechapel. He was marking them with paint as he went, giving each a short inspection as well. "What are you up to?" I asked.

The bald necromancer was happy to see my return. "Most of these buildings will need to be leveled. I have a plan for the tower you constructed—it shall serve as the focal point, the very center of the citadel's power. The structures left over from Whitechapel with the strongest foundations will be kept and integrated into the citadel itself, but all the others need to be destroyed to make way for progress."

"I like how you think. How long before we will be building proper walls and battlements?" I had a grand vision for the citadel in my head, a towering spire of swirling magic, gargoyles, and sheer power. I wanted the best guilds in all of Wonder to come across Undercroft Citadel and shake with fear.

Xollmomath smiled. "It should not be long, Master," he said.

Master? Oh. My influence skill was finally higher than his, thanks to Infernum. I was the new dungeon boss, and he was one of my loyal subjects. I checked my character sheet just to be sure, and there it was:

Undercroft Citadel

Commander: Ben Hales (Influence: 29)

Bosses: Xia (Warlock), Helvegen (Painter), Xollmomath (Necromancer)

It felt good to be in charge. If I had to guess at just how strong Undercroft Citadel had come in terms of other dungeons throughout Wonder, I figured a group would need at least a full complement—usually eight to ten players—of level twenty characters to destroy it. And at the rate Xollmomath was consistently gaining power . . . the future looked fantastic.

"What kinds of resources do you need to begin the more advanced work?"

"Stone is our highest priority," the necromancer responded. "We will need quite a large amount of stone in order to construct the core of the citadel, and then bones will form the rest. Bring me both, and I will give you a palace worthy of legend."

I was liking Xollmomath more and more with every word he spoke. He had the exact same vision that I held, and he was just as eager to see it through. I showed him the three fragments of the wooden stake that we had taken from Echelon. "What can you tell me about this? Anything about it look familiar?"

The necromancer's eyes showed a flash of awe in them. "Where did you find such a relic?"

"Some workers in the city dug it up during one of their projects," I answered. "What is it?"

He gingerly took the three pieces from my palm and inspected them, seeming lost within his own thoughts for a few moments. "I had thought the Founder's Stake to be lost. I never anticipated holding it once more in my hand. It is broken, of course, though it can be restored. It *will* be restored."

"Can you tell me what it does?"

His grin grew wider. "The Founder's Stake was the most powerful relic of my order several centuries ago. My master, a being more powerful than any to have walked this plane, created it with magic he captured in the very center of the world. The magic controls all life and death—the magic that weaves between both essences—and my master used it to create the very first necromancers. All magical manipulations of life force stem from such power, and without the stake's original formation, none of that power would exist today. You have found a truly remarkable relic. Once restored, the energy it will provide to the citadel will be boundless."

"How do we restore it?" I asked. Everything else we had to do, all the myriad of tasks that remained to be done around the grounds, could wait while we devoted every single body to our new quest.

Xollmomath lined up the three pieces to their original shape and pointed to a notch that was still missing. "The magical seal that binds the three pieces into their previous form is missing. It looks like a scarab, a small fleck of stone no larger than the pommel of your sword, and it contains all the knowledge my master ever accumulated. If you can restore the scarab to the stake, it shall awaken the true powers of necromancy once more."

Alright, only one item to get. No difficult ritual with countless to components. All we needed was a location and then a plan. "Any idea where to find the scarab?" I asked.

Sadly, Xollmomath shook his head. "When my master was slain, his most precious relic was destroyed. Wherever you found the fragments of the stake, perhaps the scarab is not far away. I do not know."

"Who killed your master? Who was it who destroyed the stake? Maybe they took the scarab to try and prevent the relic from being remade." The game's artificial intelligence had begun creating quests specific to Xollmomath's return, planting the relics within Echelon and then allowing a simple work crew to discover them, and now it was fashioning the opposite. The AI had given me a quest to recreate the Founder's Stake, and I had to imagine that it would be a race against the forces of Echelon trying to stop it. We had to move quickly.

"Soldiers and paladins from Echelon raided my master's temple when most of the other necromancers were away. If the scarab has not been lost or destroyed, perhaps it is kept within the royal depositories. It has been too long since I have seen it. Truly, it could have been spirited anywhere. Hundreds of years have passed since those days." Xollmomath looked away toward Echelon as he spoke. I could tell the memories given to him by the game designers and AI were potent. The NPC really did believe in his own backstory, and it was fascinating to watch it play out in real time.

I had to remind myself that I was inside a game—but when I thought about it, I knew even that was no longer true. The very aspect of Wonder that had made it feel like a game was gone. Now it was real. It was the only world that actually mattered.

"If we have to break into the royal depository in Echelon, that quest will have to wait. We need more strength," I said.

The necromancer shared my assessment of the situation. "Once I am strong enough to no longer be bound to the summoning circle, I shall accompany you to Echelon. Together we will bring destruction and reclaim all the power of the ancient necromancers."

"Excellent." I knew it would take a while to get to that level of strength, but I was already excited. Before nightfall, I still had one final task. The warlord's armor we had looted was all in a heap around the firepit behind my house. I knew it would be just as legendary as the sword now hanging in a sheath off my right hip.

The first bit of armor I grabbed was the helmet. The slots for the eyes were small. I wouldn't have a huge amount of visibility while wearing it. Perhaps that was the reason the warlord had been holding the helm at his side instead of on his head. The whole construction was actually three pieces of steel layered on top of each other. The base material was dark, almost scorched, and formed the foundation for the two elevated plates that gave the helmet its shape. The uppermost layer was black like the base, but the middle piece of metal was gold. The nasal guard that hung down between the eyes was welded directly to the cheek protection, and there was only a small slit between the sides to allow for breathing.

On top of the helmet rested a forged steel horse's head. It was small and not nearly as ostentatious as some of the plumage I had seen on other sets of armor. The animal's pose was aggressive, and it added a rather classy touch to the already wildly impressive armor.

When I placed the helmet on my head, the first thing I noticed was the distinct smell of blood. Though the warlord hadn't been wearing it when I had ended his life, more than a few drops of blood had splattered the inside. I rinsed it out with some water from the dinner spread nearby and dried it with the edge of my shirt. The smell wasn't gone entirely, but it had diminished a little at least.

It felt heavy on my head. I would need to get used to the weight of all the pieces, not just the helmet, and more points in physical would certainly help. I mentally planned a bit of exercise in full armor for the next few days, just to get more accustomed to everything.

Once the helmet was fully seated over my eyes, I could bring up the specifics of the item in my vision:

Masterwork Pyreborn Barbuta Helm: Solid steel protects the wearer's head and face against all but the most vicious of attacks. While worn, the helm also grants the wearer the ability to see allies within fifty yards regardless of visual impairment.

I focused my thoughts on Xollmomath to test the truesight ability, and his outline along with his name instantly appeared in my vision. He was moving in my direction, just a few houses away, and I could see him. "Damn. That's incredible," I muttered. When I looked away, his ethereal outline slowly faded from my vision before disappearing altogether.

Next came the breastplate. It was built with a similar construction as the helmet with three pieces of steel being layered in a beautiful pattern. In addition to black and gold, a deep shade of scarlet enamel also decorated the armor, giving it a sort of bloody shimmer than I absolutely loved. The breastplate was attached to two sizeable pauldrons, the right side a little larger than the left in order to better protect the sword arm.

Putting it on by myself took some effort. I could slide the front and back down over my head like a shirt, but tightening the leather straps on the sides was difficult. With some practice, I knew I would get better and faster. And in a pinch, just throwing the breastplate on over my clothing would certainly be enough. Even if the armor wasn't fastened to my specific shape, it would still offer a huge amount of protection.

The center of the breastplate sported a brilliant fleur-de-lis, and other intricate designs adorned almost every inch of it, each done in gold leaf. The price of the breastplate alone would probably be north of a million gold pieces, enough to buy a large estate, stock it with furniture and expensive art, and then hire a crew of servants to maintain it. Part of me thought to sell the whole set for a fortune and finance all of Undercroft Citadel, but there was no way I could let it go. The armor was just too amazing.

Once equipped, I could access its stats as well through my character sheet screen:

Masterwork Etched Pyreborn Plate: Inscribed with markings of the Pyreborn Legion (guild), this armor offers the wearer an incredibly high amount of damage reduction, stopping all but the finest of weapons from reaching flesh. When struck in combat, the plate reacts with a violent burst of fire. Attached bladebreaker pauldrons will shatter most non-masterwork bladed weapons.

I could barely contain my excitement. The armor was legendary, the highest level of quality found anywhere in the game. In all my years of watching high level players on their online streams, I had seen plenty of legendary items both being used and being discovered. I had never imagined that I would come to possess one—and I had a full set with a matching sword.

If Ingrid could see me now . . .

With such powerful armor, Vic wouldn't stand a chance. I would carve a path of destruction through his entire guild, murdering each and every last one of them until I had enough skulls to build a throne. Still, slaughtering Vic and his underlings would never be enough. My throne of skulls would be situated in a matching ossuary, the very walls made from the collected bones of my enemies.

Long mail tassets hung down from the sides of the breast-plate almost like a cloak, and they covered a set of steel chausses fit to black and gold greaves to protect my legs. To preserve mobility, the greaves didn't have any plating on the back, just thick leather bands running horizontally that were used to keep the armor in place. I strapped them on, barely able to reach the iron buckles with the somewhat limited range of motion offered by the breastplate, and their stats appeared on my character sheet next to everything else in my impressive raiment:

Masterwork Pyreborn Greaves: Fixed about the legs, these steel plates offer the wearer almost unlimited stamina. While in combat, the wearer's legs will not tire.

Of all the magical enchantments I had read from the other pieces, the legs were perhaps the most impressive. Being able to move and dodge in combat while wearing a full set of plate armor would give me a massive advantage. Outside of an unexpected and devastating attack like the one that had laid low the armor's previous owner, it would be nigh impossible to kill me.

The final pieces left to inspect were the gauntlets. They slipped easily over my forearms, and the finger articulations were made of scalloped steel, allowing me to fasten the leather straps on both arms without much difficulty at all. Once I got some practice putting on the armor by myself, I figured it probably wouldn't take more than five or six minutes. With someone helping, I'd be able to suit up for war in no time.

When the gauntlets were secure, I called their stats up from my character sheet to see the final piece of my prize:

Masterwork Pyreborn Gauntlets: The leader of the Pyreborn Legion commands untold strength, gaining a +30 bonus to Physical while wearing the gauntlets.

"Holy shit . . ." For as fantastic as the greaves and breastplate were, the gauntlets were probably better. My physical stat was twenty-one, respectable for my level, although nothing particularly out of the ordinary. Striking with an effective level of fifty-one, however, would be insane. That was the equivalent of a level twenty-five character who focused on physical above both other primary stats. And the bonus would continue to compound as I grew in strength on my own. The more physical points I acquired, the higher and higher my effective attack strength would become.

"A full set of legendary armor . . . and I'm still level eleven." I drew Infernum from my sheath. I willed it to life, and flames sprang up all along the length of the blade. As I twirled it through the air, the fire's afterimage left clinging to the sky was mesmerizing.

The full gravity of what I possessed was only slowly making sense in my mind. It all felt a bit like a dream. Players like me—average guys just starting out and looking forward to a lifetime of exploration and adventure—we weren't supposed to get legendary equipment and build citadels of evil. That kind of stuff was for the celebrity players with hundreds of thousands of followers watching their every move on the streams.

Who the hell was I that I deserved to get so much so quickly? Was the AI somehow working in my favor? It didn't seem likely. Especially considering how much I had lost before earning anything at all.

"No . . . the game didn't give me anything. I took it. I killed a man and took what was his. *That's* how success is born. No one is ever given anything, and only those strong and willing enough to kill for what they want ever get ahead." I realized I was proselytizing aloud, and the other members of Undercroft Citadel were watching me, confused expressions on their faces.

"Sorry," I muttered, though I didn't really care. Even if the entire world of Wonder thought I was insane, it would not matter. I had the command of an entire dungeon, one of the best sets of armor ever crafted, and an absolutely unwavering determination to build an empire atop the corpses of anyone who would stand in my way.

I returned Infernum to its sheath and set about removing the armor. I would need a proper stand to keep the gear organized and in one place when I wasn't wearing it all, though my old sword belt and new weapon would stay with me no matter what. If I was outside of my own house, I planned on always having Infernum just in case. The gauntlets would be a good item to have along as well, though I wasn't sure exactly how comfortable they would be without the rest of the armor set to compliment them. Either way, it was a decision for another day.

Everyone was finished eating. Helvegen and her brother were walking back to the guardhouse where they stayed. "Hey," I said, stopping them both with a hand. I met Ásgeirr's eyes and really tried to gauge his loyalty or at least what he was feeling. I noticed he had kept my short sword after I had ditched it in Echelon, and that was fine by me. "The warlocks found a forge in working order. We're planning on incorporating it into the official citadel grounds tomorrow so you have a workshop. We scavenged plenty of tools, so that hopefully won't be a problem. What else will you need to start working?"

The man looked me up and down, a little bit of fear on his face, but he seemed honest. I didn't get the feeling he was trying to hide anything from me or plotting something behind my back. "I'll need more raw materials," he said with a much thicker Scandinavian accent than his sister. "And . . . orders, I suppose. I need to know what it is you wish for me to create."

I couldn't help but smile. It seemed Undercroft Citadel would have a fully operational forge in no time. "Right now, use what you can from the scrap pile. Some of it can probably be fixed or modified into something useful, other pieces are just junk. I'll trust your discretion. The two highest priorities are getting some armor for the zombie soldiers so they aren't cut to ribbons the first time they have to fight, and then helping Xollmomath construct the actual citadel. As an engineer, can you help with the architectural construction of the buildings?"

He nodded. "I don't have much experience with buildings, but smaller projects should be easy enough with the right tools. I'm also close to leveling . . . What would you prefer I focus on? Engineers can do many things. Traps, battlements, buildings, gear, whatever you need should be possible going forward."

I reached out a hand to clasp the man's forearm and show him some respect. "Ásgeirr, whatever *you* want to do as a specialty is fine by me. As long as you're a productive member of the team, you have as much discretion as you need. I won't dictate your build. And please, think of Undercroft Citadel as your home, not just mine. We all need your skills, and we're counting on each other every single day."

Ásgeirr's hesitant expression turned into one I would say bordered on happiness. "Thank you, Ben," he said. "Please call me Geirr, if you don't mind. Hel said she told you a little about our past. We weren't exactly good people back on Earth. We didn't have much, you know? Ever since the wars, our homeland has known nothing but misery. I suppose I should thank you for the opportunity to be part of something larger than my station."

"Work hard, support the cause, and we'll all get along fine. I'm happy to have you aboard, Geirr. And whatever you've done in your past, I've either done worse or else I'm about to." I shook his hand, and I could tell a genuine warmth in the man's demeanor that gave me every confidence that I needed. If he was planning on stabbing me in the back or running away, his skill in deception was phenomenal. The majority of my old job at the Ministry of Health had involved being able to read people in order to manage their skill sets efficiently, and I liked to think I was pretty good at it. Geirr was one of us, perhaps even more so than his sister.

I went for a run the next morning. Clanging around in my legendary armor, I managed to make two full laps around the outskirts of the old Whitechapel buildings before collapsing. I had always been fairly fit, no athletic specimen by any means but not overweight either, and I considered my pair of laps to be rather impressive. I was still a long way from where I wanted to be, but that progress would come in time. And the more I trained my body, the faster I would gain points in physical and continue leveling.

I was pleased to see the citadel up and working without my direct input. The defensive patrol was still marching the perimeter, the charnel golem's misshapen head appearing every now and then between buildings. In the center of our establishment, Helvegen and a pair of warlocks were busy adding on to the guard tower. It looked like they were adding more wooden armor to the outsides, perhaps arrow slits for archers.

Xollmomath and Xia had the conjuror with them going over our magical resources and defensive wards. The necromancer apparently had identified a few of the items from the fight with the paladin that could be recast to fit his designs.

My first order of business after stashing my armor back in my house was to visit Geirr. His forge was about twenty or thirty feet from the other buildings, and I wanted to check it out. I also had a few questions that had popped into my head during my run.

I found the smith hard at work modifying the building that contained the forge, and the fires themselves were dormant.

"Hello," he said somewhat awkwardly when he noticed me in his doorway.

"Hey, Geirr. How's it going in here?" I asked.

"The previous owner left some supplies, but not much. I need to expand the workshop as well. Running the forge will produce too much heat, and it will be impossible to work for long without airflow." He was moving things around and planning out his workshop as though he'd just been hired by a shop in downtown Echelon to make a career from his craft. I liked his enthusiasm.

"About the raw materials. Any ideas where we should look?"

"Is there a mine in the village?" he asked.

I hadn't really thought about the possibility of mining. "I'm not sure. I'll double check. If there isn't one anywhere close enough to use, how difficult would it be to create one? And could you train a handful of the zombies to gather ore?"

"I've never done it before, but I would certainly be willing to try," he answered.

If the undead soldiers could be taught to swing picks and drop ore into carts, I had some hope. That was, admittedly, a rather difficult proposition. Still, we had to give it a shot.

I left the blacksmith's shop with a clearer understanding of Geirr. He struck me as someone who was honest, though perhaps there was more lurking in his unknown past that I simply had not seen yet. No matter how he turned out to be in the long run, I had the feeling he would be loyal for quite some time. The way he spoke made me think he was looking forward to developing the citadel's infrastructure. He was an engineer, and I was giving him every opportunity in the world to practice his craft.

Back at the center of our operations, Xollmomath and Xia had our scant magical resources organized and ready for use. Despite how little we had to work with, it still seemed Xia was in high spirits.

"We have enough magic to begin the real construction," she said even before I had inquired.

"Oh?"

Xia nodded excitedly. "Xollmomath has powers we will likely never be able to comprehend. If he consumes the remaining magical implements we've gathered, he will be strong enough to raise the core of the true citadel."

That was a new development. "What else could be done with the items?" I asked.

The ancient necromancer fixed me with his inky stare. "The implements are not strong, but they are enough. You could use them to enchant the undead soldiers, or we could begin erecting a spire to Lady Kalma's infinite glory."

A spire to please Lady Kalma had to have more rewards further down the line. I could feel it. Still, enchanting the drones was a tempting idea that I had to at least explore. "If you enchant the zombies, will they be more intelligent? Would they be able to take more complex commands to help with mining and gathering supplies?"

"I do not believe so. The wards we would be able to place upon them are combat wards. The soldiers would survive longer in battle, and that is all," the necromancer explained.

"Perfect. Let's build a spire. Set the foundation for my empire!" If the new enchantments couldn't turn my mindless horde into a skilled workforce ready to mine the ground for ore, they were useless compared to a spire.

The necromancer whirled back toward the small collection of artifacts. He stretched forth his hand, and a blast of ethereal magic drilled out from his fingertips toward the implements. The magic latched on to its target. After the space of only a few heartbeats, the magical relics vanished. Xollmomath laughed as he absorbed the power back into his palms.

"Yes . . ." he growled with a sinister voice. "We shall begin the work of the spire."

At once, whatever incantation the necromancer had cast was begun. The ground beneath my feet rumbled. Xia stepped back, and the robed warlock nearby stopped what he was doing to bear witness to the event. I scrambled out of the way as I felt the epicenter of the tremendous spell was going to be directly beneath my feet, and I only barely made it to the relative safety of the side of my own house before the earth was rent apart.

From the depths of whatever hell Kalma called home, a putrid stench emerged. Several corpses, old desiccated skeletons with random patches of flesh and hair still clinging to them, were the first to emerge from the chasm. They didn't walk or crawl as if animated like the undead soldiers under my own command, but they were *thrown* up and onto the soil like heaps of trash being tossed from an open door. Half a dozen of them came out, and they weren't just human. At least one of them appeared to be from a large animal, perhaps a bear, and a pair of the corpses were distinctly marine in appearance.

When the corpse exhumation was complete, the stench seemed to grow. With the smell came a hazy cloud of grey-ish black smoke puffing its way into the bright morning air. Between two buildings, I saw Geirr hesitantly approaching with a confused and fearful expression on his face. His sister was watching from her position in the guard tower, and I worried for her physical safety. The tremors roiling through the ground had not yet subsided. I didn't know if the wooden tower was sturdy enough to hold or if it would come crashing down, killing my painter and setting our defenses back a few days.

All the thoughts of catastrophic failure quickly left my mind. Behind the smoke and the insufferable stench came a bit of stone from the fissure that I knew was the peak of my glorious citadel. It was a curved wing, the outstretched appendage of a gargoyle, and before long its body was visible through the mist, twisted and disfigured. More of the structure continued to rise. The gargoyle turned out to be the capstone of the spire, a grotesque ornament on top of a morbid steeple.

The body of the structure itself was somewhat like a circular version of a ziggurat or a pyramid, and it evoked memories of the architecture I had read about in school. The design was distinctly classical with a very Roman feel to the vaulted ceiling and intricately carved pillars supporting the roof, but the tall, pointed windows were definitely products of the gothic style, if what I remembered from a few art history courses was accurate.

Sadly, the structure ceased its ascent when perhaps thirty feet had emerged. Similar to the church we had burned a few streets away, there was only one entrance. The door was magnificent, a carved slab of something heavy—maybe basalt or dark granite—and the scene depicted on its surface was nothing short of Kalma's horrific legacy. The two panels of the door each showed a person, a man on the left and a woman on the right, and they appeared chained to the very door itself. Their emaciated knees jutted out at unnatural angles, and their faces were twisted into pitiful screams of agony. Each of the humanoid statues was missing its chest and organs, instead being laid bare down to the spine like a pig that had only been half-butchered before abandoned. The spines jutted outward to make handles, and I almost hesitated to touch them.

Almost.

Deep down, I couldn't wait to enter my citadel. It wasn't terribly large, not yet at least, but it was mine, and Lady Kalma had granted it to me, her deathbringer. As I reached for the handle on the right, the one made from a woman's twisted spine, the hairs on the back of my neck stood on end. There was an electrifying energy in the air that forced all my body's adrenaline to start coursing through my veins at once.

I turned back to address the small group waiting silently for my next move. "The foundation of Undercroft Citadel is complete. This is where we shall make our home and begin to plant the seeds of our empire. Once I open this door, there's no going back. There's no second guessing or retreat. Any of you who wish to leave, now would be the time."

I waited for a moment, my eyes searching each and every face of the players and NPCs before me, and no one moved. "From now until we're all dead, you're with me. I'm with you as well." I pointed to the pain-filled expression of the man on the left door panel. "And anyone who stands in our way is already dead. There will be no mercy. We will take what we must—what we merely *want*—and we'll pay the price in blood. Some of that blood will come from our own veins, but when everything is finished, it will be the corpses of our enemies crunching beneath the heels of our boots." I looked directly toward Geirr and then Helvegen. "If anyone has done you wrong, we will find them. We'll add their bones to the bricks and mortar paving our streets. Wonder will learn who we are, and once they understand the power we will soon command, they will fear us."

I pulled open the door to reveal the inside of the citadel to everyone gathered with the proper angle to see. The inner walls were made of black stone like the exterior, and in the center of the circular room sat a throne. It wasn't made of wood or metal or any other traditional building material—it was made of bones. The bleached remains came out of the ground to form a dais of grasping hands and broken digits. The dais itself was perhaps a foot thick and appeared to be obsidian from the way it shimmered in the light, and atop it sat a seat crafted from larger bones than those underneath. Both armrests ended in skulls, their jaws missing, and the top of the chair's high back was adorned with two spiraling animal horns.

The center of the throne room was illuminated by a black chandelier, its eight candles made from blood-red wax that matched the shade of Xollmomath's eyes. There were no other rooms, and I had to assume that the ancient necromancer required more power in order to continue the wondrous conjuring. Eventually, the citadel would encompass the entirety of Whitechapel, becoming a castle, palace, and dungeon all at once. It would stretch high into the sky, and beneath it would be a labyrinth of tunnels and chambers curving deep toward Kalma's fetid domain.

Stepping into the room, I noticed at once that the horrid smell was gone. Perhaps the interior of the structure was enchanted in some way, though I felt like I had known the answer all along. By accepting Lady Kalma—truly embracing every evil act I had ever committed or would carry out in the future—I had become immune to it. It would still linger, of that I had no doubt, and anyone of any morally upright persuasion would be repulsed by a mere taste of it in the air, but I would not. I would call the place my home. The others stepped closer to the door, and none of them appeared bothered by the stench either. They had committed themselves to the cause.

"Welcome to Undercroft Citadel," I said with a smile. I sat myself in the bone chair and let my palms caress the rough skulls underneath my hands. I fit the chair well.

Xia stepped forward and was the first to bow. "Lady Kalma has granted you her blessing. You are her chosen one," she said, her voice wavering a little. When she stood, I saw a smile on her face that I had not expected.

Xollmomath was next to approach. He fixed me with his inscrutable stare. "I require more power to continue the Lady's work. Bring me more holy relics, Master, and I shall give you your empire."

"Thank you," I replied, and the bald man stepped aside.

At some point during my reveling, Helvegen had come down from her guard tower, and she stood next to her brother in the doorway. Geirr looked a little worried, but Helvegen wore a determined expression. At the same time, both of them kneeled before my black dais. "We will serve," the woman said flatly.

"Aye," Geirr added.

"Get to your feet." I stood myself to try and illustrate my willingness to be . . . not *equal* to my underlings, but perhaps benevolent was the word. "I know you will both be faithful subjects. Work hard, and everyone will get what they deserve. I'm glad to have you by my side."

The two siblings bowed awkwardly at the neck before turning to leave.

After they exited my throne room, the NPC warlocks pledged their fealty one by one, and the patrolling group of mindless underlings never bothered to make an appearance.

At the bottom of my vision, a new notification blinked. I figured raising the throne room—small though it was—had somehow enhanced Undercroft Citadel and changed it status.

Holdings: Undercroft Citadel (Dungeon)

The dungeon tag was certainly new. I didn't know if other players held their own dungeons or not. It wasn't something I had ever seen on any of the streams. Perhaps I had influenced the game's AI enough to start generating new functions beyond the classes of deathbringer and painter. I focused on the new bit of text to expand the menu:

Undercroft Citadel (Dungeon)

Commander: Ben Hales (Influence: 29)

Bosses: Xia (Warlock), Helvegen (Painter), Xollmomath (Necromancer)

Resources: Moderate stockpiles of food and lumber, poor stockpiles of weapons, minor stockpiles of wealth (gems), no stockpiles of exotic goods or artifacts, minor stockpiles of crafting resources

Military Strength: 4 warlocks, 11 zombies, 1 charnel golem, 1 truthbreaker paladin, 1 engineer

Defensive Structures: Wooden wall, minor defensive wards, minor physical traps (punji pits), small guard tower, necropolis

The only differences I saw were the addition of the necropolis in the defensive structures section and the dungeon tag applied to Undercroft Citadel's name once more.

Another notification began blinking to the right of my character sheet. Apparently reading the new designations had triggered another change somewhere else.

System Notification: New Event! A virulent band of warlocks led by the infamous Ben Hales has successfully constructed a necropolis amidst the ruins of Whitechapel. The priests of Kagu have called an assembly of all the righteous to meet at their temple in Echelon. New tasks related to the necropolis will be given, and groups looking to raid the dungeon are forming now.

Your Influence skill has increased to 20!

Your Infamy skill has increased to 30!

"Oh shit. Fuck me." I read the notification twice just to be certain I wasn't hallucinating. "At least it wasn't an 'all players' notification broadcast across the entire game . . ." I muttered, my head in my hands.

The AI had officially put a bounty on my head. If a bunch of high-level raiders showed up tomorrow to loot the citadel and destroy everything I had worked so hard to create, I couldn't really blame them. I was sure at least someone had witnessed the murder I had committed in Echelon—both of them—and the Pyreborn Legion had to be pissed that I had killed their leader. Kagu was the name of their deity, and that was the group organizing the raids, so I knew it was them.

We were royally screwed. Our pathetic little wall of sticks and punji pits wouldn't be nearly enough. Maybe choosing the spire had been a mistake. We could have upgraded the minions instead. Being perhaps cautiously optimistic, I figured we had twenty-four hours until the first adventurers showed up to try to claim loot. Maybe the threat of true death would stall a few of them, but it wouldn't be enough. Bands of adventurers and guilds of highly experienced players wouldn't hesitate to take up the new quests.

"Xollmomath!" I yelled, still sitting on my throne. "Xia! Hel! Get in here!"

Xia was the first to peek her head back into the necropolis a few seconds later. "What is it, my Lord?" she asked.

Helvegen came running. "You saw the notification?" Her face showed her terror as clear as could be.

"Come in," I bade. Then I realized there was nowhere for anyone else to sit inside the throne room. "Wait. Take your brother and grab a handful of chairs from the nearest houses. Bring a table as well." I turned to Xia waiting patiently just inside the door. "Go to my house and collect my armor."

"What's going to happen?" Helvegen wondered, her question only half rhetorical.

I shook my head and let out a sigh. "We need to make a plan. Go gather chairs and a table, paper if you can find it among the resource piles, but be quick about your business. We convene the war council in ten minutes."

CHAPTER 10

"Unfortunately, we don't know much. Actually, we basically know nothing."

My generals, none of whom had any experience commanding troops in battle or orchestrating a full-blown invasion defense, were just as terrified as I was. We sat around a rectangular kitchen table scavenged from one of the larger houses not far away. As we tried to figure out a plan, the warlocks were busy torching the nearest ring of houses to give us a better line of sight from the citadel.

Xollmomath didn't feel like he was cut out for tactics and planning, so I had let him leave to see to as much defensive preparation as he could.

That left the war counsel to just four of us. Xia was eager for blood and carnage, and I had the benefit of tempering her opinion with the more conservative ideas of Helvegen and Geirr. Honestly, I didn't know exactly where my own mind was settled on the matter. Part of me wanted to charge out to bring the slaughter directly to Echelon, using the element of surprise to gain the upper hand. At the same time, holing up in our fortress felt like it would give us the best chance of survival.

As our resident engineer, Geirr was determined to influence us toward a defensive posture. "If we set lookouts on the road and watch the city gates from Echelon, we can ambush them on the road. Guerilla tactics. Hit them quick, then run back to our walls," he said.

"Our walls aren't strong enough to hold against an attack!" Xia countered.

Geirr leaned further over the table. "That's why we hit them on the road first! Thin their numbers, then fall back to defend."

"And if they settle in for a siege and call for reinforcements? What if more fighters from Echelon arrive to make up for the attack?" Helvegen served as a bit of a neutral position between the two options, and she brought up a good—albeit terrifying—point.

When I spoke, everyone quieted down. "You're right, Hel. If we hit them on the road and they send word back to the city for reinforcements, our advantage will be gone. If we hit them at all, it has to be decisive. A sure victory. Leave none alive."

Nods all around. "What do you suggest? If they move against us with a full force, we can't take them," Helvegen said.

Of course, she was right. I looked to Geirr. "Anything creative rustling around in that brain of yours?"

The man thought for some time. "Perhaps there are things we can do if we move quickly," he said. "I've taken account of our supplies and tools. With enough hands working quickly, we might be able to dig a pit in the road and cover it, disguising it, and then trap our enemies within."

I could tell the man had to modify his speech a little due to the language barrier between us. I wondered how Helvegen had learned such fluid English when he hadn't, but all my questions about his past would have to wait. "How long would it take?"

Again, he pondered for a moment before answering. "If

the undead can hold shovels and dig, perhaps twelve hours, maybe more or less. But that is only *if* they can be trained to dig. If they cannot, it will take longer."

An idea came to my mind. "What about the charnel golem? I trust you have seen it. The bone monstrosity can shift its form to take various shapes suited to different fighting styles. Perhaps it can assume different forms more conducive to excavation. What do you think?"

The man hesitated for only a few seconds before allowing a smile to overtake his face. "It is worth the try."

"Alright, let's do it," I said with confidence. Moving hastily might mean sacrificing other, perhaps better plans, but I didn't care. Any further debate would only slow us down.

We left the citadel and entered the afternoon sunlight, all four of us grabbing shovels and picks from the assembled supplies. "Xia, get the charnel golem. Command it to follow us." I didn't know if the idea had any chance of success or not, but we had to try. The sooner we knew if it the golem could dig, the sooner we would be safe.

Well, we would probably never be *safe* in any real sense now that the entire city of Echelon knew what we were doing and where we were doing it.

"To the road," I stated. Xia headed the other direction to fetch our magical excavator, and we ran in the direction of the city.

At first, I half expected to see an army already on the road and heading in our direction, but I knew it was still too early. I stopped our merry band at what I estimated to be roughly halfway between Echelon and Undercroft Citadel, and we quickly set about destroying the road. "Just be careful," I said. "We have to make sure everything looks normal. If anyone suspects a trap, we're doomed. They'll just walk around."

Luckily, the road wasn't in any kind of high quality condition to begin with, so tearing it up a bit wouldn't be too noticeable. Assuming we could replace the upturned dirt and then have time to flatten it out again, I was confident the scheme would work.

About ten minutes into our digging, Xia arrived with the charnel golem lumbering along behind her. The beast was huge and clumsy, altogether the exact opposite of stealth. We hadn't seen anyone coming from the city just yet, but when they did come, they'd see the golem before we had any kind of opportunity to lay an ambush.

"Any ideas how to command the golem to dig?" I asked our resident warlock, hoping she would have more knowledge of undead amalgamations than I did.

She turned to address the creature. "Um . . . Dig!" She pointed toward the center of the road where we had already made a shallow hole.

The charnel golem began rearranging its bones into a shape reminiscent of a cone with legs. It reared up toward the sky for a moment, then, with all the grace and decorum of a falling building, began to pound away at the dirt.

The whole operation was extremely loud, but it worked. The beast carved a circular ditch into the brown soil that soon became a pit. The four of us with shovels worked to keep the edges of the pit uniform and to keep clumps of earth from getting lost in the grass and weeds along the side of the road. Even a few stray handfuls of upturned dirt could give away the entire trap. Wearing my armor made the task a difficult one. I was thankful that the others were enthusiastic about their own survival, and after about half an hour of work, we had a pit large enough to at least injure anyone who fell into it. They wouldn't die, but Xia could take care of that.

The charnel golem lumbered up from the trap and waited behind the warlock for a new command.

"We need to cover the pit. Save some of the dirt to conceal the covering, but take the rest away and dump it," I ordered the undead abomination. The creature rearranged itself once more, and it used two long, boney arms like huge spoons to scoop up the majority of the dirt before carrying it away from the road.

"If an army comes at night, we have a chance," Helvegen said. "Perhaps they will not see or suspect anything."

It was the best we could hope for. To complete the pit, I turned to my engineer. "Geirr, what's the best way to cover it?"

The man pointed to a section of the trees nearby. Echelon was mostly surrounded by flat, even plains, so the trees that did grow weren't massive oaks or redwoods but scraggly, shorter varieties that didn't need quite as much water to survive. "Have the golem rip a few of those trees out of the ground. We can cover it with those around the edges. I will return to my workshop. I have cloth and maybe a few planks we can use as well."

I nodded, and Geirr took off at a full run for the citadel. We were fairly far out, so he would be gone for a while. When the golem returned, I ordered it to harvest four of the smaller trees pretty far from the road, and the beast wrenched them up one at a time without complaint or difficulty.

Helvegen and I made a square around the edge of the pit with the trees, using our shovels to trim off the errant branches that stuck out onto the road. Still, we didn't see a single person coming up the roadway to try out the new dungeon.

We were lucky. I sent Xia closer to Echelon while we waited for Geirr to return. We didn't have any easy method of long-range communication, so I instructed her to shoot some magic into the air in our direction if she needed to alert us to anything. The flare would certainly alert our enemies as well, but it was the best we had for the time being.

Geirr arrived after another ten minutes, and we immediately set about covering the pit with some planks and heavy cloth. "Raised my . . . physical stat . . ." he said between deep breaths, his hands on his knees. He had run all the way from the citadel with the supplies held in his arms, and he was covered in sweat.

"How much weight will it hold?" I asked. Our construction efforts were decent, but it didn't look great.

"Five, maybe six men? Fewer if they are on horses," Geirr answered. He walked a circle around the pit as he inspected, sometimes moving things slightly until they were exactly where he wanted them. "If it is a small band of warriors moving closely with one another, we might trap them all. If they are spread out, we will break the ankles of the very first one. Still, it could slow them down."

The more I looked at the pit, the less confident I was in our ability to defend ourselves. I had the sinking feeling that I would need to put my legendary sword and armor to use before the end of the night. "Alright, let's cover it up and pack it down," I said with a sigh.

It took just as long to fully conceal the trap and repair the road as it had to construct the pit. By the time we were finished, the sun had fallen behind the horizon and Xia had returned from her forward scouting position. "Now we wait," I told the others. "Let's move away from the road. We can find some cover in the trees. If anyone comes along and falls into the pit, we need to rush out to finish them. They'll be trapped, but not forever."

"I am not a fighter. I should be back at my workshop making defenses and reinforcing the wall. May I go?" Geirr's voice was quiet and full of fear. I didn't know if he was more afraid of provoking my wrath with his question or of the prospect of fighting.

Either way, he had nothing to fear from me. "You're much more useful back at base. Go and get to work. Whatever you think you can improve the quickest for the most gain, get to it."

Geirr gave me a nod and then set out down the road toward

the citadel at an even jog. The rest of us crouched down behind a few trees to wait. As the sun sank lower, our natural camouflage grew in effectiveness, and the trap we had dug started to actually blend in with the road. Behind us and lying flat was the charnel golem. I was tempted to send it back to the citadel to continue patrolling the grounds, but I had to assume our most immediate threat would come from the most direct path. If we could pass a day or two without anyone coming from the road, then we would have to return to base to protect every possible incoming path of assault.

Two days turned out to be extremely optimistic.

I didn't know the time, but it felt past midnight. A small band of four, maybe five, people carrying torches appeared on the road. "We've got company," I whispered to the two women hiding alongside me in the underbrush.

"They're players, all of them," Hel added.

"We'll see how many they have soon enough. Once their player tags spread out, we'll know." I shielded my voice with my hand to keep it from reaching our approaching guests. We were so far away that I knew I was being overly cautious. My heart raced in my chest. The small group of paladins and their untrained NPC squires had been an easy test. Whatever we were about to face was going to be much more difficult.

"I count five," Helvegen whispered.

I had just come to the same conclusion. "Tight formation," I replied. "We might get lucky and catch them all in the trap."

"If it holds . . ."

The three of us watched and waited. It was so quiet in our stand of trees that I could tell exactly where the lone grasshopper making noise was hiding, though I dared not remove my eyes from the men on the road. "They're close."

Helvegen grabbed my arm, and I could practically feel her adrenaline rushing through her veins. The first player reached the edge of the pit. He stepped onto it, and then he stopped.

My heart sank as he looked down to his feet, but then the man shrugged and kept going. He held a torch in one arm, and his other hand rested casually on the pommel of an axe hanging from his belt.

The second and third men stepped onto the trap not far behind the first.

The ground beneath their feet gave way all at once. Wood splintered, the cloth tarp ripped free of its makeshift frame, and three players tumbled about a dozen feet down under the road.

"Charge!" I growled to Xia and Helvegen.

The three of us sprinted from the trees. I heard the charnel golem behind us rising from its prone form into the multi-legged shape that it used to patrol the citadel.

A few feet from the pit, I drew Infernum and willed it to life. Flames leapt up the length of my weapon. The two men still standing on the ground both shrieked and shielded their eyes, entirely unprepared for such a savage ambush to fall upon them in the dead of night.

Infernum sank cleanly through the first man's leather armor. He screeched and fought, and in his panic he grabbed my sword with both hands, and his screams doubled in strength as his flesh burned. I ripped the sword free and turned to the second player, but Xia already had him cowering on his knees with the smoking remnants of a spell lingering around his torso.

Behind us, the charnel golem hadn't even gotten into the fight yet. I almost felt bad for the undead beast. Unless another group of fighters was somewhere behind the first, it wouldn't get to taste a single kill.

The man I had impaled died with a pathetic whimper, and I used my boot to push his corpse down the side of the pit with his friends. The one still alive on the surface was a level seven alchemist—not a combat class at all. Useful, however . . .

"Helvegen, get inside his mind and calm him down. We need to take him back to the citadel for questioning." I gave the order, and the painter was quick to comply. She threw a spell at the man's head, and his terrified screams dwindled down to incoherent sobs. All the fight left his body. Hel wrapped an arm under the man's shoulder to lift him from the ground.

"Xollmomath will know where to keep him," the woman stated. She grabbed the man's sword from his belt and slid it into her own.

I nodded, and she headed off in the direction of Undercroft Citadel with a countenance of grim determination.

The charnel golem reared its shifting bone head above the pit. The creature was eager for blood, or perhaps it was after the captives' bones to sublimate into its own body. I had every intention of fulfilling its desires.

"Any of you wish to speak to save your lives?" I called into the pit.

The general air of panic subsided a bit, and one of the players looked up toward me. He was a level eight knight. "W-what are you going to do?" he stammered.

I prowled back and forth above him with my flaming sword still held in my hand. The man who spoke appeared uninjured, as did one of his companions, though the third was clutching a badly broken ankle off to one side. "Why did you come here? Who sent you, and what was your plan?" I shouted back at the terrified prisoner.

The man shook his head. "We saw the announcement . . . We were just coming out to see what was going on, that's all. I swear!"

His story seemed plausible, but I had no way of knowing for sure. In any circumstance, I knew Xollmomath would probably have an easy time prying secrets from the alchemist we had captured. I just had to figure out what to do with our three prisoners.

One of the other men in the pit nodded along vigorously. "Only coming to see what was happening, that's all," he pleaded.

"Xia, what do you think?" I asked.

The NPC warlock shook her head. "If you release them, they'll run and tell everyone in Echelon what we're doing—"

"We haven't seen anything yet!" one of the captives yelled.

I let my sword fall a little closer to the edge of the pit as I scowled at my prey. "You would be wise not to interrupt one of my senior counselors," I spat. "You were saying?"

"Yes, my Lord. Releasing the prisoners would just mean more information leaking back to Echelon. You could try to bring them into the fold. Have Xollmomath work his magic upon them." The warlock bowed as she finished speaking. I didn't know if her show of obedience was genuine or if she was only trying to bolster my image for the time being. Honestly, it didn't matter. Both reasonings were acceptable.

Bathed in the flickering light of my sword, the men in the pit looked pathetic. They reminded me of pigs headed for slaughter, something I had witnessed plenty of times in the various villages and cities within the game. They had the look of men—no, of *animals*—who knew they were about to die. That lack of resolve was something I did not want.

"You three will join me? Serve my citadel with obedience?" I asked.

All of them nodded at once, though none of them dared to speak again.

I extinguished my sword and returned it to its sheath. "Out of the pit," I commanded. The men helped each other to get out of the pit. The one with the broken ankle couldn't walk on his own, so they had to support him between the shoulders of the two healthy ones. "Drop your weapons on the ground, and Xia will take them. You'll walk in front of me, and if you try to escape, my charnel golem will run you down and add your bones to its body."

Again, vigorous nods were the only answer I received. The silence was pleasing.

We marched back to Undercroft Citadel at a painfully slow pace. I could have commanded the charnel golem to carry our prisoners if had I wanted to, but that little shred of mercy was more than anyone ever showed Ingrid, so they deserved nothing. The man with the broken ankle would suffer for as long as it took.

When we arrived, Helvegen was waiting with Xollmomath to greet me. "There was another development while you were gone," she said, keeping her voice low. "It can wait until you're done with this lot. I have it under control."

I thanked her and marched my three captives up to Xollmomath's feet. "Bow before the necromancer."

All three obeyed. The injured player winced and covered a shout with his hand.

"What shall you have of them, Master?" Xollmomath asked.

"These are not fighters. They are not strong enough to join our cause, but they shall still serve. We will put them to good use," I said.

One of the prisoners mouthed what I thought was a word of affirmation under his breath.

I pointed to the man with the broken ankle. "Consume him for your own power, Xollmomath," I demanded.

The necromancer smiled. "As you wish." He reached a boney, hairless hand toward the injured man, and flesh began melting from bone. The player dissolved before my eyes, liquifying into pure energy to feed my most powerful dungeon boss. When there was nothing left but the terrified screams of his compatriots, I looked to Xia for the next task.

"Add their corpses to the ranks of our undead," I told her. She smiled and drew a dagger from her belt. The first captive died without a fight. The second tried to scramble away, and the warlock blasted him in the back with enough magic to send him sprawling to the dirt, and then her dagger plunged through one of his eyes before he could get up to run once more.

"Two more zombies, Sire," the woman said with a devilish grin.

"Two more zombies." I turned back to Helvegen waiting patiently by the entrance to my throne room. "What other matters have arisen?"

She waved for me to follow her inside the citadel. Kneeling before the throne was another player bound with rope. He looked somewhat injured, perhaps a little concussed judging by the bruise on the side of his head. Above his head, I read his player name and level:

Elyk, Level 11

"Where did you find him?" I asked.

"One of the zombie patrols brought him in. Didn't try to fight them, either." Helvegen nudged the man's back with the toe of her boot. "Go ahead. Tell him what you told me. See if he believes it."

I walked around the man and took a seat in my bone throne. He looked up at me, and I could already tell there was more spirit in him than all three of the miserable wretches I had executed outside. His eyes told me he was right where he wanted to be, and that made me hesitate. If he was an assassin come to kill me for a quick reward, I was sitting only three or four feet in front of him. Then again, he had no class and was barely a higher level than I was. Plus, I still wore a legendary set of armor. If the man leapt up and tried to kill me where I sat, he wouldn't get far.

Finally, he spoke. "When I read the announcement, I left Echelon at once. I want to join you." He met my gaze with fire in his eyes.

"Hel, cut him loose." The woman's eyes went a little wide, but she did as I asked nonetheless.

When the man was free, he took a moment to stretch his limbs before standing. The first thing I noticed about him was his height. I was a few inches under six feet, and he was taller than me by at least half a foot. For all his towering height, he was slight of build, probably thinner than Helvegen, and she was rather fit.

"What do you think you would bring to my citadel? What value does your life hold? Dead, you could join my undead army. What use are you alive?" I maintained eye contact with the man, trying to gauge what he was thinking by the look in his face, but all I saw was determination. I had to admit that he reminded me a bit of myself. He wanted something, and he wasn't afraid to go after it. I could respect that.

"I want to serve you. I've always been attracted to the darker side of things, and you seem to be headed in that direction already. I should probably say I'm a fugitive, though I don't think you have much of a problem with that, right?" He spoke with confidence that said he had nothing to lose.

I had already made up my mind that I would be keeping him around, especially since Xollmomath would be able to give him a new class that was bound to be useful, so I only had one more question left. "What are you fighting for? What's your purpose here? When everything goes to shit and there's a knife pressed up against your neck, what's going to give you the energy to keep putting my enemies in the ground?"

Elyk's smile told me he had more than enough motivation to keep himself going. "Ahmose imprisoned a couple of my friends after a bar fight. When the servers crashed or whatever it was that actually happened, a riot broke out in the dungeon. All three of my friends died in that riot. Joining you lot feels like a good way to finally see that bastard's head rotting on a pike," he explained, his diabolical grin never waning.

I stood and reached out my hand. "Welcome to Undercroft Citadel," I said. "Glad to have you aboard. Once Xollmomath has finished converting the fresh corpses out there into soldiers, see him about a class. He's a trainer, and he has some rather impressive options."

"Thank you," Elyk said.

I left the captive to his own devices and walked back out into the darkness of the middle of the night. The air was cool, and I was tired. My armor was starting to feel heavy on my shoulders. We were probably only a couple hours from dawn.

The bald necromancer had finished the zombie conversion, giving us two additional soldiers to help swell our ranks. We were up to thirteen mindless soldiers, and that would have to be enough to last us through the night. If another attack came before dawn, I didn't know how much strength I would have left to meet it.

"What do you want me to do with the captive alchemist?" Helvegen asked, coming up to stand at my side. She looked just as tired as I felt.

"Save him for tomorrow. We don't have a jail . . . but I think your brother has some chain. Take him there and chain him to an anvil at the workshop. We can deal with it in the morning. And make sure we have some zombies and warlocks back on patrol." I gave the woman a pat on her shoulder and turned back to my house. Until we had the time to build a residence within the citadel itself, I would still have to stay in my cramped, stolen hovel.

CHAPTER 11

When dawn broke and the citadel began to awaken, I was still just as tired as the night before. Thankfully, no one had tried to attack in the few hours of darkness between adding to our zombie army and getting ready for breakfast. I wasn't sure we would have survived the night had there been a new raid.

Living through the night only meant I was out of time to prepare for living through the day. Without needing to eat with the others, I made my way first to Geirr's workshop to check on our alchemist. Geirr himself was there, as was Helvegen, both of them eating some food while watching our prisoner from a distance. "How are the food stores holding up?" I asked. It looked like they were eating hard bread with something, perhaps a cheese or type of butter, spread atop it. Honestly, it kind of looked terrible. I knew we were running low.

"Not great," Hel answered. "If we're going to be adding new people to the citadel, we'll need a new food source. We'll need it soon."

Just another thing to add to my already growing list of impossible tasks.

I let out a sigh and looked at our captive. "Did he try to escape?"

"Didn't make so much as a sound all night," Geirr said.

"Good." I walked up to the chained man and grabbed a stool to sit across from him. I drew my sword from its sheath and placed it across my lap.

The man was a seventh level alchemist by the name of Kulgun Ironfoot. "You went a bit dramatic on the name, don't you think?" I figured starting out with a bit of levity might be the best way to judge the man's potential loyalty. Alchemists were incredibly useful to any settlement, and it was exactly what we needed.

The man smirked. "Perhaps. But you're the one with a citadel made of bones and gargoyles. That seems just as dramatic, I think."

"Fair enough. So . . . what were you doing with those other men? Coming to raid my home?" I kept an easy tone, leaning back a little on my stool with a hand on Infernum's cold hilt.

"A raid? We were just a bunch of low-level players. I'm an alchemist, not a fighter. We just met in a pub and were curious, that's all. What's . . ." He hesitated for a moment. "What's become of the others?"

"They've agreed to serve Undercroft Citadel for the foreseeable future," I said. "Well, more or less."

The man only nodded. I didn't know if he knew we could turn people into mindless undead soldiers, and it felt best to save some information until I knew more about the man.

"You know, my first plan was to have Xollmomath come down here and get you to talk. Honestly, I'm too tired for a full-blown torture and interrogation right now. I just want to get things finished, and I have a lot on my list. If you're honest with me, that will be it. If not, I'm just going to cut your head off and be done with it." I stood from my stool and gave the alchemist a plaintive look that I felt conveyed my sincerity.

He gulped, and sweat was beading on his brow, but he didn't turn away. "I didn't know them well," he said quietly. "We had just met the night the notification came out. Thought it would be a good idea to come out and investigate, just to see what was happening. I didn't really have much opinion on the matter one way or another."

"I believe you," I told him honestly. "I don't think any group of just a handful of players would bother to take along an alchemist if they planned on a fight. No offense. As I said, I'm a busy man. If you want to live, I need to know how many other groups were planning on coming out to investigate. Tell me."

"Most everyone in the pub was talking about it, but I don't know how many were serious. Swear it." He shook his head and rocked a little back and forth on the ground. The chains around his legs rattled with every movement.

"Surely you must have heard of other groups like yours planning on paying me a little visit. Tell me."

Kulgun hung his head. "I didn't see anything or hear anything from anyone firsthand, but the rumors said there were two groups planning moves. The one everyone knew was the Pyreborn Legion. They're a pretty big guild running most of Echelon, surely you've heard of them."

I ordered my sword to ignite for a split second. "Ah, of course. I killed their leader and stole his sword. It makes sense. And what of the second group?"

"The priests of Ashur. They're mostly an NPC group, but everyone said they were recruiting an army of knights, paladins, and mages. They're pissed."

"Again, it makes sense. The temple here in Whitechapel was full of followers of Ashur. And what of their plans? Anything immediate?" I pressed on.

The man shook his head. "The Pyreborn guild seemed like they were recruiting as well. Neither group was ready to move; everyone was just too scared to leave the walls. That's why a handful of us thought we would come check it out. I . . . I wanted to get some information to sell to the guild or the priests."

Helvegen came into the workshop. "Sir, Xollmomath asked to see you. He said he would come himself, but he is weakened from the recent summoning. He can't walk this far from the circle."

"Thank you, Hel. I'll be with him in a moment," I said over my shoulder. The woman bowed slightly and left. I tossed Kulgun a piece of bread that had been sitting on an anvil just out of his reach. "You see, I am a busy man. You will serve me whether you want to or not. The only question is: in what capacity will you aid the citadel? One choice: either you swear your allegiance to me and serve Geirr as his assistant in the workshop, or I cut off your head right now and give your body to the cause. Choose."

Kulgun got to one knee and bowed his head. "I'll serve. I'll be your alchemist . . . my Lord. Just bring me supplies, and I'll give you potions. I . . . I swear it."

"Good. I'll tell Geirr as much. I think he has the key to your chains." I left the workshop before Kulgun could respond. Geirr had heard the exchange from his position right at the door, so I went directly for the citadel back at the center of our encampment. I hoped whatever it was Xollmomath had for me it was good news and not bad.

When I arrived, the bald necromancer was standing in front of the throne room door, and Elyk was next to him, both men smiling. Elyk had a curious new class next to his name. Xollmomath had bestowed upon him the class of 'Harvester,' and I could imagine what it would entail.

"Elyk, well met," I said. I shook the man's hand, and his grip was strong.

"I've become a harvester. Xollmomath says it is an ancient class, and I've never heard of it before, never seen it on any of the streams or in any of the guides." He smiled, and he seemed truly happy with the turn of events despite being bound and beaten as a slave just six hours ago.

"What can you do?"

"Get me some armor. Put me on the front lines," he said.

Xollmomath cut in with a sinister cackle. "He will be your harvester, taking lives on the battlefield like a scythe claims stalks of wheat. If you can armor him, he will bring you the heads of your enemies in numbers greater than you imagine."

"Excellent." I gave the man a friendly slap on the shoulder. "Armor is a top priority. But food might have to come first. We're starting to run out."

Of all the myriad things pressing on my mind, all the tasks around the citadel that needed to be accomplished, I had to address the food first. Holding off dozens of attacks from Echelon would mean nothing if we starved to death. I sent out the word to gather everyone except Geirr, the alchemist, and the zombies in front of my necropolis. As I waited for everyone to arrive, I considered just how far I had come in such a short time. When Ingrid had been killed, I was classless. I had possessed almost nothing. Now I had the seeds of an empire.

Looking out upon my assembled ranks, my chest swelled with pride. In a week, I had built a necropolis, acquired legendary armor, and become so strong the game had started making quests specifically related to my exploits. In another week, how much more would I have built? How much more would I have conquered? Every bloody step brought me closer to Vic.

Everyone stood quietly before the necropolis in anticipation of my address. I wasn't exactly sure what kind of collective noun to use for them all, so I sort of fumbled through my beginning. "Men and women of Undercroft Citadel, we have come a long way. As you know, Echelon is aware of our existence, and we have information stating that two separate groups within the city are preparing to raid us. I believe we have a few days before those raids reach our borders."

I stood still in front of my underlings, addressing them as though I had a podium or a balcony and was a famous dictator from the old days before Wonder ever existed. I needed a few banners scattered around the necropolis and the nearby buildings to really complete the image.

"Right now, our first priorities are physical security and food. We essentially have neither." I divided the warlocks into small teams, each with a handful of zombies, to finish demolishing all the remaining buildings within the ruins of Whitechapel that we couldn't use. That would give us better vision of whatever was coming. I redirected the charnel golem's patrol route to cover more ground closer to Echelon and gave it orders to kill any groups of three or less and simply retreat against anything more.

For Xia and Hel, my two most trusted advisors and lieutenants, I sent them each on solo missions. They were to scour what was left of Whitechapel for food, and when that was completed they would leave the city altogether in search of farms or other places we could safely raid. Xollmomath couldn't move far enough away from the summoning circle to be of much use, so that left just myself and Elyk.

The two of us needed to train. I had my armor and Infernum—plenty of destructive force to take down players twice my level—but I couldn't rely on items alone. I had to continue increasing my own stats if I was going to progress and protect my fledgling settlement. Elyk needed the same thing. His new class was completely unknown, and he had to master as much of it as he could before the next raid showed up if he was going to earn his keep.

I opted to leave my armor behind in favor of quickness, stealth, and the simple reliance on my own physical abilities that I needed to develop. Elyk still didn't have any armor other than the heavy shirt and few pieces of hardened leather he had come with. For weapons, Xollmomath had mentioned something about a scythe, and the pile of tools we had looted from the town included more than one. Sadly, they were all farming implements, not weapons of war. They would break against the first piece of armor they touched. Instead of carrying one, Elyk favored a two-weapon arrangement much like a fencer's, with a long rapier in his right hand and a small parrying dagger in his left.

If all went well, we would get to test our weapons before long.

To find our prey, we left Undercroft Citadel in the direction of a different starter town called Riverside not too far outside Echelon. The trek took more than an hour, but we still had the entire day once we arrived. All along the beaten path we used to get there, the man didn't say much. Being near him for an extended amount of time gave me the impression that he was a little more evil than he had let on. I believed his story about his friends being killed in a prison riot, but there was something else in the sheer level of determination he exhibited. The prospect of killing thrilled him.

But it thrilled me as well.

With Infernum hanging from my side, I burned to use it combat once more. The idea of slaughtering people—NPCs or players, it did not matter—in the furtherance of my vengeance was intoxicating. Each death added to my power, and power was the one thing I needed more than food, walls, a necropolis, or even underlings. Everything could be wiped away in an instant, but if I was simply strong enough on my own, it wouldn't matter.

We reached the next starter village a few hours before noon. Immediately, I noticed something different about it. There were guards. Players with names and classes floating above their heads were patrolling the town perimeter while the low-level players quested inside.

"Damn, they're guarding their vulnerable ones," I muttered.

Beside me, Elyk didn't seem phased. "Just need to kill a few guards first," he stated.

The patrolling soldiers moved in pairs. The lowest level group I could see from our position consisted of a level four-teen soldier and a level thirteen arcanist. If the pair had fought together before, they would still be quite formidable despite their lack of experience points. But in any case, they both still out-leveled us, and that meant we were in for an uphill battle.

"Think they'll alert the others if we try to catch the attention of just one pair?" I asked.

"Heh, with that sword of yours, would it really matter?"

"Don't forget, death is permanent now. No reconstitution outside. And I'm not wearing my armor," I said.

Elyk laughed. "I'm not wearing any either. But you're a damned deathbringer, and I'm a harvester. These bored idiots walking their patrol have never seen anything like us. We'll cut them to ribbons."

The man's bloodlust was beginning to seep into my own mind. I wanted the carnage just as badly as he did.

"Alright, let's do it. We'll target the weakest group first, the one with the arcanist." I pointed them out a short distance north of our position. In about ten minutes, they would pass through their closest point to our hiding place. "Let me take the caster. I have some unique abilities that should serve us well. At the very least, I'll be able to distract the arcanist long enough to kill him. Think you can handle the soldier?"

"They're as good as dead," was Elyk's response.

We waited until the patrol came closer. They weren't exactly at their perihelion when Elyk leapt to his feet and charged. The man screamed at the top of his lungs, and I was right behind him, flaming sword waving through the air. In all the chaos of the first few seconds, I had no idea if the defenders had been able to raise any kind of alarm.

Elyk hit the soldier first, and I activated *Pull from Darkness* just a few steps behind the harvester. My shadow demon launched forward directly for the arcanist's face. The man shrieked as the creature latched onto his eyes, and whatever spell he had quickly tried to cast in my direction fizzled only an inch from his fingertips.

Infernum tasted flesh a second later. The long, brutal sword bit into the mage's side right below his ribs, and the man toppled to the ground, my shadow pet still firmly covering his eyes and tearing at the skin of his face. I reeled back to swing again, and the flailing target was easy to hit. Infernum took him in the legs, severing the left one off at the hip. A third easy strike quieted his screams.

By the time I recalled my shadow pet in the hopes of launching it at the soldier, Elyk had killed his prey. His swords had done marvelous work, and the soldier had clearly been unprepared. Despite the level advantage, our pure savagery and speed had easily overcome the pair without either of us sustaining a single scratch.

Your Physical skill has increased to 22!

"Nice, ranked up in physical. Getting closer to another level," I said as I sheathed Infernum.

Elyk didn't bother to loot the corpses before grabbing me by the forearm and pulling me closer to the village. "Pretend we're guards," he said quickly.

I fell into step at his side without question. "What's your plan?" I whispered.

"Just pretend we're exactly where we need to be. We can waltz right into the center of town and start picking off every player we see." He led me in the direction of what appeared to be a civic building where a few players beneath level ten were busily completing quests without a care in the world.

We walked right up to a group of three classless players who had absolutely no idea anything was amiss.

"Let me have them. I'll get more experience than you. I need it more," Elyk said under his breath.

I gave him an almost imperceptible nod.

At once, Elyk activated a talent that sent him into a whirling spiral of death-dealing steel. His rapier held a spherical orbit all around his body that didn't slow by even a fraction when it connected with the first unsuspecting player. Like a whirlwind of death, he pushed through the two players behind the first, and the slaughter was finished before I had time to fully understand what was even happening.

"Harvester," I basically gasped. "I get it. The entire class is designed for one thing: to be unleashed directly into the center of an enemy's forces. Damn."

Elyk was panting from the effort, his physical stat still too low to grant him much endurance. "Like the necromancer said, if I get armor, I'll be unstoppable."

"That shoulder pad at least looks decent," I said, pointing to a blood-flecked piece of iron armor one of the low-level players had been wearing.

Elyk bent down to collect his ill-gotten spoils, but a deep, resonate voice made both of us stop. "You, stop!" it commanded from somewhere behind us. At the same time, we turned with our hands raised.

A level twenty-four marauder stood about fifty feet from us with a halberd in both hands and a buckler strapped over his left forearm.

"I wouldn't try it," I said with as much confidence as I could muster. "Two against one. Think it through."

The man took a few steps forward. "You just slaughtered those innocent players . . . those people. I'm taking you both to Echelon. You're under arrest."

Elyk stifled a laugh. "No you aren't," he calmly stated.

Infernum still in my hand, I willed the blade to life. "We'll go to Echelon when we're good and ready. That *won't* be today."

Both of us ran full speed for the marauder. Elyk reached him first. He deflected a well-timed strike aimed for his head, then ducked underneath the marauder's arm. He didn't slash out with his rapier to gut the man from the side but rather activated one of his talents, and his body began to spin once more. He was faster than the more heavily armored marauder, whirling with his blade held out horizontally.

He would have cut the marauder in half if his weapon didn't break.

Elyk's talent faded, and he staggered backward, clearly unbalanced with his momentum pulling him in the wrong direction.

Had I not been only a couple steps behind him, he probably would have been killed before I had the chance to intervene. I made it just in time. I released *A Feast of Spores* directly into the marauder's face, instantly expelling a noticeable chunk of my own energy.

The armored marauder staggered under the strange, toxic attack. As he fell backward, I slammed the hilt of my sword into his chest to help him along, and he crashed into the ground with a loud clatter of plate mail. Before he could hope to defend himself, I brought Infernum down on the top of his skull, rending it two.

"Take his armor," I said quickly. "It seems decent, at least better than nothing for now. More guards are bound to show up any minute."

Elyk quickly set about unbuckling the man's armor. The two of them looked to be about the same size, so it should fit him until we found something better. At the other end of the street, another group of guards were shouting in our direction. As the harvester worked at the armor, I stood in front of him, blazing sword in hand, and yelled back at the newcomers. There were four in total, and I didn't want to risk another fight without my own armor.

"Back off!" I shouted. "You know you can't take us. Just leave."

One of them took a hesitant step forward, but the player next to him held him back. They were too far away for me to hear what they were saying among themselves. I hoped they wouldn't all charge at once, but I felt like I could take them even if they did. The problem was how much it would cost. Without my armor—a stupid mistake I cursed myself for making—even a clear-cut victory over the entire group might mean a crippling injury that would never heal.

Luckily, the group seemed to take a collective step backward. "You're the ones from the new citadel, right? Running around killing low level players and cannibalizing their bodies?"

That was a little odd. To my knowledge, no one had partaken in any cannibalism yet. I could only imagine what other wild rumors were flying around Echelon. By the end of the week my reputation would probably be somewhere close to the devil himself.

"Yes!" I shouted back. "You know what we can do. You'd be wise to stay out of our way." I waved my flaming sword in front of me for a little bit of added dramatic effect.

The player in the center, the de facto leader of the little handful of players, began walking forward. He kept his weapon sheathed at his side and his arms held out in surrender.

His approach made me nervous. I was exposed, and I didn't have enough experience in the game to know what kind of trick or deception I was about to fall into. Not letting my outward confidence waver, I lowered my sword and held my ground.

The player was a level twenty-four knight. It was a generic class that attracted tons of players, but a powerful one capable of activating any number of talents to boost its combat proficiency.

The knight stopped about ten feet in front of me. "What do you want with our town? Why are you here?"

I hadn't really thought about that. Elyk and I had come to the starter village to get some easy experience and hopefully train a few skills to keep getting stronger. Our secondary mission had been supplies. We were starting to really need food, and every single crafting resource in the entire game was either already in demand or would be soon. If Undercroft Citadel was going to produce the materials we would need to conquer Echelon, we had to start soon.

That gave me an idea.

"I command an army of necromancers, warlocks, golems, and more undead than you would ever be able to stop," I said. "I don't know why you and your friends chose to protect this little shithole village, and I don't particularly care. It belongs to me now."

The man seemed uneasy. I couldn't read his expression at all to know whether my ploy was working or not. Finally, he spoke. "We just . . . want to protect the people. We keep them safe as they quest. All we want to do is get the world back to normal. Make it like it used to be before the error. We don't want any trouble."

"You speak for the whole town?"

The man nodded, his eyes darting around everywhere. "I think so. The players look up to me a little, and the NPCs don't really have any leadership of their own."

"Perfect. Then I'll deal with you only, alright?" I stepped forward to let the fire from Infernum reach the knight's skin. "You'll pay tribute to Undercroft Citadel every week. Today is Monday, and I expect your first payment by dawn tomorrow. Bring food and supplies, enough to fill a wagon, and I will let your village survive."

Again, the man nodded nervously, shifting his weight from foot to foot as he failed to meet my eyes. "Alright.

We'll pay. Just leave the town alone. I'll be there tomorrow at dawn."

"Come to the old village of Whitechapel. It isn't far away. And if you aren't personally there, the deal is off. I expect a wagon every single Monday by dawn. Don't forget it." I extinguished my sword and sheathed it. As I turned my back on the knight to collect Elyk and leave, I couldn't help but feel overwhelmingly arrogant—and it felt fantastic. I had cowed the man with nothing more than a flaming sword and a pair of murders. He had no idea that I was still just guessing when it came to actual combat. If his entire group attacked at once, Elyk and I would easily be slaughtered.

Being an evil overlord was starting to feel like it was a career in which I would excel.

For you, Ingrid. I do it all for you.

Without waiting for the knight to say anything else or make any kind of move, Elyk and I began casually strolling from the town. He had most of his newly-stolen armor strapped to his own body. What he didn't want to wear he carried with the ease of someone who knew they would never be challenged.

In truth, the harvester scared me. He was bloodthirsty, wild even, and I didn't know just how much ambition he harbored beneath the surface. Once again, I felt the weight of the tyrant pressing down on me from a new direction. I couldn't truly trust *anyone* ever again. Even the most loyal and battle-tested of my underlings were still liabilities.

As we walked back toward home, I made myself a promise never to leave Undercroft Citadel without my armor again. I also wanted to start building a solid core of personal bodyguards I could trust. Elyk made an obvious choice, and Xia would be useful as well. Once we had enough lodging to really have a true fortress established around the necropolis, I would need to establish a defensive squad to protect me at all times, especially while I slept. Helvegen would also very likely make a fine candidate for my inner circle of guards, but I wanted her to have more personal choice in what she did. The woman showed initiative, and that meant she would be more useful to the citadel completing projects alongside her brother without being micromanaged.

CHAPTER 12

U   ndercroft Citadel looked a little different upon my
         return. I had forgotten about the handful of corpses
         Lady Kalma had vomited forth from the earth when
my necropolis had appeared. So much else had been going
on with the rise of the building that I hadn't paid them much
attention.

Xollmomath had not shared my apathy.

"Welcome home, Master," he said, offering me a subtle tilt
of his head. "We have made great progress."

Xollmomath and the others had expanded the wall fortifications once more. With only a few more days of work, we
would have a large enough wall to contain all the relevant parts
of the settlement. We would need to expand more eventually,
of course, but that was still at least another few weeks away.

The most interesting things about the wall upgrades were
the corpses hanging from them. Every hundred feet or so,
Xollmomath had pinned a corpse to the wall with wooden
stakes and ropes. "They are enchanted," he said with a devilish grin.

I immediately pulled up the holdings panel of my

character sheet to see what exactly had been done. The first thing I noticed was that the village of Riverside was listed under my holdings as a vassal. That meant, I supposed, the man I had conscripted into weekly food service had been telling the truth when he said he spoke for the town as a whole. The AI had agreed, and Riverside had been added to my growing kingdom. Expanding the Riverside menu revealed only that they were providing tax revenue in the form of food along with the schedule.

Under the main tab for Undercroft Citadel, a few things had changed.

Undercroft Citadel (Dungeon)

Commander: Ben Hales (Influence: 30)

Bosses: Xia (Warlock), Helvegen (Painter), Xollmomath (Necromancer), Elyk (Harvester)

Resources: Moderate stockpiles of food and lumber, poor stockpiles of weapons, minor stockpiles of wealth (gems), no stockpiles of exotic goods or artifacts, minor stockpiles of crafting resources

Military Strength: 4 warlocks, 13 zombies, 1 charnel golem, 1 truthbreaker paladin, 1 engineer, 1 alchemist

Defensive Structures: Reinforced wooden wall enhanced with fear glyphs (detonating corpses), minor defensive wards, minor physical traps (punji pits), small guard tower, necropolis

"So those corpses will detonate if enemies get too close?" I asked, barely believing what I had read on my own sheet.

"Indeed, Master. They will rain gore down upon the enemies of the citadel. All who witness the event will cower before your unholy might." The bald necromancer laughed as he explained the gruesome traps, even going as far as to playfully caress the nearest body with a finger.

I liked where things were going. The exploding corpses were probably the strongest defenses we had outside of the necropolis itself. They were a huge addition to our overall strength.

We still had half the day left, a little more time than I had expected to have, which meant I could take stock of the rest of our progress. Everyone had certainly been busy. So far, there wasn't a drop of dissension in the ranks.

It seemed like we had exhausted what remained of Whitechapel in terms of food and other available resources. Scavenging the final handful of buildings had produced another couple days' worth of dried, seasoned meat. For Geirr's workshop, another few pounds of scrap metal had been recovered and were destined for the crucible.

At central command, Xia had returned from her scouting outside the settlement. Unfortunately, she had found nothing. Although, the more I thought about it, the better her lack of results seemed. It meant we were somewhat isolated, and that would only help our security in the short term. Helvegen still had not returned. Her name was still listed on my holdings sheet, so I figured she wasn't dead.

I climbed up the guard tower to survey my kingdom. Zombie and warlock crews were still busy demolishing some of the small houses and businesses at the farthest reaches of the old Whitechapel domain, and watching them brought a smile to my face. The NPCs who had lived there were gone. Their final vestiges of existence were being eradicated as I watched. Within twenty-four hours, Whitechapel would be gone.

Surveying all the territory belonging to Undercroft Citadel, I knew we had to create an actual entrance into the interior. So far, we had used a plain gap in the wooden wall to reach the center with no security whatsoever. That would have to change by dawn when the wagon from Riverside arrived. We needed a designated gate for the wagon to approach where my warlocks could look down upon it and fire if the need arose.

I took in the sights of my empire for a few more moments before descending back down to the ground and finding

Geirr. He was hard at work crafting more tools of higher quality than what we had salvaged, and he was eager to take on the gatehouse project. By his estimation, we would need two full days to complete a wooden structure large enough to serve as a gatehouse. For the first food delivery, we would simply have to improvise.

An hour or so before dawn, all of Undercroft Citadel was awake and preparing for our first wagon full of tribute. Helvegen hadn't returned from her mission the previous day. Her name still appeared on my sheet, though I was starting to worry that something had happened to her. Geirr shared my angst, and I had to tell him more than once that we wouldn't send out an expedition to find her until after our business with Riverside was concluded. In truth, I had no qualms letting the woman stay out another full day before looking for her. As long as her name was listed as one of the bosses of my dungeon, I knew she at least hadn't abandoned us or sold us out to another group.

The squeaking approach of a wagon pulled my thoughts back to the present. We assembled on the western side of the encampment a few hundred yards from the necropolis itself to await the shipment. Fearing a trap, I had left Xollmomath and the charnel golem back in the east. If anything happened while the majority of our forces were deployed in the west, we would at least be able to get back and join the battle without any significant delay.

As the wagon came nearer, I saw that only two players served as escorts. One of them was the knight I had dealt with the previous day. The other was a lower level fighter, and neither of the players carried any visible weapons.

So far so good. "Stop there!" I called once the wagon was about fifty yards away. I could see the fear in both of the men's eyes as they gazed upon Undercroft Citadel. They could see the wooden wall with its gruesome accouterments, and that was only the beginning of their trepidation. The large gargoyle adorning the top of my spire was just as intimidating as the corpses.

"We brought food. Also found two crates with iron ore. That's all you need, right?" the knight called back.

I waved to Xia, and the two of us went up to the wagon to inspect the goods. They had assembled a few small crates of vegetables and half of a slaughtered cow. Overall, I was pleased with the haul. "Take everything to Kulgun at the workshop. Have him test it for poison, if he can," I told Xia.

She nodded and began leading the horse at the front of the wagon back to our line of soldiers. I had no intentions of stealing the cart or the animal attached to it, so Xia ordered our warlocks to unload everything and carry it by hand inside the walls.

"You did well," I said to the knight and his companion.

The man's voice shook. "You'll leave us alone? For . . . another week?"

I let my imposing armor clank a little as I shifted my weight from one foot to the other, my right hand on Infernum's pommel. "That is the agreement, and you can count on it. Food every week plus more raw materials. Just what can fit in the cart, nothing more. You need supplies as well if you're going to continue to prosper. And if anyone from Echelon or anywhere else tries to intervene with our little arrangement, or should you come under attack, send word here to Undercroft Citadel as quickly as you can. Riverside is my vassal, and I protect *everything* that belongs to me. Do we have an understanding?"

The knight offered a deep bow. "Yes, of course, sir. We are . . . at your command."

I waved away his awkwardness and looked back toward my own underlings awaiting my return. "Perfect. I gave you an extra day to prepare the first shipment. Subsequent deliveries will take place on Mondays at dawn. I'll see you next week."

I walked back to my troops and dismissed them. Behind me, the knight didn't waste any time collecting his cart and horse for the return trip back to Riverside. I assigned everyone to the task of building the gatehouse under Geirr's direction and then headed toward the workshop to pay our resident alchemist a visit.

"How's the food look?" I asked. The man had been busy setting up a row of glass jars on a newly installed shelf above a long table that had also not been there the day before.

To his right, the meat from Riverside had been stacked in a neat pile atop a few empty burlap sacks to keep it off the ground. "Looks fine to me. Tastes alright as well," Kulgun said with a grin.

"You tried some?"

"Haven't had breakfast yet. I was hungry," the alchemist answered.

Well, I have a food tester now. "Excellent. I'll have it delivered to our stores. Hopefully we have some salt or something to preserve it. What do you make of the raw iron?"

Kulgun glanced at the new materials sitting next to the workshop's only anvil. "Not sure you can poison iron, if that's what you mean."

"What about the quantity?" I said with a sigh.

"Should be enough to start some better projects, but that's Geirr's department. I think he plans on making some more tools before adding metal plating and supports to the guard tower. Need to ask him about it, not me."

"And what is that you are working on?" I asked. I had no knowledge whatsoever of the alchemy system in Wonder since I had never played or watched others use it on the streams.

Kulgun turned back to me with a smile on his face and an empty vial in his hand. "I don't know too many recipes, but every alchemist can make health potions. I should have a crate of them ready by tonight, I think."

"Excellent. Keep me posted on your progress," I said, thoroughly satisfied with the progress we were making already. I had been in charge of the settlement for about ten days, and we were well on our way to building an empire.

We spent the morning continuing to improve the wall, work on the gatehouse, and make upgrades to the fortress as a whole. A few hours after lunch, one of the undead patrols around the outskirts of the territory spotted Helvegen on the horizon. The zombies began making noise, and I could see the woman coming in our direction from the guard tower. She was dragging something behind her.

"Xia, go escort our painter and help her with whatever she found," I called down to the construction crew. The warlock nodded and set down her tools to obey my command.

I watched from the tower as Xia made her way out to Helvegen and then walked by her side back to the citadel, though I still could not tell exactly what it was she dragged behind her. It looked heavy, and she had it bound with thick ropes.

Helvegen was exhausted and covered in sweat, dirt, and grime when she finally collapsed against the side of her own house underneath the guard tower. I hurried down the ladder to see what she had scored on her expedition. She didn't appear injured in any way, so I figured whatever was in her net wasn't alive.

"What did you find?" I asked. The corners of a few boxes poked through the webbing of the ropes.

"There's a mine not too far off," she said. "Some imps and other slimy bastards have taken it over, but I managed to grab some supplies before coming back."

"That's perfect." I fished out one of the heavy boxes from the ropes and pried off the lid with a hammer from our pile of tools nearby. Several bars of iron were inside. The next box contained the same, and then the third held brass. "All of these are ingots, not raw ore . . ."

Helvegen nodded. "There was a forge outside the mineshaft. I think most of the equipment is too destroyed to be of use, but they had a little bit already processed when whoever was running it bit the dust."

I opened the final box, and it did not contain any metals. Instead, three bloodied, misshapen imp heads were stuffed into it. "Uh . . . why did you bring these?"

"I thought Xollmomath might have use for them," Hel said with a laugh. "Besides, I took all the ingots I found. There was still one box left over, and the weight was nothing compared to the metals."

"Fair enough." I reached out a hand to help her up from the ground. "You need a change of clothes and a shower."

She looked around at all the new construction going on around her. "You didn't build a shower, did you? I wasn't gone *that* long."

"Well you have a point there. Just clean yourself up and get a nap if you need it. I'll make sure the metal gets to your brother and the heads find Xollmomath." Having real ingots instead of scraps of poor-quality metals would be an amazing addition to our supplies.

Before I could start dragging the ingots to Geirr's workshop, Helvegen held out her hand for me to see the final spoils of her expedition. "Rubies, I think," she said.

Three small red gemstones glinted in her palm. I picked one up and held it to the light. I was no gemologist by any means, so all I could tell was that the stone was at least beautiful. It would probably sell for a high price either in Echelon or back on Earth. A notification blinked on my character sheet, and I didn't have to summon any menus to know exactly what it was. Helvegen had found real gemstones, not garnet or colored quartz that would have nearly no value, and the citadel's information sheet had updated to reflect the new wealth.

"I think your brother has the best trade skill. We should send him to Echelon to sell these. Hell, he could hire an entire work crew for just one of them." I thought of all the possibilities the wealth was sure to bring us, but then I remembered it was impossible. Geirr couldn't just waltz into Echelon with a handful of rubies. Granted, no one would know he was from Undercroft Citadel, but his name would still appear in a different color. That conspicuous designation would raise eyebrows across the city. It wasn't worth the risk.

"I'm going to sleep for a while. Whatever you decide, I'm sure it will work," Hel said before entering her house with a yawn.

Sending Geirr right into the heart of the enemy might not work, but I still had one option left. Elyk was an unsavory kind of guy, and that meant he probably knew some sketchy characters that could potentially help us move the gemstones.

In my full armor, I had nowhere to put the rubies while I watched my team of underlings continue their work on the gatehouse. I would need to find or make a pouch for my sword belt at some time, but it could wait.

When the sun began to set, I was pleased with the progress that had been made on the gatehouse. I knew I should have pitched in and helped train my own muscles with the work crew, potentially adding experience points to my physical and craftsmanship categories, but watching from the guard tower had its merits as well. I constantly scanned the horizon for any incoming threats, and I felt like a proper overlord in charge of immense amounts of power. Perhaps distancing myself a little from the common workers and dungeon bosses would help cultivate an air of respect. At the Ministry of Health, I had only rarely seen my own superiors on the office floor. The days when the Public Health Secretary and his staff had walked among the plebeians had always been filled with terror. Everyone had worked harder, ties had been tied tighter, and our lunches were always taken at our desks instead of local pubs.

There was something to be said of a managerial style that stayed one step removed. I needed my underlings to be accustomed to my authority, to expect me to be on the tier above them looking down at all times. If I limited my casual interactions with the work teams to just the most necessary occasions, I would maintain an air of fear and awe.

Still, I wasn't sure I would need such an aura. Didn't I already command enough obedience? Helvegen was showing initiative, and that was a good thing. As to the others, I honestly didn't know. I *thought* I had a good grasp on how things were going among both my players and NPCs, but it could all evaporate in an instant.

I realized that I was still pacing back and forth across the small guard tower while everyone below was eating around the fire that marked the very first territory Undercroft Citadel had ever taken from Whitechapel. Overall, spirits seemed high despite the long day of manual labor everyone had just completed.

I went back down the ladder and sat next to Elyk, my heavy armor clanking with every step. "How is the gatehouse coming along?" I asked with a casual tone.

The harvester finished a chunk of meat before responding. "Should be finished tomorrow. I've raised my craftsmanship skill three points today since I've never used it before. Any word on some proper armor coming my way?"

The man's stolen armor would work well enough for now, though I was just as eager as he was to get him a custom set more like mine. "Hel brought in a shipment of iron and brass today. She found a mine close enough to use once we clear out the imps that have overrun it. I'm sure her brother can make something better eventually." I held out the rubies for the man to see. "In the meantime, I need to move some gemstones. I figured that if anyone knew where to move some gems, that person might be you."

Elyk eyed the rubies, and a smile started playing at the edges of his lips. "Aye, there's a fence I knew in Echelon who might be able to help."

"Think you could get a message to him? I don't want to send anyone into the city if we don't have to. It could be dangerous."

He nodded. "Give me some gold to grease a few palms. I'll arrange a meeting."

"You have a deal." I took back the rubies and stood to go search our gear pile for a nice leather pouch. "Leave in the morning. I'll get you some gold then. See if your fence can be here by noon. I'd very much like to meet him."

"Her," Elyk corrected. Without paying me much more attention, he returned to his dinner.

For the night patrols, I gave Xia, Geirr, and Kulgun shifts manning the guard tower, and the warlocks took turns marching with the mindless undead in an endless, repetitive circle.

Thankfully, no attack came from Echelon or the Pyreborn Legion overnight. Another day of safety—another day to prepare for the attack we all knew would be coming.

I saw Elyk off right after breakfast. He seemed eager to go practice a bit of skullduggery on the citadel's behalf, and I hoped he would find what we needed. Truth be told, I still didn't know exactly what I would trade the rubies for, if anything, and holding them until Geirr could place enchantments upon them for weapons and armor was still an option.

About an hour after Xia and the warlocks got to work

finishing the gatehouse, Geirr delivered an armor stand to my throne room. He was under the impression that I would eventually be staying full-time inside the necropolis itself, and I shared his vision. We just needed more corpses to fuel Xollmomath's magic. We needed more slaughter.

As work on the gatehouse continued to progress, I decided to go with Helvegen to scout the mine she had found. It was north of our settlement, more or less on the other side of Undercroft Citadel from Echelon, and there wasn't another town or village anywhere nearby that we would have to worry about. It essentially was just a hole dug into the ground with a very small amount of shattered smithing gear scattered around the outside. "Imps aren't very large or very difficult to kill," I said, peering into the darkness of the mineshaft's imposing entrance. "I wonder if Xollmomath would be able to use them or not."

Staring into the tunnel reminded me of the dungeon below the counting house in Echelon, and my heart immediately longed to have Ingrid at my side. I was thankful that Helvegen didn't share much in common with Ingrid or the constant battery of memories would have been too much for me to process. No matter what, going on a dungeon run with a single female companion would be a psychological challenge.

Helvegen's voice brought me back to the present. "Raising imps from the dead as zombie soldiers probably wouldn't be worth the effort," she said. "There's bound to be a leader, though. Whatever the boss is, its corpse will be a worthy sacrifice."

"Agreed. Let's scout through the first few tunnels if we can. Once we get our bearings, we'll know if we need to bring others or not. I'd rather commit as few resources as possible to clearing it out until we know the immediate threat from Echelon has passed." I drew Infernum and willed the steel to life, throwing a good amount of light into the mineshaft. Having a permanent torch whenever I needed it was perhaps more useful than even my lack of hunger. Thinking of my talents and the skills I had gotten from my armor made me realize how long it had been since I had levelled. Most players sank all of their time and effort into powering up one specific stat in order to gain the most talents in the least amount of time. I hadn't really focused on anything, and my progress had suffered because of it. Hopefully the dungeon would offer a good amount of experience points.

"Come on. If we move quickly, maybe we can exterminate all these vermin quick enough to make it back to Undercroft by nightfall," I said.

We started down the first tunnel at a pretty quick pace. I led the way since my legendary armor would protect me from almost anything an imp could throw at us, but we reached the end of the tunnel without needing it. Imps were naturally cavern dwellers preferring the dark and musty places under the earth to the light, so it made sense that there weren't any so close to the surface. We would need to descend deeper to find some action, and that's exactly what we did.

The first tunnel—a basic shaft about two hundred feet long and perhaps eight feet in diameter—opened up into a sharply declining path with iron tracks set into the ground for mining carts. One such empty cart rested at the top of the track.

"The ingots were outside," Hel said. "I'm surprised the cart isn't still full of raw ore. I'll bet we'll find more deeper in the mine, and my brother can probably get the forge up and running outside in no time."

I smiled at the thought. "That's perfect. Let's hope whoever used to run the mine was busy. Stumbling across a huge stockpile of ore just waiting to be taken would do wonders for the citadel."

We made our way slowly down the sloping tunnel following the rail tracks deeper into the mine complex. The dirt to the sides of the rails was loose and crumbling, and paying attention to our footing meant we had to move more slowly than I would have liked. After about a hundred feet of descent, we came to a split in the mine. Two new tunnels branched out on either side of the main cart rails. Noises came from one of them.

"Imps," Hel said.

"Perfect." I stuck my flaming sword into the tunnel's opening, but we couldn't see any of the little critters from where we were. Not too far ahead, the tunnel turned and blocked our view. "Stay a few steps back just in case we get jumped from the darkness. Let me take the hits. I want to test out all my armor."

Helvegen moved back a little while still remaining vigilant and ready to spring into action. Around the next corner, we finally got our first hint of the imps infesting the mine. I could smell them. Their stench hung in the air, and their squawking, incessant voices echoed from what I assumed to be a chamber deeper in the complex. It sounded like there were dozens of them, though I couldn't honestly tell based on sounds alone.

"What do you think? I'm not too worried about a couple imps. Just charge in swinging?" I asked.

The woman nodded. "We should be able to crush them quickly. I'm right behind you," she whispered.

I mentally counted down, preparing myself for the ensuing battle despite my overwhelming confidence, and then took off. We ran about twenty feet before blasting our way into the chamber. There were probably twenty or thirty imps happily bouncing around on their knobby, hairless feet.

The first imp casualty was rent in half by my flaming sword. I whirled to my left—two more imps were caught within Infernum's impressive reach, and they joined the rapidly growing ranks of the dead. The shrieks of the enraged imps filled the small cavern. Helvegen waited only a few seconds before joining the fray herself, adding more shouts and grunts to the already deafening cacophony.

Before long, I was covered in gore. My sword and armor were so outrageously good compared to the scrabbling imps that I didn't even need to activate a single talent. I felt like Elyk, turning side to side swinging my weapon in huge arcs and scattering enemies all around the room. They threw themselves against my armor, scraping with their claws and even biting down on the hardened steel plates, and I never felt anything other than victory.

The horde of imps was a relentless tide, but I stood among them as a god, and nothing they could do would slow my death march. When I reached the other side of the cavern, Helvegen and I were the only two living things left.

Thanks to one of the armor enchantments, I wasn't even particularly winded, either.

Your Physical skill has increased to 22!

"Ha, perfect. I levelled physical again. How'd you fare for experience?" I asked. Helvegen had been equally unscathed, though she had stayed mostly in my wake, doing a good amount of fighting while still leaving the bulk of the slaughter to me.

"Two points," she said with a blood-splattered smile. "I hit level nine."

"Excellent. Now let's figure out where the tunnel goes. There's got to be some loot the imps were protecting somewhere." I started scavenging through the nearest corpses, but I quickly realized that the imps offered no material gains. Perhaps a high-level druid or hunter would be able to make use of their remains. I, however, could not. "Maybe we should grab a few imp carcasses for our alchemist. Think he could use some of their organs?"

Helvegen shook her head. "Just leave them. If he wants a few dead imps, he can get them himself."

"Fair enough." Two smaller exits branched off from the imp chamber, and neither of them looked terribly promising. At the top of the small quarters, the smoke produced by Infernum serving as our torch was getting to be noticeable. It had nowhere to go, and I couldn't keep myself from breathing it in if I wanted to see.

Without any reason to choose one pathway over another, I selected the passage on the right and marked it with a pair of decapitated imp corpses. Getting lost in the mine shaft would be horrible. I wouldn't starve to death with my buff, but dehydration was still a thing in the game, and Lady Kalma hadn't given me any magical means by which to stave it off. I shuddered at the thought of wandering aimlessly in the dark and twisting mine tunnels, growing delirious from lack of water and sunlight.

Hopefully we would find the end soon and be able to get out.

The tunnel I chose led to another cavern, a larger one than the first, and we basically hit the jackpot in terms of supplies. There were mining picks, steam augers, helmets, lanterns, torches, and bins full of raw materials all neatly organized as though the miners who had used them were simply gone on a lunch break. "Here we go . . ." I walked over to one of the augers to see if it was still in working order. I didn't know much about them other than they were complex and somewhat rare, but nothing appeared broken.

"Once we capture this place and really make it our own, we'll be churning out ore every single day. Geirr will never have to melt down scraps again," Helvegen said with a bit of awe.

"Yeah. I just wish it was a little closer to the citadel. Still, we can send crews here every day to bring back ore. We'll be set." The auger had a coal cart and steam generator attached to it, and it even had a second blade sitting in a leather sheath not far away. Honestly, everything was starting to feel a little too good to be true. "What do you think happened to the miners? Where'd they go?" I wondered aloud.

Helvegen looked like she had never considered the prospect of the miners' return, and she was suddenly on edge. "Imps wouldn't have chased them out. They would have fought."

"Though imps would have eaten all of the bodies leaving us without any evidence of the miners at all," I added. The fiendish little critters were notorious for devouring corpses after large battles. They would show up like vultures to feast on the bodies until all the players finally logged back in and forced their own remains to dissolve. No one really controlled the imps, but they were always there. Thankfully, they weren't much of a challenge to kill. With my legendary armor, I'd be able to cleave through thousands of them.

"There's another passage over here," Helvegen called.

She had found a steel door leading deeper into the complex, and it had been left slightly ajar, saving us the hassle of searching for a key. On the other side, the tunnel narrowed and sloped deeper.

"Something is a little different about this passage," I said, running a hand along the roughly hewn walls.

Helvegen shared my assessment. "Looks fresh, but I don't think the miners were hauling ore out of here. The walls are too narrow for a cart or even some of the bigger equipment."

"Maybe they had just begun to chase a new vein when the imps attacked," I mused.

The painter shook her head. "You don't build a steel door with a lock on a tunnel you just began to explore."

"Good point." I moved a little deeper into the cavern with Infernum leading the way as our only light source. The tunnel turned sharply several times, and each new direction brought the walls a little closer together. Despite being nearly invincible in my armor, I was starting to feel rather claustrophobic.

"There . . . did you hear it?" Helvegen whispered behind me.

I stopped for a moment to focus my senses on the darkness in front of us. "Yeah . . . it sounds like . . . breathing, I think."

I hadn't fought many imps before, and none of the power gamers on the streams online had ever bothered to spend much time slaughtering the little critters, so I had no idea what to expect. If there was some sort of imp boss waiting for us at the end of the tunnel, we would be facing it without any prior knowledge to help us out. No matter our lack of experience, I was confident Infernum would get the job done in short order. Nothing would stand in my way.

It didn't take too much more to find the source of the low rumble, and our guess had been correct. The next chamber was small, barely large enough for the two of us to stand without bumping into each other, and it overlooked a slightly larger area housing a huge, sleeping imp. The creature's bulbous, pockmarked body was riddled with squirming, translucent eggs. Each one of the milky sacks contained a writhing imp waiting to be born.

"Looks like the bastards came from inside the mine and ambushed the miners. There might be a higher-level dungeon down here somewhere, some magical portal that leads to an even bigger boss with more loot. I bet the miners probably built that door back there once the first wave of imps came rushing through. But look, that's why they kept opening it up and coming back." I pointed with my flaming sword to the back of the chamber where a clear line of glittering gemstones was reflecting the light.

"A fortune . . ." Helvegen said quietly.

I knew exactly what we had to do. "If we can kill the . . . whatever it is, we can take it for ourselves. With that kind of wealth, we'll be able to grow the citadel tenfold. And once we're stronger we can come back to see if there's a real dungeon down here. You up for a little boss fight?"

Helvegen's smile told me all I needed to know.

"Perfect. I'll go straight in with all my talents and try to end it quickly. As soon as it wakes up, try to use a paint and make it see something else. I'm not sure what though, so you'll have to figure it out on your own. Ready?" I set my feet and got ready to summon my shadow pet and send it right into the imp matron's face. An all-out blitz felt like it would be effective since the colossal creature looked too large to be able to react quickly.

Helvegen nodded, and I took off at a dead sprint. About four steps before I reached the matron, she—a guess simply based on the presence of eggs—reared awake with a terrible groaning roar.

Infernum crashed down into the creature's huge face with a burst of sparks and smoke. Its roar transformed into a piteous squeal. Several of the imps incubating closest to its head burst from their eggs. The matron's heavy arms rose up from under its ponderous layers of fat like two massive, tubular tentacles. They crashed into my sides and knocked me back, but Infernum had done considerable work on the creature's face. A slab of flesh large enough to easily be lethal to any humanoid had been cleaved from the monster's head. Blood poured down its body and mixed with the sickly green amniotic fluid leaking from the egg sacks that had ruptured.

I pushed myself back into the fight and flung my shadow pet for the matron while swinging wildly for the handful of imps slashing at my armor. Helvegen shot a bolt of magic over my shoulder that wrapped itself around what was left of the matron's skull.

Three imps—born fully formed and ready to fight—died before they could do much against my armor, and then I was back in the boss's reach. I swung with both hands on Infernum's hilt and severed one of the thick tentacle arms from the beast's torso. A renewed shriek filled the room in response. It was loud enough to stagger me backward, and then the one remaining arm slammed into my chest.

Had I been wearing anything less than one of the strongest

armors in all of Wonder, I would have surely been rocketed into the cavern wall and reduced to a bloody smear on the stone. I had to imagine that exact fate had befallen the first group of miners who had tried to kill the matron, and a shudder ran down my spine.

. . . But I *was* wearing legendary armor, and the strike didn't move me more than a few inches. Hell, it didn't even hurt.

I swung again, and Infernum claimed the matron's final appendage. More and more imps broke free of their eggs, some of them only partially formed and completely incapable of surviving more than a few seconds on their own. I didn't pay them any attention. I plowed through the clamoring horde to the matron's chest and stabbed straight for her heart.

A torrent of blood and slimy, pale internal organs flooded out over my blade. Fire licked away at flesh, and the resulting smell was hideous. I ripped my sword free and stabbed again.

A tremendous shudder ran through the imp matron's body, and then it stopped moving.

Your Physical skill has increased to 23!

Your Renown skill has increased to 14!

You are now hated by Imps (wild beasts)!

I bellowed a deep, primal war cry over the corpse of the imp matron. "Fuck yes! We fucking *slaughtered* it!"

Helvegen was laughing behind me. Her own bloodlust was nearly as strong as mine, and we both let it consume us as we reveled in the flawless victory. I dropped my sword and wrapped her in a hug, my steel breastplate no doubt digging into her chest, but neither of us cared. We had destroyed a dungeon boss in the space of a few seconds. The fight hadn't even lasted long enough for my shadow pet to draw a second burst of energy from my body in order to sustain itself.

I felt unstoppable.

"We have the gems. We have the mine. It's *ours*," Helvegen said, her voice full of pride.

Before I really considered what I was doing, I pulled back a few inches and planted a quick kiss on the woman's forehead. It was something I would have done when celebrating with my wife, and instantly felt . . . Well, I didn't know.

Helvegen looked momentarily surprised, but then she kissed me back. Her long hair brushed against the sides of my face, recalling more memories of my wife's tender touch to my mind. I drank in the painter's scent and pushed the memories away, relishing the kiss and my adrenaline-fueled bloodlust at the same time.

For the first moment since Ingrid had died, I felt a small shred of genuine happiness.

CHAPTER 13

Helvegen and I used some ropes from the mine to drag one of the ore carts all the way back to Undercroft Citadel. We needed the supplies and raw materials for the home forge until we could set up an operation directly at the mine, and the extreme exertion caused both of us to gain another point in physical.

I reached twenty-four in the stat, and that meant I hit level twelve. *Finally.*

The point registered on my character sheet right about the time we finally made it back home, but there was too much to do to worry about which talent to pick. I dismissed the notification for the time being and got right back to work. Helvegen finished taking the ore to her brother, my warlock retinue was busy upgrading the defenses, and Elyk had returned from Echelon with his fence.

Always so much damn work to be done, never enough time to do it all. At least the Pyreborn Legion hasn't shown up yet . . .

My first order of business was seeing to the fence. If we could move the rubies and start bringing in some serious supplies, we'd be much better prepared for our inevitable battle against the guild I had pissed off. If the first sale went well, we'd certainly have more gemstones to move.

Elyk came up and introduced the fence before I had much of a chance to even relax my tired muscles. Everyone had finished dinner, and it was starting to get late. "Meet Toskr. If there's anything you aren't supposed to be able to buy, she's the one who can sell it to you."

The woman honestly didn't look the part of a thieving fence. She wore plain clothes, just a simple linen tunic with a pair of leather bracers, and didn't carry any visible weapons. Her class identified her as a merchant, which I figured made sense, but travelling without protection or the ability to defend herself was too out of place to ignore. Then again, perhaps Elyk was all the protection she needed. The harvester's mission was to bring the fence in Undercroft Citadel, and that relied on her remaining safe.

"You came here alone?" I asked.

The woman smiled and subtly gave me a nod. "I am but a simple tradeswoman. I do not travel with a retinue of soldiers, if that's what you're asking."

"I see. And I trust Elyk has told you what we intend to sell?"

Again, she tipped her head. "Though the market for luxury goods has taken a sharp decline since the corruption of the servers, there are still those wealthy enough to be buying pretty things to wear about their necks and fingers."

"Good. We need just about everything, but tools, supplies, and workers are a top priority. If we produced a steady stream of gemstones for you, would you be able to move them all and bring back what we need?" I liked the woman's rather straightforward approach despite being a little put off by her civilian appearance. Maybe I was being swindled out of a trio of small rubies. But when I thought about the untold riches waiting to be mined in the coming weeks, I didn't really care. Trusting the fence with a small fraction of our wealth was a risk I was willing to take.

"I assume you want NPC workers, not players, yes?" Toskr inquired. She brushed a strand of her strawberry blonde hair back behind her ear.

"Exactly. Elyk will see you safely back to Echelon in the morning if you don't mind staying here. Get what you can for the rubies, and send me strong bodies to work a mine, tools as well if you can." More tired than I had previously realized, I left the harvester to figure out the specifics of the trade agreement on his own.

I still needed to see Geirr and talk about setting up the formal mining operations, but my bed sounded nicer than making more plans. Dragging the heavy cart had taken its toll on my back, my arms, and my shoulders.

I pushed open the door to my small house next to the necropolis and started removing my heavy steel armor, thankful for the wooden rack I had to keep it all up off the floor and out of my way. In such tight quarters, there really wasn't any room to have more than my sword lying on the floorboards next to my thin mattress.

Finally, I had a minute to call up my character sheet and read through my twelfth level options:

Imperial Strength (physical): The deathbringer summons the powerful blessings of Lady Kalma for a short time. While the spell lasts, the user's Physical skill gains a +10 bonus. Active, consumes moderate energy.

Peer Through Depths (cunning): Lady Kalma sees all, and some of her unnatural sight is granted to the deathbringer. The user can see through magically hidden veils and certain auras designed to trick or confuse. Passive.

Visage of the Dark One (influence): Lady Kalma's influence is so strong that certain aspects of her terrifying countenance may be called upon to dominate, coerce, or otherwise influence any whose Cunning is less than the user's Influence. Higher levels of Renown or Infamy also increase the strength of the effect. Active, consumes minor energy.

There were aspects of each available talent that I knew I liked. If I were a normal player trying to complete quests, run through dungeons, and generally play the game, I would have immediately selected either Imperial Strength or Peer Through Depths. The strength buff would be super useful when it came to big fights and boss battles. With Infernum in my hands and a set of legendary armor, it just wasn't worth spending the talent point.

Peer Through Depths struck me in almost the same way. For an adventurer running through quests with only a small group, the ability to find hidden treasure would be a huge boon. For me, I would not likely be personally leading too many more raids. I would soon have underlings for that kind of work. That left Visage of the Dark One as the most logical choice. I had to admit, being a dungeon ruler meant I needed a lot more influence-based skills than I would have liked otherwise. I couldn't simply rely on my own skills or equipment to solve every problem. Being able to lead and direct was far more important, and it would only grow in usefulness the larger Undercroft Citadel became.

I focused my vision on the talent and unlocked it, adding the ability to my list. I thought of activating it once just to see exactly what it would mean, but I was too tired. All I wanted was sleep.

Finally out of pressing issues to address, I laid down on my thin mattress and shut my eyes. Sadly, *The Black One's Sustenance* only took away my need to eat, not my need to rest. With all the weariness weighing heavily on my body, it didn't take long to fall asleep.

A knock on my door roused me from my sleep a little before dawn. A few thin rays of light made their way through the uneven paneling, but it wasn't exactly enough for me to see much. "Hello?" I called out as I reached out for Infernum resting only a foot or so from my pillow.

"Just me, Hel . . . can we talk?"

I rubbed some of the sleep from my eyes and stretched a bit, moving my arms in wide circles to get some of the blood to return to my fingers. The morning was cold, and the air that found its way under my blanket raised gooseflesh on my legs. "Yeah, just a second," I called back.

I set Infernum on the small table that dominated the majority of the space in my house and pulled free the locking bar on the door. Helvegen was standing there with her arms wrapped around her sides against the wind. "Can I come in?" she asked.

"Uh, yeah, I guess. Not a lot of room." I stood to the side to let her enter, and when her hair brushed against my bare chest, I realized I was still shirtless from sleep. "Sorry, let me grab a shirt. Didn't expect any—"

She turned and placed a hand on my shoulder. "No, don't worry about it. I mean . . . if you don't want to."

"Um . . . alright. What's up?"

Helvegen was biting her lower lip and avoiding eye contact, her long hair covering her face. I noticed as well that she wasn't wearing any weapons or even boots, making me think she had just awoken as well. For whatever reason, there wasn't any urgency in her demeanor despite the awkward hour of the morning.

"I just . . . I want you to know that I'm loyal to you and to Undercroft Citadel. I know you don't trust anyone, but you can trust me." Her hand was still on my chest, and she didn't look up from the floor, leaving us standing in an uncomfortable position that I didn't really know how to break.

"Yeah, I get that, Hel," I said quietly. "I'm not going to kick you out if that's why you're worried. I need you to help me. We're in it together. Ok?"

She gave me an almost imperceptible nod.

"Sit down and tell me what's on your mind. If there's something bothering you, I don't mind listening." I guided her down to my mattress so that we could sit side by side. There wasn't really enough room, and the mattress itself was only a few inches off the ground, so we ended up sitting with our backs to the cold wood of the wall and our legs stretched out all the way to my table.

"I told you my past wasn't that great . . . Maybe you should hear the rest of it," she said.

My mind swam with the possibilities of what the woman was about to tell me. We were living inside a necropolis guarded by an ancient necromancer and surrounded by corpses that would explode on our enemies—there wasn't much left that would faze me.

"I'm a murderer," I blurted out before really thinking about my words. But it was true. I *was* a murderer. *I do it all for Ingrid. Everything is for her. For vengeance.*

Helvegen took in a deep breath and closed her eyes. "I've been in the game since the second month it went online. I laid low for over a year, which is why I'm still such a low level. But I've never left."

I had heard stories on the forums of people who had decided to 'live' in the game. For some, the prospect of never returning to the real world was too intoxicating to turn down. Most of the people who lived in the game did so for a reason, and that reason was never anything good.

"Was someone looking for you on the outside?" I asked. I didn't want to pry too deeply into her past, but I also felt like she was waiting for me to prompt her with a question before continuing.

The woman held back a sob. "A couple years before Wonder, when the food started running out all over Europe, my brother and I joined the looters. We stole from stores until that ran out, and then we had nothing."

"Everyone remembers the food riots," I said softly. The riots that had dominated Europe and South America for the few years before Wonder came online were still fresh in everyone's mind. I had my government job back then at the Ministry of Health, so my family had at least never gone hungry, but a lot of others had.

"During one of the riots, a group of us got worked up following some asshole who turned out to be an anarchist. We left the downtown shopping districts and stole a bus. The guy we were following drove us from Uppsala out to the coast. Ben . . . I was in the group that destroyed the Forsmark Nuclear Station. I was there. I helped." She started crying as she finished her story, and I knew exactly why.

If the opening of Wonder was the most significant event of the 2060s, the Forsmark Nuclear Disaster was certainly the most significant event of the 2050s. Tens of thousands of people had died from the resulting radiation event, and that number was only as low as it was due to the rapid evacuation the European Union had managed to pull off. Stockholm had been quarantined and placed within the exclusion zone less than a week after the attack.

"They never caught the guy responsible for it all," I said more to myself than Hel, remembering the twenty-four-hour news coverage that had blasted the event into every home and apartment across the world.

"I don't even remember his name. He fell into one of the cooling towers, so it doesn't even matter. He's dead now. But I ran. I fled to Norway and hid out there with another group of activists. Once the portal in Oslo opened, I stole enough money to buy a pass and bribed the registration agent to use a false name. I came through at Olympia City and got to Echelon as soon as I could. They sent agents into the game looking for anyone related to the attack even after all those years had passed, but they never found me."

"Holy shit . . ." I whispered. *I was living with a terrorist.*

"When you tell me that you're a murderer, it doesn't really mean anything, you know? Whatever you've done, I'm worse. A lot worse." She couldn't keep herself from crying in earnest, and her head fell against my bare shoulder.

I didn't know what to say. How could I possibly comfort someone with that much weighing on their conscience? I hadn't really kept up with much of what had happened in Europe after the disaster—my wife's cancer had taken top priority in my mind—but I knew that Sweden had been rendered uninhabitable. Denmark had been quarantined as well, though after the food shortages, no one really had any reason to be there in the first place. From what I remembered, the famine had killed somewhere around thirty thousand, and it was still in full force when Wonder had come online. The death toll from the radiation had at least matched that of the famine.

The two of us sat on my mattress for a long time. She cried against my shoulder, and I held her. There was nothing else I could do. I didn't have the words in my body that it would take to comfort her.

When the sun was high in the sky and I could hear the other members of the citadel awake and busy outside, I finally worked up the courage to stand.

"Come on, let's go to work," I said, pulling Helvegen up from my mattress. "Try to take your mind off of it all. Just focus on improving the citadel, and you'll forget all about it."

She stood, but she shook her head. "I'll never forget about it," she said quietly.

"I know."

Undercroft Citadel was alive with movement when I finally emerged from my house and let the sunlight start warming up my naked torso. I decided against putting on a shirt for the morning, preferring to enjoy the open air as much as possible after spending a few hours awake in my cramped, stuffy house.

I was happy to see that even without my personal direction, everyone seemed to know what they needed to do. A group of warlocks was busy finishing the final gatehouse improvements. Xia and Xollmomath were surveying the wall defenses and presumably making upgrades to various aspects of it as they went. Elyk and the fence were both gone, and that was to be expected. Assuming they returned from Echelon sometime in the afternoon, everything was in order.

I started my day with a visit to the workshop, and I was happy to see that Geirr and Kulgun had nearly finished creating a dedicated space for the alchemist to work. Things were progressing nicely, and with the addition of the materials we were sure to pull out of the mine, we would be manufacturing advanced gear before long.

"How are things going?" I asked the busy pair.

Geirr regarded me with a smile. "Bring me more materials like those ingots, and I'll have everyone outfitted with decent weapons by the end of the week."

"Speaking of which, Helvegen found a mine. We checked it out yesterday. Some imps had chased out the former miners, but we killed their queen and ran them out. Think you could start hauling ore out of there again?" I explained.

"I'm not a miner," the burly engineer said. "Hell, I'm not even a smith. I'm just the best one to run the forge right now, not the best one you're going to find by any means. What's that village you convinced to bring us food?"

The seeds of a plan were starting to form in my mind. I knew what Geirr was after, and I liked the sound of it. "I don't remember their name, but you're right. They're bound to have plenty of people we could . . . *convince*. How many would you need to make a mining crew?"

"We shouldn't need more than ten strong backs to hit rocks and load carts. Until we get a proper smith, I won't be able to use it all that quickly anyway." The engineer beamed at the prospect of so thoroughly escalating the citadel's production capabilities.

"Perfect. That's the plan, then. We'll get ten of them to help us with the mine, and I can set the charnel golem to protect the shipments coming back to the workshop. It should work just fine. How long until you use the ingots your sister already brought back?" It looked like the first batch of materials hadn't yet been touched on account of time being spent building the alchemist's workbench, so I hoped we had enough to last at least a few more days.

Geirr looked at the small stack of ingots with a bit of admiration in his smile. "That'll last a week, but I plan on running the forge hard. Your harvester needs better armor and a different weapon. I mean to see him properly outfitted."

"That's what I like to hear. Once our business with the Pyreborn Legion is finished or at least put on hold, I'll see about getting your mining crew." I left the workshop with a good deal of confidence that we were going to survive. I knew an attack from Echelon would be coming sooner rather than later, but we would be ready to meet it. We would survive the initial quest seekers and dungeon raiders, and then all the players in Echelon would hesitate to come against us again.

We just needed to get past that first real battle.

CHAPTER 14

A s it turned out, our first real battle came that very night.

I had spent the day with the conjuror warlock and a handful of zombies trying to get a good handle on their combat capabilities. Elyk returned right around dusk, and he was covered in sweat.

"Ben! Ben!" he yelled, sprinting up to the newly completed gatehouse with all the speed his legs could muster. "They're coming!"

I ordered the gates opened, and the harvester practically fell through them.

"Who's coming? What's happening? Tell me!" I yelled at him, but he was doubled over and too out of breath to answer right away. As he was busy sucking air into his lungs, I turned to Xia and Xollmomath not far behind me. "Send out word! Get everyone back to the citadel to defend. Everyone! To arms!"

Undercroft Citadel exploded into action. The warlocks scrambled to get their meager allotment of gear and take up their predetermined positions along the wall. The charnel golem came romping through the center of the encampment on five thick, thundering bone legs, nearly smashing into several of the interior buildings as it went.

Elyk took a long drink from a waterskin, then finally had enough composure to tell me what was going on. "After I helped figure out what we'd get for the rubies, I snuck up on a meeting in Echelon," he said. "That guild you pissed off, the fire guys in red armor with their stupid tabards, they're coming tonight. They managed to get a few more players to join their cause, but I couldn't see how many. Once I heard they were planning an attack, I left as fast as I could."

"You did well." Hands on my hips, I turned back to the interior of the compound to take stock of our complete defensive picture. What we had made was certainly impressive, but it wasn't complete. Not yet. "Did you see how many guild members there were?"

"Twenty-five, maybe thirty. Most of them are knights and paladins, really heavily armored bastards. You know the type."

"Shit." I thought of the trap we had laid for Kulgun and his group out on the road, but there wasn't enough time to pull it off if the guild would be assaulting our walls soon. We needed something else. "Get Geirr. Bring him to me on top of the gatehouse, then get ready to fight."

Elyk nodded and took off in the direction of the workshop.

I climbed the steps leading to the top of the small gatehouse. There was enough room on the platform for perhaps four archers, but that was four more than we had. As far as I knew, we didn't even have a bow and arrow anywhere in the entire settlement.

"Some damned crossbows would be nice. Another thing to add to the list . . ."

Geirr came scrambling up the steps behind me before I had time to finish the thought. "An attack?" he gasped, still wearing a leather apron and holding a hammer at his side.

"Echelon has come to collect their quest rewards. Elyk says they'll be here soon. I need an engineer. Are you with us?" I looked him in the eyes as I spoke, and I saw nothing but cold determination staring back at me.

"I'm with you. What needs to be done and how much time is there to do it?" He was all business despite having already given an entire day at the forge. I knew he was tired, and I loved his tenacity.

I turned him toward the field and road in front of our gatehouse. "I don't know what we need, but we need it now. You have an hour, maybe a little more if we're lucky, and whatever you come up with needs to kill twenty or more armored knights. Can you do it?"

Geirr extended a hand, and I eagerly shook it. "I'll do what I can," he said solemnly.

The two of us descended back down the staircase where we split. I went to assemble the undead and left Geirr to his own expertise, hoping desperately that the man could cobble together a trap to save us all. Deep down, I knew it was a long shot, but it was also our *only* shot.

I ordered the undead soldiers to my side and began walking them around the exterior of the wall. "We're expecting an attack from Echelon. There's no guarantee it comes at our front door where we're best suited to defend." I pointed to various sections of the wall between suspended corpses, and the mindless fighters took up stations. "If anyone comes to attack, run to the gatehouse."

Although the undead did not reply with any noise or words or other kind of signaling to tell me they understood their directives, I could *feel* their obedience to me as their dungeon boss. They understood my commands, and they would follow without hesitation, even to their deaths. *Very likely to their deaths*, I knew. But they were undead, expendable soldiers meant to be fodder and nothing else.

And when the battle concludes, if any of us are still alive, I'll have a whole new army at my command . . .

Once I had a ring of zombies stationed around the walls, all I could really do was wait and watch Geirr work. I felt bad not stepping in to help with my own two hands, but my time would come later. I stood on the top of the gatehouse, and he worked down below with two warlocks, Xia, and his sister at some contraption involving mildly enchanted runes and a few bins full of scrap he had hauled into small depressions on either side of the road.

He finished his trap construction before we had any sign from the guild, and then the waiting grew even more tense. Four of us sat on the top level of the gatehouse with our eyes glued to the horizon. On the complete opposite side of the settlement, Xollmomath and the charnel golem were waiting as well.

"First thing tomorrow, we need a warning bell up on the top of the necropolis," I told Geirr. "Using runners isn't efficient."

"Heh, we'll need more iron for a project like that," he answered.

Sitting cross-legged on my left, Elyk was woefully under-prepared. All he had in the way of armor was a bit of scavenged leather and plate that we had stolen from Riverside, and the sword hanging from his belt wasn't that great either. Perhaps if we survived the night, we would be able to scavenge enough supplies to make him into a proper fighter. Cobbling together pieces of armor after fights would only take us so far.

Despite the adrenaline in my veins and the quiet fear hanging palpably in the air, I felt myself starting to doze off a few hours after midnight.

Then we saw a rider carrying a red banner crest the horizon directly in front of the gatehouse.

System Notification: Undercroft Citadel is under attack by the forces of Echelon and the Pyreborn Legion!

Everyone stood. Judging by the notification, the first rider was a mere prelude to the rest of the guild appearing.

"Here we go. Get ready." I turned to Elyk. "Get Xollmo-math and the golem. Bring them here. Get the zombies as well, or at least bring them as close to the gatehouse as you can without it being too obvious. We don't want to tip our hand. Just leave one on the other side in case they try to attack from multiple fronts." In my mind, I knew a two-pronged attack would very likely be our death. Our only hope in that circumstance would come from the simple fact that the citadel was small. We could move from side to side inside the walls faster than anyone could do the same on the outside.

I descended the steps and walked out of the gate, signaling the warlocks to keep the entrance open behind me in case I needed to make a hasty retreat back behind cover. I held my helmet against the bottom of my breastplate, and Infernum was still sheathed at my side. As the rider kept approaching, I decided that being fully armored was the better choice, and I secured the helmet around my head and waited.

The player carrying the red banner stopped about thirty feet away. His name was Gordon, and the identifier above his head labelled him as a level twenty-two knight. The armor he wore was steel painted red, with a phoenix on the center of the breastplate that glittered in the light of the torch he was carrying.

My own citadel didn't offer much light behind me, only a handful of torches, and I had to wonder how well the undead could see in such darkness. If it came to fight, I had to assume my side would have the disadvantage, but I didn't actually know. Maybe undead had perfect dark vision. Heh, maybe they were night blind.

"You are the one in charge, are you not?" Gordon asked from horseback, shouting across the small expanse of no man's land.

I took a single step forward. "I am," I called back. "You're from the Pyreborn Legion?"

The man indicated the fluttering red banner waving over his shoulder with a nod. "Will you talk?"

I pretended to mull over the question as I rubbed my chin beneath my stolen helmet. "Alright. Bring your leaders here. I'll talk in front of my people."

Gordon stared at me for a few moments before angling his horse back to the other riders still waiting behind him. About half of those who had come against us were carrying torches which made them a little easier to count.

Twenty-eight. And every single one of them had a horse. I didn't know how high a horse could jump, and my confidence in our wooden wall was quickly waning. Perhaps there were even more farther behind or hiding in the darkness that I could not see. The possibilities were endless, and they all led to my demise.

While the Pyreborn Legion was discussing things among themselves, I looked quickly back to Geirr at the top of the gatehouse. "Get ready," I told him.

Six riders approached the area where Gordon had just been, crimson banners flapping behind their gleaming armor and torches. I moved back a little closer to the gatehouse in order to draw them in nearer to the traps. The darkness concealed everything Geirr had hastily put together, and I was confident that the enchanted runes on either side of the road could not been seen.

All six riders dropped from their saddles and approached, their gauntleted hands resting on the pommels of their weapons. The lowest level among them was twenty-four, far higher than anyone at Undercroft Citadel outside of Xia and Xollmomath.

"We just want to talk. No need to kill each other," one of the guild leaders said.

I drew Infernum and kept it low at my side. "I can only assume you're here for your leader's sword and armor."

"We'd like to negotiate a return of the artifacts," the man said. He looked around at his close companions with confidence in his posture. "I do not know how many you have under your command, but clearly you can see that you are in a poor position. Do not throw away all the lives you have cobbled together. If it comes to it, we'll kill every last one of you. Do not be confused about the stakes. Everything is on the line, and you have everything to lose."

By god, he was right. We risked every last drop of blood we had accumulated, and I didn't doubt that the guild was more than prepared to cut us down. Even worse, they were all outfitted with gear that made ours look pathetic.

"Alright, let's negotiate. What's your offer?" I answered.

The man didn't hesitate to give me his demands. "The guild understands how dangerous these times are for everyone, and we don't want more bloodshed. Give us back the armor and the sword, and we'll swear to leave you alone until the devs tell us the respawn function is back online. Once things are back to normal, the truce expires. Do we have terms?"

"And a truce with you means nothing outside of your guild," I replied somewhat curtly.

"Your issues with Echelon are not the same as those with us. If anyone wants to come pick the experience points off your bones, that's for you to figure out. We're just here for the artifacts. Do we have terms?" The man took another small step forward, and he was perfectly within the range of the trap.

I lifted my sword up to shoulder height. "No, we do not have terms. You ask too much."

I willed the blade to life and swung it downward like a starter girl at a drag race, wordlessly telling Geirr to spring his trap.

Four volatile runes, each holding blasts of Xia's magic

within their stone faces, erupted underneath piles of metal scrap and jagged wooden debris. At the same time, I charged forward and unleashed a shadow monster from my body, swinging Infernum hard for the nearest guild member.

Of the six who had come to negotiate, three of them were badly injured by the shrapnel blast. They writhed on the ground, some activating talents to start healing their wounds, and magic flew down upon their backs from the warlocks at the gate. The other three who were not directly caught in the blast were not unscathed either, and general chaos erupted among them as they all reached for weapons, began quaffing potions, and started activating skills.

In the space of a few heartbeats, the six leaders of the Pyreborn Legion were battered and falling back. Infernum cleaved through one man's head, and I kept up my momentum on the second. When the blade came down at the scrambling guild leader, a flare of magic pushed it harmlessly away into the dirt. I grabbed his breastplate and slammed him down to his knees.

A Feast of Spores wafted out of my mouth and into his face. Though his magical barrier had prevented Infernum from reaching his flesh, it did nothing to stop the toxic spores flooding into his body through his eyes, nose, and mouth.

I threw him to the ground and ran to the next guild leader. That one, clad in heavy steel painted red with the guild's imagery, had no such protections. Infernum didn't even slow as it shattered the man's sword and entered his chest. He screamed, and the horses the men had ridden began to flee from the chaos and noise of the battle.

On my left, two of the guild leaders had gotten their wits about them enough to stage attacks of their own. They were skilled in their classes, and their equipment was certainly above the average and beyond anything I had fought against previously.

I didn't have time to move my own weapon into place to block. As soon as the two men struck me, I knew it didn't matter. None of it mattered. I was a steel-clad juggernaut with a flaming sword, and they were practically insects when compared to my power. Their weapons clanged off my spaulders and breastplates—if I hadn't heard or seen their strikes, I would not have felt enough to know I had been attacked.

When I turned with my fiery sword poised to cleave them in half, I could see the fear in both men's eyes. They died with similar expressions on their faces a few seconds later.

My shadow pet pulled a second pang of energy from my body, and I turned to see if it was even still in the fight. The knight it had been fighting was dead among his brethren. I dismissed the pet and started to run back toward the gatehouse. The rest of the guild members were coming on strong, and they barely had any ground to cover before trampling me beneath their hooves, despite my legendary armor.

Notifications flew past my vision with experience points and increases to attributes from the higher-level characters I was slaughtering, but I didn't have time to pay any attention to them. I could figure out all that later.

I reached the open gate and threw myself inside as quickly as I could. About twenty armored knights were hot on my heels, and two of them—unable to stop on account of their speed—crashed into the wooden doors, horses and all. I was shocked when the doors held. They splintered inward, but they held. A slight glimmer of hope.

Two of the corpses attached to the outside of the wall exploded, and a rain of gore and magical poison showered down on the flanks of the attackers. Knights were leaping from their mounts to come at the gate with swords, axes, and active talents bolstering their arms.

Above the splintering gates, Xollmomath was beginning to cast. At the same time, the charnel golem shifted its bones over the left side of the wall to join the fray with huge, swinging tentacles. Helvegen added her own magic, and it was impossible to tell what was having any effect and what was being negated by counter magic from the paladins.

After a few moments, all I could tell was that we were winning.

The gate was certainly going to come down, but every second that passed brought more death with it. If I were leading the attack, I would have called for a retreat already—but the knights continued to attack. They had no leader to tell them to run.

They would all die at our gates, and they would die soon.

On the creaking, groaning gatehouse, Xollmomath issued a terrifying roar into the night sky. Magic flashed up from the earth, brilliant bursts of light followed by a cascade of suffocating darkness like the hands of a primordial titan reclaiming unworthy souls back to hell.

The knights threw everything they had at the magical onslaught. Their best efforts were not enough. Xollmomath's grasping tendrils wrenched the guild members down into the earth, and their screams filled the night air. When the magic subsided, only a small number of the men had not been crushed. Three of them wobbled about, feebly trying to drag themselves away on broken legs. A fourth knight appeared relatively uninjured, though a blast from Xia that overwhelmed whatever magical protections had been cast on him soon rendered the man no better than his crying, whimpering comrades.

As a final exclamation point on what had so quickly turned into a thorough rout, the charnel golem reared back on three spindly, bone legs and then came crashing down on top of the four crippled knights. Their cries came to an abrupt halt leaving only the clicking, rattling noises of the charnel golem's ever-shifting movements in their place.

After a few moments of quiet, the warlock NPCs began a rousing victory cheer that quickly spread among everyone. Well, everyone except for the mindless undead soldiers, of course. The zombies just stood in their places, still waiting for a command from me.

"Alright, alright, everyone calm down!" I called out over my troops after they'd had a few moments of well-deserved revelry. "We don't know if anyone else is coming. We aren't finished just yet."

"Bring me their bodies! More fuel for the cause!" Xoll-momath yelled with glee from the top of the gatehouse. He laughed and laughed, and soon his excitement was bleeding over into the others once more.

I was glad that I didn't have to try and gather everyone back under my control again, and the warlocks started dragging the corpses inside the wall for Xollmomath to use.

Using the corpses . . .

I watched as the ancient necromancer reanimated the bodies one by one, and a shiver went down my spine. We were slaughtering people—real, human people—and adding their hollow corpses to our army like shoveling coal into a furnace.

I sighed and continued to watch the bloody display unfold. Each corpse dragged before the mighty necromancer reminded me of Ingrid's body lying still and lifeless on the street in the center of Echelon. The more I saw her in my mind, the less I cared about those we had killed.

When there were only five bodies left, I called up to Xollmomath to halt our engine of death. "That's enough undead for now. I'd like to use some of these . . . some of the dead for myself. Well, take two of them to replace the corpse bombs we lost on the wall, but save three for me."

I waved to Elyk to come join me as the warlocks set about crafting a new pair of explosives for our defense system. "Want another mission back to Echelon?" I asked.

The violent grin on the harvester's face spoke volumes. "Just tell me where to go, Boss."

"I knew you'd be the right one for the job." I drew my sword and handed it to him hilt first. "These last three. I want you to take their heads to Echelon. We have some paper in the supply pile, and I want to write up a few short things for everyone living there. We'll stuff the notes in their mouths, then I want you to deliver a message. A really fucking clear message."

Elyk's violent smile didn't waver. Honestly, the guy kind of terrified me. What the NPCs were doing was in their programing—it was unavoidable—and Helvegen's motivations were largely rooted in self-preservation. What I was doing made sense to me personally, but Elyk was altogether different. I got the distinct impression that he simply enjoyed murder. He enjoyed it a lot.

In other words, I knew I could trust him. He had found a home among true evil, and he wouldn't risk losing it. He was smart enough to understand that bastions of evil weren't easily discovered or lightly joined.

Before I thought about it any further, the distinct sound of a head being separated from a neck brought me back to the present. I let Elyk and Infernum continue to work and went back to the supplies at the original three houses that had become Undercroft Citadel. I grabbed a few scraps of old parchment and found a quill with just enough ink to get down a few words.

The notes I wrote were simple. I needed to convey one basic thing to the people of Echelon: Undercroft Citadel was not a low-level dungeon that could be overrun by a group of adventurers, even skilled ones. On each of the three scraps of parchment, I wrote the words, "The Pyreborn Legion. Fucking pathetic." I signed each one as Ben Hales, Commander of Undercroft Citadel.

I knew what fear had done to the real world after Helvegen

and the other terrorists had radioactively contaminated half of Scandinavia. Terrorism was a viable method of control. I wasn't going to blow up a building or slaughter a bunch of civilians, but that was the level of fear I needed to create. Letting everyone in Echelon know my name and just how ruthless I was willing to be was the only method I had at my disposal to create the atmosphere I needed in order to be left alone. I knew there was a chance that I was provoking a war—that Echelon would see the heads and rally an entire army—but it was a chance I had to be willing to take. With true death now gripping everyone and making them all cling to their capitals for safety, an all-out war was unlikely. At least for now.

I finished my messages and took them to Elyk who was already eagerly preparing to depart. "Stuff the notes in their mouths and leave the heads somewhere effective. I'll let you figure out the details. Be back soon."

The man nodded and smiled, the wickedness in his countenance enough to make me at least slightly glad that he was going to spend some time away from the citadel. The man was loyal, but he was also insane. I wasn't sure how safe it was to have someone like him in our midst. I felt like a shepherd inviting a wolf into the pen, though none of us were exactly sheep. We were cold-blooded killers just like Elyk.

When the harvester had left to carry out his grim task, we turned to looting the battlefield and dragged all of the new gear behind the walls. Geirr and Kulgun took some of the pieces that needed repair back to their workshop while the rest was parted out among the soldiers. Xia found a few decent magical pieces of equipment among the dead as well, and she was busy analyzing them with Xollmomath to see what could be used and what was simply fit to be amalgamated into our defenses.

In the end, the haul was significant. We had a few complete

sets of well-made armor and more than a handful of weapons. I kept the best pieces aside for Elyk, eager to make him into a true harvester in accordance with Xollmomath's expectations. The general air of excited revelry continued as we went through the gear and started some minor repairs on the walls. We had passed our first big challenge, and everyone was rightfully happy about it.

Actually, we hadn't just *passed* our first challenge—we had dominated it. All we had lost were a few traps and some mindless undead, everything easily replaced without consuming many resources.

Congratulations! You have successfully defended Undercroft Citadel! New quests and pathways are now available.

The system notification brought a smile to my face. The raid was officially over, and the game was planning on giving me more rewards for my efforts. We would likely discover the new quest chains gradually as we continued to expand.

As nice as the game's rewards were certain to be, I needed a way to reward my followers as well. I wanted to keep the morale as high I could, especially with tomorrow's grim task involving the enslavement of the neighboring village to work our mines, but I didn't know what to do. We didn't have enough food for a feast, and that was the only idea that crossed my mind. I had skipped most of the retirement parties back at the Ministry of Health.

"Hey, Xia," I called to the warlock.

She handed a small ring back to Xollmomath and came over. "Yes, my Lord?"

"We need a party. We need to celebrate our victory. Any ideas?" I asked.

The warlock mulled over my question for a few moments. "In the old days, the ancient clans would offer sacrifices to Lady Kalma. Burnt offerings please her greatly. Perhaps you could talk to Xollmomath and see if he would be willing to put on a Dark Revelry. I have read about them in scrolls, but I have never seen one."

That sounded interesting. Whatever the hell a Dark Revelry turned out to be, I figured it had to beat burnt offerings left to a digital god. I went back up to the top of the gatehouse to watch Xollmomath identifying magical items for a bit and ask him how we put on a Dark Revelry.

"We shall have need of several virgins," was his initial response . . . which was rather ominous, to say the least.

"More sacrifices and burnt offerings?" I asked. "I was really hoping for something that wouldn't require us to go out and capture people. Kind of wanted to stay in for the rest of the night, you know?"

The necromancer's expression told me I had the wrong idea. "You are a strange one, Ben Hales. The Dark Revelry celebrates the pleasures of the flesh. No sacrifices are necessary."

Oh. Well that was different. Helvegen was close enough to be in earshot, and her face turned red with embarrassment in the flickering torchlight.

"Alright, I'll . . . let you know if we decide to go in that direction." Scratching my head for some other ideas, I left the gatehouse in the direction of my citadel. If we had some beer or ale, we would at least be able to get drunk for a night, and that would be good enough. I had never really been much of a drinker back on Earth, but after everything that had happened, a nice bourbon sounded excellent.

What my gargoyle-covered necropolis lacked in a liquor cabinet it sure made up for in grandeur. The fight with the Pyreborn Legion had apparently been enough to earn another upgrade to my keep. It used to be a single-story structure with a vaulted ceiling and a single room dominated by my throne, and that had dramatically changed. A second floor had risen up beneath the first, pushing my throne room about fifteen feet into the air, and a stone staircase flanked by marble statues depicting chained, twisted, naked humans in all sorts of agonizing poses. Beneath the stairs and off a little way to the right was a double door probably twice my height. I hesitantly tested the handle—unsure about what might lurk behind the ornately carved door—and found it unlocked.

The inside of the lower level turned out to be my personal chambers. The first room served as a kind of foyer with three chairs and a small table, all of which were carved from a dark wood that gleamed like ebony. Through an archway about four feet above my head was my bedroom. A huge black wardrobe stood against one wall opposite a floor-to-ceiling mirror gilded around the edges with a swirling pattern of gold leaf. The whole room was illuminated by six purple crystals hanging from the ceiling on thin chains. Though the crystals themselves were certainly a deep lavender color, the light they gave off was soft and yellow, almost reminding me of the light from my apartment.

A small collection of the crystals was piled up against the wall opposite my bed in the fashion of a fireplace, though if the magical devices emitted any smoke, there would be nowhere for it to go. The bed itself was probably the most marvelous of all the creations. It was a four-poster in the style of the old Renaissance and medieval paintings I had seen, and it was so large it dominated the room. Each post was detailed with carved scenes of battle. When taken as a whole, I guessed they depicted four sections of the same war between an army of skeletons and a world of human archers.

At first I thought the entire bed was made from the same dark wood as the furniture in the foyer, but it was cold to the touch more like marble, though the texture of it wasn't quite smooth enough to be made from stone. Regardless of the actual material of the frame, the mattress was quite obviously made of animal furs and thick cotton padding with silk sheets and a pair of heavy down pillows topping it off.

I stripped out of my armor and clothes as quickly as I could, more than eager to test out the bed and let my weary bones take a rest. I didn't remember if I had shut the door, and I really didn't care. Whatever other marvels remained inside the glorious room could wait until morning.

The moment my head hit the furs and silk was just as amazing as I had anticipated. Everything was cool to the touch and wrapped around my naked body, instantly reminding me of the bed I had shared with my wife on our honeymoon. We had gone to a resort not too far from where we lived and stayed for five days just enjoying the outdoors, relaxing in a lavish suite, and seeing a few plays.

With thoughts of my wife filling my mind, it didn't take long to fall asleep.

Judging by how noisy the citadel was when I woke up, it was well past breakfast. I took a few minutes to myself to lie on my bed and just listen to everything before getting up. My back was sore, and my legs were still dead tired. Even though the fight at our gate had only lasted about ten minutes, I was still exhausted. Lying on my back and looking up at the ceiling, I wondered how to turn off the purple crystal lights hanging above the bed.

"Uh, turn off the lights," I said to no one. The lights did not respond. "Dark!" I yelled a little more forcefully. Again, nothing happened.

Xia poked her head in from the foyer. "Do you need something, Master?" she asked.

"No, well, yes. Just trying to figure out how to turn off the lights," I said. I sat up and pulled myself back against the gleaming black headboard, then instantly remembered that I had slept naked and scooped up some of the sheets.

If Xia noticed my lack of modesty, she didn't say anything. She came into the room and looked up at the crystals, a smile on her face. "These are amazing," she said.

"Yeah, they're solid. But how do I turn them off? I was so tired last night that I didn't really care."

"Have you tried telling them to dim with your mind? Magic like that sometimes responds to thoughts more than anything else." She stepped a foot up on the edge of my bed to get a better look at the lanterns, offering me an exquisite view of her leg in the process.

Maybe I'm still thinking about my wife . . . I had dreamt of her last night, of our honeymoon, and the sight of so much bare flesh gave rise to an emotion I hadn't experienced in years. I shook the notion from my mind and tried to think straight enough to experiment with Xia's suggestion.

Turn off, I silently commanded, trying to picture the purple crystals extinguishing in my mind's eyes. Just like that, the room went from well-lit to pitch black.

"Wow, it worked!" I said. I had seen a lot of insane shit in Wonder, but somehow the idea that I had turned off a light with my mind was still extremely surprising.

Before I thought to turn on the lights once more, I felt a rustling in the sheets at the end of my bed. Xia had stepped both of her feet onto the silks and furs.

"Hey . . . u-uh . . ." I stammered.

"So, did you get to enjoy a Dark Revelry last night, Master?" the woman asked. I felt her lower down to the sheets and slide forward a little like she was sitting on her knees to the side of my legs.

"What are you doing?"

"Shhh." Xia slid the length of her body up against mine on the other side of the sheets, my naked body feeling every one of her curves and reacting to each miniscule touch.

I laid my head back down against the pillows and let my

tired body collapse beneath the furs. Xia hesitated, and then I felt her lifting up the sheets to get under them as well, pressing her body in close against my side.

"Hey . . . I'm not sure, uh, exactly what we're doing . . ." I said awkwardly.

I felt her pull away, but only by a couple inches. "I can go," she whispered into the back of my hair. At the same time she had moved her body a little farther away from mine, I felt her arm wrap around my chest, her fingers lightly grazing over my left pectoral.

Some people who played the game bragged about sleeping with NPCs. They made a sport out of it, and with prostitution being legal in most of the capital cities, it wasn't very difficult to be good at it. I never considered myself to be one of those kinds of people. And in the back of my mind, I knew that Xia's programming had made her infatuated with Xollmomath before I came along. That meant the only reason she was crawling over me in bed now was because I had become the new Xollmomath. I was the most badass guy in Undercroft Citadel, and the warlock was programmed to be attracted to power.

I couldn't do it.

At the same time, I *did* like the attention and the contact. No woman had paid much attention to me at all since my wife died, and all those years of having no one other than Ingrid to keep me company were begging to be erased by a few hours of carnal fun with an NPC warlock.

"Ben?" she spoke into my hair.

"Yeah, you can stay . . . just . . . stay like that. We can lie here for a little while. It's kind of nice, don't you think? I want to relax before I get up." I nuzzled my way back into Xia's arms, and she pressed her entire body up against mine, issuing a soft purr at the same time.

Lying there in the darkness, all I could think about were the mornings I had spent doing the exact same thing with my wife. Toward the end, I had started sleeping in her hospital bed, just wrapping myself around her and being close to her for hours. But Xia smelled different, and she *wasn't* my wife. She was warm in different places than I was used to, and her hair was a little shorter, not to mention too dark.

About six months before I had taken Ingrid on her first trip through the portal to Echelon, she had told me to start dating again. The truth was that I had wanted to do exactly that, but I didn't know where to begin. That had been the last day I had worn my wedding ring—another request from Ingrid, and I think a little bit of my soul had died when I placed it inside the urn on the mantle.

I felt a few tears start to roll down my cheeks. In the quiet darkness of another woman's arms, I tried to let go.

CHAPTER 15

The morning, when I had finally decided to get out of bed and face it, passed by quickly. Noon came before I had really accomplished anything, but that wasn't true for everyone else in Undercroft Citadel. They had been hard at work since dawn, and it showed.

All the damage to the gatehouse had been repaired, and a few more zombie proximity mines had been rigged up along the outside of the walls. In addition to all the static improvements, the knights had brought a lot more enchanted gear with them than I had originally thought. Helvegen had grabbed a bit of new armor, and we had another few pieces stockpiled in anticipation of Elyk's return from the city. The lower quality pieces had been doled out among the warlocks, adding to our overall defensive strength by a good amount. Sitting around the courtyard in front of my giant necropolis, we actually looked a bit formidable.

Curiously, the NPCs had also salvaged the banners and guild tabards brought to our gates by the Pyreborn Legion. We had a score of the red banners, all in relatively good condition, and I didn't quite know what I would do with them. If they had been trimmed in gold they would have been the perfect material to make Ingrid another dress like the one we had bought before going into the sewers.

Thinking of her dress gave me an idea. Sure, we could probably use the materials for some practical purpose, but everything I was doing was to avenge to her death. It was all for her. It seemed fitting that Undercroft Citadel would have banners the same color as her dress. "Get these tabards on flagpoles," I told the group of warlocks. "Set them up around the wall. That'll be our banner."

I rooted through the collection of pennants and tabards to grab the best piece among them to keep for myself. Then I found Xia eating alone on the other side of the necropolis—I had been avoiding her for a few hours out of embarrassment—and showed her. "Think you could enchant one of the Pyreborn Legion banners and turn it into a cloak for me?" I asked. I didn't know if she would be more suited to crafting a new piece of gear or if I should take it to Geirr and Kulgun at the workshop, but asking couldn't hurt.

She took the banner from my hands and rubbed it between two fingers, inspecting it as she pulled it along. "Probably," she said after a moment. "Enchanting runes or corpses is much easier, of course, but I have made one or two pieces of armor in the past as well. I'll see if we have the materials I'll need at the workshop and let you know. Do you mind if I hold on to it for now? It will probably take some time."

"By all means." Not wanting to make things any more awkward than they already were between us, I decided to stay and keep her company. Not needing to eat anything myself, I didn't know what to say, so I sat next to her with my back against the necropolis and enjoyed the nice weather in peace.

After a few minutes, I decided it was past time to call up my character sheet and check out all my new stats:

Ben Hales, Level 13 Deathbringer

Physical: 26

Cunning: 24

Influence: 23 (33)

Renown: 18

Investigation: 7

Trade: 9

Craftsmanship: 9

Fortune: 9

Infamy: 39

Status: unstable, shrouded by Lady Kalma, feared, hated by Echelon, hated by Imps (wild beasts)

Holdings: Undercroft Citadel (Dungeon), Riverside (Vassal), Tendershoot Mine

Allegiance: Lady Kalma, the Stench of Corpses

Besides my level going up to thirteen, the most noticeable difference on my character sheet was that all mention of the Pyreborn Legion hunting me had been removed. That was certainly a welcome change. Another interesting change came in the form of a small red icon blinking next to my name. I focused on it, and a new notification popped up along the bottom of my vision:

Congratulations! You have earned a new title: Ben Hales, Defender of the Necropolis!

Would you like to equip it now? Yes | No

Congratulations! You have earned a new title: Ben Hales, Slayer of the Pyreborn Legion!

Would you like to equip it now? Yes | No

I ran through both of them in my mind a couple times before finally settling on the first title and equipping it. Ben Hales, Defender of the Necropolis—I loved it. Next on the list was my thirteenth level talent. I opened the menu in my vision to check out my newest options:

Strength over Strength (Physical): Each kill adds more fuel to the

fire, granting the deathbringer +1 Physical, +1 Cunning, and +1 In-
fluence for one minute. Additional kills add a stacking bonus and
double the talent's remaining duration. Passive.

Devious Exploitation (Cunning): The deathbringer sees enemy
machinations before they are sprung and can better identify the in-
tentions of others. The effect is directly related to the user's Cunning
and the target's Cunning. Passive.

Advanced Production (Influence): Lady Kalma's citadels are fac-
tories of death capable of churning out massive engines of war with
the right materials. Advanced Production allows the deathbringer's
necropolis to be outfitted with either a ballista, battering ram, or cat-
apult assemblage. Passive.

My first inclination was to go for the cunning skill and
unlock Devious Exploitation. That would help in fights, and
it would certainly be beneficial the next time a guild came
knocking on door looking for loot and experience points, but
I knew it wasn't the right choice. I needed to keep unlocking
more skills based on influence if I wanted Undercroft Citadel
to keep growing stronger. And besides, my legendary armor
already made me one of the strongest fighters in the world
despite my lack of stats and combat abilities.

I unlocked Advanced Production, and then another menu
with the three options appeared beneath the talent, where I selected to build the ballista station. A low rumbling came from
the ground beneath my feet. The top of a building started
breaking up from the ground next to the rest of the necropolis. I watched in awe—along with everyone else close enough
to see it happening—as a fully outfitted workshop rose up and
settled in like it was part of the original structure all along.

"Xia, go get Geirr and Kulgun. They'll want to see their new
workshop right away," I told the warlock.

We had a proper forge, two large anvils, multiple racks of
hammers, a few sets of metal tongs, and other tools I couldn't
identify ready and waiting to be put to use. In addition to the

building itself, a small storehouse had appeared to one side, and it was already fully stocked with all the supplies we would need to start making ballistae. The only thing the workshop hadn't come with was an alchemy lab, and I felt bad telling Kulgun to move all the benches and shelves he had just made, but I didn't think he would mind. The new structure was far better than anything we could put together with the leftover remnants of Whitechapel.

The new workshop brought about the issue of securing the mine, another item on my list for the day, but I wanted to wait until Elyk had returned from his mission to Echelon before going back to Riverside for some slaves.

I decided to spend the afternoon directing the charnel golem around the outside of the wall, basically using it like a backhoe to start digging out a moat. I had a pretty specific vision for what Undercroft Citadel would eventually look like, and part of that plan involved making sure the majority of our enemies came at us from the front—right where we wanted them.

Sometime in the afternoon, Elyk came riding up the road from Echelon on horseback with a stout wagon rolling along behind him. I met him at the gate, eager to see how things had gone.

"Well, I think we got the message across," he said with a smile.

"Yeah?"

"Tossed a brick through one of the castle windows, then chucked a head right inside. You should have heard the screams, man. It was epic," he said. "I dropped off another at the portal, and I left the last one spiked onto one of the battlements right by the main gate. Two guards chased me out of the city, but I got 'em."

"And the horse?" I asked.

"Our first delivery from the fence. Sold the rubies well," the harvester answered, reaching down to give the horse's neck a friendly pat. He jumped down from the horse and pulled back the heavy canvas covering the wagon. Inside the wagon were two NPCs, both burly miners wearing leather aprons with arms the size of my waist, and they each had a pile of mining gear next to them.

"Ah, that's perfect!"

The two miners got up from the cart and started stretching their arms and backs. Their names were both in the Undercroft Citadel color indicating their loyalty, and I had no doubt they would do exactly as they were commanded, just like the NPC warlocks and zombies.

"Want me to get them started right away?" Elyk asked.

I loved his enthusiasm. "Yeah, once Geirr gets the new workshop up and running, take him and Helvegen to the mine. She knows where it is. They can get it set up. We'll go to Riverside for some more workers tomorrow."

"The new workshop? Already building another?"

"Go check out the necropolis. A lot of things have happened since you left," I told him with a laugh.

He smiled and started leading his horse into the compound, the two NPC miners trudging alongside the cart. We would need a stable at some point, but that was just yet another item on my long list of things to do in the future. Building one would take more workers, and I didn't have many to spare.

By the time night fell, I had just about completed the first level of the trench that would eventually become our moat. I had no clue how to fill it with water—perhaps I would find some magical answer later—but the trench itself was a start. With two more passes it would be deep enough to at least make any would-be invaders think twice.

Happy with the day's progress, I climbed to the top of the central guard tower to watch my small kingdom eat dinner. Everyone was gathered around the fire in front of the necropolis, and I looked down on them with pride. Then I got an idea.

I went to the base of the necropolis and closed my eyes. Commanding the lights inside my room had been easy enough, maybe commanding the rest of the necropolis would operate in much the same way. *Bring me to the top*, I thought, forcefully directing my silent words toward the imposing structure as I imagined the gargoyles sweeping down from their perches to grab me by the shoulders.

The sound of stone scraping against stone met my ears. A few seconds later I felt a heavy set of talons dig into my shoulder, and everyone eating dinner in front of me stopped talking. Heavy wing beats filled the silence, and my feet left the ground.

My heart thrumming away in my chest, I opened my eyes and watched as my underlings got smaller beneath me. The gargoyle lifted me through the air to the very pinnacle of the necropolis, and there was just enough room at the top for two average-sized humanoids to either stand or sit with their legs dangling over the edge. I opted to sit, then mentally commanded the gargoyle to perch next to me with its wings folded.

Finally, I could see my fledgling empire in all its glory. I was about forty feet up from the ground, and the view was magnificent. "Everything is mine . . ." I said to the stoic gargoyle. "All mine. Soon Echelon will be mine was well."

While my head was filled with visions of conquest, my thoughts lingered away from such glory and destruction. In the end, there was only one person's head I needed to see impaled on a bloody spike.

Vic. I didn't know where he was or if he was even still alive. Maybe he had gone back to Olympia City, the capital that corresponded to Oslo back on Earth, or maybe he had been killed shortly after the server corruption and everything I did was for naught.

No, he's out there somewhere, I repeated. *He has a lair, a hideout for his crew of raiders, and it shouldn't be that far away.*

I scanned the horizon, a pair of my new red banners flapping in the wind above the gatehouse, and saw nothing. No Vic, no band of marauders riding hard in our direction, and no huge army from Echelon coming to lay waste to everything I had built.

For perhaps the first time since Ingrid had died, I let myself truly feel a little bit of safety and security.

Take me back down, I commanded the gargoyle at my side. Like an obedient dog following its master's voice, the stone creature unfolded its wings and took to the air, painfully digging into my shoulders once more. I alighted gently onto the ground, and everyone around the fire just sat with their food in their laps and stared.

"That's a neat trick," Kulgun finally said, hesitantly breaking the silence.

I smiled. "Does anyone know if we have any booze in the stores?" I asked.

"There's an unopened barrel of mead in the cellar, I think. Should I get it?" Helvegen asked, her brown eyes lighting up her face.

"Grab it. We might not have what it takes for a Dark Revelry, but I think Lady Kalma wouldn't mind a bit of celebration the old school way." I met each of the players' and NPCs' gazes in turn. "No one goes to sleep tonight until the barrel's empty. Are we in agreement?"

The resounding cheer that met my demand told me I was in the presence of more than one drinker. Perfect.

"I . . . uh, I found a bottle of liquor under the floorboards of the house next to the old forge," Kulgun said.

"Go get it. Let's celebrate."

He went off in the direction of the old forge, and Helvegen emerged from the supply cellar a few moments later. It took the efforts of her and her brother to roll the barrel of mead up to ground level, and I suddenly wasn't too sure if our small crew would be able to actually finish it off in a single night.

Luckily, the mead turned out not to be too strong. It had a sweet flavor reminiscent of the honey used to make it, and the lack of wood notes told me it hadn't sat in the barrel very long. The liquor Kulgun had found was, on the other hand, basically pure alcohol. It smelled like propane and tasted like fire. Throughout all the festivities, Xollmomath was the only one who didn't take at least a single drink. He said something about always keeping his mind clear in case Lady Kalma decided to contact him directly, and no one seemed too keen on pressing the subject. I was actually kind of appreciative for his sobriety by the end of the night. Having the most powerful member of the group maintaining a level head gave me an extra measure of confidence in case of attack.

As it turned out, my fears were just fears, and we drank the rest of the night without incident. My head swam as I stumbled back into my new bedroom on the bottom floor of the necropolis. I basically dove into the sheets and furs. I rolled over to my back, and the crystal lights above my head made me squint to block them out. *Turn . . . off . . . dark . . .* I thought in fragmented bits. About half of the lights extinguished, and that helped, but it wasn't exactly good enough.

Come on, just turn . . . turn off! I sort of growled in my mind. The rest of the crystals dimmed to black. *Finally . . .* I dug myself into the sheets and tried to relax enough to get the world to stop spinning. Why the game creators had ever decided to make alcohol have the same effects in Wonder as it did in the real world was a mystery that I would never unravel. At the very least, they should have eliminated the spins. That would have been nice.

Hey, Necropolis . . . can you make it colder in here? I silently asked the somewhat sentient building. I had no idea if it would work, but I felt like trying couldn't hurt. A few seconds later I felt a cool breeze gently touching my shoulders. It was coming from directly above kind of like a ceiling fan, and I had to assume the crystals dangling from the ceiling were responsible for it as well. Having a mentally-controlled thermostat was definitely one of the better perks of being a dungeon boss. I decided to push my luck and see what else the magical building was capable of producing.

Necropolis . . . play some smooth jazz. But not too loud, I have a headache. Or actually I'm just drunk . . . sorry for lying to you, Necropolis. Sadly, nothing happened. It seemed music was beyond the abilities of Lady Kalma's personal fortress.

Necropolis, make the ceiling look like stars . . . I waited a moment with my eyes clenched shut before opening them to see if my command worked. The walls had at least slowed their tormenting spin, though I still felt like I would puke at any moment. When I did open my eyes, the display on the ceiling grabbed my attention and actually made me forget the spinning walls for a moment. The crystals were projecting a subtle display so similar to a cloudless night sky that it was almost impossible to actually see the hard stone. It felt real.

Wow, thanks, I mused. I tried to think of other commands I might be able to give, but I was too drunk and too distracted by the stars and the cool air that nothing really came to my mind. Eventually, the room stopped spinning long enough for me to fall asleep, though I did end up losing a healthy dose of mead in the corner of the room that I dreaded having to clean up in the morning. Maybe the necropolis itself would be able to clean it up for me. I doubted it, but there was always a chance.

Morning felt like it arrived about one minute after I fell asleep. I was still groggy, still tired, and my vomit was still sitting in the corner right where I had left it. *Necropolis, please clean the floors when you get a chance. Thanks.* I felt kind of stupid trying to mentally command my house to clean up the floor, but I had high hopes for the magic running the place. After waiting between the sheets for about ten minutes I decided that the crystals powering the air conditioning and the lighting didn't have the ability to send out a cleaning crew. "Eh, I'll get one of the warlocks to do it . . ." I said to myself. I didn't mind ordering around NPCs to do a little housework. I was their dungeon boss, and they were my loyal vassals.

I stretched and rolled to the edge of the bed, rubbing my eyes, and the cold stone floor was icy against the bottoms of my bare feet. *Necropolis, turn off the cold air. And you can turn off the stars, too. Thanks.*

My room returned to its usual dark ambiance. Not quite ready to go outside and meet the sunlight, I decided to let my head rest another five or so minutes. My stomach was churning as well. I hadn't eaten much of anything in the last week or so due to my passive buff removing the need for food, but breakfast sounded great. I really just needed some carbs to weigh down my stomach so I could get back to my typical dour demeanor and evil ways.

I made it outside, and the rest of Undercroft Citadel wasn't all that busy. Geirr was thankfully not yet awake, or I probably would have killed him the first time he struck an anvil. Kulgun was in the workshop instead, fiddling with the ballista parts and starting to get the first one set up. We'd need to make an archery range to test it out and train ourselves at some point. The NPC warlocks were all awake and going about their daily tasks, but I saw no sign of Xia, Xollmomath, or Helvegen. They were probably still asleep.

I used what remained of the morning to get in a little more exercise. My head punished me for it the entire time, but I managed to run three laps around the outside of the wall with my beast plate strapped on for extra weight. By the time I finished, I was drenched in sweat and badly needed a shower—which made me realize for the first time that our settlement had very little in the way of personal hygiene. Looking around at our supplies, I wasn't exactly sure how we were supposed to remedy that. Before the server corruption, getting clean had never been a huge issue. There were bath houses in the major cities, but most players just went home when they needed to. We had neither luxury.

Xia was awake and working with a few pieces of the salvaged gear from the Pyreborn Legion, so I figured I could ask her. "Hey, we need somewhere to clean ourselves. How difficult would it be to rig up a shower or make a bath house? Think we could do it?"

The woman looked around at a few of the nearest houses. "We need to start collecting more rainwater. I think we have a few extra barrels somewhere in the cellar. I could set them up on the rooftops, and then we could make a shower. Should I start?"

"Yeah," I told her. "Let's build a little shower station. It shouldn't be too difficult or take up too many resources. Grab some warlocks and see to it."

She nodded and went first to the underground storerooms for the barrels, and I left her to the task. Next on the list was capturing some more miners to augment the two we had gotten from the fence in Echelon.

I found Elyk sitting on the top of the gatehouse. He had a few pieces of armor spread out before him and was making adjustments to various things and testing how they fit. "Find anything useful?" I asked him.

He finished strapping a studded leather brigandine over his chest and then tried moving around in it. "Eh, nothing perfect, but better than going with just a shirt. I thought about stealing some weapons back in Echelon. Probably wouldn't have been worth the risk."

"I appreciate the restraint," I told him honestly.

"I like one of these paladin swords. Not a bad enchantment on it by my standards. It'll work for now." He grabbed a hand-and-a-half sword and gave it a few practice swings.

The harvester looked comfortable with the large weapon in his hands. Good gear combined with the man's natural ferocity was certainly a potent combination. He was the perfect choice to take to Riverside. "Ready to go get some more miners?" I asked with a smile.

Elyk returned a sinister grin. "Let's go. I've been looking forward to a little more action."

"I don't doubt it at all."

The two of us made the trip to Riverside relatively quickly. Even from a distance, it was obvious that the village had gone through a few changes since the last time we had been there. They had a few defensive embankments built up facing Undercroft Citadel, though their sparse placements were still woefully inadequate.

"Ha, think they're planning on an invasion?" Elyk remarked. He kicked one of the wooden palisades, and a bit of rotten wood broke off under his heel.

"It won't do them any good," I added. I was tempted to draw my flaming sword and cleave some of the defenses in half just to send a message, but I figured that at least starting with a bit of civility might get us somewhere. If it came to an all-out melee, we'd be fine anyway.

A couple NPC guards, both level five and wearing starter gear appropriate to the village's status, spotted us before we entered the town streets. "Take us to whoever is in charge," I stated forcefully. The two NPCs looked nervous, but they bowed their heads and started to lead us to the town hall nonetheless.

The building itself was just as weak as the rest of River-side. It was only a single story, and the wooden siding on both edges of the door was old and falling apart. The NPC mayor of the village was inside waiting for us with a handful of guards, two of which were actually human players—a fact I found surprising. The players were level ten and level eleven, a knight and a dragoon. They were all dressed up in what appeared to be the finest armor in the whole town, and it looked absolutely pathetic next to my own. Then again, everything looked that way when compared to the legendary gear hanging from my shoulders.

"Why have you come here? We sent our first tribute. We've not betrayed Undercroft Citadel," the mayor began, his voice already shaking.

"I'm well aware of—"

Elyk cut me off before I had a chance to continue. Or rather, he cut off one of the guards . . . at the waist. His big sword sliced through the player's abdomen, sending the dragoon into a shrieking fit of hysteria while the two NPC guards readied their weapons for a fight.

I pulled Infernum from my side and willed it to life, setting my feet and getting ready as well, but I didn't need to do anything at all. Elyk stepped forward to the center of the room, his blade still dripping blood onto the wooden floorboards, and commanded everyone's attention. "Now that you're all intent on listening, I think we can begin. We need strong backs and able hands to work our mine. You have people living here who will suffice for our purposes. Now, should we go door to door taking whoever we like, or should we simply wait out front for you to bring them to us?"

Wow. I had to admit I was impressed. I silently extinguished Infernum's flame and slid it back into its sheath, watching the harvester at work. The mayor fidgeted from foot to foot, and the other player continued to wail in the corner of the room.

He had thrown down his weapon and taken off his helm, his head buried in his hands. I guessed the man Elyk had just killed was at least a close friend, maybe even a brother. The death weighed on my mind for all of a couple seconds. There were already dozens like it piled at my feet, and there were hundreds more yet to come. Thousands.

"I . . ." the mayor's voice trailed off into a stifled cough. "I do not wish anyone else to die . . . Please. At least give us that much."

"And our workers?" Elyk went on, his expression as brutal as ever.

The mayor gulped and pulled at his collar like it was suddenly too hot inside the small town hall. "I'll sound the bell. Everyone will come assemble . . . and then we'll ask for volunteers to work your mine. Please, it is the best I can do."

I grabbed Elyk by the shoulder and held him back. "That'll work just fine. You have five minutes." We both turned and exited the building, leaving the screaming player and the three NPCs behind us.

Your Infamy skill has increased to 40!

"At the rate we're gaining infamy, every player in Wonder will know the name Undercroft Citadel before long. The AI will start making more and more quests, and eventually the rewards will be so enticing that all the best guilds will come running to collect," I said. We stood in the center of the street to wait for Riverside to gather its citizens.

"You want me to pull it back?" Elyk asked. He sounded embarrassed, like a scolded child caught stealing candy at a checkout counter, and it caught me off guard.

"No," I laughed, giving him a smile. "Your methods are effective. I like that."

The momentary tension evaporated, and the harvester managed a grin. "When our infamy gets too high, we'll kill them all. They'll send their best, and we'll bury them in the dirt together."

"Haha, I like the way you think. You scare the shit out of me sometimes, but I like it." A loud bell at the end of the street started ringing, mercifully drowning out the violent cries of the player still in the town hall. I figured the mayor had left by way of a different exit, and they had simply abandoned the dragoon to his own misery.

"Mind if I go eliminate all that whining?" Elyk asked with a wink.

"Have at it." I didn't really want him to just wantonly kill another player—another real human being trapped inside the game just like us—but my hesitation was short lived. The person meant nothing to me. People died every day all over both Wonder and Earth, and their deaths were inconsequential. And if it made all the crying stop, I had to say I wasn't too concerned with the methodology.

A few moments later, the wailing abruptly stopped. Elyk emerged from the town hall shortly thereafter, and much to my surprise, the dragoon was following closely behind him, absolutely silent.

I raised an eyebrow.

"Told him I'd cut off his hands and make him eat them before turning him into a zombie if he didn't shut his fucking mouth," the harvester explained as casually as if he was talking about the cloudy sky.

I looked to the dragoon. "He means it, if you haven't figured that out. And I don't honestly care what he does with you or your hands."

The captive nodded vigorously and didn't say a word.

Elyk shoved him to the ground, and then we only had a few minutes to wait for the rest of the village to assemble with their mayor in a small pack about twenty yards in front of us. They stood back, clearly scared out of their minds, and some of them were clutching farm implements or other rudimentary weapons, but none of them even took a single step forward to come fight.

The mayor was the first one to speak. "Alright," he called across the expanse. "Do what you've come to do, but be quick about it. And then leave."

He showed a little more gumption than I had expected from such an obviously weak NPC, and that was at least moderately respectable. I waved to Elyk, and we left the dragoon sitting in the dirt to go inspect our spoils.

Most of the NPCs shrank back in response to our advance. I ignored the ones who stood tall and unmoving, preferring to select my mining crew from among the more docile choices, and quickly rounded up ten of the strongest looking males.

"What do you think?" I asked the harvester.

He thought for a moment, a sinister grin on his face. "We'll take these, but we need insurance as well." A few of Riverside's women were starting to cry, and Elyk grabbed two of them out of the crowd. "I'm guessing they know some of our new miners. We'll keep them in Undercroft Citadel to ensure compliance." He gave a hard stare to all the others assembled in the street. "If the miners rebel, we'll kill one of them. If the food shipments stop, we'll kill the other."

The mayor looked like he wanted to protest, but his chest deflated and he hung his head instead.

Not surprisingly, there weren't any human players left among the population of Riverside. I figured they had all run back to the safety of Echelon, and for that I was glad. The village would certainly send word back to the capital of what had transpired, and they might even be able to raise a small militia of other NPCs to come help defend the city, but they wouldn't be any more trouble than that. Actual players would probably have a lot better luck rousing others to their cause. That was something we wouldn't have to worry about.

I let Elyk do the majority of the work for the return trip, most of which revolved around scaring the piss out of our captives, something that fit his particular set of skills rather perfectly. We made it back to Undercroft Citadel a little before nightfall without any problems at all.

Elyk herded our miners to a couple houses that still remained near the outskirts of the compound, making what essentially amounted to a livestock pen on the inside section of the wall. I left him to his business, content that he would be the right one for the job and get our mine fully operational within a couple days. Ideally, we would be able to lay more cart tracks all the way from the mine's small forge to the workshop attached to the necropolis, and then the flow of ingots would be constant. Once everything was running smoothly, we'd need to find more engineers and blacksmiths to be able to utilize everything, and that was certainly a welcome problem to have.

The two women Elyk had selected to be our hostages were both healer classes—one an herbalist and the other a hospitaler. They were treated better than the miners, and we found enough room for them to get set up making medical supplies under Kulgun's direction. We needed more healing potions, and crafting basic items would lead to more advanced recipes, so the sooner we started fortifying our stockpiles the better.

Overall, Undercroft Citadel was really coming along. We had a steady supply of food, a rainwater collection system, a mine bringing in raw materials to a fully functional workshop, and an army of undead and warlocks to defend us against any attacks. We were making steady progress. What we needed next was going to be tricky.

"Hey, Xollmomath, you have a minute?" I called to the ancient necromancer as he finished his evening meal.

The bald man bade me to sit next to him around the fire. "What is it you desire?" he cryptically asked.

"You remember the Founder's Stake?"

The gleam in the man's eye told me he remembered it

fondly. "Of course, Master. Has the time come to restore the Founder's Stake to the glory it rightly deserves?"

"Exactly." I gave the man a friendly pat on the shoulder, and his skin was ice cold beneath my touch, even through his linen shirt. "Once we get the mine operation fully underway, that's my next plan. We can go back to Echelon and break into the royal vault, steal the last part of the Founder's Stake, and bring back all the necromancer magic you used to have. Sound like a plan?"

"What you speak of will be no easy feat," Xollmomath warned. "The scarab containing my master's knowledge is not something that can be trifled with by untrained hands. It consumes life, and without proper care given to the artifact's handling, it will consume more. All who touch it will be in great peril."

That changed a few things. I had planned on taking Xia, Helvegen, and Elyk with me to storm the castle, but now I wasn't so sure. "How strong does someone have to be to resist being eaten by the scarab? Will Xia be able to handle it safely?"

The man rubbed a pale hand across his beardless chin. Even the backs of his fingers were hairless—perhaps a lingering side-effect of being dead for several centuries. "I do not know," he finally said after some time. "She is a strong one, but perhaps not strong enough. Only the most infamous and corrupt, the blackest of heart, may truly resist the scarab's call. I believe you would be better suited to the task, Ben Hales."

Ah ha! The game's AI was trying to tell me that my infamy score would directly affect how I would be able to interact with the scarab, and it simply didn't allow any of the NPCs to break character or speak in any kind of meta terms. I didn't know what exact value of infamy I would need to safely handle the scarab, but I had to be getting close. Xollmomath probably would have just told me to back off and wait to recover the relic if I wasn't even close to being ready.

"Alright, I think I know what to do. I'll take Xia, Helvegen, and Elyk into Echelon soon, and we'll bring back that scarab. You'll know how to reassemble to stake, right?" A new plan was forming in my head, one that involved a lot of bloodshed and slaughter on our way to the royal archives inside the king's castle—one that would result in a huge amount of experience and infamy gain before we ever got into the treasure rooms. It would be tough, but it would work. It had to.

The bald necromancer grinned. "Bring me the scarab. Leave everything else to me."

That night I went to sleep in my perfectly air-conditioned room with a better idea of exactly what we needed to do. I mentally allotted a week, maybe ten days if we needed it, to preparation. Then we would storm Echelon, and the city would kneel before me.

CHAPTER 16

I got started early the next morning. My first stop was with Geirr and Kulgun at the workshop. I set the engineer to making gear from all the resources we had and the equipment leftover from the fight with the Pyreborn Legion. We needed more armor, full sets of armaments for all four of us who would go into Echelon, and he was the only one with the skills for the job.

I set Kulgun to roughly the same task. While Geirr hammered away on his anvil, Kulgun would work with our newly acquired herbalist to craft potions. He had already finished about a third of the first ballista, but that project could wait. Healing potions and other alchemical buffs were the top priority.

Once Helvegen and Elyk had finished their breakfast, the three of us gathered a handful of zombies and a pair of warlocks, and then led our forced labor group out toward the mine. It wasn't a long trip, and I trusted the harvester to handle everything on his own, but I wanted to do some more exploration. We had only ventured through a small section of the mine on our previous trip. There were bound to be more enemies lurking beneath the surface.

Elyk and Helvegen split the miners into groups with only a couple of them swinging picks against stone. The rest were busy gathering up the unused cart track and laying it down outside, slowly extending the existing path from the forge back to our workshop. Completing the new track would take some time. Luckily, the supplies we received from Lady Kalma's kind graces when I had built the ballista workshop would last until we got the supply line up and running.

Once everything was set and the warlocks were serving as taskmasters to keep the NPC slaves busy, I took Helvegen and Elyk down into the bowels of the mine's darker passages. Infernum illuminated the tunnels well, though deep shadows lurked around every turn.

"You cleared out all the imps, right?" Elyk asked as we moved past a small chamber containing a dozen or more broken eggs.

"Killed their queen, too," Helvegen answered.

"Let's hope there's something left down here to kill. I know it may come as a surprise to both of you, but slaughtering humans can get old. We need a good hunt! Some wild beasts to track and kill!" Elyk's tone and choice of words when talking about the sight of human blood getting stale for him wasn't necessarily convincing. Regardless, I liked his enthusiasm and shared a bit of it myself.

"Just remember to fight intelligently. We're here to train, not to throw our lives away," I said quietly. "If a fight seems too hard, we'll retreat and come back later. We just need to grab as much experience as we can."

I toyed with the idea of telling them the grander plan involving King Ahmose's personal treasure trove and the absolute slaughter I intended bring down upon the city. Though I didn't think either of them would be opposed to the overall mission—especially not Elyk—I decided against telling them. We still had a week or more left to prepare, and plans could change. I didn't want everyone in Undercroft Citadel getting ready with one specific goal in mind just to have to change it on them later.

We moved deeper and deeper into the underground mine complex, and the air took on a stagnant, musty quality that told me no one had ventured into the lowest levels in quite some time, possibly years. Some of the old wooden supports had fallen from the walls and roof as well, making me question just how deep we could go until we were stopped by a cave-in.

Luckily, the tunnel we were in widened and the floor levelled out, and we found what we had been looking for all along. At the other end of a long, natural chamber stood a swirling portal. It was somewhat familiar in appearance to the portals that used to bring players from Earth into the game, but it was much smaller and it actually showed a bit of the other side through its translucent barrier.

"A real dungeon," I said with a bit of awe. The small dungeon beneath the counting house had been cordoned off from the rest of the building by a hole in the basement wall, and that was pretty typical for lower-level quest areas. Higher-level dungeons were often protected by magical barriers like portals that could keep out unprepared players and prevent them from racking up tons of needless deaths in zones far beyond their skills.

The other side of the portal showed a vague, blurry image of a castle battlement. Beyond the parapets was a dark forest, deep and foreboding in a splash of moonlight, and I could hear a faint noise that sounded like the chirping of crickets coming through the barrier.

"A sealed dungeon beneath a mine. I've heard of them before, but I've never been inside one. Either of you guys seen one on a stream before?" Elyk asked.

I nodded. "Yeah, I used to watch one of the crazy geared

hunters from Echelon. He ran raids through dungeons all the time. I don't think I've ever seen one in a mine before, and I most certainly haven't seen one with my own eyes."

"Geirr used to watch one of the popular streamers," Helvegen said. "There was a guild he followed that went on dungeon runs all the time. But they always had at least five people, usually more. Think we can even do it?"

I walked up to the translucent skin covering the portal and let my fingertips brush against it. The magic made my hand tingle. I had no idea what it would feel like to step through to the other side. No one on the forums had ever talked about that part of the raids. "We might have a small party, but I think we can kill whatever lurks on the other side."

"Come on, quit dicking around," Elyk said with a laugh. He stepped forward and disappeared through the portal.

"Well, that settles that. Let's go!" I followed quickly behind him, and Helvegen came through just a second after I did.

As the barrier between locations touched my body, it felt kind of like slipping underwater at the edge of a pool. There was a little bit of a temperature difference since wherever the castle was, it happened to be night time, and the change made all the hairs on my body stand on end. It was a little like being shocked all over, but it didn't hurt—actually, it felt good. Though I had never done any of the drugs that had been coded into Wonder, I had to imagine that crossing the barrier was at least somewhat similar to that kind of experience. I knew at once that if I had the opportunity, I would become addicted to dungeons raids.

We were standing on the top of a castle battlement. I had expected the building to be in ruins, a classic dungeon depiction that had been popular since the first day Wonder had come online, but it was intact. Deep blue banners streamed from the parapet down the front wall, and a pair of painted statues depicting armored warriors flanked either side of the battlement, their paint unblemished by time.

I remembered the sewers beneath the counting house in Echelon and how Ingrid and I had come across another group. Dungeons in Wonder existed in the game just like castles from the Middle Ages existed back on Earth, so there wasn't any programming to ensure that we were the only group of players present. "Give it a moment," I told the others, crouching down between two of the parapet's protrusions. "Just listen. I don't want to go charging in if another group is already here. We need to be careful."

As I spoke, the magical doorway behind us faded into nothing, and my heart sank through my chest.

"Uh . . . Well, that sucks," Elyk said under his breath.

I shared his sentiment. "There's always another way back," I reminded him. "We just can't exit the same way we came in. We'll need to find another portal."

"Unless we aren't in a dungeon . . ." Helvegen whispered.

"I . . . I hadn't thought about that." I pounded a fist down on the top of the stone and cursed my luck.

"That might have been a regular magic portal set up by some random mage. It could have been there for years just waiting for some stupid band of idiots to come stumbling through," Elyk added.

"Optimism, guys," I said, though I knew they could both tell the sentiment was forced. "No matter what, we still have a castle to pillage. Let's get moving."

I decided that getting moving was the best course of action. Sitting on the battlement and wondering if we would ever see Undercroft Citadel again wasn't going to do any good. We crept toward the far end of the stone walkway to where a short wooden door presumably led inside. I kept Infernum ready at my side in case either of the painted statues flanking us decided to magically animate, but they both remained still as stone.

The door was unlocked, and it squealed on its metal hinges. The other side opened up to a tightly spiraled staircase heading down. There were a few narrow arrow slots letting in moonlight, but it wasn't much. "What do you think, should I light the sword or should we stay hidden?" I asked.

"I'd rather tell everyone we're coming than step on a trap, break my ankle, and *then* tell everyone we're coming," Helvegen answered.

I ignited Infernum once more to give us a view of where we were stepping, then continued down around three full turns of the staircase.

"I wonder which continent we're on. I've only ever been to Olympia and Echelon." Helvegen's voice was so soft I could barely hear it, and yet it still managed to echo off the stone walls.

"Shhh." I was thinking the exact same thing, but I cringed at the idea of giving away our intrusion to careless chatter.

According to the developers, each of the seven main continents had the same land area as Earth—a little over a million square miles. Earth had been bigger at one point a long time ago, but then the oceans had risen to reclaim huge swaths of every continent's coastline sometime in the 2030s before the war. Or maybe the flood had been after the war, I couldn't remember. That part of history had never been my forte back in school; my whole life before Wonder felt so far away now that I had trouble remembering the things I had once learned. It was hard to imagine a time when my hometown of Atlanta didn't have a thriving tourism industry built up around the beach that cut through the heart of the old downtown.

Perhaps if the castle we were in housed a library or some maps we would be able to figure out exactly where we were. Honestly, I didn't really care. If we were on a different continent altogether, we were screwed. If I was right and we were in a dungeon, we'd be fine.

We reached the bottom of the stairs, and there was no door to block us from view, but we also didn't hear or see anything in the next room. The spiral staircase had ended in a great hall dominated by two long tables running side by side through the length the room. Against the opposite wall was a hearth with logs stacked up in a neat pile to one side. Where we were crouched, we had a decent place to hide behind a tall chair at the head of one of the tables, and we could see both exits as well.

Two voices echoed off the stone walls a few seconds later. The three of us pushed back up the stairs a bit, leaving me to tank in the front and also be our only set of eyes into the hall. I quickly extinguished Infernum and waited.

A regally attired man and woman came into the hall from one of the side passages. ". . . but where are we going to get that much meat this time of year?" the man was asking. He started loading a few logs into the fireplace, then pat down his shirt and pants, presumably looking for firesteel.

"I've told you before, James, the butcher in Iverstead has more than we need. If you'd only let me—"

"No!" the man interrupted fiercely. "Be quiet about that bastard, woman. I'll have no word of him while in this castle, do you hear me?"

The woman let out a sigh and turned toward one of the paintings lining the wall, her hands on her hips.

The man finally gave up searching for something to light the fire and threw his hands in the air. "Just light the damn logs, Marissa," he shouted before storming out of the hall through the same doorway he had used to enter.

Still looking upset, the woman moved to the front of the fire and waved a hand in front of it, and the wood roared to life with flame.

"A wizard?" Helvegen whispered behind me.

I was wondering the same thing. The woman held out her hands presumably to warm them on the magical fire for a few seconds before following her husband out of the hall. "Come on, let's move. They'll probably be back soon."

We scampered out of the spiral staircase toward the end of the hall, moving through the same doorway the couple had used, and we found two more paths in the next room. One of them led into a kitchen, and I could still hear sounds of the argument coming from that direction.

The second door held more promise. It was partially opened, and it led down deeper into the castle, dark and foreboding. "Let's go," I whispered. I eased open the door and slid through, the others following close behind me.

Elyk pulled the door partially closed behind us, leaving it more or less as we had found it. The staircase was pitch black. I didn't know how to ignite Infernum only partially to reduce the risk of giving us away. After easing myself down a single step, I figured making the light once more would be more beneficial than risking a broken ankle or a broken neck, so I willed it to life. The blade's fire reflected off the walls and gave us a good idea of where we were going. The floor beneath us was damp, like we were underground with poor protection from the rain.

A gentle voice came up from someone out of sight. "Hello?"

All three of us on the stairs stopped.

A few painful moments dragged by, and then the voice spoke again. "Hello? Are . . . are you here to rescue me?"

It sounded like a woman, though the voice was so frail I couldn't really tell.

I eased down another two stairs to get a better view around the corner at the landing. We were in a small dungeon, and it smelled like stagnant water and death. A pair of skeletons dangled from chains in the center of the room, and the only living specimen was shackled to the far wall. She was a frail woman, probably around my age, wearing nothing more than a simple linen shift that went down to her knees. Just about every inch of her skin was covered in dirt and grime. Her arms were restrained above her head, her fingers limp.

The three of us made it to the landing, our boots splashing in the inch or so of water that had pooled atop the stone floor. There was a single window set into the top of the wall to my right where I figured most of the water had come in, judging by the brown stains running down beneath it. The woman recoiled at the sight of us, not that she had anywhere to go.

"Are . . . are you here to kill me?" she weakly called.

I shook my head and lowered my fearsome weapon. "Not exactly," I said. "What is this place? Why are you here?"

"You're from the village?" she asked. Her cheeks beneath her eyes were just as streaked with brown as the stone beneath the solitary window.

I took a few steps closer to her, giving the two dangling skeletons a wide berth. "Which village?"

"They . . . kidnapped me from Iverstead. That was a month ago, maybe more . . . I don't really remember." The woman fought back sobs as she spoke, and her frail, emaciated body shook from the effort.

"We saw two people upstairs, a man and a woman. They're the ones who kidnapped you?" I asked.

She nodded. "They're werewolves, both of them. A couple of us in Iverstead were planning on getting together to storm the castle, but there was a traitor, and they attacked before we could. I think . . . I'm the only one who survived. I don't know. If you could get me back to the village, maybe there are more people willing to come fight."

"You guys up for a little escort quest?" I asked my party. Elyk and Helvegen both looked eager for the challenge. Rescuing kidnapped NPCs and taking them back to their villages was a common trope throughout the whole game, so I wasn't too surprised that that was what we had stumbled upon. It did feel a little odd, though, for a group from Undercroft Citadel to be involved in the rescue of anyone. We were evil, but the game didn't really care. We could still find and complete quests just like all the other players around Wonder.

I leveled Infernum across from the woman's chains and swung hard. Her shackles fell to pieces, and her arms collapsed by her sides. They were pale and thin, and the woman could barely move her fingers. It would take some time for her to recover. I reached a hand down to help lift her from the ground, and Helvegen did the same from the other side. "Is there anyone else still alive down here?" I asked.

Maybe there were some other rooms or hidden chambers waiting behind unseen doors that the woman would know of, but she only shook her head. "I'm the last one," she said quietly.

"Let's go kill some werewolves!" Elyk said with a bit of a laugh.

The only way out of the dungeon was back the way we had come, and I had a few reservations about the proximity of the door to the banquet hall where the couple had clearly been preparing for some kind of party. At the top of the stairs, Elyk eased open the door a few inches, then quickly shut it once more. "About a dozen people around the table," he whispered. "They look like servants just getting things ready, not guests or our two werewolf friends."

"Ready for a little house cleaning?" I asked, a sinister smile on my face.

Elyk gave me a solemn nod as he drew his sword. Before anyone said another word, he blasted through the door and started activating talents, whirling his blade in a wide arc around his body. The first two servants were rent to pieces in only a few seconds. The others started to scream, and I moved out of the staircase with Helvegen behind me ready to defend against the werewolves should they come running back to the banquet hall.

Serving platters, wine goblets, and parts of the servants themselves went flying all over the room. In a matter of moments, Elyk turned the once opulent dining area into what looked like a slaughterhouse. He kept spinning, thrashing through what flesh remained, until the only sounds left in the room were coming from his own boots sloughing through the slick gore that now covered the stones.

"My god . . ." I muttered. Seeing all that carnage up close was a little overwhelming. The servants hadn't been difficult NPCs—basically just mindless mobs that barely yielded any experience at all—but it was just so *much*.

Elyk's chest was heaving. His arms were both covered in blood, but not a single drop of it was his. Heavy footsteps sounded from above the harvester's head. "The werewolves," he blurted out, running to the side wall and pressing his back up against it to remain hidden from the hallway.

I pulled Helvegen who in turn grabbed our rescued prisoner, and we all made a line to the side of the doorway. We had a couple seconds before the werewolves would reach the hall, so I pushed Elyk to the front of our column, eager to watch him execute the first attack of our ambush. "Whirlwind is on cooldown," he said quietly between breaths, his lungs still struggling to replenish his energy.

"Doesn't matter," I told him. "Just swing on the first thing that comes through, and I'll be right behind you the whole time."

"Hey, I need some experience too. Don't leave me out!" Helvegen added.

Before I could answer, a hairy beast maybe eight feet tall charged through the doorway, the tattered remnants of a fancy tunic hanging from its bulging, muscled torso. Elyk was almost quick enough, and he managed to give the beast a nasty gash down its back, though he was far from incapacitating it.

A mighty howl filled the room, and the harvester charged after the first werewolf.

The second beast wasn't more than a dozen steps behind the first. She charged into the room with a little more tact and defensive thought, coming in with her claws held wide and slashing at the sides of the door frame where I was still hiding. Her sharp claws raked against my legendary chest plate, and one of them violently broke free from its hairy paw. The armor reacted with a burst of flame, though it only singed her fur as she was too quick and dodged the brunt of the reaction.

One of Helvegen's spells shot over my shoulder and landed right on the werewolf's face. The creature reeled backward, its eyes wide, and I pushed in low to tackle it to the ground. It staggered backward, but it didn't lose its footing and instead shoved me by the shoulders, creating just enough separation to be free from my blade.

Helvegen continued to cast, and I shot out my shadow pet, feeling the familiar drain on my lifeforce as the small entity rocketed into the werewolf's chest. The shadow monster, combined with whatever horrors Helvegen was sending into the wolf's mind, finally stole the fight from her claws. She swiped at the little creature clinging to her fur and took her eyes off Infernum, the real threat.

I took a single step forward, my blazing sword high above my head, and cleaved it down on her shoulder. A bloody arm thudded to the floor to join the rest of the mangled human bits from the servants. I swung again, shearing off the werewolf's other arm, and she fell to her knees.

"Take her, Hel," I said to the painter. "You'll get more experience if you land the killing blow."

The woman drew a small dagger from her belt and stepped

forward, offering me an appreciative nod. Then she slit the werewolf's throat, and its painful howls came to a merciful end.

Elyk was squared off against the first beast, his sword held in both hands in front of him instead of whirling in a circle of death all around. He looked tired, and though I couldn't tell for sure, I thought he had taken a bit of damage to his forearms from the wolf's claws.

From our position near the doorway, Helvegen and I both had a clear shot at the beast's back. We could strike it down in an instant, ending the fight and potentially saving Elyk from any more damage. But we waited. All three of us had one of Kulgun's healing potions on our belts, and I didn't want to steal any more valuable experience from my party. I had my armor and sword, so they needed the levels and talents far more than I did.

"If he starts to falter, go in and help," I told Helvegen.

As it turned out, the painter's skills weren't needed. Elyk deflected a series of three wide strikes, then stepped forward and turned his body, throwing all of his weight into the hilt of his sword. The weapon's pommel connected with the werewolf's chest, and all the air was driven from its lungs.

Elyk reeled back and chopped downward, lodging his blade about three inches into the top of the werewolf's skull.

Your Infamy skill has increased to 41!

"Nice!" I said, sheathing Infernum and starting to check the corpses for loot. With so much blood and gore coating absolutely every surface in the entire banquet hall, it was hard to tell what was bone and what was a potential trinket or other valuable item.

"Got an enchanted ring," Elyk said, lifting up a bloody silver loop for the rest of us to see. "Adds fire damage to all of my attacks. It might be how the woman started the fire in the first place. I don't think she was too skilled as a wizard or she never would have transformed to fight us."

"Ha, or else we just killed them both too quickly for either of them to start using much magic," I replied. Our little band was small, but we were more ruthless than any of the NPCs could handle. The problem was, I knew at some point our advantage would run out. We would come across a group of either players or NPCs that would be strong enough to stand against us and have the mental fortitude to do it without wavering. I knew that day was coming, and I didn't want to face it.

Our rescued villager was whimpering in the corner, hiding her face from all the carnage.

"Was there anyone else?" I asked her. "Anyone else in the castle we need to kill to keep Iverstead safe from their attacks?"

She hesitated to answer, and I could tell there was more that she was hiding. I started to ask her again a bit more forcefully, but she finally opened up and spoke.

"There's a sorcerer, a powerful one . . . He made the baron and baroness into werewolves. He lives here somewhere, I think," she explained.

I looked to Elyk and Helvegen, and both of them were just as confident as ever. "Let's go kill a sorcerer."

"Wait!" the woman weakly called. "Be careful. He isn't . . . like the werewolves. He's so much stronger than them. You need more people if you hope to escape with your lives!"

The game was trying to tell us that we didn't have enough players for the final boss, and the AI refused to let the NPCs speak in such plain meta terms, so it made the captive plead with us to turn back. While I appreciated the warning, I didn't let it me slow me down.

"Do you know where the sorcerer lives inside the castle?" I asked.

"The highest tower," she answered, meekly nodding with her head in her hands.

The woman continued to protest, issuing more warnings about the danger we faced and how she would be killed if we were to die before getting her home to Iverstead . . . and her voice faded into the background.

We found the staircase leading up to the tallest tower of the castle pretty easily, and I moved to tank at the front of the group once more. By my count, we ascended four stories to the highest tower, and the stone flared out on the sides to accommodate a rather large upper room that was much wider and longer than the hall we had been in below. The three of us more or less burst into the chamber and came to a quick halt right in front of the door.

The sorcerer was standing at the far end of the hall, probably at least seventy feet away, and he had his back turned. He was moving items around on an alchemical table, and my first thought was that we'd get some good loot for Kulgun back at the workshop. If we could take down the magic user without the supplies being destroyed in the process, I'd be sure to grab as much as I could carry.

Flanking either side of the alchemical bench were two stone archways that looked like dormant portals. I hoped one of them would take us back to the mine. If the game's AI had the dungeon coming to an end with the sorcerer being the final boss, one of them would no doubt take us home.

Scattered around the rest of the room were various trunks of all different sizes, a few stone statues, and more than a pair of crumpled heaps of human parts that appeared to be failed experiments of some kind. Perhaps they were other werewolf experiments that hadn't turned out to be viable. Maybe they were something else altogether.

The sorcerer at the end of the hall continued to move things around, pouring liquids from beaker to beaker, making small notations on a sheet of paper, and casually humming to himself without a care in the world. I was certain he would have heard us coming up the stairs—we hadn't really given much thought to stealth—but he didn't turn around.

I took the first step into his chamber, and *that* turned out to be the key. All at once, two nearby statues leapt to life, and the sorcerer himself whirled around with a glass vial in his hand, shouting something incomprehensible at the same time.

A field of gloom descended on all three of our heads. I immediately felt sluggish, like my mind was clouded once more with too much mead, and it was hard to keep putting one foot in front of the other. "Hel, throw off his aim!" I called through the fog, unable to fully articulate exactly what it was that I wanted the painter to do.

Helvegen groaned. "He's too far away," she answered.

Before I could tell her to just get closer before casting, there was a stone statue standing directly in front of me, its small carved wings illuminated by the moonlight streaming in from a row of tall windows behind it. The animated marble resembled an angel . . . or maybe it didn't. With my mind in such a befuddling swirl of confusion, I wasn't exactly sure what it was.

A heavy marble fist crashed into my breastplate. The stone screeched against my steel, and a blossom of frost erupted from my attacker to encase me in a cold chill, further slowing both my body and mind. I couldn't even look to my sides to see how Elyk and Helvegen were faring, and I knew one of the statues had gone for them as well. My legendary breastplate reacted to the attack, and a powerful burst of flame leapt out to meet the frost. The heat countered the cold, and my mind cleared just a little. Sadly, it wasn't effective at all against the statue.

I staggered backward a step to try and get some room to swing my sword. I shuddered to think what would happen to Infernum as it came crashing down on the solid stone statue, but I didn't have a choice. Either I attacked and made some progress or I waited until I was dead. Infernum clanged off the statue's shoulder, and I winced from the sharp noise echoing around inside my helmet.

The statue wasn't fazed. My sword clattered off, and all that it had left was a minor scratch and a bit of black char.

Luckily, the confusing fog the sorcerer had brought down upon my head was starting to clear. I could see him at the end of the long room working on some new incantation, but for a few seconds, I could think clearly. I dropped Infernum to the ground at my side and curled my right hand into a fist. My gauntlets gave me a huge bonus to my physical stat whenever I attacked—I just needed to use the right weapon. A sharp instrument like a sword would never get the job done. My fists, however, managed to knock the heavy creature back a step or two.

I kept pummeling the statue with both hands, offering absolutely no defense against its counter attacks, and I started slowly working the creature backward like a boxer on the ropes. All the while, my own armor kept taking hit after devastating hit. It was only a matter of time before my breastplate started caving in and ripping apart my skin. If I made it back to the citadel, Geirr would have a hell of a time hammering out the dents.

Little by little, I pushed the statue back until it was directly in front of the nearest window. I wasn't sure if the thing would even fit, but I didn't care. If it took out some of the window frame as it fell, all the better. I gave the statue one final slam with both of my hands laced together, and my staggering bonus to physical was enough to get the job done.

Your Physical skill has increased to 27!

The heavy statue crashed through the glass window, and I spun back to see what had become of my two companions. They were both badly pressed. More black fog was clinging in a heavy sheet around their heads, and it looked like the statue they were fighting had made so much frost that the ground itself was turning to ice. I didn't know if either Elyk or Helvegen were still alive.

Then I saw a flash of yellow magic, and Elyk erupted from the thick haze with his sword spinning around his body. He held it by the blade, using the large crosspiece of the hilt like a sledgehammer to chip away piece after piece from the statue. It worked, and bits of masonry were flying in every direction through the room.

Helvegen wasn't so fortunate. She was lying on her back, her body wrapped in a sheet of ice and her head dangerously close to being stepped on by the massive statue. I grabbed Infernum from the ground and willed it to life, then raced to the woman's side. The blade's fire easily started to chew through all the ice that had wrapped around her torso. In a short moment, I had Helvegen standing on her own feet once more, though her left wrist and arm had been severely battered. "Drink your potion," I told her.

The fog that hung thick in that part of the room was starting to cloud my own mind again. I helped Helvegen grab her potion from her belt before turning to the statue, eager to move away from the debilitating miasma and think clearly once more.

Sword in my hand, I rushed at the statue to help Elyk . . . and I couldn't remember how I had beaten the first statue. I knew I had done it, but I couldn't bring the details of the fight into my mind. Whatever was hanging in the air was all I could think about. It stole my focus and wouldn't give it back.

A huge force thundered into my chest, knocking me to the ground and sending me skidding across the frozen ground. I didn't know if Elyk had hit me with his whirling sword or if the statue itself had shoved me away. In either instance, the pain it brought was massive. I heaved as my lungs struggled for air.

Away from the miasma, I remembered. If I used my fists, I could push the thing out a window.

I fought back all the pain coursing through my body and

got back on my feet. The ground beneath me was slick with frost, but I trudged forward and hardened my mind to the mental confusion threatening to overwhelm it.

I slammed a fist into the back of the statue, and the animated stone lurched a foot closer to the nearest window. Elyk seemed to understand my strategy—or at least I thought he did—and he began hammering on the creature in the same direction that I was. We pushed it from two sides, and under the joint onslaught of both of our attacks, we sent it plummeting down to its death far below.

Elyk tossed his sword to the ground. The blade was so bent and disfigured that it was almost closer to a hook than a straight weapon.

"Here," I told him, handing him Infernum by the hilt. "I don't know if you can get the fire to work, but it'll be better than nothing."

"A lot better," he said, rubbing his left hand across his forehead. The fog was starting to lift toward the higher reaches of the room, and both of us were coming out of it at the same time.

At the far end, the sorcerer didn't seem too upset that we had beaten his statues without taking a single casualty. He held a clear flask full of dark liquid in one hand and a short wand in the other. "You dare to disturb my progress!" the man yelled. His voice was high-pitched and frenzied. I couldn't tell if he was simply deranged or just overly confident. Either way, he was going to die.

I led the front of our little death triangle, Elyk to my left and Helvegen a few steps behind, still recovering from her wounds. Kulgun's healing potion had not been particularly strong, and she needed more time to fully recover her faculties. I hoped she wouldn't need to cast more than one or two spells. If all went well, Elyk and I would be able to easily overcome the sorcerer's physical defenses, and the battle would end quickly.

The crazed man's confidence didn't falter as we approached. He drank about half of whatever was in his bottle and wiped his mouth on one of his sleeves. "Come, my pets!" he yelled, throwing the rest of the bottle onto the ground where it shattered.

Instead of little shards of broken glass, the bottle exploded into a huge swarm of tiny, impossibly fast spiders. They were everywhere, hundreds of them all at once, and I started smashing them under my boots with impunity. "Hel, give us a distraction!" I called.

Elyk was busy smashing the spiders as well, though his own armor wasn't nearly as impenetrable as mine, and some of them had clearly gotten to his skin and started biting him. He yelled through clenched teeth, tossed my sword back to me, and started stripping off his chest armor, eager to rip the arachnids from his flesh.

I charged forward, leaving my two companions to deal with the rest of the spiders. With Infernum once more in my grasp, I knew it would only take a single hit to kill the boss. The man was unarmored, and my legendary sword would almost certainly cleave through any magical wards he had enacted to protect himself from physical attacks. A few steps from the sorcerer, I felt the first sting on my body. One of the spiders—or at least I hoped it was only one of them—had worked its way beneath my left gauntlet. I could feel its tiny little mandibles crunching through the skin over one of my knuckles, and then a stinging pain flared through my entire arm. The solitary bite was painful enough to make my eyes water. I couldn't imagine what Elyk was going through.

Despite the pain, I charged forward and swung down hard for the center of the sorcerer's chest. My flaming sword passed right through the man without slowing as though he was made of nothing more than detailed light. Some of

Helvegen's magic landed on his body at the same time, but we were fighting an illusion. None of it would have any effect.

I spun, keeping Infernum level in front of me in case the sorcerer had teleported, but he wasn't behind me, either. He stepped out of the portal on my right, and he had two swirling balls of ice held in his hands.

The magical orbs shot through the air before I had a chance to react. Both of them slammed into my chest where they were met with a blast of fire from my armor. Just like my reflexes, the fire was a second too slow to counteract the ice, and a deep, unforgiving cold encased my entire body. It was so cold I could barely move. My muscles contracted violently, sending more and more pain cascading all over my bones.

Another two spheres of magical ice appeared in the sorcerer's hands. I saw the attacks coming, and I had just enough time to activate Forsaken Barrier before they landed, instantly shifting me about six feet to my left while leaving behind an illusion of my own to take the hit.

Helvegen shot another bolt of dark energy toward the sorcerer, and that one seemed to have an effect. The man's eyes went wide, and he shot forth another two waves of punishing ice at a spot on the floor in front of his workbench. The orbs shattered harmlessly against the stone, and then the man turned and sprinted back through the portal.

When he didn't emerge anywhere else in the room, I figured he had fled for good and we would need to hunt him down through whatever place he had gone.

"Get what we can for our alchemist, and then let's chase him," I said. Elyk was panting heavily and struggling to get up off the ground. At least it looked like all of the spiders had finally been killed.

"I'll make it," he stated, accepting a hand from Helvegen to regain his feet. "Just fucking hurts, no real damage, I think."

"What about getting that prisoner back to her village?"

our painter asked. She was looking toward the stairs, but the woman we had saved was nowhere to be seen.

Going after her would take time, and I didn't want to let the sorcerer prepare any kind of defense on the other side of the portal. "Just leave her. She can figure out how to get back home on her own. Better loot if we kill the boss. The escort quest won't be worth much. Let's go," I said.

Helvegen and I grabbed a couple of random bottles from the workbench, careful not to lose our balance on all the fresh ice underneath it, and I pocketed a scroll as well. We could figure out what it all was later.

When Elyk had recovered enough to fight once more, I led the way through the portal where the sorcerer had disappeared.

The wall behind the stone ring was visually just as solid as all the others. When I touched it, my hand sank through the false image.

The other side looked more like the mine where we had started than the castle we had just left. I was the first to make it through, Helvegen and Elyk spreading out to either side. We were in a softly illuminated cavern covered in wet moss and a sticky tangle of white silken webs. The chamber itself was large, and I could hear water flowing somewhere up ahead, though it wasn't loud enough to make me think we were coming up on a waterfall.

"Stay on your guard," I said quietly, taking a few steps forward. Shadows played against the wall at the far end of the cavern. Something up ahead made a clicking noise.

Then I saw it. A huge, eight-legged beast with dripping mandibles was waiting for us at the end of the cavern. Its massive abdomen was highlighted in red like a black widow, and it had a pair of monstrous spinnerets hanging down to the ground. Behind it, the far wall was so thoroughly coated in silk webbing that I couldn't see if the room continued or not.

Perhaps the sorcerer had fled to another chamber and left the spider as a little treat for us.

We wouldn't know until we killed the black widow and started carving through the web.

As was becoming the usual format of our combat, I took the lead. I charged right for the center of the horrific beast, Infernum blazing brightly before me, and swatted two flying globs of spider spit out of the air. I reached the clacking mandibles, and they were too big for me to dodge. Luckily, my armor held through the first powerful bite, though I felt it starting to bend inward. Fire exploded out in all directions from my breastplate, and I added to it with Infernum, quickly severing the spider's left jaw from its face and taking out a handful of eyes at the same time.

The beast shrieked and squirmed backward, its legs thrashing out in front of it to knock me away, and I was launched back about ten feet. The extensive net of webs covering the floor helped break my fall, though my helmet still cracked painfully into the stone and sent a dizzying clatter of noise through my brain.

I watched Elyk run past as I struggled to get my mind back under control. He scooped up Infernum from the ground and charged in almost the exact same manner I had. If the beast had still held both of its mandibles, he would have been sliced in half at the waist almost immediately. As it was, the only remaining mandible clacked into his side, and then Infernum punched down through the top of the spider's head. The trio of eyes that remained on the side of the spider's dripping face were shorn off, and they scattered against the cavern wall.

The beast didn't have much fight left in it. Our relentless attack had already come close to killing it, and all it could do was flail its legs side to side in a desperate attempt to escape the onslaught. I got back to my feet and rushed in to join Elyk, though he didn't need any help using my legendary sword to slay the boss. He hacked and slashed through the center of the spider's thorax, throwing fire and arachnid guts all over the chamber with every swing. Its clawing legs shuddered twice at its sides, and then it died.

"One hell of a sword," Elyk said, tossing the blade to my outstretched hand. He was covered in bug gore and smelled terrible. As I extinguished the blade to sheath it at my side, the spider's corpse started convulsing and twitching like something inside it was having a seizure or trying to break free. We all backed away slowly, waiting for whatever was happening to conclude.

"I think it's getting smaller," Helvegen said.

She was right. The corpse was shrinking, its hard exoskeleton cracking and rupturing as it compressed in on itself. Before long, the carcass had been reduced to the size of a man—the sorcerer—still just as dead as it had been before. We had killed the boss, and the dungeon was finished.

"Ha, leveled up!" Elyk announced. "Nice."

"That wasn't too bad. A solid fight." I used my boot to roll the corpse over, moving the robe to inspect it for any more loot. The man's belt had a couple more glass flasks on it, though they had all been crushed against his chest.

Helvegen was pushing aside some of the spider web at the back of the room and peering into whatever lay beyond. "Use your sword to carve through here," she said. "There's more loot."

I took Infernum over to the back wall and started carving through layer after layer of spider's silk. It fell away in great heaps, and before long what remained wasn't strong enough to hold itself up. The entire barrier came falling off the ceiling like snow from a roof.

The room beyond was small. Two corpses dangled in more webs just beyond the entrance, but they weren't terribly interesting. What caught my attention was a wooden chest banded with iron and sporting a steel lock. The chest was about half the size of the sorcerer's corpse, and it looked heavy.

"Think you could bust it open?" Elyk asked.

"There's no doubt that Infernum would carve right through the lock, but I don't want to risk damaging whatever is inside. Could be fragile, you know? Everything else from the sorcerer is alchemical. There could be a whole set of implements and alembics inside. Let's just try to get it back to the citadel," I explained.

With my huge buff to physical, it wasn't too hard to lift the chest. The only challenge was getting my arms to stretch far enough to grab both handles, but I managed nonetheless.

"Back through the portal?" Elyk asked.

There wasn't anywhere else left to go. "Sure thing. Let's do it."

We walked back through the portal that should have taken us to the top floor of the highest tower in the castle, but instead we appeared back in the mine where we had started, the dungeon run complete. "Well, we didn't finish the escort quest, but who cares? I'm ready to check out our loot!"

The journey back to the mine's entrance was a tough one. The chest was a little too bulky to be easily maneuvered through the tight subterranean quarters of the twisting mine shafts, and Elyk had to help me more than once. Finally, we made it to the top, and the progress our mining crew was making was noticeable. They had a cart full of raw materials waiting to be turned into ingots at the small forge, and two other miners were busy extending the iron tracks in the direction of Undercroft Citadel.

I was tempted to order our NPC slaves to carry the heavy loot crate back to the base, but in the end, I wanted the physical practice. Moving something so heavy for a good distance would at least get me close to improving my physical stat, and that would get me to level fourteen.

Sure enough, the notification flickered across my vision at just about the same time we returned to the necropolis. I dropped off the lockbox at the workshop for Geirr and Kulgun to figure out, and they both seemed more than happy to take a crack at it. I left the potions we had claimed from the castle in their possession as well before going into my room to sleep. It was maybe an hour or so after dusk, and my body was tired. Our jaunt through the dungeon had taken a lot more time than the three of us had realized.

CHAPTER 17

When I awoke the next morning, the first thing on my mind was my new talent choice. Being level fourteen already felt like I was progressing quickly, which was exactly what I needed to do. If my empire was to grow powerful enough to take on Vic and his gang of lowlifes, I needed to be unstoppable. With a smile on my face, I lay beneath my sheets and accessed my new options:

Bear the Heavens (Physical): Lady Kalma's most stalwart warriors never falter. The deathbringer gains the ability to use all shields without becoming encumbered. Additionally, foes attempting to push or grapple with the deathbringer will be easily overcome. Passive.

Malignant Putrescence (Cunning): The deathbringer can implant a vile poison sack in the flesh of enemies. The poison sack ruptures after three minutes, spreading a noxious cloud of deadly spores through the air. Active, consumes minor energy.

Subjugation (Influence): The weak are culled, and even the strong learn to bend their knees. Lady Kalma's deathbringer can readily identify those whose lives are only suitable to be ended. Such insignificant beings can be instantly consumed with a single touch and raised again as zombies to fight at the deathbringer's side. Active, consumes minor energy.

My initial thought was to ignore the physical skill and focus on the other two. I had more sheer strength than I would need as long as I had my gauntlets, and using a shield felt like something I wasn't about to try. Both Malignant Putrescence and Subjugation felt like they had a lot of potential for useful application. Being able to turn weaker enemies into zombies in the middle of a fight could potentially turn a battle from a loss into a victory, though I wasn't exactly sure what the game would consider to be weak enough. The skill could turn out to have tons of targets, or it could be a wasted talent depending on where the AI drew the cutoff.

Malignant Putrescence was starting to look a lot better. I liked the idea of being able to plant a toxic seed inside an enemy, watch them run back to their own allies for cover or protection, and then infecting them all with poison from afar. My only reservation was the requirement of melee range, but the skill still outshined both of the other choices for level fourteen.

I focused on the cunning talent and unlocked it with a thought. Honestly, I was eager to test it out, but I didn't really have a supply of willing subjects waiting to be infected with toxic spores. I could go back to Riverside and try it on one of the NPCs there, but I still needed them as a source of food. Killing them all wouldn't bring me much gain, tempting as it was.

With a sigh born mostly of contentedness, I mentally commanded my room to bring up the lights and turn down the air conditioning. I stretched, tossed on my clothes, and went first to the workshop to see if my engineer had managed to open the chest from the spider den without damaging the contents. Geirr was happy to see me, though the chest remained locked atop one of the anvils.

"No luck on the box yet, Boss," he said, a smile on his face. "But those scrolls you brought back are worth the trip on their own."

"Oh yeah? What are they?" I hadn't bothered to check out the two pieces of parchment we had stolen, and since I wasn't a class focused on production and didn't have much in the way of craftsmanship myself, whatever schematics or patterns they held probably wouldn't have made sense to me anyway.

Geirr ushered me over to the alchemy workbench where both of the scrolls had been laid flat with a few stones. "The first one isn't too much, just a recipe for a resist frost damage potion, but the second one . . ." He pointed to the next parchment and practically beamed. "It's a schematic for a trap the likes of which I've never seen. Let me show you how it works."

It turned out that Geirr had immediately been able to read the two parchments last night when we had brought them back, and he had stayed awake through dawn making parts and figuring it all out. How I had slept through him hammering away in the workshop less than thirty feet from my bed was a mystery. Perhaps I had been more tired than I had thought.

He had a big square frame set up on the ground outside the workshop, and crisscrossing the metal bars were long strips of studded leather that looked like they had been salvaged from some of the knights' armor after we had killed the Pyreborn Legion. The whole assembly reminded me a bit of bear trap.

"How does it work? I can't really tell how close it is to being ready, sorry." I didn't want to bring down the man's spirits with my complete lack of engineering knowledge, though he took my ignorance in stride.

Geirr pointed out a small pair of springs on the top and bottom of the frame that I had missed. "We bury it a couple inches below the surface and cover it with dirt. The leather should keep the ground somewhat solid above it. Then, once someone steps on the inside, these springs snap closed to capture whoever is on top. But that's just the beginning!"

So my bear trap idea seemed to be rather accurate. Still, something like that wasn't terribly complex. "What's the rest?" I asked.

Geirr lifted up one of the leather straps to reveal a small row of glass pouches on the other side. What I had thought were studs in the leather were actually the tops of fixtures designed to hold vials in place. "Once the trap closes, these little canisters fill up bladders with a special chemical compound that's lighter than air. As long as we don't catch more than two people in each trap, it should lift them right out of the ground and send them into the sky!"

"Oh, nice! That's awesome! And how long will the gas last? How long before they come plummeting back to the ground in a steel death cage?" I asked. I imagined a huge army from Echelon coming to sack the citadel, surrounding our walls with knights and catapults and battering rams. A few of these traps placed at strategic intervals beyond the moat would certainly be a sight to behold.

"I'm not exactly sure yet," Geirr answered. "I think it will depend mostly on how much chemical compound we can produce and how heavy the target is. Kulgun knows more about that kind of thing than I do, and he thinks we should be able to lift an armored attacker at least fifty feet before the gas runs out and drops them back down."

"Ha, fifty feet is plenty! Good work. I know you have a ton of other projects to complete, but once you get one of these fully operational, I want to test it with something. Keep me posted on your progress." I gave him a slap on the back and let him return to his work. From what I could tell, the first trap wasn't too far from being finished, though I wasn't sure how long it would take Kulgun to render the proper compounds to make the chemicals we needed. Hopefully I'd get to see one in action sooner rather than later.

As Geirr returned his attention back to the trap, I silently commanded one of the gargoyles from the necropolis to take me back to the top. I got it to dig its claws into my shoulders a little less, and then I was sitting at the apex of my empire once more. I could see it all, and I couldn't help but smile.

Tendershoot Mine was in sight, as was Riverside, though both were far enough away that I couldn't actually make out any details of what was going on at either location. In a few days we would receive another shipment of food through the front gates, and at the rate we were expanding, we would need it more than ever. Luckily, it looked like our herbalist was already making progress setting up a little patch of farmable soil for us to raise our own medicinal plants. If it worked well, I could see us expanding the area to include a crop or two, though that would have to be pretty far in the future.

There was also the issue of getting enough soldiers together to defend the supply train we were building from the mine to the workshop. I had a handful of gargoyles at my disposal, but I didn't know if they could fight.

Only one way to find out.

I mentally commanded the two nearest gargoyles to take flight from the necropolis and hover in front of me. They obeyed, their stone wings beating the air and making some of my hair fly around my face. I realized I hadn't cut it in some time, and it was probably longer than it had been since . . . since my wife had told me to grow it long because she liked how it looked on me. After she died, I had kept it a lot shorter. I don't know why, but growing it out long just hadn't felt right. Now, sitting atop my necropolis and surveying my kingdom, I decided that I liked it.

When my thoughts finally returned to the task at hand, I was excited to see what the gargoyles could do. I mentally commanded them to spar, and they turned in midair to face each other at once. The fought, but I wasn't exactly impressed. Their heavy fists didn't deal much damage, and maintaining their altitude made their balance precarious, giving them nothing for purchase to be able to throw the full weight of their massive bodies into one another. I knew that if I told them to land and really go at it I'd see a much more impressive display, though I didn't get the feeling that the necropolis would simply regrow destroyed gargoyles like a tree bearing fruit. Still, knowing they could fight was at least beneficial.

It had been a few days since I had investigated my character sheet and the building pane available to me as a dungeon boss, so I decided to see if anything had changed. I got the feeling that testing the gargoyles' combat abilities—or rather discovering that they had them in the first place—would add them to the military strength of Undercroft Citadel.

Ben Hales, Level 14 Deathbringer, Defender of the Necropolis
Physical: 28
Cunning: 24
Influence: 23 (33)
Renown: 18
Investigation: 7
Trade: 9
Craftsmanship: 9
Fortune: 9
Infamy: 41
Status: unstable, shrouded by Lady Kalma, feared, hated by Echelon, hated by Imps (wild beasts)
Holdings: Undercroft Citadel (Dungeon), Riverside (Vassal), Tendershoot Mine
Allegiance: Lady Kalma, the Stench of Corpses

I scanned everything to make sure there were no surprises before opening the sheet for my empire:

Undercroft Citadel (Dungeon)

Commander: Ben Hales (Influence: 33)

Bosses: Xia (Warlock), Helvegen (Painter), Xollmomath (Necromancer), Elyk (Harvester)

Resources: Moderate stockpiles of food and lumber, moderate stockpiles of weapons, minor stockpiles of wealth (gems), no stockpiles of exotic goods or artifacts, moderate stockpiles of crafting resources

Military Strength: 4 warlocks, 17 zombies, 1 charnel golem, 1 truthbreaker paladin

Specialists: 1 engineer, 1 alchemist, 1 herbalist, 1 hospitaler

Defensive Structures: Reinforced wooden wall enhanced with fear glyphs (detonating corpses), minor defensive wards, minor physical traps (punji pits), small guard tower, necropolis, moat, 5 stone gargoyles

Active Production Facilities: 2 forges, 2 crafting benches, 1 engineering bench, 1 alchemy bench, 1 herbalist grove

That pane had a few new items. I was a little surprised to see that the gargoyles had been placed into the defensive category and not as members of the citadel's military, though I figured it just meant they couldn't stray too far from the structure itself. The more I thought about it, the more I realized that Xollmomath had the same limitation. Perhaps the necromancer's ability to grow stronger and eventually leave our territory was the key difference, and the gargoyles had no such option available to them.

Our stockpiles of weapons had increased since the battle with the Pyreborn Legion, and our number of zombie fighters had increased as well. Most notably different was the addition of the active production facilities category. It was nice to be able to see everything the citadel had acquired. If everything went according to plan, we would keep adding more and more to the settlement, and eventually there would be so many active production areas that I wouldn't be able to take a quick survey of them all each morning.

As I sat on the top of my necropolis and watched everything

going on down below, a flutter of movement caught my eye. Someone was coming. They were still pretty far away, but they were coming nonetheless, and from the direction of Echelon. I mentally commanded the two gargoyles that had just been fighting to go and warn Xia and Xollmomath while a third took me back down to the bottom, but the stone constructions had no lungs or voices. I had to trust that they would figure it out.

I ran into my room as soon as my feet hit the ground and raised the lights inside the necropolis. I started strapping on my armor as quickly as I could. Outside, it didn't take long for the citadel to go into a controlled panic. Everyone was strapping on gear and getting ready, and confused shouts were coming from every direction as my underlings tried to figure out exactly what was going on.

It took me a little under five minutes to get ready for war. Had our visitor been riding hard, they would have easily reached the moat and the wall by then, but as I emerged from my room, I saw no breach. No one was inside our walls laying waste to the NPCs.

"Xia, Elyk, Hel—with me. Xollmomath, take the warlocks and the zombies to the front gate. Everyone! Get ready!" I yelled. There was no hesitation.

I led my small band to the guard tower, hoping we could see whoever was approaching without needing to climb up the inner part of the wall and get too close to any potential combat.

"There's just one?" Elyk asked when we had all reached the second floor of the small tower. He had a hand over his eyes to shield his vision from the morning sun.

"Anyone else see anything?" I asked. So far, it was only a single rider carrying a banner and moving slowly.

The rider continued to come forward until they were about a hundred feet from our walls. Curious, the four of us watched on as the rider took their banner and threw the pole into the ground, then dismounted and sat down on the dirt next to the flapping cloth.

"A challenge?" Helvegen wondered aloud.

"Or a trap," I added.

We waited for quite some time, and whoever was out there did not move.

Elyk was pacing back and forth with his hands on his hips. "If it was someone else from the Pyreborn Legion looking for their friends, the banner would be red, right?"

I couldn't tell exactly, but it looked like the banner they had planted in the soil was either white or grey. "Come on. Us four. Let's go see what the hell is going on."

I led the way down from the guard tower and toward the front gate, Infernum hanging at my side and giving me unmeasurable confidence. Xia attempted to protest my leaving the safety of the walls, saying I should remain with Xollmomath in case there truly was a trap, but staying behind felt cowardly.

To the warlock's dismay, I kept my position at the front of our diamond formation as we exited the gatehouse. The road was still a little beat up from the last fight, and more than one splotchy bloodstain marred the otherwise brown and green tones of the grassy countryside.

"A player, not an NPC," Helvegen said quietly. Sure enough, the person sitting on the grass had a name printed in Echelon's colors above their head.

"A woman, and no armor," the harvester said.

Bringing up the rear of our formation, Xia was the only one displaying any outright nervousness. "Feels like a trap," she muttered more than once.

Secretly, I shared her assessment. Everything about the strange encounter felt too strange. But the field beyond where the woman and her horse remained was flat. If there was an army of mounted knights waiting to ambush us, they would be so far away that we'd easily make it back to the walls before we were in any real danger.

Despite my inner reservations, I kept up my outward air of absolute confidence and arrogance. Finally, I stopped my retinue about twenty feet from the unmoving woman. Her horse was grazing idly behind her, far enough that if the woman tried to make a run for it she wouldn't be too quick.

For a long moment, no one said anything. The woman just kept looking at me, a slight smile on her otherwise inscrutable face.

"Well," I said after growing tired of the tension. "What is it you've come to do?"

The woman gave a brief glance to the grey banner at her side. "King Ahmose II requests an audience with the leader of Undercroft Citadel," she said evenly.

That caught me a bit off guard. I hadn't expected the unarmed woman to be an emissary from the king at all. But . . . could I believe her?

"Certainly you must have some proof that what you say is true, that the king truly does want to meet and you aren't just here as some elaborate trap, yes?" I asked.

She raised an eyebrow. "You think ahead. The king appreciates such qualities." The woman uncrossed her legs and stood—eliciting a bit of tensed muscles from my allies—and then plucked a small item from one of her pockets. She held it flat on the palm of her hand, and I couldn't see it from such a distance. "Here. A token of the king's sincerity."

"Xia, go see what it is. If you think it's safe, bring it to me," I commanded. Risking an NPC, powerful as she was, felt like the best choice.

The warlock sauntered forward, and Elyk took a few tentative steps toward the emissary as well, ready to snap into action at a moment's notice should the need arise. I kept my right hand on Infernum's pommel in what I hoped was a stance that exuded confidence. If I truly was going to meet with King Ahmose II, I wanted his emissary to report back that I was not some idiot out in the sticks messing around with a few NPCs. I wanted him to fear me if possible, or at least treat me with the respect I had earned.

Xia kept one hand back as she plucked the small item from the emissary's hand. I half expected the object to detonate in some huge explosion, sending Xia's scattered remains all over the field, but nothing of the sort happened. In fact, nothing really happened at all. The warlock inspected the item for a while, turning it over in her fingers and holding it up close to her eyes, then returned to my side.

"What is it?" I asked. It looked like a green gemstone, perhaps an emerald, though a simple token of wealth seemed like it would be an odd choice for the king to send as a demonstration of his honesty. There wouldn't be any meaning to something like that.

I called up the item's information to my vision to see exactly what it was:

Favor of the King: The leader of Echelon, King Ahmose I, imbued this emerald with a small part of his soul upon his death. Anyone possessing it may approach the king's grave and use the gemstone to communicate with the fallen monarch for a short period of time.

"The king does not give you such an artifact lightly," the emissary called when she was sure I had read the item's details. "It is his most treasured possession, and he fully expects to receive it back at your meeting. Do you believe me now?"

I nodded. The relic was truly something of infinite value, allowing the king to talk to his dead father. My mind thought first of Ingrid and then of my wife. Of course, neither of them had made such an enchanted gemstone before dying. I hadn't even known things like that existed. In any case, it probably would have come with a price tag in the millions or higher. I sighed and handed the artifact to Elyk for safekeeping.

"Alright, I accept. I'll meet the king, but not in his castle. Neutral ground," I called back to the emissary.

She looked like she had anticipated my demand. "There is a village not far from here: Riverside. Do you know of it?"

Ha, that was my vassal. A bunch of their NPCs were my slaves working in Tendershoot mine at that very moment. "Sure. I'll meet there," I said.

"The king will find you tomorrow at dusk. He will bring a full regiment of his most powerful guards, but he will not attack you or your companions." The woman grabbed her banner from the ground and returned it to the leather holder on her horse's flank before climbing back into the saddle.

"Tell him I'll be there," I said. "We'll come armed, but he has my word that I won't try to fight. We don't need any more bloodshed."

The woman tipped her head. "I will deliver your message to the king. Be well." With that, she kicked her horse into a light trot and started back toward the city.

When she was gone, our small group finally relaxed a little bit.

"You're going to the meeting?" Elyk was the first to ask. "I don't know, it seems risky."

I couldn't help but laugh. "Of course not. And none of you are going either. He's pulling all of his best guards from the castle, and there's a vault in Echelon that currently holds something I need. *That* is where we will be."

The violent harvester joined my laughter. "Damn, Ben. Alright. Let's go sack the castle while the king is away."

CHAPTER 18

We spent the day and a half before the scheduled meeting with the king in a frenzy of activity. Xollmomath and the warlocks worked around the clock to ensure our defenses were as stalwart as possible, while neither Geirr not Kulgun left the workshop as they got everything ready for our trip. Geirr's first floating trap was finished, though he didn't have enough chemicals to reload it, so a demonstration would have to wait.

When we were finally ready to depart around noon the next day, I felt confident. I had my armor and legendary sword, of course, and the others were as thoroughly outfitted as they were going to be.

Elyk finally had a full suit of reinforced leather armor. It wasn't entirely covering his body like my steel, but that's how he wanted it. His talents required him to move quickly, and the less restrictive studded leather would let him fly through the battlefield doing what he did best. Geirr had also made him a scythe. The weapon stood as tall as he did, and its curved blade was probably four feet long. Helvegen had heavier armor, wearing a breastplate and greaves stolen from the Pyreborn Legion. She also carried a sword and a kite shield, though she was admittedly not great with them. If all went well, she would stay more toward the back of each fight and fling her spells from afar.

Xia wore her customary robe, and she had as many defensive enchantments cast on her body by Xollmomath as she could withstand. She would be formidable, there was no doubt about that. She also kept five of our zombie soldiers under her command, and each of them was rigged with magic essentially as suicide bombers, ready to run into the fray and detonate in a fiery explosion of rotten human parts.

We kept two of the NPC warlocks with us as well, the conjuror and one of the unspecialized ones. They were outfitted similarly to Xia, and they would help push the front lines. Leading our little band was the truthbreaker paladin we had resurrected. He was still a fragile zombie, but he wore more armor than any of the rest of us. The soldier was basically one solid sheet of steel from head to toe, and Geirr had been able to add an array of sharp spikes to it that I was eager to watch in action.

For potions, we didn't have as much as I would have liked. Kulgun still didn't have the materials he needed to really start producing high-end elixirs in quantity. Still, we had four healing potions between us, two resist frost potions just in case, and three different low quality elemental grenades that we could throw. Kulgun had also been able to make a single vial of magical smoke that would probably be more useful than even the healing potions. The smoke would come out thick almost like ink from a squid, clinging to everything it touched and hopefully blinding our enemies. If we needed to escape or to simply ratchet down the difficulty of a fight, it would be perfect.

Geirr had also managed to open the chest we had brought back from the castle dungeon. The loot inside wasn't as exciting as I had hoped it would be. We received a handful of more potion recipes—a little expected since the boss had been an alchemist. In addition to the scrolls and a few empty potion vials that we used to store Kulgun's new brews, we had also gotten a delicate wand with a single charge of a power spell: Fill with Spiders. The spell had to be lined up perfectly as it would only generate an effect if it hit living flesh. If any of our zombies got in the way or the spell accidentally collided with a wall or even armor, it would be wasted. The effect, however, was drastic. It implanted a swarm of the vicious spiderlings that we had fought in the castle inside a host. When the host was killed, the spiderlings erupted from their eggs to cause havoc, and we would hopefully be far away from the action by the time that happened. The prospect of being bitten by more of the nasty little arachnids was something I didn't want to face.

Despite our preparation, I was nervous. Everyone except Elyk was nervous too. The harvester was eager, excitedly shifting his weight from one foot to the other and pacing like a dog about to go on a walk. He was ready for more bloodshed. He'd get it soon enough.

It rained on our long walk from Undercroft Citadel to Echelon. The cold droplets easily snaked underneath my armor to soak my clothes, and the steel chafed my skin as it moved back and forth and clamped the wet cloth tight to my skin. I needed a cape or a hood of some sort to keep the rain from drenching me. I had given one of the Pyreborn Legion's banners to Xia for exactly that purpose, though she had not made anything with it yet.

We approached the huge city from the west, the side closest to the keep. The castle itself was absolutely magnificent. Huge spires reached up toward the rain clouds overhead. Battlements stretched between each tower with soldiers dutifully patrolling their walkways, crossbows in their hands and swords hanging from their sides. Pennants fluttered in the rain from the peaks of the towers, and Ahmose's banners hung from the stone walls.

"We can't hope to climb all the way over," I said. The curtain wall in front of us was probably forty feet high, built directly into the back of the castle. Luckily, none of the guards were looking our way, though I had no doubt that some of the men patrolling the battlements would soon turn to face us.

"Come on. Let's go through the stables," Helvegen suggested. The stables weren't far away, and they had an arched exit carved into the wall where the horses could be led out to graze. The problem was, the door to the pastures was barred.

"How do we get in?" I asked. We moved up alongside the stable entrance so we were close enough to the wall to stay out of sight from the guards above.

The bars covering the entrance formed an iron lattice work that would take hours to hack through, if it was possible at all. Besides the time and effort it would take, the noise we would make would alert the entire castle to our presence.

"We could wait for them to open it," Xia suggested.

Our little pack of groaning zombies lined up against the wall were already starting to make more noise than I wanted. "No," I said. "We need something quicker."

Of everyone in our party, I figured Helvegen—being the most objectively attractive—had the best chance of luring someone close enough to kill. "Hel, pretend your lost. Go rattle the bars and see if you can get one of the guards to come close enough to grab."

The woman nodded, her long hair matted to her face in the rain, and ran up to the door. She grabbed the rusted metal gate and shook it, calling into the stables for someone to let her in.

Only a moment or two later, a pair of NPC stable hands

wearing daggers on their belts began to warily approach. I ducked back to the side before they could see me, eager to let the painter work.

Surprisingly, a little bit of magic left the woman's fingertips. From my position with my back flat against the stone wall, I couldn't see what she had done. I just had to wait.

"Please, I got lost out here in the rain. I'm just ... so cold ..."

"Uh, what were you doing out in the king's pasture?"

"Just let me in, won't you?"

"Maybe ... I mean, I guess."

There was a long pause, and all I could hear was the rain beating against the side of the castle.

"McKinnon! Get this woman a blanket or something from the barn!" The sound of keys rattling against metal accompanied the man's rough voice.

Helvegen shot me a quick glance, and I nodded to Elyk on the other side of the gate. The harvester swung his scythe with all the force he could muster right as Helvegen leapt backward out of its path. The blade lodged deeply in the man's chest, nearly coming out of his back.

"Here," Elyk said, reaching through the bars. He pulled a ring of keys through to our side and jingled them between his fingers. "Got our way in."

We unlocked the gate as the second stable hand started screaming at the top of his lungs. Piling through the archway into the covered stable grounds, our little crew stormed the area in a matter of seconds. By the time our five trailing zombies had come out of the rain, four stable workers were dead in the mud. We stood in a rough circle in the midst of the carnage, no one saying a word.

After a moment, when I was sure that no other sounds of alarm were coming from elsewhere in the keep next to the stable, we started to move. "This way," I said, pointing to a stone staircase that led up to the side of the castle. "Kill anything that moves. I don't care who it is or what they're doing. As soon as one of the guards raises an alarm and alerts the others, the AI will probably send out a message to everyone sworn to defend the king. Once that happens, I don't have a clue how long we'll have. Ahmose's crew might storm the citadel. We have to go fast."

The staircase I had chosen basically at random led to a kitchen. We burst through a wooden door, Elyk and his bloody scythe leading the way, and basically trampled a woman carrying a basket full of uncooked bread toward an oven. There were probably a dozen NPCs working in the large kitchen. I stood back by the door with my sword still sheathed at my side and let my party devour the easy experience points. Sadly, the workers didn't yield much as they died.

Elyk and the truthbreaker handled just about every kill between the two of them, and that was just the way I wanted things to go down. The longer we could reserve our magical abilities, the better off we would be.

When the quick slaughter was over, I took a moment to relish the scene. We had been inside the king's keep for all of two or three minutes, and we had already eradicated a good chunk of his serving staff. *Every corpse brings me closer to vengeance, Ingrid,* I silently whispered to my daughter. I saw her face in my mind, so full of life one minute and then so full of pain and anguish the next.

I was standing with one heavy boot on the corpse of the older woman we had trampled to death, and I ground my heel through her bones.

"Two doors out, Boss," Elyk remarked, bringing my thoughts back to the task at hand.

"Check them out," I told him. To the others, I commanded them not to bother trying to loot any of the servants. Even if one of them happened to be wearing a magic ring or necklace, it wouldn't be worth the lost time to recover.

"This one," Elyk said only a few seconds later. He stood in front of a wooden door two steps up from the kitchen floor.

"Where does it lead?" I moved up beside the door to get a peek through the gap. The next room looked like a hallway, the walls lined with a few paintings in nice wooden frames.

Elyk ran his gauntlet along the four-foot length of his scythe, coating his hand in fresh blood. "I don't know, but the other one just goes to a storeroom."

That was good enough for me. Elyk pushed open the door, and I waved everyone through. I stepped into line behind the main party, right ahead of the five walking zombie bombs. As we ran down the hallway, Elyk smeared each of the paintings with blood from his gauntlets. He was already the most violent person I had ever met, and the way he didn't just kill our enemies but desecrated them and everything they owned was terrifying—and beautiful. It sent one hell of a clear message.

The end of the hall opened into a dining space, one I figured to be a more intimate reception area where the royal family could entertain a small number of guests without using their man banquet area. Luckily, the hall was devoid of living things for us to kill.

Serving as the main nexus for food and other items from the kitchen to be delivered throughout the castle, the hall had several doors along its walls. "Check each door. We're looking for something that goes down, probably to a crypt or some other kind of underground vault, I'm guessing." The party fanned out and began easing open doors to peer through.

With the rain obscuring the sun, there wasn't much light filtering through the high windows overhead. I hoped it wouldn't take much longer to at least get on the right track toward wherever the scarab jewel we sought was located. Every minute we spent stampeding through the castle halls was one we were essentially stealing. I didn't know how many we would get.

The undead truthbreaker paladin wrenched open the door it had checked and then issued forth a burst of black magic from its mouth and chest. An armored guard collapsed inward a second later, groaning and reaching forward with an outstretched hand. The paladin wrapped both hands around its sword and swung down, severing the guard's head from his shoulders with a single strike.

Groaning, the truthbreaker pointed in the direction from which the guard had come. I poked my head through the door, then waved for everyone to follow. The undead had discovered a path downward, and that was good enough.

The staircase was tight, high-walled, and dark. I willed Infernum to life so we could see, though I wasn't too keen on being in the front of the pack without at least an NPC going first. In the tight space of the stairs, there wasn't enough room to maneuver the truthbreaker to take point.

We reached another door, and I held up a fist to keep everyone behind me quiet. I listened for a moment with my ear pressed up against the wood, and I could make out a few voices coming from the other side. I didn't know what they were saying.

"Sounds like two or three," I whispered back toward Elyk and Xia behind the truthbreaker.

I gingerly tested the doorknob, and it was unlocked. Sadly, the rusted metal screeched as I turned it, and the voices on the other side instantly quieted.

"Let's go!" I yelled, shouldering through the door at full speed.

I spilled into the next room, and my breath caught in my chest. We had just charged headlong into the castle's barracks. About twenty or so guards, each of them wide-eyed and scrambling for weapons, stared back at us. Without hesitation, I swung hard for the nearest soldier's waist, and Infernum cut him in half.

System Notification: New Event! The forces of Undercroft Citadel are laying waste to Castle Echelon! Undead are terrorizing the halls, and a powerful band of warlocks is slaughtering the guards!

Elyk loosed a primal scream and started spinning somewhere to my right. A piece of human flesh and bone smacked into my face, leaving a bloody smear down the side of my nose and over my mouth. I spat to clear the taste from my lips, then plowed onward to the next guard.

It looked like the king had been true to his emissary's word and taken plenty of guards with him to our meeting. The barracks had enough beds and equipment chests for at least eighty or a hundred men, and we were fighting less than a third of that number—though I didn't know how many more were scattered throughout the rest of the castle and currently charging toward us. At least the system notification hadn't told everyone which room we were in.

I hacked through two more guards, slicing one man's sword in half as I cleaved through his shoulder, and by then my party had fully entered the barracks. Two of the walking zombie bombs were running into the thick of things right past me on either side, and I used their distraction to dive back a few paces and hopefully get out of the blast radius.

Magic from the warlocks was flying over my head at the same time. In all the chaos, it was hard to figure out exactly what was going on. Then I felt a heavy sword slam into my breastplate, turning me a few inches, and I saw an unarmored guard with fear blazing in his eyes. He held his short sword with both hands, but he was too terrified to pull it back and swing it again—likely as a result of how thoroughly my armor had negated his best efforts.

I reared back and slugged him with Infernum's hilt. My gauntlets and the sword's cross piece combined for a devastating hit. Clearly, my insane level of physical stat was far beyond anything the NPC guard could ever hope to survive. He didn't even reel backward. My fist blasted *through* his skull, and the rest of his bloody corpse simply collapsed to the floor, his head nothing more than a pulpy red mess covering my gauntlet.

The zombie bombs reached their destination, and they exploded at the same time in the very center of the barracks. Parts went flying in every direction. Most of them were from the zombies, but a good number also came from the three guards that had been hacking at them and trying to take them down. I didn't know if the magic turning my expendable soldiers into bombs was dependent on the zombies being animated when it went off or not. Frankly, I didn't care. The detonation worked, and the effect it had was extreme.

Maybe ten guards were still standing. A few of them had already been wounded by fiery warlock magic, and all ten of them were running for the rear exit.

"Cut them down!" I bellowed. I watched from the center of the room as my party swarmed over beds, trunks, and corpses. They ran forward like demons, slashing the fleeing guards in the back or burning them alive with powerful spells.

In the space of a few heartbeats, the room was devoid of enemies. "Did any guards escape?" I asked.

Elyk had his head out of the next door. "No," he called back. "The coast is clear, but we're headed outside again."

There wasn't anywhere else for us to go, so I commanded everyone onward into the castle's bailey. The rain had turned the ground to thick mud. What was once a magnificent, grassy area dominated by four huge cherry trees anchoring the corners now looked more like a cemetery. We were covered in blood and gore, sloshing through mud that came up to our ankles, and our mere presence in the typically serene bailey was a blight upon its beauty.

From the wall and battlements across from where we had emerged, a crossbow thrummed. The bolt hit one of my warlocks squarely in the chest, and the NPC went down without a word. A handful of guards were running back and forth on the parapet, pointing down at us and shouting commands.

There wasn't a staircase up to the battlements from the inside of the bailey. There was a door near the main gatehouse not too far away, but crossing the mud under crossbow fire just to enter a tight staircase would be suicide. To my left, the main doors to the castle had been shut and no doubt barred from the inside. To my right . . . we found our prize.

A small marble mausoleum stood with its outer gate open, and I could see stairs leading underground beyond the first row of square tombs. "There!" I yelled, pointing with my flaming sword.

Elyk led the way, rushing for the small structure without hesitation. Another crossbow bolt rocketed down from the battlement, and I thanked my lucky stars when it thudded into the ground a few feet between Helvegen and me.

Your Fortune skill has increased to 10!

We pounded into the mausoleum and down the stairs to the underground crypt. It felt like the rain was picking up, and small rivers of it were cascading down the stairs underneath our boots. "Spread out! We're looking for artifacts, anything that might be on display or otherwise look important," I yelled.

I stayed in the middle of the crypt, surrounded by lavish tombs on all sides, with Infernum held high above me to give everyone light. My party made quick work of the area. They smashed urns, knocked decorations from the walls, and even slid the lids from a few of the sarcophagi. In a matter of moments, the entire crypt was ransacked. Elyk even went as far as to throw around some of the remains he had exposed.

"There's nothing here!" Helvegen was the first to shout. Xia and another warlock offered the same sentiment from their side of the crypt.

"Fuck . . . Back to the top!" I yelled. I grabbed the truth-breaker roughly by his undead shoulder and shoved him to the front. "Go! Up the stairs as fast as you can! Kill the first thing you see!"

The undead minion obeyed without hesitation. It stormed back up the stairs and out of the crypt with its huge sword held above its head. The moment it hit the rain, a pair of crossbow bolts slammed into its heavily armored upper chest. The truthbreaker didn't slow. I couldn't see if the bolt had punctured through the truthbreaker's armor or not. Either way, it wouldn't matter. The zombie didn't need lungs to breathe and fuel its muscles, and no blood seeped out of its wounds. It charged onward, completely unfazed, and then removed the head from a kneeling crossbowman right in front of the mausoleum entrance. The guard had been a player, a tenth level archer.

Your Influence skill has increased to 24!

A small group of four guards were assembled in a little defensive knot behind the dead crossbowman. The truthbreaker kept up its relentless pace, issuing forth more magic from its mouth and chest as it ran. The spell stunned the first guard, breaking the enemy formation, and I came on right behind the undead with a flurry of fire and steel.

I swung side to side, easily ripping apart two of the guards. Another bolt of fire magic slammed into the remaining enemy, knocking him back and making the man scream as his clothes ignited. I pushed into him, slamming the hilt of my sword down hard on his helmet, smiling as the metal cracked. He fell to his back, and the truthbreaker's sword laid waste to his chest before I could finish the kill.

I ripped my attention back to the battlement above the gatehouse, but no NPCs were there. The parapet was silent, save for the rain. Then the castle's heavy front doors started to open. I waved everyone back behind me, pointing and silently mouthing for Elyk and Helvegen to get to the side where they'd be able to perfectly ambush whatever was about to come out.

The doors opened farther, and I could see torchlight glinting off steel.

A player stood in the doorway, a huge shield in one hand and a three-headed flail in the other. Her name was Briggan, and the text floating above her head said she was a level thirty-one paladin. Her shield and every inch of her impressive armor was painted with Echelon's crest. All I could think about was ripping her armor from her corpse and giving it Elyk. If it was even half as good as mine, we would be unstoppable together. Hell, we already were pretty close to unstoppable.

Briggan spoke first. "This as far as you get, traitor." Her voice was even and loud, deadly serious.

I laughed. "Traitor? I was never sworn to Echelon or the king. I betrayed nothing."

"Echelon gave you quests and a home, did it not? And you've betrayed the truce. While the servers are corrupted, no one is killing. You're a murderer." I couldn't see her face behind her helmet to know how she was reacting.

"Ha, that one I'll give you. I've certainly killed more than my share. But you still got one thing wrong."

Briggan started to speak again, but I launched my shadow pet right at her face before she had the chance. A burst of light cascaded down through the rain an instant later, searing the four remaining undead in my party. Paladins excelled at fighting abominations like those I had brought to the castle, and the first spell was clearly an effective one. I ordered the three walking bombs to charge into the keep before they died. If the holy light was going to kill them, I wanted them to die as close to the paladin as possible.

My four undead charged, their rotten flesh smoking and

rapidly disintegrating under the punishing magical light. I stayed back, not yet wanting to throw myself against the paladin until I had a clearer picture of her abilities. If at all possible, I wanted to bait her out into the bailey so Elyk and Helvegen could kill her from the side.

Briggan met the four undead with her flail thrashing in front of her. The first zombie bomb blasted apart, and I couldn't tell if the detonation was from the force of the woman's flail or the stored magical power being unleashed.

No matter the source of the fleshy explosion, the woman didn't falter. In fact, she appeared to become imbued with strength, and her armor started shining with more glorious light like that coming down with the rain.

Another zombie bomb detonated, and then the third. In the midst of it all, the truthbreaker had lost both of its legs. It was still fighting from bloody stumps, hacking vertically with its monstrous sword, but it wasn't inflicting much damage at all. As the carnage started to clear, Xia and her three warlocks began launching a cascade of fiery magic at the woman.

Fire and darkness splashed into Briggan's armor at a furious pace. *Finally*, she faltered. She lost her footing for a moment, and her flail slowed its murderous pace.

I charged in to the truthbreaker's side, swinging my own sword as the woman staggered, and Infernum smashed a huge dent into her shield. She fell back again, and I could hear her grunting under her helm.

I swung down two more times in rapid succession, never giving her even a second to adjust her shield or rethink her footing. She slid backward as her boots struggled for purchase on the marble floor. Then a new burst of light shimmered out of her armor, and it was so strong I had to cover my eyes lest I risked going blind in a single instant.

Covering my face, I skittered back into the rain and tried to shake the dizzying blast of pain from my mind. When I finally looked up, the paladin was standing tall once more amongst the corpses of my undead minions. Other than a massive dent on her shield, she looked unharmed.

She stared right at me. "I will only say it once more, traitor: this is as far as you get. Turn back now, and perhaps you shall live."

A little bit of motion behind Briggan caught my eye. There was someone else deeper in the keep, hiding behind a tapestry that ran the length of the wall. When I focused on them, another player name appeared their head. It was a man, a level twenty-four cleric. He'd been healing the woman through the entire onslaught, and I hadn't seen it.

But now I did.

Your Cunning skill has increased to 25!

I shot a brief glance to Elyk, hopefully conveying my desire for him to be ready, and then charged in once more. I immediately took up the offensive, battering Briggan's shield with hit after hit from Infernum. I knew she wanted me to be relentless, to tire out against her armor and lose my resolve. With a healer pumping her full of magical endurance, she could easily outlast me and then bash my skull to pieces with her flail. My legs would never fatigue so long as I stayed in combat, but my arms certainly would.

Now that I knew what she had planned, she was falling right into my trap, not the other way around. I kept up my furious attacks, my arms burning in protest with each swing, and pushed her toward the wall where her companion hid. More magic flew from the tapestry, and now that I was keeping an eye out for it, I saw every spell. Still, the woman gave up ground and was forced back toward the wall.

When Briggan's back was nearly touching stone, I screamed for Elyk and peeled off to my right, leaving the entire left side of my body exposed to the paladin's immediate counterattack.

Three heavy, spiked balls crashed into my breastplate. A few of them punctured through, and I could feel the massive amount of concussive force radiating pain through my entire side. My armor responded with a gout of flame, but I wasn't facing the woman to see if it did any good.

Infernum blazing in both hands, I swung for the tapestry with all the force my incredible physical stat could provide. The beautiful woven artwork was rent in two. Behind it, a much less beautiful man met the exact same fate. A pair of magical defensive wards flared to life, one of them trying to deflect my strike and the other trying to quickly undo the damage I had wrought, but they both amounted to nothing before the sheer power I commanded. The cleric died without so much as a whimper.

I turned back to face the paladin, and Elyk had her fully engaged. With her personal healer slain, the woman's body language was starting to exude a serious amount of fear. She fought more conservatively, trying to angle her own body away from her shield while swinging her flail toward the harvester's head.

None of Briggan's altered fighting style mattered. She grunted and groaned under Elyk's whirling, tempestuous attack, and then his huge scythe slipped past her shield and into her chest. She yelped once, then fell to her knees.

Elyk wrenched out his blade, towering over the woman.

"You want the honors?" he asked me. His face, at least what I could see of it under his helmet, was covered in blood. He hadn't even bothered to clear the red flecks from around his mouth.

"Take it. You earned it," I told him.

The harvester grinned. He took a step back, and Briggan began raising her hands in front of her like she was still trying to fight or at least protect herself. Elyk's aim was true, and the woman's head tumbled to the ground like a cut stalk of wheat.

Your Physical skill has increased to 29!
Your Influence skill has increased to 25!
Your Renown skill has increased to 21!
Your Infamy skill has increased to 44!

Underneath all of the stats on my character sheet, I noticed that another change had taken place. Where I had been listed as hated by Echelon, I now read that I was also feared.

I couldn't help but take a moment to drink it all in. My infamy stat was astronomical. My renown was starting to rival some of the mid-tier streamers from well-known guilds that I had watched back on the forums. The rest of my stats were still about average for my level, but a few things were getting to be extreme. With higher and higher infamy, I would start attracting more sinister allies to Undercroft Citadel. More people like Elyk, both players and NPCs. My empire would continue to grow.

I dismissed my character sheet and took stock of the tangible force we had left. The truthbreaker was dead—or perhaps it was *more* dead since it hadn't been alive in the first place—and all of our walking zombie explosives had been expended. We still had Xia, a powerful warlock in her own right, and three of the other warlocks as well, plus Helvegen. Overall, we were doing exceedingly well.

Our rain- and blood-soaked party stood in the first room of the royal keep. The audience chamber lay beyond, and I could see the opulent throne sitting at the end of the long entrance. It just looked so . . . arrogant. "Want to send another little message?" I asked the harvester.

Elyk nodded and started reaching for Briggan's head.

"No, leave the head. Or better yet, grab her helmet and then toss the head into the mud outside. Help me bring the rest of her up to the throne," I said.

Elyk tossed his own helmet to one of the warlocks before looting the paladin's, and then we began removing the rest of the woman's armor as well. Helvegen and the warlocks stood guard, and we had the full armor set free of its former host in a few minutes. "Chest piece is a little small, but I bet Geirr can fix it up," the harvester said once he was standing in his prize. In truth, it kind of looked ridiculous on him. The armor had clearly been made for a woman. Still, it was leagues better than what he had been wearing, and the warlock who got his old armor was grateful for the upgrade.

We dragged the now armorless body to the throne, and Elyk hefted her into it with a grunt. She looked like a queen sitting on the royal chair, surrounded by gemstones, gold in-lay, and all manner of other wealth. But her blood was staining the marble. The gold was turning red.

Elyk started prying one of the opals from the back of the chair, but I grabbed his arm to stop him. "Leave it," I said. "Sends a little clearer message that way. Besides, we aren't here to expand our treasury."

"Right. Sorry, Boss," the man said, a little crestfallen.

"Alright. We have a bunch of doors, check each one. We're looking for anywhere that might house some ancient relics," I told the party. The audience chamber was obviously the cen-tral hub of the entire castle, and it had a handful of exits lead-ing out in all different directions. One of them had to take us to the scarab, I could feel it in my gut.

Sure enough, Xia found our first lead. "Got a locked door here, and there's a sign above it that says 'The Gallery of Rel-ics,' so I think we found what we're looking for," she happily announced.

"Perfect." I had expected the scarab to be stored in some sort of museum-esque area of the castle, but I hadn't expected the door we needed to actually be labeled. I went up to it and tested the knob, and the lock seemed firm.

Summoning all the strength gifted to me by my legendary gauntlets, I made a fist and punched the metal plate housing the lock. The resounding crack vibrated up my forearm, but it didn't hurt. The armor absorbed any potential damage to my fingers without letting me feel any of it. I punched it two more times, and the lock plate dented inward, splintering the heavy wood behind it. After three more strikes, we were in.

The castle's museum, at first glance, was large. There were multiple rooms, and the first entryway was crowded with glass cases along the walls. Several of them stood in the center of the room as well. There wasn't much space for the whole party to spread out and investigate everything. As it turned out, we didn't need it. Elyk came storming into the museum like a bull, indiscriminately smashing every glass case within his reach.

"Hey, hey," I shouted, grabbing him by the arm. "Don't break the scarab, remember!"

The harvester settled down a little, though he only stopped in front of each case for a moment before smashing it and moving on to the next. At least I had convinced him to slow down.

We whirled through the first room of the museum quickly. The majority of the artifacts stored within were artistic rather than magical, and we left them in ruins on the ground without stealing more than one or two items.

The next part of the little museum was through another stone archway, but luckily it wasn't locked. It was smaller than the first room, perhaps only half the size, and it looked to be a lot more promising. Swords hung on the walls with fine steel shields, and helmets rested on wooden stands with small placards beneath them detailing their various histories. "Elyk, wait at the first door. Yell if anyone is coming that you can't handle," I told the harvester. I was glad to have him away from the more delicate artifacts, and I also didn't want any guards sneaking up on us while we were still looting.

"Understood," he answered, turning back for the front of the museum.

Helvegen took the left side of the room, and I scoured the right. "Grab anything you can carry that might be useful," I said.

The first object of note that I found was a small round shield designed to be strapped to a wrist and used with a two-handed weapon. The buckler's face was painted with a hard coating of enamel, and the whole thing vibrated with magic beneath its glass case. Using Infernum's hilt like a hammer, I smashed the glass and grabbed the shield. Once I was touching it, I called up the item's description in my vision:

Lord Bazrath's Radiant Targe: Holding significant magic within its steel, this buckler protects the wielder from all forms of harmful magic up to level 21 while also significantly decreasing the wearer's ability to be seen by enemies.

I instantly thought of Elyk whirling through a battlefield strewn with corpses, cutting our enemies to bloody pieces without even slowing. I flipped the shield straps around my own arm and loosely buckled them just to hold it in place while I looted the rest of the room.

At the end of the museum, I found what we had come to claim. A small scarab gem sat on a plush velvet pillow underneath another locked glass case. It was next to several other precious stones and a pair of golden coat buttons. The small description underneath the row of items described the scarab as having unknown origins and being part of something much larger that was once housed in the archive but was lost some years ago. I knew it was exactly what we were looking for.

I smashed through the top of the case and reached down to take out the pillow, pushing aside as much of the glass shards as I could. I had a leather pouch on my belt, and I slid all the artifacts from the pillow into it before tying it shut and then tucking it underneath my tassets for safekeeping.

"Come on, I got it," I said. "Let's get out of here before we have to fight again."

Your Investigation skill has increased to 8!

Helvegen followed me out of the room, a small wooden chest held under one arm. At the main entrance to the archive, Elyk was standing near the throne, towering over two fresh corpses that hadn't been there before. One of them was dressed like a guard, and the other was a woman, probably around eighteen or nineteen years old. She wore simple clothing, though it was obvious to see it was finely made and had likely been expensive.

"Did the king have a daughter?" I asked. Since I had never been one of the millions who had watched the royal family on the streams, I didn't know.

Elyk laughed and nudged the corpse with the end of his scythe. "I think he used to. Not anymore."

"Come on, let's move." I wanted to be gone from the castle before my mind could turn to Ingrid as I knew it would. Seeing the man's daughter so plainly butchered was bound to bring back a wave of painful memories that I had no interest in confronting.

We ran out of the front door and into the bailey once more. The rain had slackened, though the ground was still one giant field of mud.

Someone new was standing on the top of the battlements above the gatehouse that led into Echelon. He was alone, and he was surrounded by magic. Above his head, I could see his player name, level, and class:

Kevin, level 68 Ranger, Defender of the Realm

He held a bow at his side, an arrow nocked on the string and ready to fire in an instant. The bow itself was made of pure magic, being incorporeal and untouchable by any other than the powerful ranger. The arrows he used were the same, and his enchanted quiver was capable of producing an unlimited supply of them, each new missile becoming a different magical element according to whatever the ranger wanted them to be. He simply had to think of a damage type, and the next arrow he pulled from his quiver would be made from the very essence of that element.

"What do you want?" I yelled up at the ranger.

He didn't move. The aura shimmering around his body—there might have actually been more than one, I couldn't really tell—pulsed as the seconds ticked by.

I moved everyone back a foot or so closer to the castle. If we needed to make a run for it, going through the dry halls of the keep would be much easier than sprinting across the muddy bailey directly under the ranger's fire.

Finally, Kevin broke the tense silence. "The king is dead?" he yelled down. Somehow, his voice didn't quite match the sheer power he exuded. He sounded normal, not like the god his reputation on the Echelon forums made him out to be. I had watched him play for hours and hours. Though the rest of his guild, Resurrection, had been active online doing voice-overs for their own streams and interacting with the community, Kevin never really had, so I hadn't heard him speak before.

"No, the king is in Riverside," I shouted back through the rain. "He isn't dead."

The ranger seemed to study me for a moment. He wasn't wearing a helmet at all, so I could see his eyes and watch them as they looked me up and down, judging me. "You're speaking the truth?" he called.

I didn't want to invite him down and openly offer for him to get any closer to us than he already was, but I didn't really see any other way. "Come see for yourself. The king isn't here, and that wasn't our goal in the first place. We got what we wanted. We're leaving."

Kevin mulled it over a few moments, still silently staring at me like he was looking right through my soul. "What did you steal?" he asked.

"Don't tell him," Elyk quickly whispered.

I sheathed Infernum and slid the buckler I had taken from my wrist down to my hands. "Magic gear!" I called back. "We need more gear if we're going to survive, so we tricked the king into leaving and then looted the armory."

I passed the targe to Elyk and readjusted my gauntlets. The lie felt believable, and it wasn't even entirely untrue. We *had* needed armor and other gear.

"What do you expect Resurrection to do?" Kevin shouted back. "We cannot let you rampage through Echelon whenever you please. Our guild has protected the city for years, and we won't stop just because your death will be permanent. Do you understand?"

I nodded. The guild was probably the most powerful organization in the entire city, and I imagined a few of their members were likely close to the king himself. Perhaps even a few of them had traveled with the king to Riverside and were there right now waiting for me in the rain. If we provoked the guild into a war, we'd never win.

"Undercroft Citadel has no quarrel with your guild," I shouted.

Kevin appeared to relax a little, but his posture did nothing to ease my fears. If he wanted to kill us all, I had very little hope that any of us would be able to escape. Perhaps if Xollmomath was with us, we could stand our ground and fight. The ancient necromancer had been strong enough to slaughter an entire middle-tier guild more or less on his own. He would at least give us a fighting chance against someone like Kevin.

"What's the plan, Boss?" Elyk whispered. Behind him, Helvegen was nervously shifting from foot to foot.

We could all feel our impending doom. The hour of our reckoning was getting closer and closer. I grabbed the small leather pouch from under my armor and pulled it off my belt. After I handed it to Elyk, I looked back to the top of the gatehouse. "Again, we have no quarrels with you or your guild. We got what we came for, the king still lives, and we're going home."

Kevin made a motion with his hand, and the heavy doors of the main gatehouse started creaking open. Behind them, the iron portcullis was slowly raising skyward on loud, rattling chains. The rest of Resurrection stood in full armament, banners and tabards streaming in the rain, blocking the main exit. There were around forty guild members, and the minimum level required to join Resurrection had always been thirty. Xia was the only one in my party who could match them for level.

Kevin raised his bow a few inches. He still wasn't pointing it at me, but he wasn't looking any friendlier, either. "As long as you live, you're a threat to Echelon. Any threat to the city is a threat to my brothers and sisters. We don't let threats just keep walking around and getting stronger. You're going to die today."

That brought a spark of a plan to my mind.

Actually, it didn't just bring a simple spark. I knew what I needed to do, and it would work. By god it was a stretch, but it *had* to work.

Your Cunning skill has increased to 26!

I thought it over, and I could see all the pieces coming together neatly.

I started unstrapping my armor and letting it fall to the mud. "Take my armor back to the citadel. I'll handle the guild by myself. You guys need to run. Just get out of the keep any way you can, and then get to Undercroft Citadel. Get the scarab to Xollmomath and tell him to get ready. When I return, I'll very likely have an entire guild chasing me."

Helvegen's breath caught in her throat. "You're just going to give up? Let them kill you?"

I handed her my greaves and met her eyes. "I told you I would return. You have to trust me. One way or another, I'll see Undercroft Citadel before nightfall. Now go!"

My party snatched up all the pieces of my legendary armor and started running back into the keep. When they were out of sight, I closed the castle doors behind me. It was hard to get my footing in the slick mud without the extra weight of my steel raiment giving me added traction.

Finally, I felt ready. "Alright, I agree with you," I yelled up to Kevin. So far, his guildmates hadn't come charging through the open gate to cut me down. I felt like that was a good thing.

Kevin jumped from the battlement. The fall was least twenty or thirty feet, though he barely even seemed to notice. Mud flew up in all directions upon his landing, splattering across the ground but altogether deflected by one of his magical auras so that not a single spec of it landed on his armor.

"You come willingly?" the ranger demanded. His even voice now held malice. I knew he suspected some sort of trick or trap, and he was on high alert.

I shook my head. "No, that wasn't the deal. You said I would die today, and that's fine. *I* am the threat to Echelon, not my friends or my dungeon. Kill me, and you'll remove the threat you fear so much, but I'm not going anywhere with you. I never agreed to that."

When it was clear that Kevin didn't exactly understand what it was I had proposed, I took a few steps forward. I ripped off my soaking wet shirt and threw it to the ground. The rain felt cold against my skin, but it was better than the cloying fabric sticking to every inch of my flesh.

"One on one. You can even keep your armor and weapons. I'll fight you, your guild leader, or anyone else from Resurrection that wants a shot. I only have one demand." I tightened the thin drawstring on my cheap pants to keep the sodden garment from falling down my legs, though part of me wanted to fight naked. I felt like I would get a little more trust if I showed them I wasn't concealing anything, but in the end I kept my pants in place. Ingrid wouldn't have wanted her father running through the streets of Echelon naked.

"Enough of your stalling. If you have something to say, just come out with it," the ranger spat back. He drew back his bowstring and leveled the arrow right at my chest. It glittered in the hazy afternoon light with a sheen of red magic. I figured the arrow was imbued with fire. Regardless of the element Kevin chose, my only hope was that it would kill me quickly.

I spread my arms wide and smiled. "One on one, and if I die, you leave my body here. Leave me facedown in the mud so that King Ahmose II knows that I am dead. I betrayed my word to him, and I'd like the good king to know that I am dead. If my body is moved or burned or destroyed, he'll never know for sure. I wouldn't want to live always looking over my shoulder just in case, and I'm sure the king does not want that either. And if I kill you, Resurrection leaves me and Under-croft Citadel alone forever. Are we agreed?"

Kevin's face was contorted with confusion. "The hell are you up to?" he asked.

I offered him as sincere a look as I knew how. "I just want to do right by the king. My daughter—my only daughter—died in the server crash. She's gone, and I don't think I can go on doing that to other people. I'd like to go see her once more, but I won't just let you kill me. Let me die with a little bit of honor in proper combat."

Finally, Kevin gave me a disinterested shrug. "If death is what you want, I won't hesitate to give it to you," he said.

Before he could change his mind or think any more on my strange request, I lowered my head and charged at him, throwing mud up onto the castle doors behind me.

Kevin let his fiery arrow loose, and it streaked in toward my chest with impossible speed. Anticipating the shot, I rolled to my left as soon as it left the ranger's bow, and I managed to come through with only a graze. It hurt like a bitch, but the wound was essentially superficial.

Reaching to the quiver on his back, Kevin pulled forth an arrow made of pure lightning and nocked it to his magical string. I kept running for him, my hands balled into fists, when he shot a second time. Since I was so much closer than when the first arrow had nearly killed me, I didn't have any time to dodge the second one. The lightning missile slammed into my exposed sternum.

I flew through the air. The force of the arrow was so strong that it lifted me off my feet and catapulted me backward. My body slammed into the closed castle doors. When I didn't fall into the mud below, I looked down and saw the end of the magical shaft protruding from my broken and bloody chest. The arrow had pinned me to the door like I was some medieval piece of parchment being nailed to the town bulletin board.

Electricity rattled through my body. It made my teeth slam together as all the muscles in my chest, head, and neck clenched at the same time. Blood slurped out of my mouth and down my torso to join the rest of it pouring out in rapid spurts. It hurt more than I could describe, but all I could do was laugh.

Kevin took a few steps closer and nocked another arrow. He looked intently into my eyes from about five feet away. All around him, his multitude of swirling auras still shimmered. The protection surrounding him was so thorough that it even kept out the rain.

"Well, if you're trying to tell the king that you're dead, nailing you to the door seems like as good a way as any," the ranger remarked.

He pulled back on his magical bowstring and shot me again, that time in the meat of my left thigh. The arrow was made of darkness, and the black toxin instantly crept through my entire body, staining my flesh with sticky corruption. He nocked another arrow, one made from ice, and my vision was too blurry for me to see where he was aiming. A fresh blossom of pain coming from my right leg told me where he had fired.

Two more arrows rocketed into my body, one into each arm. There was too much pain flooding my senses for me to determine which elements had been used. All the pain just mixed together, overwhelming my entire consciousness.

The last thing I saw as the world faded to black was Kevin turning away from me with a smile on his face. "Not even any loot," I heard him scoff. "What a waste. Let's go."

In the deep, unending blackness of death, I summoned my character sheet to what remained of my tattered consciousness.

Status: shrouded by Lady Kalma faded from my list of other modifiers as my lungs gave out.

Death was somewhat peaceful, though it didn't last nearly as long as I had hoped.

If you enjoyed this novel, please consider leaving a review at your favorite book retailer's website. Reviews from enthusiastic readers are vital to authors everywhere. Your support is greatly appreciated!

ABOUT THE AUTHOR

Stuart Thaman is the international best-selling author of almost twenty novels. He writes epic fantasy and LitRPG, trying to find unique plots and bring them to readers everywhere. He holds degrees in politics, classical philosophy, German, and law.

He spends his days playing with his cats, going to metal shows, smoking cigars, collecting tattoos, and trying to learn card tricks.

Check out all the latest books at www.stuartthamanbooks.com where you can grab a free download just for signing up on the email list.

THE ADVENTURE CONTINUES IN
FORSAKEN TALENTS: A BLACK SOUL

Get a free copy of *The Minotaur King*
by joining the mailing list!

https://dl.bookfunnel.com/lt2mw0eidx